Creekside

F•re Ant Books

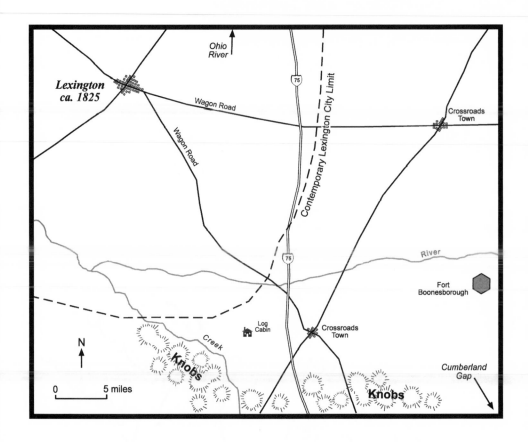

Lexington
ca. 1825

Ohio
River

75

Contemporary Lexington City Limit

Wagon Road

Wagon Road

Crossroads
Town

75

River

Fort
Boonesborough

Log
Cabin

Crossroads
Town

Creek

Knobs

N

0   5 miles

Knobs

Cumberland
Gap

Creekside

An Archaeological Novel

KELLI CARMEAN

For Shirley,
Enjoy the past ~
Enjoy the present.
Enjoy
Kelli Carmean

THE UNIVERSITY OF ALABAMA PRESS
Tuscaloosa

Copyright © 2010
The University of Alabama Press
Tuscaloosa, Alabama 35487-0380
All rights reserved
Manufactured in the United States of America

Typeface: ACaslon

∞

The paper on which this book is printed meets the minimum requirements of American
National Standard for Information Sciences-Permanence of Paper for Printed Library
Materials, ANSI Z39.48-1984.

Library of Congress Cataloging-in-Publication Data

Carmean, Kelli, 1960–
Creekside : an archaeological novel / Kelli Carmean.
p. cm.
"Fire ant books."
ISBN 978-0-8173-5661-3 (pbk. : alk. paper) — ISBN 978-0-8173-8350-3 (electronic)
1. Archaeologists—Fiction. 2. Kentucky—Fiction. I. Title.
PS3603.A75376C74   2010
813'.6—dc22
2009050552

The past is a dangerous place to visit. It is beauty. It is also burden. It is where we go, many of us, to remind ourselves who we are, and even sometimes to find out.

—Eddy Harris, 1996

Author's Note

Archaeologists know that the material remains of the past not only are important, but also can tell us a great deal about the lives of past peoples and the broader societies in which they lived. Sharing that message with the public, however, has not always been high on the discipline's list of priorities.

Although I surely hope *Creekside* entertains with a good story, a parallel, hidden agenda for the novel is public outreach in archaeology. The stories told within these pages provide a human context for readers to engage a bit with the realities of archaeology: daily experiences on a dig, tight contract deadlines, the use of heavy equipment, damage from looters and collectors, report writing and artifact analysis, and the reality of site destruction in the path of modern development. The stories also allow the reader to ponder the region's history: early Euro-American settlement of Kentucky, Indians defending their land, the immigrant stampede down the Ohio River, and the persistent question of social class and land.

It is my hope that archaeological fiction set in a doomed pasture in the suburban sprawl of the United States is appealing because of its immediacy. Such is the reality we see each day; pastures like this are everywhere in our country and are disappearing fast. If *Creekside* causes readers to think differently the next time they pass a new subdivision development, or any new development that alters the land, if even for a moment they reflect on the past that could potentially be destroyed by the bulldozer, the book has made an impact. This book also puts forward optimism. The story offers the hope that despite the undeniable and perhaps inevitable loss of the past, certain essential elements of it persist around us, even in the face of their immense alteration. We have only to recognize it in our midst and value it actively.

Acknowledgments

I owe a great debt of gratitude to Cherril Sparks and Tom Rice. Having first surprised me by reading my nonfiction book *Spider Woman Walks This Land: Traditional Cultural Properties and the Navajo Nation,* both friends sat me down and insisted I consider what at the time seemed like an impossible plunge into fiction. Thanks to you two, I gave it a try. Thanks also to Cherril and Jim Sparks for reading and commenting on a very early version of this book.

Many thanks also to Jill Marie Landis for her guidance and professional comments and for giving me the opportunity for regular chapter drops at her house. Thanks to Greg King, Monica Udvardy, Bonnie Plummer, Isabelle White, Ann Stebbins, Lucrecia Guerrero, Kurt Barbieri, Liliana Barbieri, Willard Carmean, and Kim Carmean for reading drafts at various stages and offering encouragement and helpful comments. Thanks also to Liliana for being willing to share her artistic skills. Thanks as well to two anonymous reviewers for their helpful comments and to Karen Johnson for her savvy editing. Thanks, of course, to my husband, Mike, for his patience, love, photography, and great cooking, and to the Westerfields of Nonesuch for their pasture. And thanks to the historic family who once planted irises up their walkway and "shared" them with me. In a preemptory apology to potentially irate gardeners, while *I* know irises have rhizomes and not bulbs or roots, a non-gardener like Meg, or uneducated Estelle, would never have called the underground parts by such a term.

Kentucky archaeologists Bill Sharp and Wayna Roach, along with two anonymous archaeologist reviewers, offered encouragement and helpful guidance as well. Finally, it is truly heartening that The University of Alabama Press sees the potential for creative public outreach in archaeology. Thank you. I alone, of course, am responsible for all historical, material, cultural, grammatical, plot, and any other kind of error, miscalculation, or stretching of the truth.

Creekside

Chapter One

Meg Harrington's grip on the datum stake was tight as she first started hammering it in the ground, but then her grip had better be tight, or else the darn thing wouldn't go in straight and she'd have to set it all over again. But with each new strike of the hammer, the skin of her palm grew colder as it gripped the rough iron rebar on this sticky early summer day. Meg frowned at the stake: It was as if the deeper it sunk the colder it got, even as it slid obediently through the thick green sod of the pasture. But once the stake surged into the earth itself, cold streams of air burst forth from this newest wound in the land.

Meg dropped the hammer and stood up, the hairs on the back of her neck prickling. Something was wrong. She sensed that some strange probing creature had just now found her, gazed at her from some unknown place. Meg narrowed her eyes and searched the pasture for the source of her sudden wariness—and some explanation for the stake's strange behavior.

There was a surveying team from the highway department working near the edge of the road, laying the centerline for the grand stone entryway bridge for the expanded Creekside subdivision. A bulldozer dumped a fresh load of fill dirt at the far fence, while a bright yellow backhoe reached out its long mechanical arm to dig a new sewer ditch deep and straight. A lazy creek meandered across the pasture, nearly hidden from view by a thick line of trees on either bank. A farmer's cattle still grazed in a distant field, one of the few that had not yet been transformed into perfectly square quarter-acre lots with elegant new Creekside homes.

Meg turned toward the truck. Several of her students were busy hanging sifting screens from tall wooden tripods. Others were unloading shovels and buckets and wheelbarrows and all the other excavation equipment from the pickup, its bright gold and blue doors emblazoned with the official Commonwealth of Kentucky seal: a buckskin-clad pioneer shaking hands with a gentleman.

As far as she could tell, nothing seemed out of place. Everything she could see was typical for an archaeological site about to be excavated, and where an expanded housing subdivision would soon stand. No shadowy figures stood hidden at the trees along the creek; no one watched her from the road.

Still perplexed, Meg dropped a knee back to the sod and retrieved her hammer. She glared for a moment at the stake's metal head, then, without clutching the shaft, she held the hammer with both hands and pounded its tip. But even the clang of metal on metal—barely audible above the distant roar of bulldozers—sounded strange that morning. This time it was the thin, pensive echo of striking metal that made her pause—hammer mid-stroke—and listen to the reverberation. The metal gave off a lonely, insistent ring that seemed to emerge from the dark, silent layers that rested beneath the sod of the pasture. Meg tilted her head; her hand reached toward the greenness, and with open palm she stroked the fresh lush grass, buried her fingers deep within, contemplating for a moment the silent layers beneath.

Then she yanked her hand back. How could she think of stratigraphic layers like that? They were data; that's all. She would dig each one carefully, analyze and classify their artifacts, and draw logical conclusions about past human activities. She would write a detailed report and submit it to KYDOT—the Kentucky Department of Transportation. Of course the layers of the earth were dark and silent—why wouldn't they be?

And of course KYDOT would get their report—on time as always—just like they got their sites excavated at absurdly minimal cost. In return, she got to train her students in the applied, "real world" of contract archaeology, rather than rely on the broad theoretics of the classroom. Under Professor Margaret Harrington's dedicated guidance, several generations of Bluegrass University students had already passed through her summer archaeological field schools and learned what needed to be done in preparation for a site's ultimate destruction under the sharp blade of the bulldozer.

And this time, out here in this green pasture, KYDOT had given her six weeks to do it—just six weeks to excavate the Creekside Subdivision Expansion Site—before the roaring bulldozers tore it to shreds.

Meg glanced toward the far fence, at the heaving piece of heavy equipment, at its lurching yellow hulk as the operator threw the massive machine into reverse, prepared to strike again at a small determined outcrop of hardpan. A quick rev of the engine, an enormous plume of black diesel belch . . . and the bulldozer rolled forward.

Meg turned her attention back to the stake and began hammering again, forcing herself to ignore the strange ring. With only six weeks, she couldn't allow herself to engage in such ridiculous flights of fancy or ponder such quaint melodrama. However dark and silent the layers beneath the pasture may be, it was her responsibility to dig them—and she had best dig them fast.

The rebar sufficiently secure in the ground, she unfurled a length of bright pink flagging tape and wrapped it around the tip. She slid a Sharpie from behind her ear and wrote the coordinates on the tape in perfect block print. The metal datum stake stood at exactly 0 North and 0 East—the main reference point for their grid across the broad green pasture.

Meg leaned back, gazed at the gentle flapping of the long pink tape in the warm breeze. A familiar feeling of confidence welled up inside her. Now that the grid's main reference point—an absolute and logical framework of space and time—was in place, she would never be lost. With a grateful impulse she reached out and grabbed hold of the stake with both hands. It felt solid, unmoving in her hands, firm and fixed in the ground. A point in the earth unyielding to the vagaries of change.

"Dr. Harrington? What are you doing?"

Meg jumped at the sound of Emily's voice. Her hands flew to her old Dodgers baseball cap and started fiddling with it. Emily must have walked up from behind without her noticing.

"Is everything all right?" Emily asked.

"Uh yeah, sure," she mumbled, embarrassed. "Everything's fine."

"Are you sure?"

"It's nothing," Meg said, chastising herself for letting her mind wander so foolishly. "Datum stake's in. Come on—let's go check on the crew."

As they walked back across the pasture, the two made an interesting pair. Dr. Meg Harrington was tall and lanky and quick with a smile despite big brown melancholy eyes set deep in a long oval face. A thick brown braid of long unruly hair escaped out the back of her old Dodgers cap. Emily Rothschild, Meg's former student and current field assistant, was short and pretty with a pert blond ponytail that poked from beneath a floppy fisherman's hat. Both wore jeans, boots, and old T-shirts—unlike their young student crew in shorts and flip-flops—for them this pasture was a worksite, not some summer picnic.

As they walked, Meg's gaze was drawn out beyond the green folds of pasture and off into the distance. She slowed to linger at the crest of a gentle rise of land, stilled by the quiet majesty stretching out before them.

It was from here Meg could best appreciate the steep jagged knobs that spilled out in a long gray line as they tapered off into the horizon. A gust of wind rose against a distant wall of rock, ruffled the tufts of trees that sprang up from the most improbable cliff-line crannies. Meg even liked the name of the landforms, the knobs, as the early settlers in the region had so aptly called them. A sudden magical landscape of giant doorknobs protruding skyward—the earth, a mosaic of immense doors to open and enter at will.

"Beautiful spot for a dig, huh?" Emily asked.

"Sure is," Meg said. How many projects had she worked in flat and dusty, hot and ugly places where the highlight of the day was returning to a rundown motel with a buzzing neon Vacancy sign and a not-so-enviable view of the parking lot? Always on the move to yet another contract, to yet another archaeological site scheduled for annihilation.

Meg gazed out across the quiet folds of green, to the long line of sudden knobs, admired the resilience of their hard gray stone, imagined the depth and strength of their long rock roots. The warmth of the sun drew closer, climbed up to caress her back. The last drops of dew on the grass twinkled in the brightness of morning. She breathed in the lush freedom of the pasture; even the earthy aroma of drying cow patties was a pungent, welcome simplicity after another demanding academic year. Overhead, a thin curl of a single cloud adorned the crisp Kentucky sky. Meg closed her eyes, lifted her face to the sun, and sighed over toward the ancient knobs. Perhaps this would be a good place to put down some roots of her own.

"Hey, good job you guys!" Meg said, her head nodding with enthusiasm. Her eyes swept the organized rows of shovels and screens and wheelbarrows and plastic trunks containing the surprising variety of equipment they would need during their pasture sojourn. Her students had arranged the field equipment neatly against the rough trunk of an old oak, tucked within the tree's tight ring of leafy shade.

"Alright! May the fun begin," Meg said, swinging both arms to point toward the metal rebar. "Meet me at the datum stake. Let's grid this puppy!"

Under Meg's and Emily's direction, the crew worked fast. By early afternoon they were able to stand back and observe their handiwork: A series of long, perfectly spaced, perfectly straight rows of bright pink pinflags swept due north and south, due east and west across the length and breadth of the pasture. The grid resembled a giant chessboard rolling and tumbling with the soft green swells of the land.

"Looks like we're ready for the next step. Find a buddy and each team grab a shovel, a trowel, a screen, some paper bags, and a Sharpie," Meg instructed, enumerating each item on her fingers as she spoke. "Then meet me at 10 North 10 East. That's where we'll dig our first shovel probe."

Once everyone stood around her in a tight circle, at exactly 10 meters North and 10 meters East, Meg punched the shovel's sharp tip in the ground. With practiced ease, she jumped up and landed hard with both booted feet square and certain on the shovel's rolled end. But as the earth swallowed the shiny metal, sadness breathed up from that long thin crescent of cut. Balanced on the end of the shovel, she actually felt it—a slow cool exhale rising from the narrow slash in the earth. Unexpected tears welled in her eyes, and she blinked hard to keep them from falling.

Meg jumped off the blade, jerked her hands from the shovel handle. She looked back and forth from her hands to the shovel in bewilderment. The long wooden handle swung back and forth from its blade, still wedged solid in the ground. With each tight swing it slowed until it stood motionless in the sod. An innocent tool, a thin, solitary tether deep into the silence of the past.

"What was that?" gasped Meg.

"What was *what*?" Emily asked, stepping closer. The crew glanced at one another in uncomfortable confusion.

Meg pointed an accusing finger where the shovel met the earth. She gestured at it, her voice tinged with alarm. "I don't know! A burst of cold air! Didn't you feel it? It just . . . sprayed out at me!"

"What do you mean *sprayed out at you?*" Emily asked under her breath. She shifted her position directly in front of Meg, shielding her from the crew.

"I don't know, it just came out, a sudden wave of, of—" She wanted to say *loneliness,* or maybe even *sadness,* but she couldn't quite seem to form those ridiculous words in her mouth.

"Did you hit a rock, or a pocket of . . . clay . . . or . . . something?" Emily asked.

"A rock?" Meg asked incredulously. "No, that was no rock—or clay!" She shook her head. "Weird. That's never happened before." She ran both hands along her head, shook it again.

"Do you want me to dig the probe?" Emily offered.

"No, I'll do it—it's okay," Meg said. "Ah heck, who knows? Maybe it *was* a rock. I suppose it coulda been. Helluva rock, though, maybe from a different

planet or something—maybe a rare chunk of meteorite. Kryptonite or something." She was muttering to no one in particular, working hard at being jovial
in a self-mocking kind of way, making a valiant effort to mask her own odd behavior.

Meg grabbed the bill of her old Dodgers cap and snatched it from her head.
She dipped her forehead to her shoulder, wiped off some tiny beads of sweat,
then snugged her cap determinedly back down on her head. She stepped to the
shovel, yanked it from the ground, scowled at the curved blade. She punched
the tip back in the sod, alongside her first thin sliver. She jumped on the rolled
metal edge and again the shiny blade cut deep into the ground. Then she kept
going, shifting the blade in a circular fashion until the last slice met the first—
a perfect brown circle carved in the bright green of the pasture. Meg set her
voice and brain on autopilot—a skill learned long ago—as she described the
size and depth of a shovel probe, the reasons for digging them in the first place.
She talked some more about the grid, rambled on for a while about the significance of site size.

But her heart wasn't in her words. Each time she sank the blade, the cold
wave rose back up to greet her, bringing with it that odd feeling of loneliness and loss, of sadness and silence. And the vague, inarticulate sense of being watched. But midway through, Meg sensed that the cold wave, bizarre as it
was, held no malevolence, that the distant watcher, whoever it was, meant her
no harm. The watcher simply watched, held her lightly in its gaze—a strange
mute witness that merely observed her from afar.

When Meg heaved down on the handle, her curved blade surfaced again
with a perfect wedge of compact soil. She dumped it in the screen Emily held
at her side. Emily stabbed it several times with her trowel, and then her lithe
body shifted back and forth as she shook the screen, her blond ponytail flapping against her back as soil rained down through the quarter-inch wire mesh.
Together, Meg and Emily broke up clods of dirt, poked around in the remaining soil, pulled out artifacts, passed them into the young eager waiting hands of
the student crew that encircled them, peering over their shoulders to see more
of what the shovel may have divulged from the earth.

But after completing the shovel probe demonstration, Meg sent the students off to dig their own probes, with Emily supervising. Standing there, she
watched them head off to their next grid coordinate locations.

"Did Dr. Harrington mention that archaeology is truly ground breaking?"
She heard Emily joke with the crew, heard their muffled chorus of answering
groans.

Meg walked to the quiet shade of the old oak. The equipment not currently in use was still stacked in neat reassuring rows against the tree's rough trunk. She rummaged around in her backpack, tugged out her notebook. She turned a bucket upside down, sat on it, and slid her favorite mechanical pencil from behind her ear. She settled down to take some notes on the progress of their first day in the field at the Creekside Subdivision Expansion Site.

Pencil poised above paper, she thought about what to write. She stared down at the blank white lines of the blank white page in front of her. She brushed the paper a few times with the edge of her hand. This excavation was beginning like no other.

Surely she couldn't write about a cold datum stake or some strange exhalations from the earth that only she had experienced. Nor could she write about the lonely silence of the stratigraphic layers that rested mere centimeters below her booted feet. Could she really write about some persistent watcher that even she could not find? She would banish these outlandish thoughts by letting the facts take over her mind, infuse it with welcome reason. Logic would force out anything else that might be tempted to intrude. She would transcribe only the facts—neatly, orderly—on the blank white lines of the blank white page in front of her.

Slowly, still shaken, Meg began to write. Reassuring herself that reason was all that mattered, she detailed only the important information, the data specifics as currently known about the Creekside Subdivision Expansion Site. She sketched the layout of the grid in relation to the creek, the road, the fence line, convinced the precision of the grid was all she needed. She indicated magnetic north with a dark confident arrow.

But even as she wrote and sketched from her shady perch on the upturned bucket, her unease still lingered around the edges. It crept back from the tiny spaces, from the minute seams that existed between the hard objective facts. A new uncertainty sprung from the depths of the earth, seeped up through that ancient land now slated for destruction. Lying just below her booted feet, it surged from the darkness of the ground to find her and brought with it the possibility of a new opening—one that reached far back through the persistent cracks in reality and stretched far forward through the silent fissures of time.

Chapter Two

The rifle's sharp retort slapped the steep gray rock of the knobs, then echoed into the forest. Virgil Mullins followed the tangled tracks and fresh trickles of blood on snow to the base of the knob where the deer had finally fallen. When the man came to stand before the fallen animal, their eyes met in a glimmer of shared anguish as the dying deer writhed in the quickly reddening snow.

Virgil swung his horn from behind his back, poured a stream of black powder, and tamped it in place with swift practiced hands. As he lifted the rifle to his cheek, a thin shadow stretched long across the snow. He placed his sight on the broad span of brown between the sad eyes of the wounded deer. When he pulled the trigger, flint struck metal and a spark lit the powder in the pan. Black smoke billowed up as the explosion propelled the lead ball through the deer's skull, shattering it with a fast loud crack. Then the deer lay still, sprawled face first, neck sharply twisted, ignoble in the bloody snow. It had happened fast, since Virgil Mullins was a man who could never bear to see an animal suffer.

Virgil walked back to the cabin and together with his young son, Thomas, led the mule back out to the base of the knob. With skilled hands and sharp knives they gutted the deer, its hot steaming organs spilling out onto the sudden cold of the ground. As they heaved the carcass on the mule's back, the old farm animal shifted under its weight. The doe was a decent size and would be a welcome change to the long winter weeks of salt pork still ahead.

Snow crunched loud underfoot as father and son wound their way back through the forest and up the narrow wagon lane toward the cabin. Occasional flakes caught the sun, a fresh sprinkle of bright glitter strewn across the quiet of the white earth.

"Next birthday, son, you'll be gettin a rifle," Virgil announced. "After that you'll come a-huntin with me." A man of few words, Virgil's voice was low and rough. He spoke matter-of-fact, but he knew his son was eager to join him in the forest, shoot his first deer, and have his own rifle. How many times had he watched the boy take up his father's rifle, slide his thin fingers down the long sleek muzzle, touch the cool swirling brass inlay of the patch pocket, feel the honeyed softness of the smooth worn wood?

Virgil had kept Thomas at home helping his mother longer than he probably should have. It was still Thomas's chore to haul the water—the rope handles of two battered wood pails tied to the heavy shoulder yoke. Already that morning he had made two trips to the creek, broken the thin crust of ice, and plunged the pails into the frigid water. The boy had nearly leapt for the door when his father called him to help retrieve the deer.

But Virgil had kept Thomas at home not because he didn't want his son at his side, but because he knew the forest was still too dangerous for a man who couldn't properly defend himself. Just last fall, the Tackett family on the other side of the river had lost a man to a party of Indians. The victim was Ruth Tackett's youngest brother, a man only just arrived on the Kentucky frontier.

"Can I get a .45 caliber bore? And I sure do like them hex stars. Think I can get one on the cheek piece, Pa?" Thomas asked, his young voice full of excitement. "And them crescent butts sure is nice on a Kentucky." As his son spoke, the expression on Virgil's face changed to one of surprise. How was it his boy knew so much about long rifles?

He turned and looked at his son, walking along on the other side of the plodding mule. A brown crumpled felt hat rode so low over his head it nearly hid his freckled face, his fine blond hair—hair just like his mother's. Thomas looked up at his father just then. His son's pale blue eyes were also like Estelle's.

A proud grin broke across his face as Virgil realized his boy was growing up fast. "Sure, son, I think them's all mighty fine ideals," he said, careful to keep any hint of patronizing from his voice. His son was becoming a man. He'd have to get used to that. Curly maple—he'd buy his son a rifle with a sturdy stock of curly maple, like his own. Together they would sit near the hearth, clean and polish their rifles, admire the gold of the grain as it jumped and shimmered in the firelight.

"Come spring we'll ride over to the fort and have us a visit with the gunsmith. I'll see to it he fashions you up a real fine muzzle loader . . . as long as it's not too costly, now," Virgil added, always the frugal man not inclined to luxury, especially now that they finally owned land here in Kentucky.

The Mullins family had begun clearing the land beside the little creek some eight years earlier, back in the spring 1779. They built a cabin out of tall chestnuts and poplars felled by Virgil and some other men from the fort and hauled from the forest chained to the sweating backs of mules. With axes swinging they notched the log ends and hoisted them in place, chinked them tight with broad sweeps of thick mortar.

At first they lived in a one-room cabin, but after Thomas was born Virgil added another, building out from the same stone foundation. Now, one room served as kitchen and living area, while the other was for storage and sleeping. Estelle's cooking hearth separated the two rooms, keeping both warm in winter.

The years had been endless work—felling the trees, building the cabin, planting an orchard, and plowing the land.

Each spring, Estelle sowed her kitchen garden on the sun side of the cabin, where the soil was rich and deep, and they ate well all through summer. Each fall, his wife put up a plentiful share of vegetables, arranging the deep rows of heavy crocks on the springhouse shelves. She always dried plenty of peaches from the orchard as well, and hung them in gunnies from the springhouse rafters, ready for the day she felt inspired to bake a pie. They were both thankful to finally have land. It was here they could set roots as deep and strong as the blooming peach trees in an orchard that was all their own.

Their affection had grown even deeper here. Once, on their fifth wedding anniversary at the cabin, Virgil had surprised her with a full bushel of gnarled iris roots. It had been a large expense for such an extravagance, but he was sure his wife would prize them for years to come. They planted the irises in two long rows—a winding pathway to their front porch step. And then, in the midst of planting, she had wrestled him to the ground, and he had happily obliged, dragged her skirt high, irises and dirt and digging tools flung all around. He had been surprised—his wife would never have done such a thing back in Virginia. She was a different woman here, and it was the land that had changed her.

Virgil and Estelle were one of several determined families that had trudged their way over Cumberland Gap with great difficulty. They loaded only essentials on the packhorses at Sapling Grove, but even then they had been forced to abandon several baskets along rugged Boone's Trace. She had hauled a bundle on her own back and kept slow but steady stride up the steep slopes of those unforgiving mountains. But even after they crossed the Appalachians their troubles had not been over, and they nearly lost two pack animals in a difficult river crossing on the long western slopes. But when their weary party at last stood overlooking the Bluegrass, all eyes brimmed with tears. They laughed, clapped each other on the back, dropped to their knees, and raised loud thankful prayers to the Lord. Never before had they seen such vast stretches of prairie and forest so ripe and full and yearning for the plow. This beautiful wilderness—and the stony gray knobs that ringed it—was to be theirs. Best of all, these new lands lay far beyond the grasp of the wealthy tobacco planters of the Virginia Tidewater and Piedmont who had long since claimed all the good land east of the mountains for themselves.

At first they lived in a dirt-floor room at Fort Boonesborough, and it was there they heard the tales of those ten long days of siege just that September—and their joy began to fade. Clearly, the land developer back in Virginia had told them terrible lies about the treaties. They found the forests could teem with Indians who might appear by foot or canoe or horseback and surprise an unsuspecting work party even in the middle of day, strike fast, and then vanish back into the wilderness. Life on the frontier was risky and unpredictable, and it fell to the settlers to survive despite their own hard losses.

But they had sweated and toiled in other men's fields back east, scrimped and saved and gone into debt to put down coin on their own tiny parcels here in the west. They had not trudged long and hard over Cumberland Gap to turn around and go back to tenant farming in Virginia or Carolina. They finally had land of their own, and they were going to keep it.

Alerted by the chorus of dogs, Estelle opened the cabin door and walked to the porch rail. As she waited, a thick wool shawl drawn about her shoulders, her breath formed little puffs of white in the early winter air. One hand clutched the shawl, while the other stroked her belly; at last she was pregnant again, and due in spring.

She smiled and clapped her hands as the three figures rounded the lane, one weighed down with the heavy carcass of the deer. "Ah, she sure is a beauty!" Estelle cried as they neared the porch. She laughed, hopped down the steps, and started circling the mule, nodding her head as she admired the doe. The mule snorted and flopped its ears as a beaming Thomas held the reins.

Then, from the opposite side of the mule, Estelle turned and dashed. Virgil saw her coming right away. He swooped off his hat and opened his arms, and she rushed into them and tousled his hair. He picked her up and swung her full circle, her feet pulling with the draw of the turn. Then she stood smiling, one arm around her husband's waist, and with the other she hugged her son to her side. All three gazed at the fine animal slung over the mule. They'd eat well tonight and for the weeks ahead.

"Well, you two, go on now and cut me out the loin." Estelle said, rearranging her wool shawl. She tucked a few strands of hair back in her thick blond coil of braid. "I'll roast it up for supper tonight."

"Yes Ma'am, we sure will," Virgil said, putting his hat on and snugging it back in place. "Tomorrow we'll start some meat to smokin. Before we wash up proper I'll take a leg on over to the Tackett's. I don't think theys had much fresh venison for a spell."

Estelle nodded her head in agreement. "That'd be real nice."

Virgil leaned over and gave his wife a peck on the cheek. "Come on son; let's us get to work," he said, starting toward the smokehouse.

About an hour later, Estelle heard her son's footsteps bang across the porch and then a few gentle kicks at the door. When she opened it, a big red slab of fresh venison looked her in the eye. "Here's your loin, Ma," Thomas said, a proud grin on his face. "Pa let me cut it out myself."

Estelle took the loin and admired its weight in her hands. "Why thank you; that's sure a fine cut a meat, hain't it?" She looked past her son. Virgil and the mule stood ready at the bottom of the porch step.

"Sure is. Ma, since we's goin to the Tackett's, can I stay the night with Isaac?" He looked at her with big pleading eyes, hopeful with the prospect of spending some time with his friend again. "Please, Ma?"

"Well, I don't know. What about supper? You don't want any of this here-meat?"

"Sure I do. But I can eat some tomorrow, cain't I?"

"Well, you talk about it with your pa on the way over. See what he says." Although Thomas took any opportunity to be with Isaac, she knew Virgil liked it better when his son was home.

"Alright," Thomas said, jumping down the steps. He mounted the mule, a generous cut of deer haunch tied tight behind the old saddle.

"Give my best to Ruth," Estelle called, still holding the loin. She leaned against the door frame and watched as they headed down the lane. She was glad her son would soon have a little brother or sister to play with, to help him pass the time.

Even though the work of building a farm had seemed endless, they had also discovered that life on the frontier could be lonely. Neighbors were far away and the roads rough, especially in bad weather. It was such a change from Virginia, where neighbors and relatives were always close by.

Of all her family, Estelle missed Elizabeth, her eldest sister, the most. Growing up, it was her eldest sister who had braided her hair each morning, taught her to tie her shoes, and curled up beside her in the same tiny bed for warmth in winter. Estelle had begged her sister to come with them to Kentucky, but she had refused, unable to imagine a life so far away and in a place like the frontier. They both cried hard as the wagon wound its way out of town, westbound and off the face of the earth. In their last tearful embrace, Elizabeth pressed a handkerchief in her hand and whispered, "Don't forget me."

Only after several hours on the rutted road did Estelle feel brave enough to pull back the corners, see what the handkerchief held. And, indeed, it held a treasure—a beautiful silver locket edged with filigree. The gift must have cost her sister a small fortune. On the locket's shiny silver face she recognized her own initials: EEOM—Estelle Elizabeth Osterfield Mullins. Her sister had even gone to the trouble and expense of having the locket engraved.

As she clutched it to her chest her mind once again flooded with doubt: Were they making a mistake leaving Virginia? Perhaps they would eventually be able to buy land there. People always said never go west of the mountains— it was too dangerous over there, life too uncertain and the living just too hard. How would they ever make it so far from family?

It took several more hours of jostling along in the old wagon to muster the strength to look inside the locket. But as she clicked open the two shells of silver and peered inside, her tears began anew when she recognized a tiny lock of her sister's hair curled inside—a soft round nest of love. Estelle squeezed the locket shut and clutched it fast and tight to her chest. This was all she had of her beloved Elizabeth now, her precious sister whom she knew she'd never see again.

As Estelle lifted the heavy iron lid, a mouth-watering aroma wafted up from the fresh venison roasting in the baking dish. She tossed in the potatoes and carrots, humming softly as she moved between hearth and table. She plucked several fresh coals from the fire, arranged them on top of the cast-iron lid. The chorus of barking dogs began just as she finished wiping the table, and she knew her men had returned. But then she heard a swell of urgency in the barking that had not been there moments before. She jerked her head in alarm as a rifle shot rattled the window glass with a fast hideous jolt.

Estelle flung back the door and ran to the rail just in time to spot a small party of Indians flash from the clearing. Their faces were painted red and black and tall black spikes stuck straight up from their hairless heads. As they ran they raised their rifles, and piercing cries shattered the cold winter air. Then they were gone, vanished into the silence of the forest.

It was then she saw a heap on the ground at the bend in the lane. She leapt from the porch, looked frantically about the clearing, and shouted as she ran: "Virgil? Thomas?" Then she was kneeling beside her husband. She grabbed him by the shoulders and turned him over. Tears leapt from her eyes as she searched for Virgil's face in the glistening mass of red before her.

Thick streams of blood poured from a dark ominous gash on his head where a large jagged piece of scalp was missing. Blood stained the front of his shirt where the bullet entered his stomach. The stain was round and wide and growing rapidly from a dark center of ragged cloth. He coughed, and blood sputtered from his mouth. He clutched his belly and rolled into a ball. Blood had already started to soak the snow around him and was expanding fast.

"Oh, God, no!" Estelle screamed, gripping the cloth of his coat. She looked in disbelief at the mass of red at her knees, at the soft pink edges of gaping flesh. She shoved her hands down on what might have been the center of the wound on his head in a desperate attempt to stop the bleeding. She shifted a hand to the broad red stain on his shirt, tried to apply pressure.

"No, Virgil, no!" she begged the groaning man. "Thomas!" she shouted to the clearing, "Thomas, where are you?" Then she remembered her son had asked to stay the night with Isaac; her husband had returned alone.

Virgil's breath was coming rough and labored, and his body was twitching in erratic spasms of pain. For many dreadful moments she remained there, cradling her husband in her arms, unable to fathom what had just happened and unwilling to accept what she dreaded was about to take place. She flung her head back and shook her hands at the sky in ferocious bursts, then stared in horror at her own blood-soaked hands. Stunned, she muttered a fast prayer—small whispered breaths of desperate pleading white.

She rocked back and forth, weeping. As she touched her cheek to his, she felt his soul drifting away. It was raw instinct that caused her to turn her head and peer intently around the cold, empty clearing. When she searched deep in the snowy forest, her eye caught a quick flash of red. It came from a cardinal in the distant woods, flapping its bright wings against the white of snow, hovering just within the shadow of the leafless trees. She drew an instant reassurance from the quiet of the red flitting bird, found a thread of comfort in the snowy land. As she watched the movement of wings in the forest, stillness descended around her. She stopped the rocking; the sobbing ceased as well.

She looked down at the bleeding man in her arms, understood what to do.

She bent over, her tear-streaked face nuzzled in the familiar crook of his neck. "Virgil, my love, you wait here. I'll be right back." The startling tenderness in her voice made the man breathe more evenly; his body eased its struggle and relaxed a little onto the frozen ground.

Estelle ran back to the cabin, emerged with an armful of blankets. She slid one under her husband's head and piled the remaining blankets over top. Then she slipped underneath, curled around him from behind, and wedged her arm below his. She laid her hand where the bullet had entered his stomach and felt the damp warmth of his blood below her palm. How many nights had they had slept like this? Woken like this? With her other hand she stroked Virgil's hair, hummed in his ear. As she turned to kiss his shoulder, she felt the baby inside the curve of her belly move as it sensed the nearness of its father, as if reaching out for the man who would not live to know its face.

Nestled in his hair, Estelle breathed deeply—first once, then again. She savored his familiar scent, drew it into her, committing his smell to memory even mingled as it was with the sharp tang of blood. She matched her breath to her husband's ragged breathing, absorbed into her own body whatever pain she could wrest from his. Even when the breaths became more labored, she stayed curled tightly behind him, breathing calmly beside him on the cold bloody ground, until the life left him.

Only when the tears were dry on her cheeks did she rise up from beneath the blankets. She stood, alone and dazed, in the soundless clearing. Again she looked around, but this time it was through stunned eyes devoid of comprehension. Numbness had fallen, taken her away, and enveloped her with thick, clouded vision. She turned and stumbled, one foot before the other, following the tangled path of footprints on the snowy wagon lane. The fresh flakes of brilliant white had ceased to glitter.

When finally she reached the riverbank, she stood at the edge and peered blankly at the water's glassy surface. The river ran dark and cloudy, obscuring any object that may have rested even slightly beneath its skin. Dirty foam frothed up where the edges of currents met, each struggling with the other to dominate the river. She stared at her feet, perched on the sodden riverbank. Frost twinkled in brittle uncertain patches; blurred hoof tracks of mule and jumbled boot prints of man disappeared on the shoals just beyond the river's cold watery edge.

To one side, wet twigs and crushed leaves circled in a stagnant, ice-encrusted eddy. Its surface formed a still pool that reflected the pale sickle of the moon that hung behind her in the gray winter sky.

All of a sudden Virgil's face appeared behind her shoulder. Not the dark bloodied face of the man whose lifeless body lay in the clearing—it was his familiar face and tender eyes that smiled back at her from that still pool. She caught her breath; he was there with her after all. For one cherished moment their eyes met in an intimate flicker of recognition, but when she wheeled around to embrace him, only the bare trees and the gray winter sky hung before that pale sickle of moon.

Estelle sobbed only once as she forced herself to face the river again. She stepped one foot in, and then the other, and instantly the cold spilled over into the warmth inside her boot. It climbed her calves, groped upward to her thighs as she kept moving. She raised her hands as the water rose; it rushed fast and close in welcoming embrace. When she reached the midpoint of the river, she turned upstream. The insistent pull of the current tugged at her skirt, pushed determinedly against the front of her legs. A glimmer lit her face as she felt the power of the moving water.

She lowered her hands, brown and flaky with her husband's dried blood, until they hovered just above the skin of the water. She dipped her fingers, watched in stunned fascination as the wet surface rippled and parted and pressed past, innocent of all it carried downstream that cold winter day. But the river called out for more. She bent her knees and crouched low in the frigid water. It swirled swift around her waist, close at her breasts, and splashed as if in play against the bottom of her chin. She smiled as the exhilarating coldness tingled her skin, caressed her with icy fingers. She took a breath and lowered her head beneath the river's dark cloudy surface.

The cold penetrated her thick coil of braid and offered instant relief for her tired face, for her worn and swollen eyes. Under water, the incessant thundering in her head was transformed to a welcome silence, and with it, dim, thankful darkness. The cold enveloped everything and dangled before her the enticing image of deep, eternal stillness. Estelle tried to imagine her life without Virgil. She reached her arms to the bottom, to consider with her hands the loose rock of the shoals. Small and slick. Soft with muck. Nothing to grab hold of. She could just lift her feet . . . drift away into that stillness.

But her feet remained in place, two thin shaking tethers to the murky river bottom. She brought her hands to the wet bulge at her belly, felt the life of the growing child within. And Thomas awaited her at the Tackett's. Slowly, distraught, she finished crossing the shoals and dragged herself up the edge of the muddy bank. Dripping and spent, she stumbled at last into the Tackett clearing and collapsed in a shivering heap at the icy foot of their door.

By the time Mr. Tackett made his way to the Mullins cabin, Virgil's body was frozen solid. Knee bent to the red icy ground, the neighbor paused at the side of the contorted corpse of his friend. He rested a large calloused hand on Virgil's unmoving shoulder, bent his head.

Then he went to the barn, swung open the door, and grabbed a shovel from the wall. He strode around the edge of the clearing until he settled on a location: A gentle rise of land not far from the creek. A gentle rise scattered with dogwoods and redbuds, a few small oaks that in time would put on girth, leaf out in broad dappled shade. A rise with sufficient room to grow: while his friend's grave might be the first, it would not be the last in this new cemetery. That is, if the family was even able to return to this broad stretch of land beside the creek.

As he dug through the cold earth that day, the shovel's shiny metal blade scraped against the frozen ground with a cruel, high-pitched ring. Thin lonely echoes of sadness, the bitter sound of loss lingered in the air, reverberated against the hard, bare trunks of the chill winter forest. Tragedy had once again struck another family on this dangerous frontier.

Chapter Three

It was not a difficult decision for Meg Harrington to decide where to place her excavation units. Although the data gathered from several days of shovel probing were helpful, they were relatively minor compared to the most obvious evidence of all: two thick rows of irises thrust up through the pasture sod. It was an "X Marks the Spot" on a pirate's secret treasure map, a kind of "Dig Here" for archaeologists.

"I guess the front door was right about there," Meg said, pointing a finger at the wide swath of green at one end of the thick rows. The crew stood beside her, gazing at the invisible house. She squinted, trying to visualize the old place against the bizarre backdrop of newly built subdivision houses: It must have been a beautiful home with the irises in full bloom.

"Hey, let's do the path!" yelled Scott, the class comedian. He started a conga line, and the rest of the crew fell in behind, sashaying up the iris rows, kicking their legs out to either side, everyone comically out of sequence. Scott struck up a pitiful rendition of Tiny Tim's "Tiptoe through the Tulips." When he reached the end of the iris path, he pushed an imaginary doorbell, shouted, "Ding Dong, anybody home?" The crew erupted into laughter as Tonya yelled, "Avon calling!" from midway along the conga line.

Meg pretended to laugh along with her crew, although she didn't find their light-hearted antics funny this time, even though she couldn't quite say why—apart from the fact that Avon would never have existed on the Kentucky frontier; nor did this simple cabin ever have—or ever need—a doorbell.

Metal blades again sliced the pasture, but this time the crew's straight shovels skimmed off the sod to form one-by-one-meter excavation units—perfect squares of flat brown soil cut through the green sod.

"Alright everyone, gather over here, if you please," Meg called, plopping herself cross-legged on the ground. "You're all ready to excavate so you need to take elevations first. Scott, pound this in the sod beside the unit," she said, handing him a short wooden stake. "Then tie this string around the top—really tight, so it doesn't move."

When Scott finished he held the string in his hand, its long length of slack dipping down to the tip of the stake.

Meg unfurled a tape measure and held it flush against the stake. "First we measure the height of the string above the sod. Everybody look. What does the tape read?"

Scott squatted and read the numbers on the tape: "Fifteen centimeters."

"Good." Meg held up a line level between her thumb and index finger. As she dipped it back and forth, the tiny bubble of air ran down one side and then the other. She handed it to Scott. "Hook this on the string and pull it taut. Raise or lower the string to get the bubble in the middle."

When Scott got the bubble even, Meg moved the tip of her tape measure to the soil at the bottom corner of the unit. Together, tape measure and string made a perfect right angle.

"Okay—now what does it read?" she asked.

"Twenty centimeters," answered Scott.

"So that means the sod was five centimeters thick, right?" Meg asked. She gazed around and waited for the crew to nod. "So if you start level 1 here," she patted the soil, "what is your top measurement for level 1?"

"Twenty centimeters," said Tonya.

Nodding, Meg passed out excavation forms to each student. "Good. Write that measurement on your form." Then she waited for the question.

"Umm, what corner is that?" asked Tonya.

Meg patted the soil in the corner with her hand. "Ah, yes. What corner is this?" she asked the crew.

As they stood staring at her, it was only Suzy who raised her head to consider the grid they had established—the orientation of the bright pink pinflags as they swept due north and south, due east and west across the pasture. "That's the northeast corner," she said, and then blushed.

"Exactly. Northeast corner." Meg smiled at Suzy, then scanned the other faces to gauge their comprehension. "Since this is Suzy's unit, she'll write twenty centimeters in the blank for the northeast corner. We'll dig in ten-centimeter arbitrary levels. So if you *start* at a depth of twenty centimeters for level 1, what should the depth be when you *finish* level 1?"

Again it was Suzy who spoke: "Thirty," she offered, then blushed again. She had to be the shyest student Meg had ever known.

"Excellent on the math!" Meg said, nodding. "Okay everybody, back to your units. Emily and I'll be around to check your elevations."

It was then Meg noticed the tiny movement on her leg. "Ah ha! I see we have a guest!" she said, watching the tick crawl on her jeans. It reared back, its tiny front legs waving as it tasted the air, smelling its way toward warm embeddable flesh. "And now I will demonstrate the technique of dealing with unwelcome visitors at the site."

The crew observed as Meg plucked her Marshalltown trowel from her back pocket. She brought the weapon close and with a dramatic thrust impaled the tick with her trowel's sharp pointed tip. She raised the skewered creature in the air, examined the writhing insect for a moment, then stabbed tick and trowel into the sod, twisting it a bit for good measure. She wiped the blade on her jeans and then slid it down in her back jeans pocket. "Okay, got it everyone?"

A day later, midway through level 2, the dull sound of Scott's scraping trowel changed to a high tinny ring: He had hit something solid. Further excavation exposed the edges of a wide flat rock, then another wide flat rock, and then another. Soon, Scott had exposed ten wide, flat, irregularly shaped limestone slabs, each set puzzle-like into a neat rectangle. The stones in the center were charred a deep sooty black. It was the fireplace pad of an old log cabin, and at three feet by five feet, it had been the cooking hearth of a rather modest one.

For the next several days they excavated out from the fireplace pad, following easily the outlines of the cabin's narrow limestone foundation. By the end of the week they had a clear view of two rooms separated by the dark fitted stones of the cooking hearth. They also discovered the outlines of two front porches— one small and one large—as well as a small rear addition. It had been here, in this place, within these humble rooms and before this fireside, where so much of life had unfolded for the people who once made their home beside the creek.

Many kinds of broken glass and ceramic sherds began to appear in the screens. Suzy dug up some broken redware with dark angry cracks across the interior's brittle, low-fired glaze. Tonya's unit was full of pieces of pearlware with scalloped blue edges, as well as a few pieces of creamware. Joe's level 2 began to yield a few sherds of a lavender willowware transfer print with a pastoral Chinese pagoda scene. They found the sharp, uneven fragments of brown salt-glazed stoneware and dark olive-green glass bottles. The earth also gave up a wide assortment of iron nails and other strangely twisted scraps of corroding metal.

According to the reference books in Meg's lab, these were historic artifacts that spanned the late eighteenth almost through the middle of the nineteenth centuries. Redware stretched well back into the early 1700s and continued through the end of the century. Creamware dishes first began appearing on dining tables around the mid 1700s and were quite common until they were replaced by the more costly pearlware beginning around the 1780s, and creamware was relegated to more humble vessels like the chamber pot. Willowware transfer print was manufactured initially in England and was imported to grace the finer tables of North America, and it was found in an increasing variety of colors after about 1825.

Trained craftsmen at smithies hammered out the square wrought nails prior to 1790, while later hardware makers cut the square shanks out of rolled metal plates. Glassblowers in growing cities like Pittsburgh blew the bottles—liquid sand glowing hot at the ends of their long spinning tubes. Overall, the range of artifact dates revealed that several generations had made their home beside this little creek, below the shadow of the gray stone knobs.

Meg gulped some Gatorade in the shade of the old oak and studied the crew. They were hard at work excavating new units downslope from the limestone cabin foundation. Under Emily's capable supervision, they were doing fine without her.

The irises had been calling, and today Meg could finally answer. Each day they lured her; she detoured through the thick rows on her way to the truck and on her way back. Sometimes she even walked to the creek via the irises, which made little geographical sense. She had observed their slow progression each day, noted the swelling of new cones, the bursting of bright new blossoms, and the lengthening of their sturdy stems as the irises stretched further skyward. Today was the day.

Meg pulled her clipboard from her pack, snapped a sheet of graph paper to the front. She grabbed a fifty-meter tape and strode to the bright pink pinflag at grid point 80 North 20 East. She secured the zero end of the tape at the foot of the pinflag. From there she walked backward, unreeling the tape, staying oriented with the bright pink pinflags along the 80 North gridline before her. When she reached the start of the irises, she squatted and laid the tape flush with the ground. "Humm, that's interesting," she mumbled. "They start at exactly 80 North 25 East."

She kept walking backward, unfurling the tape. But with each step her eyes grew wider: She was backing down the absolute center of the iris pathway.

When she reached the porch foundation—and the end of the irises' rows—she again snugged the tape flush with the ground. It read exactly forty-five meters.

Meg stood up and narrowed her eyes at the unfurled tape. She strode back along its length, making sure it lay perfectly flat on the ground, until she reached the 80 North 20 East pinflag. The zero end of the tape was still secure. She lifted her clipboard's metal lid, pulled out the site map, and studied the grid's perfect directional chessboard of pinflags across the pasture. She couldn't believe it; the tape was right and so was the grid. She let out a sigh; whoever had planted these irises had done so on a perfect east-west angle with her grid, and for an exact twenty meters.

Shaking her head in surprise, Meg walked back along the pathway. She stepped up on the foundation stones of the porch enlargement and stood gazing out across the two thick rows of irises. She pulled her favorite mechanical pencil from behind her ear, clicked it a few times, and then touched the lead to graph paper.

The thin, delicate petals were translucent in the morning light, splendid against the bright, dazzling green of the sod. Some blossoms gleamed broad centers of yellow—the color of radiant sunshine. Their frilly edges were pale, reminiscent of the shade of sweet creamy butter. She entered the pathway; she mapped the location of the first royal purple iris, a hue deep and majestic. Its fringes were light lavender, with long daring stamens of gold. Another step and another bearded iris of shimmering yellow, and then back to purple—the color of a ripe summer plum. Tall and strong they stood, these proud seasonal keepers of this green, rolling land.

Meg was in their midst and breathed in their brilliance as her eyes fluttered closed. Poised between her fingers, the smooth lead of her mechanical pencil glided across the straight, logical lines of graph paper, and her hand was the follower.

The subtle, fleeting fragrance of iris and the striking memory of brilliant color sought entry to her senses and discovered open passage there. The delicate scent transported her away from the noise of passing cars and the constant rumble of heavy equipment. The sounds grew indistinct, receding into the distance. She heard the buzz of a bee in search of warm summer nectar, the languid flap of the painted wing of a Monarch. Was she really able to hear the pink-spotted lady beetle creeping up the sturdy stalk?

When at last she opened her eyes, she had reached the far end of the pathway. She gazed down at the clipboard; the paper before her revealed the precise location of each clump of iris, transcribed for posterity. She had rendered the precise orientation of each thick row without a single fault; each bloom of purple was marked without flaw, each burst of yellow labeled as such. No ugly erasure marks blemished the fine lines of graph paper; no careless blunder of pencil lead marred her faultless illustration of that perfectly placed pathway of brilliance.

"Dr. Harrington? I think I found something." It was Tonya, calling from her unit just downslope from the cabin foundation.

On a dig, "I think I found something" was a rather amusing phrase and was at best an understatement. Usually, it meant the speaker had unearthed something other than the ubiquitous ceramic sherds, broken pieces of glass, or thin corroded metal. Something a little more unusual. Meg knelt on the matted grass beside Tonya's unit and peered toward the dim corner where the girl's tattooed arm pointed. "What is it?"

"I don't know." As Tonya shrugged, the New Age dragon across her arms and shoulders shrugged along with her. "Some kind of weird glint—it just appeared out of nowhere. I scraped my trowel over it. I think it sounds like metal, but I don't know."

"Well, excavate a little more—see if you can find some edges."

As Meg watched Tonya carry out her instructions she was reminded of the incident that almost dissuaded her from a career in archaeology. She had probably been about Tonya's age.

Her supervisor on the dig more often than not hijacked a unit when anything out of the ordinary appeared. One time he grabbed the trowel right out of Meg's hand and scooted her off to the side. She had stared over his shoulder as the man finished unearthing a 3,000-year-old eagle bone flute fragment she had begun to expose—and whose unexpected emergence she dutifully reported. It was terrible archaeological etiquette on his part, but such behavior was nevertheless common. Unless there was a legitimate reason otherwise, proper archaeological protocol was to allow the thrill of unearthing an artifact to accrue to the finder.

"Anything different?" asked Meg, hoping she sounded nonchalant, but knowing glints were relatively unusual.

"Well, I think I found an edge. Whatever it is, it's gotta be real small." Tonya said.

"Okay, get an elevation, photos, and map its location in the unit."

As Meg waited she wished yet again she had found the courage to tell her ill-mannered supervisor to buzz off, but however much she regretted it, those words had not passed her lips that day. But once the tears had dried that evening, she realized she had learned a valuable lesson that day in her unit: She would have to figure out a way to stand up for herself; otherwise people would just scoot her off to the side for the rest of her life.

As if sensing something unusual in the air—a kind of archaeological osmosis—the crew had wandered over, gathering at the edge of Tonya's unit to see what was going on. It was the archaeological equivalent of rubbernecking, brought on by the whiff of something special on the cusp of discovery.

As Meg waited, that same cold sensation she felt that first day seeped up from the ground around her, a slight chill on her skin. She glanced around—Tonya didn't seem to notice it, nor did the rest of the crew. This time it felt calmer, and Meg didn't try to resist, accepting instead its strange coolness as it gathered in the air around her. She took a deep breath and smelled the age of this place, then shivered a bit as the chill deepened. "Okay, go ahead and pick it up," she blurted, and Tonya reached out her tattooed arm and plucked up the strange glinting object.

It was about the size of a walnut and small cakes of dirt still adhered to its surface. Once Tonya removed it from the shade of the unit, Meg could see the object wasn't really shiny at all, but the relative lack of light had only made it appear that way. Full sunlight revealed a heavy tarnish coating a metal surface. Even as it sat in Tonya's hand, she could make out the artifact's basic features: oval and flat. Definitely not a nail or even an odd piece of irregular glass.

Meg could contain herself no longer. She thrust out her arm, requesting the retrieval of this unknown glinting artifact from Tonya. And then she was holding it. It was close to weightless and very cool to the touch. As she turned it over with gentle fingers, laid it forward and back in the palm of her hand, the identity of the blackened metal slowly gathered in her consciousness. It was a piece of old silver jewelry. No, it was much more than that—it was a silver locket.

At the moment of the object's naming, a cool tingling sensation began in the palm of her hand. Meg's eyes grew wider as the tingling grew stronger. It tickled her hand, radiating out from the patch of skin where the locket lay. The sense of being watched came back, and she turned her head toward the trees along the creek bank, then the other way to the gray knobs in the distance, and then looked back down at the dirt-caked locket sitting in the palm of her hand.

The crew was standing around her, expectant. They were waiting for her next move; eager for her to utter for them the identity of this new find, say something profound about this unusual new discovery. "I think it might be a locket," she said weakly. Even as the words passed Meg's lips they felt meager and insufficient, a wholly inadequate description of the wonder resting in the palm of her tingling hand.

But Tonya was staring at her. Now that she knew what it was, the girl standing before her wanted to hold it again, experience the sensation of this rare item for herself. Meg frowned as she looked at her palm. She didn't want to give it back, but she knew she had to. Archaeological etiquette demanded she give it back. Proper protocol allowed the opportunity for every crew member to hold in their very own hand whatever marvel was unearthed on their project. While the thrill of excavation may accrue to the digger, once removed from the ground, the artifact belonged to all. Everyone present had the absolute right to hold it.

Meg felt dizzy as she extended her reluctant arm toward Tonya, who plucked up the little locket with fast grubby fingers. "Careful! It's delicate," Meg quickly cautioned. Immediately the perspiration rose on the small of her back and her armpits felt wet and clammy. She forced herself to focus on the tip of the tail of the tattooed dragon on Tonya's wrist as the girl brought the locket close to her face for examination. Meg pursed her lips—the strange juxtaposition of the New Age dragon and the tradition that was this old silver locket irritated her.

After Tonya was finished she passed the locket to Scott, who also inspected the new artifact. The class comedian held it up to the sky, ludicrously testing whether he could see through it. And then it went to Suzy, who looked at it and then passed it to Bob, who looked at it and then passed it to Jessica, who looked at it and then passed it to the next person.

Meg tracked the path of that tarnished silver oval with her eyes, scowling to herself as each new pair of grubby crew hands groped and grabbed the little treasure on its long obligatory round. She felt the sudden urge to pounce for the locket and dash away. She looked toward the old oak. She needed to get control of the situation before she did something so foolish. "Scott, go get a little box from the yellow trunk. Tonya, make a separate bag and write the coordinates on it," she ordered.

Meg gritted her teeth as she watched Tonya scrawl across the bag in her sloppy student writing. She tried not to snatch the box away from Scott when he brought it, although she might have. Once the locket was finally back in the safety of her hands, she opened the box, wadded soft cotton around the locket, put the lid back on, and slid the box into the labeled bag.

And the crew was still standing there, gawking at her every move. "Okay everybody—show's over. Back to the trenches!"

But even as she had watched the locket make its slow and painful circle back to her, Meg understood the object that passed from hand to hand was much more than some mere artifact. As she opened the box and slipped the locket inside, she recognized it for exactly what it was—a very personal and vital piece of the past and the very essence of so much of life that had once taken place along this broad stretch of land at the edge of the creek, beneath the shadow of the tall gray knobs.

Meg's footfalls sounded anxious that Saturday morning as she strode the long university hall to her archaeology lab. She stopped at the door and glanced back up the hall, checking that no one had followed her. Satisfied she was alone, she stuck her key in the door, entered, and locked the door behind her.

An old clipboard with a smudged sheet of paper hung from a hook on the wall beside the door. A frayed piece of dirty string was tied to the clipboard, and the gnawed stub of a dull pencil dangled glumly in the air. Grumbling under her breath, Meg batted for the pencil, logged herself into the lab, dutifully noting name, date, and time, and cursed the name of Ross Landers as she scrawled on the smudged sheet of paper.

She tested the doorknob; it was still locked. Who was she locking it from, exactly? No students were likely to come by on a Saturday, especially not during summer. Emily wouldn't stop in because she and her boyfriend had driven to Cincinnati for his big introduction to her family. But still Meg wanted the door locked—she didn't want to have to contend with any surprise visitors.

The archaeology lab of Bluegrass University was functional but far from elegant. Low stools sat in rows along counters, and a white enamel sink and drain board sat midway along the wall. A variety of mismatched tables, a hodgepodge scavenged from across campus, provided workspace in the center of the room. Meg had run long extension cords so lamps could sit on the tables and render sufficient light for proper artifact identification. Always conscious of safety, she had duct-taped the extension cords onto the lab's warped linoleum floor tiles. As she crossed the room, she noted the duct tape had again curled up at the corners and was dark with grit. She would need to replace it again soon.

Colorful posters covered the lab's institutional beige concrete-block walls. One poster read, "Archaeology: More Than Meets the Eye," superimposed over an undulating landscape. Another poster depicted a man opening his trench coat as if to sell stolen watches, only to reveal a stunning cache of prehistoric weapons, including an atlatl, or spear thrower. The byline was "When Atlatals Are Outlawed Only Outlaws Will Have Atlatals." Meg's favorite was the close-up of a hand holding a potsherd and an arrowhead, "Our Nation's Past: Held in Trust."

Heavy rain had forced the crew to the lab for the last couple of days. A veritable beehive of washing had produced long neat rows of Styrofoam trays burgeoning with clean and drying artifacts ready to be labeled, sorted, counted, weighed, recorded, bagged, and boxed. But Meg didn't even glance at the long waiting rows of Styrofoam trays. Rather, she walked straight to her desk in the corner. She tried the lower right drawer. It was still locked.

Meg found the proper key and turned the lock with a dull metallic clunk. She opened the drawer and there it was—the bag containing the boxed locket. Her own neat block printing now graced the rewritten bag, duly noting all relevant information: site number, unit coordinates, depth, date, Tonya's initials as excavator. She picked up the bag and took it to the sink.

She walked to the cabinet, poked through the shelves until she found what she was looking for: boxes of baking soda and coarse salt. She carried the boxes to the drain board and pulled up a stool. She mixed large portions of salt and baking soda in a heavy bowl of steaming water, stirring it to create a gentle acid wash.

Meg plucked the locket from the cotton and placed it on the white enamel drain board. She dunked a Q-tip into the thick mixture and let a heavy drop fall onto the locket's heavily tarnished surface. She rubbed the swab across the dark metal with slow circular motions. As she rubbed, the last grains of dirt dissolved and the tarnish lightened a shade as the acid began eating away at the thick oxidized coating.

She dipped the Q-tip, rubbed some more, followed by more vanishing tarnish. Again she dipped and rubbed, little by little peeling back each thin layer darkened by time. Working methodically, she removed tarnish from both surfaces, from hook and hinge, and along the narrow crevice where the two silver oval shells plunged deeply inward. A series of sharp broken ends ringed the circumference of the locket and was all that now remained of delicate filigree decoration. At one time it must have been a fine piece of jewelry. She cleaned the broken ends as best she could.

She recalled descriptions of similar filigreed lockets in the reference books. She made a mental note to investigate whether this might be one of Mr. Asa Blanchard's pieces, an early Lexington silversmith as famous in his day as Boston's Paul Revere. She'd also check the estimated value at manufacture for such a piece, but even without that figure, Meg guessed the locket's cost had been high in comparison to most of the other artifacts they had recovered thus far from the Creekside Subdivision Expansion Site. How could a family of humble settlers have afforded something so expensive on the early Kentucky frontier?

As she continued rubbing she noticed a tight cluster of shallow scratches was beginning to appear on the silver surface. Her eyes narrowed as those random lines began to take on more regular, curvilinear shapes as they rose from below the tarnish. These marks were too uniform to be just some haphazard scrapes against some hard object. The pattern was too even, the depth too consistent, the width of the lines too regular, the spacing too precise.

Slowly, it dawned on her what she was seeing: Those weren't scratches, but the intentional incisions of a flowing motif that crossed the locket's silver face. Was it some kind of floral design? But as Meg continued examining what she now understood was the front of the locket, four elaborate cursive letters materialized from the confused jumble of lines, leaping out from beneath the long years of tarnish. She laid down the Q-tip, picked up a pin. She traced the pin's sharp tip along the lines of the letters as they swung and looped until she could decipher each one: EEOM. Initials? Could these really be initials?

At Meg's discovery of the initials, the pin poised in her fingers trembled just a little. A strange surge of intimacy rose in her chest, and with it came a familiarity, an unexpected ease with this long-ago woman—this EEOM—who must once have worn this silver locket on a chain around her neck. Before she was able to yank it away, Meg's heart was touched by the image of this nameless faceless woman.

Only at that moment did she begin to comprehend why she had been so moved by the locket's discovery. As she traced once again the swirling initials, Meg reflected on the undeniable truth that she herself had never owned anything so special, anything so traditional, and nothing even remotely resembling a precious silver locket. But as she gazed at the flowing initials, she realized she had yearned for such a wonderful thing her entire life. What would it be like to have a locket with her own initials curling across a bright face of shining silver? Her heart jumped at the thought.

But a locket would be a gift her father would never have given her, although not because he wouldn't. Rather, in his always-busy world, such a gift would simply never have occurred to him; books and science kits had always been his idea of appropriate presents. Then later, as an adult with a salary of her own, the thought of buying a locket for herself had never occurred to her either, caught up in her own demanding world of academia. Besides, lockets had to be gifts, didn't they?

With the exception of the filigree, the locket was in good shape for being buried for well over a hundred years. The oval loop was still intact, as was the hinge element—the two most delicate parts. If the locket were to break, it would do so at one of those locations. Meg picked up her Q-tip, dripped more of the cleaning solution over the hinge, soaking it thoroughly.

She knew she shouldn't try to open the locket. She was not trained in jewelry conservation and would not be able to repair the hinge if it broke. She got up, retrieved a bottle of lubricating oil from the cabinet, and turned its nozzle to hover just above the hinge. She watched as several drops of oil seeped into the tiny crux of silver pivot teeth, saturating the locket's delicate turning axis.

She really should not try to open the locket. Besides, there was nothing to be gained from opening it. She wouldn't be able to learn anything more from the inside that she didn't already know from the outside—or wouldn't soon be able to find out from the reference books. Even if she did open it, she knew nothing inside would be preserved—the acidity of the soil would have long since caused the decomposition of any organic material that might once have been tucked inside the locket's paired silver shells.

But still, against reason, as she sat on her stool at the white enamel drain board, she wanted to open the locket, and desperately so. She wanted to open it not necessarily to gratify the urge of discovery that drove so much of archaeological science, nor for the simple fact that no one had glimpsed the inside since it dropped to the ground so long ago. Meg wanted to open it just to find out what treasure this woman—this EEOM—had chosen to carry inside her cherished locket. What was it that had warranted such a place of honor?

Even as she assessed the strength of the hinge, Meg wanted to open it and discover every trite thing that has ever been tucked into a locket to be inside this one. Maybe a photograph or a poem on paper folded small. Dried flower petals from a special bouquet. A bedtime story. A mother's comforting arms and her warm beating heart. Meg wanted to find all these things inside these paired silver shells as if the locket contained an infinite number of immense chambers.

As a girl, Meg harbored hopes that her mother—even as she lay dying—had left something behind, some special gift for her daughter to open at some indeterminate time in the future. Young Magpie—her mother always called her that—imagined she would discover that special gift inside a colorful box with a fitted lid, tied with a long pink ribbon. When she loosened the ribbon and peered inside, she would find the treasures of her mother's cherished mementos, each deep with meaning. There would be a hand-knit scarf for cold winters. A cup of steaming cocoa. A special letter just for her. The box would hold a great magical hand imbued with the ability to consider the temperature of the forehead of a feverish child or wick away any tear that dared trickle down a cheek. And, of course, a silver locket would be the most marvelous gift contained within that colorful box. What would Magpie have tucked within its paired silver shells?

Meg took a dental pick from her drawer, and braced the locket against the white enamel drain board. Her hands trembled as she inserted the pick's sharp tip into the dark crevice plunging between the silver ovals.

She pushed. Nothing happened. She inserted the pick at a different spot, tried again. She pushed a little harder, prying down against the delicate edge of a silver shell, then checked to see if she left a dent. On the third try the locket popped open with a peaceful click . . . and the swift release into the present of memories lost and forgotten, buried beneath the passage of time.

Holding her breath, Meg pushed open the top shell. It moved with a stiff resistance, forcing her to gain entry with an intention she would never be able to deny. Then she sat upright on her stool. The silver locket lay on the drain board, spread wide and gaping, deprived at last of its final intimate secrets. It was an absolute invasion of privacy—the epitome of intrusion. It reminded Meg of a dissection project in biology class, the dead frog pinned down and splayed, utterly immobile on the ignominy of the dissection table.

Nothing was there. The paired silver shells held nothing beyond more thick layers of black tarnish.

Meg set the dental pick on the white enamel drain board with a dull thud of finality. She let out the breath which she hadn't realized she was holding— and with it, an unmistakable sigh of regret. She looked up at the clock, buzzing without interest on the institutional beige concrete-block wall of her archaeology lab. She had been immersed in her work—no, in her absurd and futile fantasies—for well over an hour.

She frowned as she stared through the lab's solitary window, her eyes locked in a hard blank stare. Cars whizzed by on their important Saturday errands— fast blurs racing back and forth, oblivious and unmoved by the mere artifact lying on the white enamel drain board, indifferent to her disappointment. She clenched her teeth against rising emotion.

Well, of course there's nothing there. What did she expect to find? A sudden flush of humiliation coursed through her. As if discovering the initials wasn't enough, she still had dared to want more—to be greedy and hope for some impossible miracle to emerge from the ground. But more was not forthcoming, nor would it ever be. She recognized the too-familiar shape of unmet longing—that strange laughing monster that lurks and teases, tempts and dangles before your eyes that which can never be yours, then snatches it away the moment you reach a hand to claim it. She was ashamed of herself for coming up empty-handed even when she knew she would—for letting sentiment triumph over objectivity.

No, there was no colorful box tied with a long pink ribbon, nor would there ever be. No letter. No magical hand. No beating heart. There would be none of it, no matter how much she wished it otherwise. A tear welled in her eye; she wiped it away with the back of her hand. She knew exactly what her father would say right now: "Buck up Buttercup."

Jaw clenched, Meg picked up her Q-tip, dunked it back into the cleaning solution. She began rubbing away the tarnish from inside the locket's paired silver shells. Where hope and optimism had only just so recently reigned, melancholy now prevailed. When the occasional tear tingled up in her eye, she blinked it away. It was her own fault for giving in to such silliness.

After she finished rubbing, Meg began the locket's documentation—a mere consolation prize compared to the grand one that might have been.

But even as she wiped and measured, weighed and photographed and recorded each objective attribute of the locket—determination smeared across her expressionless face—the initials EEOM snuck back in thin wisps. They crept up beside her as she worked, twirling around her lone bent figure like a magical shimmering dream, a lost ghost now released, at last curling its way out of the darkness and making its way home. While one side of Meg's brain concentrated on the task at hand, the other was borne away with the swirls of flowing script as they turned and twisted over and around, conjuring new images of this now-silent woman. She would not be turned away.

Chapter Four

Thomas woke to find his world completely changed. His hands rushed to the painful throbbing in his head, but the instant he tried to move he realized he was bound tight, feet and hands roped behind him like a farm animal ready for slaughter. He lay on his side, someplace dark and warm and full of strange smells—of smoke, of fresh animal pelt and parched rawhide, of dried blood and sweat, and the pungent tang of his own stale urine.

Dimly he recalled confusing images from the last indeterminate stretch of days. Being slung down on the ground—the coldness of the snow—loud voices shouting things he did not understand. Opening his eyes to the blank bright sky—bare leafless trees that seemed to move on their own. The steady shifting of a mule. A bruising rain of heavy clubs on his back. Thirst. A dull ache in his legs and arms. The throb in his head. But the images were blurred, incoherent, running together like long chaotic piles of loose tangled rope—no beginning and no end of continual drifting delirium.

He groaned, shifted his legs, and touched something solid in the dark. Then he fell back into a long dreamless sleep.

He woke again as the hide flap, covering what appeared to be an entrance, was thrown back. Piercing rays of unexpected sunlight shot across his eyes, and he winced from their rapid stabs of pain. A wall of coldness hit him, forcing him back toward the brink of consciousness. He struggled against his restraints, bringing an instant tightening of the rough rope and new jolts of hurt in his arms and legs. Someone grabbed the rope and dragged him into the sunlight. The cold hard ground was shocking after the recent warmth.

A cacophony of strange voices yelled strange words at him. Women's voices, men's voices, some deep and rough, others shrill and angry—a deafening circle of dissonance from all directions. He thrashed about to face them, only to hear the voices at his back; he struggled to turn again, but they were everywhere, and soon he lacked the strength to resist against the hurting.

Suddenly the voices stopped, and an imprecise shape appeared abruptly before him. It was a face, brown and wrinkled. As his vision brought the strange face into focus, two old sharp narrow black eyes penetrated his own. Gradually, he understood the eyes to be those of an old woman, regarding him with an indecipherable mix of curiosity and suspicion. The old woman's face disappeared and then reappeared again further away, this time apparently connected to strong knotted hands that urged him to turn his head. His head moved in the direction of command, and his dry cracked lips brushed against something firm. The hands lifted his head, poured a trickle of cool water at the corner of his mouth. Instantly his parched tongue thrust out to find more, and soon he was licking greedily at the musty gourd bowl the woman held to his lips, thankful for the cool wetness that rushed into his dry mouth.

When he coughed and sputtered, laughter erupted from all around. Only then did he look out beyond the old woman to see a mass of unfamiliar brown faces watching him as he lay tied and helpless on the cold ground.

The old woman's knotted fingers pried his teeth apart, squeezed mush between them. It was soft and warm and sweet, and his mouth filled at once with saliva. He opened his mouth for more, and again a wave of laughter burst from the watching brown faces. The woman again pushed in fingers with mush— his was the wide maw of a helpless baby bird, its pleading mouth agape. He swallowed everything she gave him without argument, staring blankly into her strange dark eyes, into her strange wrinkled face. Once more he slept.

Soon after, she cut free the ropes that bound his hands and feet. The faces still watched, erupted again into laughter when she removed Thomas's damp bloody clothes and threw them into the fire. She wiped his thin pale body with a coarse wet cloth, dipping it occasionally in an iron kettle of water. Her movements were firm and deliberate, and he knew better than to resist them. She dressed him in a simple cotton shirt and deerskin breeches and wrapped a plain wool blanket around his shoulders. Again she fed him, and again he fell into a deep dreamless sleep.

And so it continued for many days, until he could at last stay awake and sit upright beside the fire.

It was much later that Thomas learned that a man named Old Bear had hit him three times on the head before he fell face first in the red tangle of snow beside his dying father. Impressed by his strength to resist such powerful blows, Old Bear had claimed the blond boy, right there at the edge of the white settler's clearing. In time, Thomas understood he was the replacement for Old Bear's youngest grandson, who was killed some years earlier by a group of Long Knives—white men who had shot the boy in the back as he gathered bulrushes for his grandmother.

He came to learn that the Long Knives were crossing even deeper into the lake country now, to carry home deerskins by the horse load, skins for which the white people east of the mountains seemed to have an endless desire. Yet the Shaawanwa—Old Bear's people—had never agreed to allow the Long Knives into their territory, and they had been given no trade goods for the many fine deerskins that left their land. When Old Bear and his people had demanded payment, the Long Knives had raised their rifles without hesitation.

It had been Old Bear's wife, Black Crow Woman, who fed him that first day and the many days that followed. It was she who tended his head wound, put there by Old Bear's heavy rifle butt. She chewed up roots and spit the wet pulp on his scalp, packing it tight and deep in his wound, even though he winced from the pain. It was she who had tied soft leather strips tightly around his head. Soon a thick scab had formed over the wound, and the pain had left him.

At first, Old Bear kept the boy tied to the house post with a long rope around his ankle. But even tied he was helpful to his captors. From his tether he became the fire tender for the household, learning without difficulty the manner of heat required by Black Crow Woman for her cooking, swiftly grasping her technique to conserve wood by encouraging coals to glow rather than allowing flames to shoot in the air. When he offered his help in chopping firewood, the old woman handed him a hatchet and then, later, an ax.

Still tethered, he helped her prepare the fresh deer hides the hunters brought to the edge of her fire—proved his skill with the sharp skinning knife. Although the other boys his age laughed at him as he chopped the wood or scraped the hides, Thomas was glad he could help this kind old woman who had cared for him during those odd, painful, bleary days when first he arrived.

One moonless night several weeks after he came to the village, Old Bear placed him in the center of a great circle of people. They spoke many words and wailed and sang and passed their hands over him, chanting in a strange tongue Thomas could not understand. They ate deer meat from curving lengths of tree bark and sweet corn mush from deep gourd bowls. They played drums and thick wooden flutes, and a man blew long puffs of thick tobacco smoke against his naked chest. First men danced around the fire, then women danced. Again they ate their fill. And from that strange moonless night, everyone in the village called him Strong Bear.

Spring arrived early that year. Even by the last week of February the redbuds near the Tackett cabin had started to open their tiny purple flowers up their limbs. The dogwoods came next, their four petals of white hanging suspended above the cold, still sodden earth.

Estelle studied the progress of spring as again she paced the edge of the clearing. When she had first paced there, all she could do was relive each terrible shriek when they told her Thomas had not stayed the night with Isaac. With boundless patience, Ruth Tackett had sat mute beside her, held her arms, and waited as each dreadful shriek raked through her friend's wet shivering body.

Estelle prayed quietly as she paced the warming edge of the clearing. The shrieking was behind her; now she sought solace in observing the force of the forest blossoms—their beauty and tenderness in such contrast to their strength and hopefulness—especially the earliest ones, those that led the way despite the danger of a final killing frost.

Estelle had stayed on with the Tackett family, as Ruth had insisted. Although at first she had wanted to return home, even Estelle had soon realized it would have been foolish to live alone and pregnant in her cabin over winter. But as she stayed on with her neighbors, she was glad of it, and for more than sheer survival. That winter, Ruth and Estelle came to appreciate each other in new ways. They spoke of hardship and resentment at the injustices heaped upon them. Her husband out of earshot, Ruth had the freedom to speak of her brother's death—also at the hands of the Indians. Over the coldness of that winter they spoke in ways that helped Estelle begin the long task of mourning Virgil's death and accepting the heartbreak of her son's disappearance.

Grateful for the help and newfound friendship, Estelle lent a hand as best she could, given her advancing pregnancy. She took over the cooking, which left Ruth able to clean the cabin and teach her children the few letters and figures she knew. Many an evening the women simply sat and darned woolen socks by the hearth or turned a calico skirt, content to sit in silence as the flames jumped and crackled on the warm stones at their feet. Estelle had not known such closeness since she had left her sister back in Virginia—and Ruth had never known it at all.

Estelle had been relieved when the new pastor had finally been able to make the journey in mid January and recite a proper funeral service over Virgil's grave.

At that time of year, greenness lay nowhere near the earth, and Virgil's solitary mound of dirt stood grim and lonely on the gentle rise of land beside the creek. But just as the pastor had begun reciting his solemn prayer, a bright red cardinal appeared at the edge of the clearing, offering up the only splash of color in the bleak day. Mesmerized, Estelle had watched as the bird flitted back and forth near the gray slab of upright stone, alighted on a leafless branch. Then she closed her eyes in disappointment when it winged its way back into the dark forest.

Then, early one cold February morning Ruth had sent her husband to bring the midwife. Together they helped Estelle push her baby daughter into the world, and little Lizzie Mullins heralded her birth loud and unmistakable to all in earshot. Once again happiness made its way back into the quiet folds of winter life at the Tackett cabin. The sound of a healthy new baby, along with the glad flurry of activity it brought, was a welcome change from the sorrow of the previous months. But even as Estelle paced the warming edge of the Tackett clearing, little Lizzie swaddled tight and slung at her side, she knew her joy could only begin again once her son was back and they had returned to their own spot of land near the banks of the winding creek.

Thin clouds streaked the brilliant March sky the morning the pastor arrived without warning at the Tackett cabin. Estelle's heart jumped when she recognized his thin figure riding up the lane—perhaps he brought news? She was surprised to see him again so soon. He had visited last week with little to report concerning her son. Instead, he had informed her that the situation might proceed in a number of directions. Their best hope was for the Indians to turn him over as bounty, "which is what we should pray for," he had urged.

Estelle watched the pastor through the window's swirling glass as he dismounted his horse, then took what seemed like unusual pains to make sure his black hat and long black waistcoat were properly arranged after his ride. She saw him pat his horse's neck, noticed his lips move as he whispered something in the mare's ear. She blinked: Had the pastor really just spoken to his *horse?* Before she could consider it further, the man leapt up the stairs on stiff spindly legs and strode across the porch, his heavy footsteps reverberating against the cold wooden floorboards. He knocked on the cabin door.

"Good morning, Reverend. So good to see you again," Ruth greeted him.

The man stepped inside and again tugged at the dark cloth of his waistcoat. "Good morning, Mrs. Tackett, Mrs. Mullins," said the pastor, bowing a little to each of the women.

"Can I get you a cup of coffee?" Ruth asked, already heading toward the hearth.

"Yes, thank you," he said. He removed his hat and coat and held them a moment before reaching over and hanging them on a peg beside the door. He glanced uneasily at Isaac and the other Tackett children as they sprawled across the cabin floor, playing a rousing game of marbles.

"Please have a seat," Ruth said, handing him a cup with black coffee. She pulled a chair from the table.

"Thank you. Yes, thank you very much." But the man kept standing, holding the steaming cup in his hands. The coffee was much too hot to drink and the tin of the cup must already have transferred the heat to his long thin fingers, but the pastor just stood in the middle of the room, holding the cup with unmistakable embarrassment.

"I'm terribly sorry to be impolite, Mrs. Tackett, but I've actually come to have a private word with Mrs. Mullins."

"Why, I'm as rough as a cob, hain't I," Ruth said. She walked over and opened the door to their sleeping room. "You two talk in here."

Estelle got up from her seat near the window. She plucked the sleeping Lizzie from her cradle and passed into the room, followed by the pastor, who closed the door behind him. Estelle sat in a rocking chair beside the window. The baby fussed a bit, but then quieted down as her mother's rocking lulled back sleep. The pastor pulled up a small wooden chair and sat in it; with his feet flat on the floor, his long legs thrust his bony knees well up above his lap. He looked uncomfortable in the small chair.

"As you know, Mrs. Mullins, I have corresponded with the Northwest Territory authorities," he said. "I have finally learned that Thomas is alive."

"Oh, thank the good Lord," Estelle gasped. "How is he? Is he hurt?"

"Thomas is being held in a Shawnee village . . . several days' journey north, across the Ohio," the pastor said, watching her reaction from the corner of his eye. "I was informed he is being treated well."

"When's he comin home?"

"I believe the negotiations can gather speed as soon as the roads open up with the spring thaw," he said, glancing quickly out the window.

"Well, cain't you write again now . . . get 'im back sooner?"

"I'm afraid these matters are very delicate and move on their own time, Mrs. Mullins. I must work through the local authorities, and they have any number of pressing issues to address."

"Yes, of course they do. I knows it. Well, please do write as soon as you think it proper, so I can get my son back," Estelle urged.

Since the pastor was one of the few fully literate members of their community, it went without question that he would handle the negotiations. It was rumored he had learned his letters despite an improbable start—abandoned at the doorstep of a Boston church at the height of a cholera epidemic. They found him one morning, his hands tied to the church's cross-shaped brass door-knocker. After the terrified boy was cut free, his hands had clutched the dark cloth of the minister's coat so tight his little fingers had to be pried away. But within days he had revealed an unexpected intelligence and was transferred from the scullery to more important tasks in the orphanage office.

"I'm afraid I also bring news that you may not want to hear," the pastor began. He ventured a faint smile, although the effect was more like a grimace on the man's thin, serious face. Estelle remained silent, steeling herself against the news. "The letter from the territorial authorities also informed me that Thomas has been adopted."

"Adopted?" she asked, peering at him with incomprehension.

"Yes, adopted. By the Indians," he said, replacing his spectacles back into their grooves. "Apparently, he was adopted by a man to replace a grandson killed some years ago. Killed, it appears, by white hunters." The pastor peered intently at the coffee in his cup.

The irony of his last statement was lost on Estelle as she reacted to the first. "But, that just cain't be possible. That's plain silly! My son already has a family—his mama, and now his sister!" Estelle protested, gesturing with a jerk of her head at the swaddled infant in her arms. "Thomas hain't no orphan!"

"Yes, Mrs. Mullins, I understand," the pastor said in a careful tone of practiced patience. He put his cup of coffee on the table.

"Well, they just cain't have 'im. It's simple as that," she said, as if she somehow had the ability to disallow her son's adoption.

A long silence settled between them as Estelle rocked back and forth, as if her chair was propelled by a force far greater than the small woman who sat in it. Her faced was etched with outrage and anger burned behind her eyes. After a time, once the ferocity of her rocking had subsided, the pastor spoke again.

"Mrs. Mullins, you must try to understand that Indian families have also experienced great loss. Adoption is just their custom. Thomas is unhurt—indeed, the correspondence was written by the official who actually saw him. The man took great pains to assure me that he is being well cared for. Your boy is in no danger."

The pastor's voice was calm and compassionate, with almost a pleading quality to it. The sincerity of his words touched her, if only for a short while. She forced the corners of her mouth to rise in an unconvincing smile. "Yes, that's real good, I suppose. But, what do we do now? They cain't just keep 'im."

"No, of course not. One possibility is to offer a ransom directly to those holding him. They may take it. However, Mrs. Mullins, if they accept it at all, the ransom could be quite costly." Even though the family had been frugal, wisely guarding their hard-earned resources against an uncertain future, the pastor knew the sum would likely require their entire savings, and more.

"Whatever it takes, I'll pay. I'll even sell off my land if I got no other choice. I just needs to get my son back." Estelle turned to gaze at her infant daughter, sound asleep in her swaddling blanket. She lifted up the tiny bundle and clutched it tight.

"I understand, Mrs. Mullins." The pastor paused, then yanked off his spectacles. For several moments he rubbed the bony bridge of his nose where the eyepieces had begun to wear angry red grooves. "I suggest we simply proceed with ransom negotiations. Situations can change, although I'm afraid the Indians actually do have the upper hand," he said matter-of-factly. "And we continue to pray," he added. "We remember what our knees are for and have faith the Lord will keep Thomas in His care while he is away."

Estelle nodded at the pastor's words, but still frowned as she continued her rocking. She looked away, and silence again fell between them. She expected the pastor to take his leave now that he had delivered his news, but he remained seated in the chair at her side, his hands resting awkwardly on his knees, arms straight, shoulders rigid. All of a sudden he reached over and rested his thin bony hand on her arm.

The previous pastor at the fort had been a warm man who had a natural ease with every individual with whom he came in contact. He was the kind of man who could effortlessly, without a moment's hesitation, place an agreeable hand on an arm for comfort, or in a simple, unfettered gesture of friendship. But the new pastor was not like that. He was stiff and reserved, visibly ill at ease with even the most basic of physical demonstrations. He must have sensed Estelle tense beneath his touch, and he jerked his hand back to his knee. Again he tore his spectacles from his face, again rubbed the bridge of his bony nose.

"I have something else I would like to discuss with you, Mrs. Mullins," he said, a newly serious look crossing his already serious face. He replaced his spectacles, glanced warily at the infant in Estelle's lap. Little Lizzie had begun to fidget.

"I wanted to speak with you about this matter when last I was here, but I thought it too soon after . . . after your loss," the pastor said.

He spoke with precision, but the words had a practiced air to them. It seemed as if he was making a deliberate effort to hide the nervousness that had crept into his voice. He drew his clay pipe and pouch of burley from his pocket, apparently thought better of smoking, and returned the items. He picked up his coffee cup from the table, stared down into the strong black liquid.

Estelle remained silent, eyes downcast. She anticipated his next words with sadness, having guessed they would come during one of their conversations regarding Thomas's return.

"I am sure you understand that you cannot stay here indefinitely, nor can you tend your farm alone," he began, returning to his matter-of-fact manner of speech. "You need a husband to provide for you."

Estelle was not surprised the pastor would broach such a topic. As a circuit rider he was in the unique position to know the personal situations of every individual in their scattered community. She had seen pastors act as go-betweens any number of times, as fate had shifted and early death ripped spouses apart or as young people came of age and needed assistance finding a mate, suitable or otherwise.

Estelle was resolved to the fact that she would marry again. Given the circumstances, she also realized this time it would be out of necessity rather than love. Although she had a newborn—which was to her disadvantage—she also had a sturdy cabin and good land that was already cleared, even if its acreage wasn't large. She was still young and attractive, which worked to her advantage as well. Everything combined, her marriage prospects were good.

"I earn a respectable salary," continued the pastor, a clear edge of defensiveness in his voice. "Although I am not as experienced with farming as your late husband, I can hire a man for the heavier work and to tend the place when I am called away on ministerial rounds." He paused to let the meaning of his proposal become clear. He lifted his chin, jutted it toward the window. He didn't look at her.

Estelle's eyes widened as she grasped the implication of his words. She had assumed he would arrange a marriage for her to some recent arrival in Kentucky, most likely a man in search of land or a mother for his children. She was fully prepared for such an arrangement, but a marriage to the pastor himself? She had never imagined that possibility.

As her stunned mind regained control, she realized she had never quite thought of the pastor as a man—of even having an interest in a woman other than in some vague spiritual sense. She knew his cooking and cleaning were taken care of by women at the fort—women who were compensated for their efforts—so he did not require a wife for the completion of necessary household chores. He was not in need of land, since he did not earn his living by farming. He had plenty of contact with all kinds of people, and his circuit brought him many different places, so he could not lack for sociability. But, apparently, the pastor was a man and did have his needs.

Unsure of what to say, Estelle said nothing. Her mind searched for some kind of appropriate response. Confused, uncertain, she turned her head even further away from him and stared down at a knot in the wood flooring. She had stopped her rocking. Perhaps sensing the tension in the room, little Lizzie began twisting on her mother's lap. Her cranky noises soon grew to full-fledged crying as her tiny body writhed inside the blanket's tight wraps. She wanted to be fed.

Under normal circumstances, Estelle would simply have turned away, unbuttoned her blouse, and discreetly fed her baby, continuing the conversation with the pastor. Under normal circumstances, the pastor's downcast eyes would have turned discreetly in the opposite direction, careful to avoid any visual contact with the necessary activity transpiring beside him. But all that had now changed, and for both of them.

For her, even the idea of exposing her bare breast, heavy and swollen with milk, however inconspicuously, was enough to still her hand in her lap. For him, a new and troublesome temptation had crept into his mind, and he wondered whether he would be able to keep his eyes chastely averted from something he so very much longed to see. Several moments passed, moments in which Lizzie's crying increased its intensity.

It was the pastor who spoke first. "I understand this must come as a surprise to you, Mrs. Mullins," he said flatly. He placed his coffee cup on the table, rose from his seat. "I am a man of the Lord, and you can be assured I would treat you well and care for your family as my own," he said, glancing at the wailing infant.

Without further comment the pastor left the room, closing the door behind him with a quick thump of the door. After exchanging polite but speedy good-byes with Ruth, he strode from the cabin and across the narrow porch. Through the window Estelle watched the pastor's stiff, thin frame as he mounted his horse, yanked the reins toward the lane, and kicked harsh heels at the sides of his mare. The brilliant blue of the morning sky had given way to a tense blank gray. She glanced at the pastor's cup beside her on the table. He had not drunk a sip.

As she unbuttoned her blouse and gave her breast to her baby, tears surged from her eyes. They drained from a new well of fresh sadness she had not known existed. As Virgil's only daughter and last child suckled greedily, one single, hot tear trickled with great and prolonged leisure down the pathway of Estelle's cheek. It dangled slow and long in midair, hanging from the sharp edge of her jaw, before finally dropping in silence on the swaddling blanket below.

For many days following the pastor's visit, Estelle paced the edge of the Tackett clearing. She needed to consider her options with great care.

Married to the pastor she would have an even better chance of recovering her son, stolen by the Indians. He mentioned a good salary, which she would need to pay the ransom. Her neighbors had been kind to let her stay, but she couldn't impose much longer. And as she gazed into the greening forest she felt a growing urgency: Time was fast approaching to sink her shovel, turn the rich warming soil, and prepare it once more for another season of bounty. Despite the continued Indian threat, she wanted to return to her own land, live beside the deepening roots of her own peach orchard. After several days of pacing, she decided she could do far worse than marry the pastor.

The following week when Mr. Tackett rode to the fort, Estelle sent word she would accept his offer, and one month later they were married in a brief ceremony. With Ruth's help, Estelle had returned to prepare her home for the arrival of her strangely transformed family. The women swept the floor and washed the windows and dusted the rooms and ran the broom along the rafters. Ruth helped her remove Virgil's clothing from the drawers, fold them neat to give to charity. They made space for the pastor's belongings as best they could. They crammed his trunk into the crowded sleeping room and his bookcase and desk into the cabin's front room, shifting the pieces several times before they finally fit.

Ruth did her best to make the event as special as she could for her friend. She had sent her husband to the surrounding farms to announce the marriage and to invite them to the ceremony, followed by dinner. The women brought their covered dishes—soup beans and cornbread in a skillet, mustard greens stewed with hock, and the last of the thick-rind cushaw cooked down with bacon. Ruth killed a hen and fried up the cut pieces, grease popping as the fresh meat hit the hot lard. Estelle carried a gunny of dried peaches up from the springhouse and baked a pie. Although the neighbors said how good it was, she was barely able to taste the sweetness of the peaches as they crossed her tongue.

For Estelle, the only bright moment of the day was when Ruth surprised her with a wedding gift: a white muslin dress. How had her friend managed to hide its stitching from her? When she put it on, a tidy row of bone buttons graced Estelle's long thin neck and curving back. She clasped the silver locket, her sister's cherished parting gift, around her neck; it nestled with grace atop the plain white ruffle of the bodice.

But it was only the cardinal that drew Estelle's complete attention. She was certain it was the same bright red bird she had seen before. The bird was there again, waiting at the edge of the forest. It flitted past the window, landing here and there and cocking its head as if considering the goings on from all angles. She saw it alight on her husband's gravestone, its bright red hue stark against the grayness of the limestone slab.

Estelle slipped through the cabin door, leaned out over the porch rail. "Hey little bird. Pretty little bird," she chirped. The cardinal cocked its head and whistled back at her. "Hey pretty bird," she called again, sudden tears on her cheeks. She tried to whistle, but her throat was tight with emotion. The bird rested on the gravestone for a time, chirping at the lone woman at the porch rail, then it took wing, vanished again into the shadows of the still cold forest.

After the newlyweds said their good-byes, the pastor closed the door of the cabin, and they entered an awkward silence. It was their first time alone since he had suggested their unlikely union.

Without a word, the pastor busied himself with moving in. He unpacked his clothes in the sleeping room, folding them in the drawers where Virgil's garments had recently sat. In the front room, he pulled out his books and papers and arranged them meticulously on his bookshelf. Frowning, he slid each leather volume into position, sorting repeatedly until finally satisfied they stood in precise order. He placed his inkwell and white feather quill to the exact front and center of his desk, and then scowled at the window nearest it, apparently not pleased with the light that shone across the smooth wooden surface. He worked with an efficient concentration, usurping space for his effects without hesitation, his lean lips drawn tight.

Dusk fell slowly over the cabin. Estelle lit a candle as darkness gathered in the corners; but as soon as she set the candlestick on the table, the pastor picked it up and carried it toward the sleeping room. He paused at the door when he did not hear his wife's footsteps behind him. He turned and, without glancing in her direction, opened his long arm toward the room, signifying she should pass before him.

They were silent as they changed into their bedclothes. Little Lizzie lay fast asleep, snug in her cradle in the corner. The pastor was quick to climb beneath the cold bedding, then lay motionless on his back.

The candle—a dirty stub of gray wax in a dented candlestick—stood on a table beside the bed. Its dim glow cast long, grotesque shadows against the rough-hewn wood of the cabin wall. She could feel the slits of his eyes follow her as she changed out of her clothes, folding and refolding her dress before finally opening a drawer, putting it in, and sliding the drawer closed.

Unable to delay any longer, she walked to the far side of the bed—Virgil's side. As soon as she tucked her legs under the bedding, his cold hand moved at once to her waist. As she laid her head on the pillow, he slid his hand to her belly and quickly up to her breasts, groping furtively from one to the other, squeezing them hard. Within moments he had pulled himself on top of her, pinning her against the bed. A tall man, the pastor had to hunch his back to find her mouth; and once he did, he pressed his thin cold lips hard against hers. His breath was sour and tinged with the sharp bitter taste of burley. He slid his hand between her legs, yanked up her nightdress, and shoved her legs apart with great and clumsy haste. He snatched up his own nightclothes, then thrust himself inside her. Within seconds he was grunting in shallow rhythmic gasps beside her ear.

As quickly as it had begun, it was finished. He slid off, turned on his back, and fell immediately to sleep. Soon, loud abrupt snores intruded on the silence of the dark night. Estelle turned on her side, away from him. She was grateful it had not lasted long: Virgil's tenderness—and the quiet joy of their long and gentle lovemaking—would be allowed to linger in her memory.

Ever since that strange, moonless night when they passed their hands over Thomas, Old Bear no longer kept him tied by the ankle, and he had been free to wander.

A few other white people also lived in the little wigwam village, which he decided must lie some distance north of Kentucky due to the thickness of the snow that still blanketed the forest and the low path of the sun as it crossed the sky. The other white people—some captives, others adoptees like himself—

helped him learn some Shaawanwa words, although it was Black Crow Woman who taught him the most.

By the time spring and summer had passed and autumn had again returned to paint the wilderness, he was hunting in the bright woods alongside Old Bear and his sons and grandsons.

Thomas helped the old man work his trap line, catching beaver and mink and fox in the iron teeth of the leghold traps. He helped skin and butcher the animals they killed, working fast with his sharp knife—but no longer did he scrape the hides, because that was work done by women and children and old people. Like the other men in the hunting party, he roasted fresh venison on long green sticks held over the crackling fire and let the warm juice trickle down his chin and arms—and like the other men he reached out his tongue to lick his skin and savor more of the warm delicious liquid from the fresh warm meat.

One chill morning, Black Crow Woman walked over to him as he sat beside the fire, a thick skin robe draped about his shoulders. The first snow of the new winter had fallen the night before, and a dusting of fresh white glitter rested on the bare trees of the forest. He had removed the long muzzle and was polishing the shiny brass fittings of his new rifle—a recent gift from Old Bear.

"Here," said Black Crow Woman in a low grumble. She thrust a pair of moccasins at him, gestured just once toward his feet.

The moccasins were made of thick elk hide and decorated with colored glass beads sewn tight to the leather. She had arranged the beads with skill to create a bold floral pattern—swirls of bright reds and dark blues and vivid dazzling greens were all stitched firm to a background of white, placed with great care in neat perfect rows. Thomas took off his old pair of worn boots and put on his grandmother's gift. He stood and admired his new moccasins. They were warm and soft and sturdy around his feet. The bright colorful beads twinkled in the light of the morning sun. She had made a perfect fit.

Long strands of fine blond hair hung loose around his sun-browned face. "Thank you," Strong Bear said softly, in Shaawanwa, his eyes downcast in a proper sign of respect.

Over time, Estelle grew to consider the pastor a reliable man, if not a particularly kind or talented one. At first he made an honest effort at the life of a farm husband, but it soon became apparent he had neither the knowledge nor the physical stamina it required. The pastor also lacked the patience and quiet determination that was necessary to gently coax food from the land.

Before long, Estelle realized her innate abilities and hard-earned experience were far greater than the pastor's could ever be. Most of their conversations consisted of instructions on some farm task—how to harness the mules, when to plow and plant, and how long to let the cut hay dry in the field before stacking it in the barn for winter. Since she offered her guidance with kindness, he accepted it without meanness.

Eventually, the pastor came to spend less and less time at the little farm beside the creek. Instead, he devoted ever-increasing amounts of his boundless energy to his religious responsibilities as he tended not to the farm, but to the unending spiritual needs of his far-flung and ever-growing flock.

It did not take long for Estelle to understand it was in the religious realm that his true passions lay, not with farming—nor with her. Yet as time passed, she found it comforting to realize her husband took pleasure in having a family and a home to call his own—a place to which he could return in gratitude after a long absence. Nor did he ever fail to arrive on the porch with a piece of hard candy or some little trinket in his pocket for young Lizzie—or later, for his own two sons once time brought their arrival in the world.

As it turned out, the pastor did earn a good income, every last penny of which he turned over to his wife. With the money she was able to hire men to work the land, often men who had lost their land to others with greater learning and awareness of how to acquire proper title, or men who came by wagon over the Gap, since the widening of the trail they now called the Wilderness Road, in 1796. Although not prosperous exactly, the little farm near the creek soon brought a decent return.

Although Estelle gained a certain unanticipated respect for the pastor—perhaps even a begrudging admiration for him—she was not disappointed when he stayed away for longer stretches of time.

But as the pastor's interest in the farm waned, Estelle's grew. In time she took on many of the tasks Virgil had once done. It now fell to her to thrust her hand deep within the womb of a goat and pull out the struggling kid when its mother lost the strength to push. Whereas before she disliked wringing the necks of chickens, soon she was butchering hogs, hoisting them to the barn rafters with pulleys, jumping back before the hot blood drenched her, and then holding her ears to escape the agonizing squeals of the dying animals. Once, when a deer wandered into the clearing, she pulled Virgil's rifle from the wall and, with a steady aim, felled it in one shot.

Despite the sometimes oppressive heat, summer became Estelle's favorite time of year. It was then that her and Virgil's winding rows of yellow and purple irises burst open and filled the clearing with memories of a love undiminished by the passage of time.

When Lizzie was still a little child, Estelle taught her to cut an armful of fresh irises and arrange them in a thick, red pitcher. "First you put the tall stems right here, in the middle," she instructed her daughter. "And then bring the shorter ones down the sides, like this. But you wanna make 'em go every other one—one yellow, one purple." The girl watched, her pudgy child's mouth agape, as her mother took each flower and arranged it just right in the thick red pitcher.

Estelle leaned back to observe her work. "There, now hain't that pretty? Okay, honey, go on an' take up the pitcher." As soon as the toddler's little hands neared the sides of the pitcher, she clasped her own strong hands overtop the tiny ones. "Now walk on up the rise, gal." And Estelle bent at the waist and shuffled behind, matching her own stride to the small tottering steps before her.

"Put it on down right here, at Pa's headstone. That's a good girl. Now I want you to take up a flower and lay it down over ther at that little oak. That one's for your brother Thomas, stolen by the Indians. As you lay it down on the ground, say a prayer for his return."

Later, when she grew older, Lizzie carried the thick red pitcher herself. She walked on her own up the gentle rise of land, placed the pitcher before the rough gray headstone of her father's grave. And always she pulled one bright stem out for her brother and, with a prayer, placed it at the foot of the little oak.

Not by accident, Estelle believed, Mr. Tackett had chosen to bury her husband in sight of the blooming irises. During those long warm stretches of early summer, she spent every spare moment out on the porch. She imagined that Virgil could just turn his head and look out over their long curving rows of yellow and purple. Because he could see them each year, she reasoned, he slept at peace with the knowledge that their love continued, season after season, still strong enough to push aside dirt and grass and proclaim its proud devotion.

Even the pastor enjoyed an evening on the porch overlooking the curving rows of irises, although perhaps for far different reasons than his wife.

It was there twilight would find him, packing his clay pipe with burley and drawing with leisure on its long stem, little puffs of glad smoke escaping from the tight corner of his mouth. Amid the rising chorus of crickets and whippoorwills, he watched the irises' crooked shadows as they lengthened across the clearing, their yellows and purples becoming darker, less distinct with the gathering dusk. He preferred to sit in silence, ponder the slow amber flash of lightning bugs that rose with the fall of night. As a family they sat on the porch and basked in the radiance of the evening sky, watched as streaks of blazing orange and lengthening crimson were all that remained of the sun's fiery orb as it dropped from sight behind the tall gray knobs.

It was at moments like this the pastor was wont to say, "It was as if God, in all His magnificence, had reached out with His paintbrush and adorned the very dome of the sky."

Chapter Five

She appeared every day without fail. Sometimes Meg glanced up several times in one day and there she was just sitting on the back deck of her new Creekside home. Occasionally, the old woman even stood at the rail, leaning out toward the excavations as if to get a better view, even though the distance was too far to see much. Why didn't she come for a visit?

Meg had already given her site tour to plenty of visitors in the last few weeks. She was always quite careful to explain their excavations in the pasture with no more than the very simplest of narratives, focused only on the high points—usually pertaining to the function of the artifacts themselves. Long ago she had learned her lesson about delving into obtuse topics like unsolved discrepancies in overlapping date ranges or the many characteristics of indeterminate soil anomalies. Such subjects were certain to inspire the layman never to visit again. Once, on a first, and last, dinner date, Meg had launched into recounting the details of a remarkable new method for establishing teacup date ranges using handle angles, but failed to notice her would-be beau's eyes glazing over by her third sentence. Once she realized its potential, however, she came to consider her unique ability to bore as quite the latent talent. She had even been known to stoop so low as to conjure up long, dull details of imaginary artifacts so she could observe the growing discomfort, the squirming, and the covert checking of watches.

But she would never be so cruel to a visitor at her site. She would even laugh politely if someone asked if they were digging for gold; and although it was difficult, she would even manage to smile and bite her lip if a guest started chatting about dinosaurs.

Surely the old woman on the back deck had seen scores of visitors come and go from the site. Most had been residents of houses already built at Creekside, curious to discover what the archaeologists were finding in the pasture at the edge of the creek. But the old woman never came, even though she seemed quite interested in their work. She would just appear and disappear several times a day and observe them intently whenever she was out on the deck.

At last, curiosity got the best of Meg. One day, once the crew was settled in their units and the morning's excavation routine had begun and the old woman had appeared on the deck, she made her move.

Trying to appear nonchalant, Meg sauntered over to the broad shade of the old oak. Hidden to some extent behind the tree's rough trunk, she rummaged around in her pack and slid out a small pair of binoculars. She peeked at the old woman, whose attention was firmly fixed on the crew, then she flipped the bill of her Dodgers cap and brought the binoculars up to her eyes. Meg moved her head until she located the tall piers of the blurry deck and turned the knob until the field of vision jumped into focus.

The old woman was a light-skinned black and around seventy years of age. She wore a sleeveless, bright pink top with what looked to be a hand-crocheted green shawl draped over plump shoulders. A long swirl of carefully coiffed, frizzy salt-and-pepper hair emerged from behind to swoop up and over the top of her head. She had a pleasant smile on a cherubic face as she looked toward the excavations. Her cheeks shone brightly in the morning sun, and a quiet wisdom was etched in the folds and wrinkles of her cheerful brown skin. Her smile conveyed a profound sense of belonging, of a certain and deep rootedness. Even despite the distance from the old oak to the back deck—and the odd disconnect of a binocular lens—Meg liked her immediately.

The woman seemed to exude such patience, such dignity as she sat near the rail, poised like a queen on her throne, taking in the goings-on in her realm at the edge of the creek. It was as if she had always sat there and gazed out across this green rolling land, even though Meg knew that was impossible since her particular block had only been built about a year ago. The woman seemed oddly out of place on the uninspiring back deck of a bland Creekside home. Was she the elderly mother of a child successful enough to buy a house in an elegant new subdivision? Had she been born into money and, having led a life of leisure, was now happily ensconced in her enviable retirement home? Had she won the lottery and wisely invested her prize in a coveted Creekside address?

And what was she thinking as she watched the archaeologists dig and sift through bucket after bucket of pasture soil? Did she ponder the loss of fertile farmland as it was slowly—or quickly—converted to suburban sprawl right before her eyes? Did she reflect on how the original American dream home—like Meg's 1950s red brick ranch—was now deemed woefully inadequate for the modern American family? A woman her age may even have traveled winding farm lanes, now converted to four-lane highways that ran straight and certain to a new shopping mall. Did her wry smile convey bewilderment about such things, or was she nostalgic about the past at all?

Meg watched with fascination as the expression on the woman's face began to change. It did so only gradually, transforming to a visage filled by mirth, with a bright sparkle of mischief in her eyes. Deliberately, at the pace of a tired snail, she turned her regal head to look straight at Meg, and there they were, eyeball to eyeball. It must have taken the woman sitting on the deck a moment to make out what the woman in the backwards baseball cap beneath the broad shade of the old oak had pressed against her face, but once she did, the bright sparkle of mischief was joined by a grin of utmost hilarity.

Meg was mortified. A wave of embarrassment poured over her, flushing her cheeks a vivid red. All of a sudden she couldn't believe what she was doing. What had ever possessed her to snoop around like that, spying on an innocent old woman just minding her own business as she sat on her own back deck? Meg stood stock-still—a deer caught in the headlights. Thoughts raced through her mind as she sought some reasonably graceful exit to her awkward predicament. Might she pretend she was bird watching?

Ashamed, her cheeks still burning, she lowered the binoculars. There was just no way of denying it: she had been caught red-handed. What was there to do but laugh, grab off her Dodgers cap, and fling her arm straight up in the air? She sailed her cap from side to side in an exaggerated wave, a wide smile smeared across her conceded-to-guilty face. And the old woman returned Meg's wave, although she could only do so intermittently since she was rocking back and forth on her throne and slapping her knee, holding her broad belly in what, even from that distance, Meg knew were great peals of laughter.

Meg rose from her crouched position down in the excavation unit, threw her arms over her head, arched her back, and emitted a groan of pleasure in the stretch. She turned her arm and looked at her watch. It was still a bit early, but it was Friday and it was hot and the crew had worked hard all week. She cupped her hands to her mouth and yelled, "Lunch!"

As they had each noon since the dig began, the little crew meandered down their pasture path to the cool shade of the creek. Peanut butter and jelly sandwiches, cold pizza, bags of Cheetos, and little cans of Vienna sausages and Boston baked beans appeared; and contented chatting soon filled the air of the shady banks. As usual, Meg ate her lunch from a Tupperware container: last night's stir-fry chicken. Her cooking was a science of efficiency merged with nutrition, a strategy learned during her time-crunched, poverty-stricken days of graduate school.

As the crew ate and chatted, Meg's eyes swept the vegetation hugging the creek banks. The daughter of a forester, she had grown up in the woods. Numerous childhood photographs of her and her older brother, Nick, had been taken in front of trees—for scale. Wide-girthed redwoods in California, towering ponderosa pines in Colorado, great spreading red oaks in the Appalachians, and majestic white pines in her own home state of Minnesota. In some photos the children pointed sticks at the annual whorls on lofty conifers, identifying for the viewer the amazingly rapid growth achieved in a single year. Her father was always the scientist, even on summer vacation.

An earlier era of black-and-whites captured a scrawny, grinning Magpie dutifully grasping her pointing sticks, unruly hair disheveled from the recent and inevitable roughhousing with her older brother. Meg's mother—dead from uterine cancer—was glaringly absent from photos taken after Meg turned ten. The more recent color photos showed a girl less scrawny, but one whose pointing sticks were straighter, more obedient, poised in a manner more eager to please. Those photographs caught the vigilant face of a newly uncertain girl, revealing that the bitter lesson of impermanence had visited early and left its mark.

Meg noted that their lunch spot at the creek harbored mostly young oaks and sycamores, although a few twisting cottonwoods also lined the curving banks. Thick tangles of honeysuckle and Virginia creeper gripped the tree trunks, their heavy fragrant vines cascading earthward. Just before the creek curled away in the distance, Meg made out the dark shape of a crumbling stump of some once mighty tree, possibly one of the grand American chestnuts that fell to the blight in the early 1900s.

The creek was beautiful in the cool shade. It was a delightful Shangri-la veiled by a quiet ribbon of trees winding through the uniformity of a modern housing subdivision. The constant trickle of water was a welcome relief after the glare of full sun and the distant drone of bulldozers. It was a peaceful respite from all of that.

Just then a high-pitched chorus of bells startled everyone. It was Emily's cell phone. "Oh God, I'm sorry," Emily muttered, rummaging through her pack.

She located her phone and the bells got louder, even more obnoxious as she pulled it out and flipped open the lid.

"Hello?" said Emily. Pause.

"You're back! How was it?" Emily said again, turning away slightly. Very long pause.

Meg knew that Oliver, Emily's boyfriend, had been out of town at a conference, some big meeting on the comparative psychology of animal behavior.

Oliver Kearns was a young, still untenured psychology professor and a distant colleague of Meg's at Bluegrass University. He was everything a woman could hope for—tall with broad shoulders and a generous head of thick brown hair. He had a bright easy laugh. When he smiled, straight white teeth gleamed behind perfect lips and tiny dimples formed in his cheeks.

"Uh-huh. Sounds great." Emily said. Emily was always so positive; even many years ago as a young freshman in the front row of the classroom, it was something Meg had liked about her.

Oliver and Emily met last winter at the Rosebud Bar, at an impromptu celebration in honor of a colleague's successful tenure decision. It seemed like half the faculty showed up that afternoon, hoisting beers and toasting a grand welcome into the esteemed club of the tenured.

"Congratulations," Emily said.

Meg snapped the lid on her empty Tupperware container, glanced at her watch. She had even been present the moment Emily and Oliver's romance started. Those first sparks had flown over fried banana peppers and onion rings at the Rosebud's shuffleboard table, its gliding chrome shuttlecocks glinting in the artificial stained glass of the overhead lamp.

"Hey, that's wonderful." Emily stuck her finger in her ear, nodded her head.

Meg looked at her watch again, zipped open her pack, tossed in her empty Tupperware container, and zipped her pack closed. They had been playing teams that night at the Rosebud: Meg and Emily against Oliver Kearns and the chair of the psychology department, an aging hippie with a round belly and bright red suspenders. The women were ahead, the men ribbing them good-naturedly about the evolution of authority leading to the female of the species, when Emily broke out in a loud fit of laughter.

It was an odd, self-conscious laughter, tinged with overcompensation. The sound made a place in Meg's heart wince with uncomfortable familiarity. She turned just as Emily tossed her long blond hair over her shoulder and laughed again, her bright eyes flashing at Oliver. And Meg had grinned as she sent the shuttlecock gliding down the shuffleboard runway. She was happy for her young friend. But then a bittersweet shadow crossed her face as she felt old and undesirable, even if the shuttlecock had just made a perfect landing, suspended in midair on the far edge of the sandy runway.

"Sound's great. Hey, Oliver? I should really get going. Lunch is probably over." Emily turned to shrug apologetically at Meg, who was clasping the strap of her pack, snugging her cap back down on her head, impatient to give the order to return to work.

"Sorry, what was that?" Emily asked her phone. Apparently Oliver hadn't finished talking.

As Meg had gotten to know him better, she had discovered something about Oliver Kearns that made her slightly uncomfortable, just a little suspicious. What was it exactly? Surely he seemed too good to be true, but that wasn't quite all of it. Was he trying too hard? Overcompensating for something? Although Meg couldn't quite put her finger on it, she had of late begun avoiding Oliver whenever possible.

"Oliver, I really gotta go. But hey, Dr. Harrington and I are headed down to the Rosebud after work. You wanna meet us there?"

When Meg pulled her mail from her nook in the departmental office that Saturday morning, one quick glance nearly sufficed as an accurate inventory of its usual contents. The week's mail contained the predictable sampling of new book catalogs, a flier announcing an upcoming fall film series, a history department brown-bag lecture schedule, and the usual notice from the campus bookstore requesting faculty to confirm the status of their fall textbook orders. There was also a memo from the director of Institutional Effectiveness that all academic units were to prepare an updated progress report of their program-planning objectives prior to the visit of the re-accreditation team that fall. "Oh, great," muttered Meg, placing the memo on her desk's to-do pile, already anticipating the dubious joy of preparing yet another planning productivity update.

Near the bottom of the stack she found an official envelope from the Kentucky Department of Transportation. "Oh Jeez, what do those KYDOT jokers want now?" she grumbled. She picked up a pen, ran it through the edge of the envelope, and slid out the letter.

Dear Dr. Harrington,

We have recently received notice from the federal highway department that the timetable for construction at the Creekside subdivision access road has been moved two weeks earlier due to conflicts with heavy equipment scheduling elsewhere in the region. Construction will now commence on Monday, June 26, near the main entry gate. We regret any inconvenience this unavoidable earlier scheduling may entail. We will, however, provide you with $400.00 to assist with additional analyses. Please provide proper receipts for this additional funding and fill out the enclosed supplementary budget amendment form and return to our office before the close of the fiscal year.

Stunned, Meg dropped the letter, which lofted back and forth to drop soundlessly on her desk. She shook her head in disbelief. Construction beginning two weeks earlier? There must be some mistake. She snatched up the phone, started punching numbers. Then she remembered it was Saturday and government offices were closed. Disgusted, she slammed down the receiver. She sat back in her chair and crossed her arms on her chest. She stared at the institutional beige of her concrete-block office wall. The muscles in her jaw began clenching as she ground her teeth.

"Damn bureaucrats," she muttered to the wall. "Those assholes don't give a goddamn about archaeology." She leaned forward, sank her head in her arms, then dropped it all the way to her desk. She shook her head in disgust, then spun around in her chair, turning her back to the accursed letter. "Assholes," she grumbled.

Meg always talked to herself when she was upset. She didn't normally swear, except when she talked to herself. Talking to herself made her feel that at least her misery had some company, and perhaps she could give herself some good advice since no one else was around to provide it. Besides, swearing just made her feel better.

"I'll call those bastards first thing Monday. Tell them I need those two weeks. Construction will just have to begin as originally planned," she said matter-of-factly, but her voice was defensive, with an air of futility creeping in. She knew she wouldn't make that call.

She got up from the desk and started pacing. Her footfalls sounded hollow against the yellowing tile of the office floor. She felt a fast surge of pain strike her forehead, a tiny spike entering the tender space between her eyes, and she recognized the early pangs of a rising migraine. She ran her fingers through her hair, burrowed them hard in her scalp in an effort to prevent the pain from mounting.

"Ah shit—why even bother?" she fumed, her voice full of frustration. "There's no way they're reinstating the original timetable. That's why the peckers sent you a letter in the first place, you idiot!" She hit her head with the heel of her hand. "You know full well arguing with Frankfort is just going to get you more angry, not more time."

She flopped back down in her chair. "Money," she huffed. "Money'll fix it! It's a goddamn bribe—and a cheap one at that—$400 fucking dollars. Gimme a break!" She sank her head back into her hands with a moan.

Sure, some sites did manage, against all odds, to get preserved, but usually only because it would cost too much to excavate them. Mostly, the powers-that-be just threw money at sites—and then as little as possible—and that was that. As she sat at her desk and reread the letter, she was no longer convinced the massive amount of documentation that was such a standard feature of her profession was an adequate remedy for the massive numbers of sites destroyed each year. And for what? Faster roads? Bigger houses? More electricity? Was she really teaching her students archaeology, or was it the slow, well-honed techniques of well-documented, deliberate, cold-blooded murder?

As she scowled at the letter in her hands, assisting the highway department in its decision-making—which sites should live and which should die—seemed like a true devil's bargain. Once she had considered her arrangement with KYDOT so perfect, but that was no longer the case. What had changed? Was she becoming soft and no longer up to the task? Or were government bureaucrats pushing for more destruction these days? She shook her head in confusion.

An accelerated timetable meant she'd have to try and hurry things up out at the site. Maybe she could rustle up some volunteers, but even if she did, she'd have to train them fast so they could move dirt quickly as well as carefully—a skill that usually took quite a bit longer than a few days to acquire. Besides, once volunteers realized how tough fieldwork actually was, dentist appointments and sick relatives seemed to materialize out of the woodwork. No, volunteers would not solve her problem.

She could tell the crew that lunch would be shorter. They'd have to start half an hour earlier and quit half an hour later. She'd have to drive them harder out there, allow fewer Gatorade breaks. No more tiptoeing through the tulips either.

Then she had a brilliant idea. She would require each student to fill and screen twenty buckets of dirt a day. She would tally each bucket—keep a clipboard with student names and check off each bucket as it went to the screens. That would get things speeded up. Or she could get a stopwatch and give them one hour to fill and screen the twenty buckets; maybe that would work better. But then she might end up spending all her time tallying or timing buckets of dirt and would have difficulty making her rounds as she assisted her students as they inevitably encountered a wide and unpredictable array of archaeological deposits buried beneath the pasture. Besides, someone excavating simple fill would always move more dirt than someone excavating a feature, so the twenty-bucket requirement would be tricky to impose across the board. She might be able to devise a sliding scale to determine how many buckets were required for each type of feature—it would be hard, but she could figure something out. Maybe devise some kind of chit system.

But then what was she going to do—dock points from a student's grade if they screened nineteen buckets and not twenty? What about eighteen buckets? No, the simple fact of the matter was that the fast movement of dirt required a smoothly functioning, engaged, experienced crew operating with high morale, a complicated intersection of qualities that was difficult to achieve and could deteriorate in a heartbeat. Now that she thought about it, if she even attempted such a scheme, mood and morale would plummet and complaints would start and even less dirt would get moved. She shook her head as she realized how preposterous her brilliant idea really was.

Even if she did manage to pick up the pace, an accelerated timetable meant only one thing: Less would be saved; that's all. Less of EEOM's life beside the creek. And ever since that tarnished silver locket had shown up, Meg had become increasingly protective of that woman, or all that now remained of her—those broken sherds of glass and plate, those brittle corroding nails, those crushed thimbles and broken rusting scissors—all resting innocently there beneath the silence of the doomed pasture.

The following Sunday afternoon, Meg was back in her office. She'd dropped everything the day before as her migraine fanned out to invade each and every corner of her head. She'd gone home, buried herself under a thick mound of blankets, and tried to hide from the relentless stabbing lights.

As she sat at her chair, her head still felt achy and fragile as she continued through her stack of mail, flinging items in the blue recycle basket beside her desk. Her hand was poised to fling when she spotted her handwritten name and campus address. A quick glance at the sender: the dean's office, the new dean's office.

The new dean was proving himself an unusually energetic academic leader. He had surprised faculty and administrators alike with his planning, rather than pulling things from a hat at the last minute, as was more common in academia. He had made it his mission to bring order to the institution with stricter policies. It was a quixotic venture unlikely to succeed in a university setting; certainly that was the conclusion the old dean had eventually reached.

Meg ran her pen through the flap and slid the dean's letter from the ragged opening with a sigh. A personalized letter from the dean's office was likely to carry either bad news of another funding cut to her program or a request for more paperwork. Maybe both. As she read the letter, the muscles in her jaw again began to clench.

> Dear Dr. Harrington,
>
> Congratulations on your appointment to the university Promotion and Tenure Committee for the upcoming academic year. I appreciate your time and dedication on this important committee. In an effort to make the process flow more smoothly, my office has compiled the candidate's portfolios early so that committee members will have a longer period in which to review materials. Although candidates may add to their portfolios, as of this writing, the majority of materials is available to the below-listed committee members, and will be placed on reserve in the library. I thank you in advance for your confidentiality as the committee undertakes the candid discussion of these portfolios.
>
> *Candidates for Tenure and Promotion*
> Anita Halprin, English
> Willard Henson, Political Science
> Oliver Kearns, Psychology
> Michelle Mattingly, Economics
> *Committee Members*
> Stacy Clemment, English
> Margaret Harrington, Anthropology
> Michael Hensley, Biology
> Ross Landers, Political Science

Still clutching the letter, Meg raised it up to the ceiling. She shook it at the florescent light that hung from the sagging ceiling tiles of her office. A generous collection of dead insects had accumulated at the bottom of the light's aging fixture. "Now, what the hell have I done to deserve this?" she implored the bulb, shaking the letter for emphasis.

Of all university assignments, the Promotion and Tenure Committee was the most difficult and time consuming of all. It took so much time because it required committee members to read outrageously thick candidate portfolios heralding their accomplishments. The last time she served, Meg found it difficult to separate fact from embellishment and embellishment from pure fiction in the self-evaluation section. She was almost convinced the candidates walked on water, which was what they wanted her to believe.

An additional difficulty centered on the fact that the criteria for promotion and tenure were loose at best. Each and every year the committee had to confront the inherent problem of making a subjective process—of comparing artists and historians and mathematicians—an objective one. What kind of evidence was considered and how much should it weigh? Older faculty tended to weigh teaching evaluations more heavily, while newer faculty typically deemed publications more important. Were three co-authored articles in mid-level journals sufficient? Whose definition of mid-level was used? Why three and not four or two? How many co-authors and what was the author order? It was a perennial issue revisited every year at academic institutions across the nation.

Meg's dislike of the committee wasn't so much the concept itself, since candidate quality did have to be carefully assessed, and it was certainly best that faculty—and not administrators—assess it. She grasped full well that those tenured now chart the course of the university for years ahead, and at the end of the day the strength of the institution rested squarely on faculty quality. One of the truisms of academia held that if a professor was mediocre before tenure, he or she only got worse after. Ross Landers was a perfect case in point—someone who had likely not worked an honest day in his life following tenure. He was one of those atypical but egregious exceptions that cast doubt on all university faculty in the eyes of state legislators—the very individuals that set funding levels for higher education.

Another reason Meg hated serving on the committee was because it could be wrought with unpredictable conflict. Festering animosities among committee members might express themselves in cloaked ways during the discussion of candidate strengths and weaknesses, revealing a tangled underlying web of unsavory political intrigue. At its worst, the whole process could spiral down to the point where "an enemy of my enemy is my friend'" carried the day.

Meg sighed as she slowly, dismally, pushed her chair away from the desk. She walked to the window and leaned her head against its frame. A sharp pang stabbed her forehead. Her migraine was threatening to return.

The view from her third-floor office window was onto a cozy grouping of wooden benches dappled by the shade of leafy trees. A solitary student sat reading on one of the benches, her legs crossed beneath her. Meg watched as the girl read several pages, a half-eaten apple poised, apparently forgotten, in her raised hand. Oblivious to all else, the girl turned one page after the other, apparently transported to an absorbing place full of fascination and wonder. Meg shook her head as she took in the idyllic scene below her office window, gazed with regret at the eager young girl. Then she turned abruptly away. She didn't want to look at the reading girl anymore. She turned her attention instead to the desk, where her neat to-do pile awaited her undivided attention. She frowned at it. She just didn't have the stomach for any more that day.

Not only would she again have to serve on the university promotion and tenure committee, the dean's letter had informed her that Ross Landers would also be serving.

It was several years earlier that she and Landers had sat on the committee together, and they had butted heads in a big way. The particular meeting in question had dragged on for nearly three tedious hours. Ross Landers was sitting opposite the window in the library's conference room, gazing at students as they passed. Earlier in the meeting he had let out a long, barely audible whistle of approval as a particularly nice pair of shapely female legs strode past the window.

He had already glanced down at his arms—an artificial brown from the tanning salon—and flexed his biceps half a dozen times that afternoon in the hopes his former body-builder self still appeared strong and fit despite skin that had long since begun to sag with age. He sat with his arms propped before him on the table, his fingertips in an annoyingly pensive steeple formation, his fingers opening and closing pedantically before his chin.

"But, how can you say his scholarship is weak?" Landers said out of nowhere. "He has three publications! That is more than many others at this stage, I dare say." As he spoke he turned his head down and to the side, ran his hand along the side of his head so as not to disturb his hairspray. His cheeks were pocked with the vestiges of a bad case of teenage acne. The smile on his face held just a hint of wryness. He was baiting them.

Invariably, Ross Landers revealed that he had not adequately prepared for whatever agenda item was up for discussion, and this meeting had been no exception. The entire committee had gone silent when Landers spoke, everyone staring blankly at the artificial grain in the library's faux wood conference table. The issue of the candidate's three would-be publications had already been amply discussed and subsequently dispensed with, after which the meeting had progressed on to a consideration of the candidate's teaching evaluations for some twenty minutes. Clearly, Ross Landers had not been listening. Or maybe he had.

Landers was the kind of colleague most faculty simply learned to ignore. Everyone knew his teaching evaluations were terrible, and he was notorious for the quantity of classes he cancelled each semester and the ease with which students earned an A. As a result, the weakest students from across Bluegrass University flocked to his classes. His reputation meant his enrollments were strong on paper. It was rumored among faculty that sexual harassment charges had been filed against him several times, but none had stuck. Clearly, Ross Landers would have to do something utterly egregious—and get caught red-handed at it—to get fired. But he was too smart for that.

Although he had been eligible to retire for many years, he always opted to stay on. He relished the suspense of keeping his colleagues in the dark about his retirement plans. His peers had become accustomed to working around him and tried to avoid soliciting his views on anything of substance. Yet when he discovered he had not been consulted on some matter, he would orchestrate a terrible uproar, protesting the lack of democratic participation in decision-making at the institution. But he always stopped short of swearing and calling people names to their faces. Ross Landers was a man who knew how to bide his time and stay just shy of actionable misbehavior.

When Meg reflected back on that fateful meeting of the university Promotion and Tenure Committee, she mostly pondered why she had been the one incapable of keeping her mouth shut. Certainly, her colleagues had been able to do so. Why hadn't she also pondered the artificial grain in the library's faux wood conference table? Did it irk her more that Landers was able to get away with such behavior and get away with it for so long? He was everything a professor shouldn't be, and she knew there was a very long line of vastly more competent individuals eager to occupy his institutional beige, concrete-block office.

Her fingers had gripped the arms of her swivel chair as her knuckles turned white. Her jaw clenched and her face turned red. Despite the cool setting of the air conditioner in the library conference room, dampness rose in her armpits. She leaned forward and dropped her head in her hands, shaking it in amazement, wishing Ross Landers would just disappear. She willed herself to stay quiet—to let someone else bite the bait Landers dangled before the committee that day.

He had a smug, daring look on his face as he waited to sink the hook. He formed that infuriating little steeple with his fingers again, opening and closing them, feigning deep thought. He pursed his brow, turned his head in contemplation. He snorted a little—a haughty, contemptuous kind of snort—and at that moment Meg knew she would not be able to stop her mouth.

"Haven't you been listening?" she demanded.

As soon as she spoke, Landers swiveled his chair to face her. His eyes danced with the pleasure of a newfound hunt. The corners of his lips turned up in a smirk. His next adversary had just appeared.

"We've already talked about that!" Meg yelled, thumping her hand on the table in exasperation. "Three publications, my ass. They're encyclopedia entries, for Christ's sake! Didn't you even *look* at them? They're worthless! Pure fluff!"

"I believe that is merely your opinion, which, of course, is highly debatable," Landers said leisurely, a man in complete control. "Moreover, his service contribution is quite commendable. Do you not recall, my dear Dr. Harrington," he continued with disdain, "that he created our entire departmental brochure single-handedly?"

Everyone recalled the candidate's work on the glossy brochure requested from the university public relations office. How could they possibly forget? It was a task no one wanted and everyone gossiped about once it was finished because Landers's full-color photo was plastered on the front cover after it arrived from the printing office. It was not out of the realm of possibility that the weak, untenured candidate currently under discussion had put Landers on the brochure because he recognized a colleague who could easily be bought, and thus he would be assured at least one supporter at tenure time.

Disgusted, Meg shook her head with visible contempt. Caught up in her anger, she failed to notice that the other members of the university Promotion and Tenure Committee had all fallen conspicuously silent.

"Yeah, sure he did, but does *that* earn him tenure? No one wanted to do that stupid brochure, including you. But no, the one contribution you *could* make because it required minimal intelligence—you dodged out of! Besides," continued Meg, utterly unnecessarily, but she was on a roll she couldn't seem to jump off, "you only like that damn brochure because your picture's on it!"

When Landers narrowed his eyes, she finally grasped the undeniable fact that she had just become the next casualty in his long string of people to target, to seek out and destroy, the next individual whose name he would smear at every available opportunity. Much to her dismay, she came to learn that Ross Landers led a small but hardy contingent of like-minded cronies, a cohort of the disdained who were nevertheless capable of extending their poisoned tentacles and creating deep chasms of damage in the most unlikely of places.

Landers had even persuaded the new incoming dean that Meg Harrington rarely used her archaeology lab—a patently false piece of misinformation—and perhaps such valuable space might best be reassigned to someone who needed it more. The new dean, desperate to appear neutral in the bewildering array of constantly shifting university factions in which he found himself, had requested she keep a log of the lab's use in an effort to assess its future disposition. And in a classic weapons-of-the-weak maneuver, Meg had complied by fishing out the ugliest gnawed stub of a pencil from the back of her drawer and tying it to the clipboard with the dirtiest piece of string she could lay her hands on.

It wasn't long after that fateful university promotion and tenure meeting that Meg experienced her first strangling fantasy. It surfaced as an innocent, non-premeditated strangling, but since then it had proceeded to grow ever more elaborate. Not surprisingly, it always played out in the library conference room.

Meg walks in and finds Landers alone, but, of course, she knew he would be alone because she followed him there. She closes the conference room door; when it clicks shut, he turns around. He's surprised to see her. "Well, hello Dr. Harrington," he says sarcastically. "What a pleasure to see you."

She leaps at him suddenly. Her hands encircle the brown sagging skin of his neck and she squeezes her fingers. Then she squeezes tighter, and their eyes flare in a fierce battle of their iron wills.

His acne-pocked cheeks turn pink and deepen to red. His arms flail wildly in a desperate attempt to make her release her merciless grip. But no—Meg's thin arms have far greater strength than those of the former body-builder and his arms flail in vain. Her swift knee to the groin halts the flailing arms completely.

When his eyes begin to bulge, staring at her in shocked incredulity, she erupts in laughter. She tightens her grip further, and his face turns purple. He begins trembling. It's slow at first, but then mounts to violent jerks as his dwindling oxygen supply reaches critical. And then he crumbles to the carpet in a pitiful pile of humanity, but not before hitting his head against the library's faux wood conference table on the way down.

Still turned away from her office window, Meg buried her face in her hands, shook it in disbelief, and then stared up at the collection of dead insects in the ceiling's florescent light fixture. Beginning in the fall semester, she'd have to serve on the university Promotion and Tenure Committee again with Ross Landers. To make matters worse, one of the untenured candidates up for consideration that year was Emily's boyfriend, the dashing young Oliver Kearns.

Chapter Six

The pastor unfolded the letter and cleared his throat. "My Esteemed Sir, I have recently returned from travels through the Indian villages to the north," he read officiously, peering over the thin gold rim of his spectacles.

Standing at the porch rail, both Estelle and Lizzie listened carefully. Only moments earlier, the pastor had ridden his horse up the lane, returning that late afternoon from an absence of many weeks. It was the first word they had received from the local authorities concerning Thomas in many years, from a region of the Ohio Country now known as Indiana Territory.

"I write to inform you that the individual known to you as one Thomas Mullins continues to reside in my jurisdiction. I am pleased to report that he remains in good health." The pastor glanced up and smiled uneasily, nodding his head to emphasize the good news. Having read the correspondence beforehand, he knew the information that was to follow would be less well received.

Despite the pastor's persistent efforts to win Thomas's release, by the summer of 1810 the boy had still not returned. But by then Thomas Mullins was not a boy any longer. He was now a man capable of making his own decisions, which apparently did not include coming back to live with his family in Kentucky.

The pastor looked back down, frowned as he continued reading. "I am also obliged to report that the adoptee in question has now married. I am led to understand that his wife currently carries their second child."

Lizzie clapped her hands, happy for her older brother. "Oh, Thomas is married, how exciting!"

Estelle glared at her daughter. "It's a squaw he's married, don't you know?!"

"Well, I'm sure she's real nice. And didn't you hear? You're a Mamaw now; hain't that wonderful?"

Without glancing up from the letter, the pastor again cleared his throat, the sound this time signifying he did not appreciate the interruption. Estelle looked away, watched for a moment as her two young sons dashed across the clearing, shook her head when she noticed the fresh mud splattered on their clean britches. She still chose to remember Thomas as that sweet, blond-headed child she last saw riding a mule from the clearing with a deer haunch, bound for the Tackett cabin. Despite abundant evidence to the contrary, she still envisioned her son as a poor unwilling captive, tied to a tree somewhere, still desperate to escape and return home.

"Take your blessings where you find them, my dear," the pastor said dryly, without looking at his wife. "Indeed, you might consider giving thanks the Lord has provided the opportunity to even have word of Thomas. You are aware, are you not, that it is unusual to have news concerning most adoptees so long after their original seizure?"

Estelle crossed her arms and grunted. She hated it when her husband spoke to her like that, scolding her for the views she held, dismissing them as unenlightened. She didn't want to hear his opinion on the matter—she had heard quite enough of it already.

"Shall I continue reading?" inquired the pastor, a rhetorical ring to his words.

"But that means Thomas hain't comin back, don't it, Ma?" asked Lizzie, ignoring her stepfather's question.

"Yes, that's right," Estelle said, her voice filled with resentment. With the news of her son's marriage, her last vestige of hope for his return had at last been snatched away. She could no longer continue to fool herself that he was coming home. Now that Thomas had a wife and family, he would never be back.

Letter in hand, the pastor dropped his arm in exasperation. But he had to turn his head in surprise with the next words out of his wife's mouth.

"But I guess we should've expected as much, seein as how he's been stolen from us so long ago," Estelle said, lowering herself into a rocking chair. The sullenness of her words hung heavy in the summer air. She lifted her head to look out over the irises, arrayed again in their bright blooms of yellow and purple. Their late afternoon shadows were just starting to snake their way across the darkening clearing.

"He's old enough to make his own decisions now," said the pastor without condemnation. "We should accept them, whatever they may be. It will be God who judges us all in the end." The pastor's voice held an odd, pensive quality. He glanced over to the gentle rise of land where a solitary slab of limestone jutted from the ground, noted the yellow and purple irises arranged as always this time of year, in their thick red pitcher.

Estelle grunted again as she rocked. She found it odd that a man who could spout such fire and brimstone from the pulpit could have such dispassionate feelings on such a subject. How could he tolerate the fact that heathens—the very ones who had murdered the boy's father in cold blood—had raised her child? But then again, Thomas was not his son; he could not be expected to be bothered as much.

"I sure would like to meet his wife," Lizzie announced. "I'd like to meet Thomas—you know, I've never even met my older brother? Couldn't we take the wagon on over—"

"No, we couldn't!" interrupted Estelle. "I've already lost one child to the Indians, and I won't be losin another!" She turned and glared at her husband, daring him to contradict her.

"But, Ma, he's my brother!" Lizzie protested.

"Shall I continue reading?" inquired the pastor again, decidedly less kindly. Surely he didn't want to get in the middle of *that* argument again.

"Yes, sir," Lizzie murmured.

Just as Thomas was no longer a boy, Lizzie was no longer a girl. She had grown into a handsome young woman and, like her mother when she was young, wore her blond hair pulled behind her head in two long braids. She had pale blue eyes like her mother and an affinity to the land and to hard work in the garden. Lizzie was always eager to hear word of her older brother. She was certain he would have made a better childhood companion than her two young half brothers, those annoying creatures whose presence she had simply learned to endure.

But as the pastor continued reading, the tone of his voice changed. Rather than officious, it took on an ominous quality: "I also must report that the individual in question has moved with his family to the Indian settlement of Prophetstown on the Tippecanoe River, not far from Lafayette, also in my jurisdiction in Indiana Territory." The pastor glanced up at the two women, gauging whether this last bit of information had made any impact on them. It had not.

What should he tell them of the goings-on at Prophetstown? Should he inform them of Tecumseh and his brother, a man they called the Prophet, and how they had already united many Indian tribes? Why, he had read just last week in the *Kentucky Gazette,* right beside John Quincy Adams's latest Federalist diatribe, that close to a thousand warriors had now gathered at Prophetstown. The Indians seemed determined to defend the land around it. If they failed, they would have little left in the Ohio Country.

The pastor sat down on a chair beside his wife, pulled out his clay pipe, and filled it with burley from his old leather pouch. He chewed pensively on the long stem for several moments, considered how much he should tell them. He was fully aware that he was much more knowledgeable than either his wife or stepdaughter on most every matter. His ministerial circuit-riding brought him into wide contact with the outside world, while the women spent their entire lives on the farm near the creek, only occasionally venturing out to run the odd errand at the crossroads town. Seldom did they make the long wagon ride to Lexington, whereas, in contrast, he was often in that fast-growing town. It was at a table in the corner of Postlethwaite's Tavern on Main Street that he frequently engaged in lengthy discussions concerning a variety of important events of the day.

The pastor folded the letter, slid it in his pocket. He glanced over at his sons as they tormented a dog near the edge of the clearing, also noticing their mud-spattered clothes. He scowled to himself as he thought of his sons, hoped they had managed to behave reasonably well during his most recent absence. When he spoke, it was to no one in particular.

"There are many among us—most importantly, many in Washington—who would like nothing more than to see not one single Indian village remain standing east of the Mississippi." His tone indicated both his disagreement and his annoyance with Washington. He frowned disapprovingly, pulled off his spectacles, and rubbed the bridge of his nose. The worn grooves on either side had only deepened, gotten angrier and redder with the passage of time.

"What's worse, there are reports of a standoff that seems to be developing at this very place called Prophetstown, where Thomas and his family now live." The pastor chewed again on the hard stem of his clay pipe, allowed time for the meaning of his words to become clear. "It seems that hostilities could break out at any moment," he continued, grumbling in large part to himself. "The Indians are, of course, unable to win such a confrontation, regardless of their courage and determination, admirable as they may be. It's a simple matter of arithmetic, you see, and the numbers are overwhelmingly against them, as is the inferior technology of their antiquated firearms."

He paused to light his pipe, drew hard on its clay stem to start the burning in the bowl. "And Thomas is now living at Prophetstown," the pastor continued, repeating himself. "I am really not at all pleased to learn he is living in that place. That is very bad news, indeed. It would be much better if he were to take his family and move west of the Mississippi. That is the Indian's best chance of retaining any semblance of . . . " Uncharacteristically for him, the pastor actually stopped mid-sentence, suddenly lost for words.

What, exactly, should the Indians be trying to retain a semblance of? With teeming boatloads of immigrants pouring every day down the Ohio, he didn't envision a bright future for any Indian in this country, even those already west of the Mississippi. Ever since the news of Captains Lewis and Clark's expedition to the Pacific had hit the papers, ever greater numbers of fur traders had crossed that mighty river, and short on their heels came settlers as the frontier moved constantly west. How would the fierce Sioux and Blackfeet respond? The kindly Nez Perce? Why, he and Lewis had discussed just that the night he was feted in Lexington. Between toasts, they had agreed these United States would someday span both oceans. What role for the Indian then? Even if they managed to not get themselves all killed, what customs might they try to retain some semblance of? Such a thought was entirely out of the question. Confused, the pastor took another long draw on his pipe, again mulled the thorny situation in his mind.

Just last week at Postlethwaite's he had argued to a group of gentlemen that the Indians should seek to learn a trade, to make a greater effort to adjust, to try harder to mold themselves in the polite habits of civilized Christian life. He had advocated that such a path—one of vigorous and relentless assimilation—was their only hope for survival, and it was the responsibility of modern education to provide just that path. But he knew better than to engage in such a discussion with Estelle. For her, all Indians were savages, plain and simple.

They sat in silence on the porch, watching as twilight fell and the first stars began flickering in the sky. Somewhere along the creek a whippoorwill began its loud incessant calling, echoed by another somewhere deep in the forest. The pastor's still-muddy sons had turned their attention to catching lightening bugs—and then crushing them in their hands with great delight.

"I was thinkin we can all head on over to the dance Saturday night," Estelle said out of the blue, intent on changing the subject. "We hain't been for a good spell, so I think I'd like to go stretch my legs a bit." She stuck her feet straight out from the chair in front of her, tapped her ankles in the air.

Ever since Virgil was killed and her son captured, she had little sympathy with "the plight of the Indians," as the reformers called it. Now even her husband had started talking that way, ever since he converted over to the abolitionist cause. It irritated her to no end. Those people—those self-righteous reformers—hadn't suffered the losses she had. They hadn't held their dying husbands in their arms, nor had their sons snatched from their very bosom. But she knew better than to discuss such things with the pastor. For him, slaves and Indians were just unfortunate victims in some vague moral struggle that made little sense. She watched her husband draw on his pipe's long stem, wryly noted that he had yet to obey the reformers and renounce his beloved burley. "Will you be here to take us, or are we gonna be drivin ourselves?" Estelle asked, needling her husband.

To his wife's amusement, the pastor actually liked to dance. More than once she had seen him leap up and perform an Irish jig when the spirit moved him, playing his tin whistle as he jumped about on long spindly legs still unexpectedly spry for his advancing years. Despite his love of music, he refused to take part in the dances—wicked and sinful is what he called them—but favored play parties, those tame dulcimer affairs in a staid front parlor that always remained under tight restraint. Estelle knew her husband disliked it when she and Lizzie attended the Saturday night barn dances, which was one of the reasons she insisted on going.

But before the pastor could respond, Lizzie interrupted. "Oh, Ma, I forgot to tell you—I'll be ridin to the dance with Isaac." She gazed out over the irises, hoping her announcement sounded like the most ordinary thing in the world.

"Oh, no you won't missy. You'll be comin with me or you won't be goin at all," Estelle said. And Lizzie knew better than to argue with her mother on that point.

Isaac was Ruth Tackett's boy. After Virgil's death, Ruth had sent her son to Estelle's farm to help out from time to time; and in due course Estelle had offered to pay him, although only after he proved himself a hard worker. Since the Tacketts had plenty of other sons to tend their farm, they were glad to let Isaac continue on with Estelle and were quietly pleased to have a few extra coins coming in as well.

Nearly every one of Lizzie's earliest memories included Isaac. Picking ripe blackberries on a scorching summer day with Isaac. Inside the henhouse with Isaac, sliding their hands under feathery bellies to seize eggs. Isaac holding the last of the winter ice from the springhouse to her eye when she was stung by a bee. And roaming for miles down the creek with Isaac just to discover what might be around the next bend. By far their favorite spot in the creek was near the low chestnut branch that bowed wide over the water. After Isaac tied an old, knotted rope from the branch, they spent many a summer afternoon swinging out and dropping like cannonballs into the pool below.

It was Isaac who taught her to ride the horse, both bareback and with the old saddle. She even got good enough to stay on as the horse jumped the creek near the chinquapin grove. Lizzie liked to help Isaac harness the mules—or at least helping is what he called it when she braided black-eyed Susans and Queen Anne's lace into old Queenie's mane. And Isaac would chuckle and shake his head because the old gal really did love all the attention, and he swore she pulled better around the sorghum press all done up with Lizzie's handiwork.

Although the two were nearly raised together, there had never been a time when they thought of each other as brother and sister. No, they had always been best friends. Only on one occasion had Lizzie felt distant from Isaac, and that was the time blood first fell from between her legs.

The blood had rushed forth in a hot burst and then started a slow trickle down the soft inside flesh of her thigh. They were in the orchard near the cabin, Isaac perched high in a tree plucking ripe peaches and tossing them down for Lizzie to stack in the basket at her feet. Lizzie's annoying half brothers hovered beside her like overgrown grasshoppers, leaping about and jostling one another in a tedious effort to beat their older sister to the peaches as they dropped from Isaac's hand.

At first, Lizzie made a determined effort to ignore the wet, peculiar tickling sensation between her legs, but finally she bent over, raised up her calico skirt, turned her knee out, and dabbed her fingers at the dribble on her leg. Only when she looked at her hand did she realize her fingers were covered with dark red blood. Isaac, waiting to drop another peach, saw it too.

"Lizzie, what happened?" Isaac called from the tree. Alerted by his words, her brothers' attention shifted to their sister and to her inexplicably bloody fingers.

Puzzled, Lizzie stared at the moist smear of red as Isaac dropped from the tree, landing nimbly at her side. Flushed with an odd embarrassment, she turned and ran toward the cabin, where Estelle was hanging the wash, knowing her mother would understand this strange new occurrence. Isaac and her brothers followed on her heels.

"Ma, I's bleedin!" Lizzie called, waving her bloody fingers in her mother's face. "It came from here," she added, preparing to raise her calico skirt to show her mother.

Estelle dropped the shirt she was about to peg on the line. "Isaac, I want you to take them boys an' get back to them peach trees right now," she demanded. She put a fist on her hip and pointed a finger to the orchard. "And I don't want you back here 'til you've done picked me four whole bushels."

"But, she wasn't even climbin the tree or nothin," explained Isaac.

"Right now—all three of you!" Estelle ordered. Bewildered, the boys walked back toward the orchard, Isaac glancing behind a time or two.

"Over to the washhouse—right now," she ordered Lizzie. She clasped her daughter by the arm as she spoke and helped move her quickly along in that direction. Uncertain, the girl let herself be towed along, tears of confusion beginning to well in her eyes. All of a sudden she didn't feel so good—a little achy around the belly.

Estelle grabbed a wooden bucket off a high nail, dipped it in the rainwater barrel, and hauled it inside the washhouse. She shut the door and turned a worn wedge of wood to lock it.

"Oh hush, girl, there hain't nothin wrong with you," she said as a few tears slid down her daughter's cheeks. "Now wash yourself down there. I'll bring you everythin you need, but quit your blatherin. Christ Almighty, you'd think the end of the world was come with all that carryin on!"

When Estelle returned from the cabin she thrust a handful of rags toward her daughter. "Stuff these at your privates to catch the blood. When theys soaked, you wash 'em yourself, in this here bucket and no other, hear? And when you're done with it you put it right back on that nail." Estelle pointed to a solitary iron nail pounded into a high log of the washhouse, glowered at her daughter to make sure she understood.

"And toss out the dirty water far away—out in the forest. You're a woman now, and that means you can up and get yourself pregnant, so you stay away from boys. And yes, missy, that means Isaac too. And don't never wash your hair when you're bleedin 'cause you'll get Quick TB if you do. Understand?"

Rags in hand, Lizzie stood and stared at her mother. Surely she didn't want to get Quick TB—whatever that was—but why did she have to stay away from Isaac? Uncertain, she looked down at the jumble of old rags in her hand, wishing she could just go back to the orchard and help pick peaches.

"Alright gal, you go on and take care of all that, and then come up to the house," said Estelle, kindness creeping back into her voice. "I'll fix you a nice cup a sassafras tea. It'll make you feel better, honey. I got a little pie left, and you can have it." She patted her daughter on the shoulder, then left the washhouse to put the kettle on.

After that day, Estelle kept a much closer watch over her daughter. Although Lizzie was still allowed to wander down the creek with Isaac, her mother insisted her brothers always go along.

But one afternoon, as the boys seemed content to swing on the knotted rope and drop in the pool below, Lizzie and Isaac slipped off on their own to explore down the creek. Without realizing it, they went further that day than they ever had, drawn ever onward by the magic of the trickling water.

They went past a thick, yellowing canebrake and then a seep where slow-moving water oozed from the muddy, algae-covered bank and trickled into the creek in a wide fan. They went past a hollow bursting with a tangled slick of leather-leaved rhododendrons ablaze in lavender and pale pink. They rounded a sharp bend in the creek where they lobbed pebbles at each other across the little spit of land and then took cover as they waited for the next missile to come careening over the edge. They picked ripe pawpaws and squeezed the sweet yellow custard in their mouths, spat the seeds in the air, and followed their small brown arcs until they disappeared into the water with tiny plunks.

They only stopped when they came to a little waterfall—a place where the creek plunged over a narrow edge of the earth. As it fell the water spread out, plummeting downward in fleeting white cascades before smacking the wet rock below and turning back into the creek. The sharp slant of late afternoon sun caught the fine spray, transformed it into tiny rainbows suspended in the golden air, illuminated against a backdrop of mossy velvet green. Caught up in the wonder of nature, Lizzie and Isaac ducked up underneath the thin veil of plunging water, spread their arms wide—and were drenched by its wetness.

By the time they got back to the knotted rope swing, Lizzie's brothers were gone. Apparently bored of playing in the water, the boys had returned to the cabin on their own.

Estelle halted her furious pacing at the head of the creek trail the instant they entered the clearing. Isaac's mule was saddled and ready to go. She thrust the reins in his hand and turned her back to him, silencing him with a hard, raised hand when he tried to explain. Speaking with her back to Isaac, Estelle narrowed her eyes, glaring at her daughter. "I'll be havin a word or two with your mother before you set foot in this clearin again; you hear me? Now git."

Isaac mounted and reluctantly pointed his mule toward the lane. He turned several times to look back at Lizzie, who stood before the porch, her still-damp dress clinging in ripples to her thin quaking frame. Her eyes were glued on the ground, and she clutched one arm to the other in dread. Lizzie's brothers snickered into their hands as they peered from around the corner of the cabin.

Estelle stood glowering at her daughter until she was certain Isaac and his mule had disappeared down the lane. When at last she spoke, her voice was shrill. "What's the matter with you, girl? You know better'n that! Why'd you disobey me?"

"Ma, we wasn't doin nothing bad; we's just walkin down the creek," Lizzie began, tears already building in her eyes.

"I don't want any of your lip, girl, or you'll be gettin it twice as bad," Estelle said, her face red with anger. "You go cut me a switch," she demanded, thrusting a kitchen knife toward her daughter's trembling hand. "And it better be nice an' green!"

Estelle stood, hands on hips, scowling at her daughter's slumped back as she walked dejectedly to the edge of the clearing.

For Lizzie, this was the worst part of the punishment. Not only did she know she was about to get whipped, but she had to select the actual implement of her suffering. It was a technique designed to further shame the guilty party, to compel the wrongdoer to further contemplate their terrible crime, and to dread even more the consequences of their actions. Experience had already taught Lizzie that if she were foolish enough to present her mother with a less-than-painful switch, she'd end up paying double—once for her original transgression and then again for attempting to deceive.

Head bowed, eyes downcast, Lizzie walked back to stand before the porch. She dragged a long thin green switch on the ground beside her. It was fresh and supple. She had begun to cry.

Her mother threw back her head and jutted her chin in her daughter's direction. "Now, don't you go cry those crocodile tears on me! You know better'n anybody you earned what's comin."

Estelle grabbed the switch from Lizzie. She studied it for a moment, whipped it dramatically in the air a few times to make sure it would render sufficient sting. The thin green switch whizzed as it sped back and forth through the air. Apparently satisfied, Estelle walked to the girl's side. From a safe distance, her brothers squealed with delight, but then retreated back to hide behind the cabin after their mother glared at them and took a few livid strides in their direction.

"Raise up your skirt!"

Slowly Lizzie obeyed, revealing two thin white trembling legs. Estelle swung the switch and struck the first of many quick stinging blows to the back of Lizzie's legs. Then she swung the switch again. And then again. She didn't stop until a wide patchwork of narrow red welts rose up on the soft white skin, all along the back of her calves and knees, until she was convinced her daughter's sobs were genuine. Only then did Estelle fling the switch away and seize her daughter by the arms. She jerked her around, their faces inches apart. Lizzie's nose was running and the entire flushed expanse of her cheeks glistened with tears. She was making a brave but fruitless effort to prevent sobs from escaping past her trembling lips.

"Now, don't disobey me again, girl, or you'll be gettin a whole lot worse!" Her mother threatened, and then let loose of her daughter.

Estelle's hands returned to her hips as she watched Lizzie slink off toward the barn. But despite her anger, she was grateful her husband hadn't been home to witness the girl's misbehavior. For if he had, her daughter would have fared far worse, particularly for an offense as grave as this. The pastor's philosophy of "spare the rod, spoil the child" would have meant a thick leather strap applied unflinchingly to the back of Lizzie's tender legs, and for far longer. It would have been wielded with a fury beyond imagination. For her daughter's sake, Estelle hoped her sons would conveniently forget about this incident before their father returned, because she certainly had no intention of telling him.

Wave upon wave of spiraling religious fervor swept across the land. Countless heads of white-clad, newly saved believers were plunged beneath Kentucky's brown baptismal rivers to emerge Christ-like from the depths, their worldly sins cleansed and floating to the sea. Among the thousands of sinners caught up in those swirling waters were the residents of the little cabin beside the creek.

As a younger man, the pastor had been among that immense sea of converts saved during that fateful August way back in 1801, when the newly faithful shouted their repentance at the now-legendary camp meeting at Cane Ridge. God had surely triumphed over Satan and his serpent during those four glorious days of frenzy.

Following those heady days of the Cane Ridge Revival, the pastor had helped found one of the countless new churches that sprang up during the bewildering Protestant fragmentation of the era. Residents in and around the little crossroads town could now worship with the Baptists or the Methodists or the Lutherans or Presbyterians or at the Christian Church or any of the other meetinghouses that had come to thrive here. Several times a week, great crescendos of passion and fury rushed forth from Church Street, bursting into the world through tall beckoning doors to envelope all within reach. Theirs was a zeal as strong and unstoppable as the great hissing steam trains that had begun thundering closer and closer even to the quiet farm hills of Kentucky.

"Let us pray for the president, for our country, for our soldiers who protect us from our enemies," intoned the pastor, his shirt clinging to his thin bony frame with sweat. Although he was no longer young, in the years since Cane Ridge the pastor had established himself as a stalwart leader of the community and had become a powerful force to be reckoned with.

"Amen Brother, Hallelujah!" shouted Brother Albert.

"But there are enemies right here, in our very midst, that we must also fear," the pastor continued, a convincing surge of apprehension flooding his voice. "There are enemies right here!" As he shouted his arm flew dramatically to indicate everyone present. He leaned over the edge of the pulpit, perched above the rows of narrow wooden pews. The congregation had already sung several hymns and the pastor had already been preaching for some time; he showed no sign of tiring.

A chorus of "Yes, Brother, amen!" rose up from the pews.

"Make no mistake my children—the work of Satan is all around us. He toils right here in our very midst," the pastor continued darkly, his voice sinking to a conspiratorial whisper as if the devil himself might be lurking just beyond the last pew, laying in wait for the opportunity to strike. "He seeks to turn you away from God! But who? Who will you follow? Who will you choose?" he implored his flock.

"Jesus! We'll choose Jesus!" cried the congregation, some of whose hands were beginning to rise up and tremble with the power of the Lord.

"And who will the sinner choose?" The pastor narrowed his eyes and looked straight into the face of every person in the pews that sweltering Sunday morning. But, of course, it was a rhetorical question he posed; and they took the bait, as, of course, he knew they would.

"Lucifer! They will choose Lucifer!" wailed the congregation.

It was then that old lady Monroe—still quite nimble for her years—jumped up and began circling briskly around the pews. She swung her arms wide and strong. "Jesus! God! Jesus! God!" she cried with every fervent swing of her arms. Old lady Monroe was always the first to begin the Jericho March.

The pastor paused, anticipating how the scene would unfold. Widow Sizemore got up and fell in behind old lady Monroe, matching her pace as they swung their arms together like well-practiced oarsmen. She, too, cried, "Jesus! God! Jesus! God!" but to her very own unique rhythm. By their second sweep around the pews, old Elias Barnes, who owned the gristmill, felt the call and followed in behind widow Sizemore. Soon others joined as well, all anointed in the spirit as they marched fiercely around the room.

In the last pew Brother Jones—an elder with the gift of healing—laid his hands on the sobbing gray head of an old man distressed by the recent death of his only son. Elder Jones cried up to the Lord to cast out the poor man's demons and to bring blessed salvation to his dead son.

From a side door of the meetinghouse, Brother Albert hauled an old wooden box and flapped back its lid. He reached in and pulled out a writhing mass of timber rattlers and diamondbacks and copperheads. As he strode back and forth along the narrow aisle he offered the slithering serpents all around. Yes! He presented them all with the opportunity to be graced by the Holy Ghost that morning—to feel His presence right there on the skin of the palm. Brother Albert held his proud hand aloft, revealing the lack of several fingers. For Brother Albert and those around him, the missing digits served as testimonial to the utter enormity of their faith.

The pastor had sat back and watched from his pulpit, gratified at the rising momentum of their frenzy. But now it was time for him to enter the fray, to provide a shepherd's guiding hand. His flock seemed to need a little extra push that hot August morning.

With one quick lunge, the pastor leapt down the pulpit's steep, wooden stairs. There, perched on the last step, he paused, perusing the chaotic scene stretching before him—a hawk hovering in midair, waiting for the plunge. He adjusted his spectacles, shifted them in their angry red grooves at the bridge of his nose. He glowered at them, one by one, seeking out the wayward sheep hidden amidst his perpetually vulnerable flock.

It was at times like this the pastor had a remarkable eye for mere pretenders in the true fervor of the Lord. Last week it had been Bessie Stapleton, a young and pretty but easily influenced farm girl who could never seem to keep her knees together. "The flesh is weak!" he had thundered, his crooked finger wagging in her face.

Today it was Everett Erlanger's turn, a pint of whiskey sticking out of his back pocket. The pastor strode in great haste down the aisle, then pulled up suddenly when he reached Everett's pew. He turned on his heel, leaned over three people, and shoved his foreboding countenance into the man's shocked face.

"Quit the drink, man!" he bellowed at the terrified Everett, and the man reeled back against the pew in sudden distress. "You and your worldly ways— the sins of the flesh will destroy you!" The pastor pointed his finger skyward, looked there, took a deep breath. "As Proverbs 20, verse 1, tells us, 'Wine is a mocker, strong drink is a brawler, and whoever is led astray by it is not wise.'"

Then his voice turned quiet and imploring, and he glared at Everett with narrow eyes. "Face your fears, my son. Be brave like Daniel, who walked into the lion's den. Will your pitiful, *pitiful* soul be damned to wander *alone* and *endlessly* through the barren lands of eternal damnation?"

Then he returned to piercing shouts. "Brother, the fiery furnace awaits you! Your worldly ways—the ways of the flesh—will lead you STRAIGHT INTO that fiery furnace! You must REPENT!" the pastor boomed, red in the face.

Foam had appeared at the corners of his mouth and with the word REPENT" was propelled out in great bursts of spittle as he screamed into Everett's anxious face. "He waits for you there, right now," the pastor said, reverting back to his soft, imploring tone. He pointed his finger toward the front of the meetinghouse. Everett's terrified eyes progressed their way along the pastor's straight, unyielding arm until they came to rest on the humble wooden altar at the head of the aisle.

It was a rare soul that could resist the pastor's skillful combination of terror and heartrending pleas for long. In the end, faced with such harsh and powerful entreaties, nearly all fell on their knees and wept repentance before his humble wooden altar, even if they did go back to their worldly ways afterwards. Much to the pastor's grudging annoyance, it wasn't uncommon for him to have to save the same lost soul four or five different times. It was a long and ceaseless toil that He bestowed upon the pastor, His humble servant, and an immense burden of responsibility, although, of course, he did so gladly.

As Everett rose to begin his slow, guilty walk of repentance to the wooden altar, a cheer for his newly saved soul welled up from those nearest him. But few others in the meetinghouse that sweltering morning paid much attention as he strode the aisle because by then most of the congregants were caught up in their own unique expressions of Christ's great passion.

Some tore their hair and clawed their faces, moaning in an indecipherable jumble of ecstasy and agony. Some rocked back and forth, sobbing as they sat huddled in their pews, reliving each terrible moment of Jesus' crucifixion. Others rolled and writhed on the floor as if wrestling great, invisible bears. Some stood on their pews, whirling hands raised in the air in a desperate effort to clamber closer to the glorious throne of heaven. Strange utterances tumbled from mouths in a deafening cacophony that rivaled the very tower of Babel itself. The entire building shook with a force far greater than the sum of the congregants gathered within, as if the epicenter of a mighty earthquake rested just below the very stone foundation of the little crossroads church.

Chapter Seven

Meg looked at her watch and rolled her eyes. The crew had already been milling about ineffectively for fifteen minutes that Monday morning, inventing myriad and ingenious forms of procrastination.

Some were slowly pulling their equipment together, only to realize they forgot some item and had to rummage through the colored trunks to find it. Others accidentally squirted copious amounts of sunscreen on their skin or sprayed themselves with great clouds of Deet, making certain to cover every square millimeter of skin and clothing. Meg recognized it immediately: Each individual swarming around the old oak that morning was trying to delay the inevitable, even if only for a few seconds.

She looked at her watch again and knowingly eyed the most egregious of the Monday morning dawdlers. She knew she had to give her crew at least some unproductive milling time—it was expected, a tacit agreement between supervisor and supervisee, and particularly so for a novice, variably dedicated student crew at a field school. But she was in a bad mood from her irritating, unproductive weekend, and the crew's prolonged dilly-dallying threatened to again tip her over the edge. What's more, the clock was ticking faster that Monday morning than it had been Friday afternoon, and every sweep of the second hand resonated as a dull thud in her exhausted brain.

Meg jerked her head at Emily, motioning her away from the old oak. "Bad news," she said, once out of earshot. "The peckers at KYDOT have pushed D-day two weeks earlier. Looks like we're going to have to pick up the pace a bit."

"Ah, man," said Emily, shaking her head.

"I'll try to find some volunteers," Meg continued, her eyes on the ground.

"But I'm not holding out hope. Can you ask around and maybe find a few? Preferably some with experience, but at this point warm bodies would be better than nothing."

Meg glanced back at the crew. They were still milling and dragging and poking fruitlessly about here and there, zipping open a backpack pocket, rummaging around in it, zipping it closed before zipping open another backpack pocket. She looked at her watch again and strode resolutely back to the old oak. "Okay everybody, let's get to work! Time's a wastin'!"

Emily nodded to Scott as he swept the flat electronic head from side to side. "Yeah, that's perfect," she said. From a distance, the casual observer might have thought Scott was buffing the pasture sod, making sure each blade of grass shone like an emerald in the early morning light. In reality, the crew had just commenced the metal detector survey.

Emily walked at his side, carrying on with what she hoped was useful instruction and just the right level of encouragement. "As you swing, keep the head as close to the ground as possible, but level with it. That's right, about two inches would be perfect—a nice even distance. But keep moving, because pretty soon this whole place will be gone—flattened for another round of houses," Emily said, gesturing to the pasture in general. "And we wouldn't want them to build on anything cultural, especially graves," she continued, hoping she didn't sound too pedantic. She was enjoying the feeling of having her own crew to supervise, even if it was just two people and even if only temporarily.

"What—ya mean no poltergeists?" asked Scott and Tonya simultaneously, and then they cracked up laughing, sending the metal detector's flat, electronic head smacking into the sod. "Great minds, you know," Scott said, tapping his index finger against his red do-rag.

Scott and Tonya were both happy to be out of their units. By the start of their third week, the crew now realized completely that excavation was difficult physical work. The body was always bent at the waist or kneeling on hard ground. It demanded hand muscles to clutch a trowel for long hours as again and again steel shaved through compact soil. Throughout the day, heavy buckets of dirt had to be hoisted to the screens, which then had to be shaken with sufficient vigor to get dirt to fall through the mesh. Only after blisters had popped and calluses had formed and muscles had strengthened could the mind concentrate on something other than pain and fatigue. Not only that, but the metal detector survey also provided a welcome change from the tedium that was excavation.

Suddenly, the electronic head let off a shrill screech. "Hel-lo!" said Scott. He glided the head back across the same stretch of pasture, and again the shrill noise pierced the air.

"Hello is right," Emily agreed. "Tonya, mark this location on the map."

Emily pulled her Sharpie from behind her ear, wrote the grid coordinates on a bright blue pinflag, and stuck it in the ground. "Okay—onwards," she said, mindful of the newly shortened timetable.

After several hours of systematically sweeping the metal detector, Emily and her little crew paused to look at the results. Their map revealed a creative constellation of screech locations superimposed over the chessboard regularity of the grid. The pattern of screeches would have made an interesting Rorschach test: Was it a bat hovering over a mosquito, or was it a bulldog chasing a cat?

"Okay you two, back to the trenches," Emily said as they walked toward the main excavation area. "Who wants to dig screeches?"

Crew hands shot in the air, trowel tips pointing skyward. "Jason and Jessica, come on down," drawled Emily, putting on her best game show host imitation. "Alright. Grab the regular: a shovel, trowels, a screen, paper bags, Sharpies. Then follow me."

Emily's new crew walked to the first blue pinflag. "Okay, let's see what's makin' all that racket down there!" Emily said, plucking the flag from the ground. "Jason, you want to run shovel first?"

Jason displayed the era's current fashion statement: circular plugs in his earlobes that stretched the skin into gaping holes. Jessica—a thin, blond girl—was also up to date: a silver tongue stud that caused people to stare at her mouth whenever she spoke, oddly hoping to catch a glimpse of the wet bobbing orb.

Jason's ear plugs jiggled as he dug, and Jessica screened the soil through the quarter-inch wire mesh. "Hey, look!" she said, plucking a small round metal object from the screen and offering it to Emily.

"Humm, an old slug," said Emily, turning the object in her fingers. "I think this might be from the Civil War. That's odd—everything else we've found predates the war. Oh well—bag it, label it, and let's move on."

At the second blue pinflag they dug up another slug, this one from a modern, high-powered rifle wielded by some orange-clad hunter, deer flung in the bed of a Ford pickup.

The third blue pinflag brought them closer to the main excavation area, but still some fifty yards away. On the map Tonya labeled this spot as a loud screech. Even as Jessica sunk the shovel, she scraped against a large object. When she stood with a load of soil in the blade, the culprit was already visible. As Jason cleaned off the caked dirt, they saw the cause of the loud screech: an iron ax head.

Emily picked it up. "Would you look at that—usually you don't find these things out so far from the habitation zone, but, well, here it is!" She said looking at the ax head. "Hey, you know what? Check this out." She held up the ax so Jessica and Jason could see its profile. "The cutting edge is really dull, and it's been sharpened so much that the doggone blade's just a stub. I mean, look at this." Emily's index finger drew in the air the shape of the original blade. "Spent. This ax head is utterly spent. Humm. Okay, bag it, label it, and let's move on."

They walked to the next blue pinflag, and as Jason sank the shovel in the ground, Emily's eyes wandered the pasture. A truck hauling another load of shaped limestone blocks for the subdivision's grand entryway bridge idled on the side of the road. The bridge was about halfway complete, soon to arch in full over the little creek. A steamroller smoothed out a fresh coat of glistening black tarmac on the road; not a single pothole marred its flat perfect surface. The creek continued its amble across the pasture, while in the distance the long row of gray stone knobs jutted up against the deep greens of summer.

"Hey Emily, you're gonna freak when you see this!"

Emily brought her attention back to her little crew. She looked at the object Jason was holding in his hand—holding it exactly the way she had just held a virtually identical object. The caked dirt was already cleaned off.

"No way!" said Emily, her eyes widening. She took the iron ax head out of Jason's hand. It, too, was dull and spent. "That's amazing. Well, I bet you doughnuts tomorrow we don't find another one at the next flag," Emily offered, believing it a safe wager. She once heard Meg present a paper on the statistically probable quantities of various artifacts at sites occupied for given date ranges. Based on that study, and the date range for the Creekside Subdivision Expansion Site—and since they had already recovered two iron ax heads—Emily concluded more should not be forthcoming.

But at the next blue pinflag, Jason jumped on the shovel, and Emily watched as he wiped the dirt off another dull, spent, iron ax head. "Okay—you win! I guess you guys want Krispy Kremes, huh?" Emily laughed, shrugging her shoulders.

And then at the next blue pinflag they found another dull, spent ax head. At the next pinflag they found another. Then a worn hammer head. Already perplexed, Emily grew more uneasy as they proceeded through the pinflags. Meg had requested she lead the metal-detector survey and write that chapter of the report. It was her first solo undertaking, and Emily was eager to please her mentor.

She bit her lip as she studied the map. The hammer head and five ax heads were scattered across the pasture in no discernable pattern. Why didn't they cluster in some well-defined area behind the cabin that she could interpret as a woodpile? Nor were they enclosed within a small, stone foundation she could suggest had once been a tool shed. What could account for so many dull, spent ax heads at a site with a three-generation date range? And why were they simply strewn all over the place? Back then metal was far too valuable to just fling around.

By late afternoon, they had one final blue pinflag to go. "What do you want to bet now, Emily?" Jason chuckled, jumping on the shovel. "Are we going to pull out a sixth spent, iron ax head?"

"No, I don't think so," Emily said, again studying the map. Tonya had recorded the screech at this pinflag as faint, producing just a low buzz from the metal detector. Emily remembered it had been so weak she had considered not recording it at all, thinking the machine might simply have registered some small natural chunk of metal. Surely this location wouldn't yield a sixth ax head.

"How about all or nothing?" suggested Emily. "I'll bring pizza for the whole crew tomorrow if it's a sixth. If it isn't, my losses are cancelled."

"All or nothing," agreed Jason, sinking the shovel blade with obvious anticipation.

Anxious, Emily glanced toward the main excavation area. It was clear Meg had called clean-up some time earlier. The crew was either screening their final buckets of dirt or packing up equipment. Meg was helping spread heavy black plastic across open excavation units in case of rain; Scott lugged concrete blocks to anchor the corners. Emily noted the crew was moving considerably faster than they had that morning, despite the afternoon heat. It was time to get her own little crew packed up.

And then Jessica's hand was stretching before her, holding something cupped in the bottom of her palm. "Emily—look at this!" she said, her silver tongue stud bobbing with excitement.

As Emily peered into Jessica's hand, an involuntary gasp escaped her mouth. She reached cautious fingers into the outstretched palm, pulled out a fragile and tiny brass cross. It couldn't have measured more than three inches long by two inches wide. The brass was hammered thin and a perfect row of small, evenly spaced holes lined the cross's outer edges. It was unbent, and not even one of the narrow edges beside a hole had broken or corroded away. The artifact was re-markably delicate—indeed, it was a miracle such an object had survived in such good condition, buried in the ground for centuries.

"Wow. Wow," was all Emily could say as she stared at the unexpected arti-fact poised between her fingers.

"What do you think Dr. Harrington's going to say when she sees *that?*" Jes-sica asked.

"I don't know, but I think she's gonna like it. Let's go show her. Bring the equipment—we're outta here!" Emily said. She turned on her heel and strode toward the packed up and waiting crew, cupping her hands to make sure she didn't drop the little artifact on her way across the pasture.

The rest of the crew, waiting with their backpacks on, could tell the metal detector team had found something unusual by the way the trio approached. Emily and her crew were so deliberate in their stride and wore such earnest expressions on their faces. Either that, or Emily had caught a mouse since her hands were cupped tight and she was walking toward them so fast. Jason and Jessica kept pace as they lugged the equipment over the hilly pasture.

The crew gathered round as Emily walked straight to Meg. She uncupped her hands, thrust out her palm—and there lay the little brass cross, safe and sheltered at the bottom of it.

"Holy Smokes!" gasped Meg, and then chuckled for a moment at her own silly joke.

Then her smile faded, and her eyes grew inquisitive. She lifted the deli-cate artifact from Emily's outstretched hand, held it up between her long, slen-der fingers. She leaned her head to the side, an expression of wonder spreading across her face. She turned it from side to side, examining it from all possible angles. It was paper-thin and fragile, miraculous in its incredible will to sur-vive; the metal, startling in strength and endurance. The little brass cross was astonishing, glinting in the gold slant of the afternoon sun.

"Hey, buddy," Meg called with relief as she recognized the backhoe operator standing beside his flatbed at the side of the tarmac. She strode to the truck and pumped his hand. She had worked with the man several times before, and they had become instant friends after she commented on his oversize belt buckle: first place at the backhoe rodeo's barrel-racing event.

Slack-jawed, the crew watched as the impressive machine rumbled from the flatbed and down its ramp. Then the operator revved the engine; the back-hoe belched a cloud of black diesel and rolled decisively across the green pasture swells. A shortened excavation schedule meant one certain addition: heavy equipment.

The man swung the eight-foot bucket through the air like the graceful arching neck of a Brontosaurus seeking a high mouthful of leaves. When he lowered the bucket, it landed on the ground with a solid metallic shudder. A brief rev of the engine, and the bucket's sharp teeth curved easily under, burrowing deep in the sod. Another shifting of levers, and the bucket peeled off the sod in one effortless cleave. And then once again the incredible hulking machine reached out its great hydraulic arm, flexed its great hydraulic elbow, and bent its great hydraulic wrist in one continuous motion.

In a single morning, the backhoe accomplished what would have taken at least ten people an entire week to complete. In a matter of hours, the machine stripped the sod and the plow zone from the broad expanse of pasture out behind the stone foundation of the cabin's two rooms. It was there, in the wide stretch to the rear of the cabin, they were most likely to encounter features like a barn or any other of the myriad assortment of outbuildings necessary to farm life.

But immediately after the machine rumbled back to its flatbed and disappeared down the road, Meg ordered her crew to work. Impressive as it was, the passing of the mighty bucket had left a thick glossy smudge across the entire surface of the stripped soil. It was impossible to see anything through such an opaque glaze.

"Okay everybody—get in one long line," Meg directed. "Right here, where the backhoe started. Marshalltowns ready? Remember, we gotta go fast!" she called, brandishing her trowel like a badge of honor.

By hand, the human line troweled down or flat-shoveled the entire surface of the machine-stripped area, stepping backwards as they peeled off the heavy rind of glossy soil. In their wake they left a much clearer window into the past. Despite its brute force advantage, no sputtering machine, however powerful, had yet been invented that could adequately substitute for a trowel-studded or flat-shoveled human hand or for the trained human eye.

"Alright, let's have a look," Meg said. She scrutinized the soil for many long minutes, pacing back and forth on the sod alongside the stripped and troweled area, Emily following close behind, the two engaged in a continuous, ongoing stream of consultation. Baffled, the crew straggled around in their wake, peering as well at the odd blotches of soil that held such keen interest for their supervisors.

"Okay—everybody come over here," Meg finally called. "Follow the shadow of my hand on the soil." She lifted her arm in the air and moved it diagonally. "Notice anything?"

The crew tracked the shadow with their eyes. Meg kept moving her arm, looking expectedly at the crew. "Can anybody see anything different from the soil on the left side of the shadow as compared to the soil on the right?" No one spoke.

"Look at the texture, too," Emily suggested.

It was Suzy who noticed the somewhat darker staining of the soil, defined only by a subtle discoloration that—if it registered at all—would have meant nothing to the inexperienced eye. "Well, it's really faint, but isn't the soil on the left a little darker and chunkier than the soil on the right?" Suzy said blushing.

Meg nearly shouted. "Yes! Excellent! And how about here?" She strode forward several steps, moved her arm to cast its shadow across a different section of the stripped and troweled area. "What do you see here?"

Scott squinted, squatting down to get a closer look. "Is there a line right there?" he asked.

"Yes indeed! A line too straight to be natural. So that means it must be . . . ?" She paused, with her voice encouraging her students to fill in the blank.

"Cultural," offered Suzy.

Meg threw both her hands in the air and nodded enthusiastically. "Excellent! What you're seeing is the edge of a feature—the location where some past activity occurred. I want you to break into teams, and each team take a section. Map each and every soil anomaly you see." From beneath the bill of her Dodgers cap, Meg glanced up at the sun. "But you're going to have to work fast because this heat is going to bake the soil in no time and you won't be able to see anything, so everybody get moving!"

With tape measures and graph paper, each team mapped each faint stain in the broad brown expanse of soil. When they pieced the map together, the intermittent placement of limestone pilings lined up, identifying the place where a barn may have stood. A round ring of rocks enclosing jet-black soil likely identified a privy. They mapped the partial foundation of a springhouse—an interpretation based on its proximity to the creek—and, after excavation, an abundance of thick, salt-glazed crockery and redware milk-pan sherds. Since the corner nearest the creek was missing, the crew decided the water must have leapt the banks at some point. But had the springhouse been damaged while people still lived in the cabin? After reflection, the crew supposed the creek must have flooded after abandonment, because it did not appear as if anyone had bothered to repair the broken foundation.

Three features had them all puzzled: a potential henhouse, a potential corn-crib, and a potential smokehouse. As they excavated, they referred to them simply as outbuildings A, B, and C because their foundations were of similar size and their contents had apparently all been perishable. But after Tonya unearthed a fragment of a large, rusty iron hook from outbuilding B, the crew began referring to it as "the smokehouse," since a leg of cured meat might once have dangled from that lone iron hook.

"Pee-uueewweey," Scott and Jessica said in unison, exaggerated looks of disgust on their faces. Kneeling on the ground, they fanned their hands melodramatically before their scrunched up noses.

Peering down from the relative safety of the sod, Meg laughed along with the two best sports on her crew. "Okay you guys—very good, you both get high marks for dramatics, but if it was that ripe, I wouldn't have you digging it. The smell's long gone, so I'm afraid it's like they say, it's all in your mind."

Scott pulled his red do-rag from his head, tied it over his nose like a bandit, and Meg chuckled. Although she had been sorely tempted, she had decided against assigning Tonya or Bob to the rather psychologically delicate task of privy excavation.

Even after only a few weeks of fieldwork, various crew phobias had already become obvious. Bob—a close-cropped nerd with thick glasses—seemed to have an irrational fear of spiders. He continually scanned the vicinity in case one of them had the temerity to approach within trowel radius. Although Tonya apparently had no terror of the tattoo needle, she had a devastating earthworm phobia. Workdays were punctuated by unexpected screams whenever Tonya's trowel sliced through a worm or Bob spotted a spider—followed by snickers from the surrounding units. No, it was best she had assigned neither Tonya nor Bob to excavate the privy, even though observing the outcome might have been amusing.

Scott laughed from beneath his do-rag. "But it's better than our Blue Room port-a-potty. That thing's got enough chemicals to pickle our turds for posterity! You think we should go ahead and document the fragrance of Blue-Dye #41 for the archaeologists of the future?" he joked. "Hey, is there a Munsell color code for that shade of blue?"

An hour or so later, Scott and Jessica had exposed the rough rock walls at the top of the privy and had begun mapping their placement. Coarse pieces of jagged limestone formed an imperfect circle at the bottom of the unit. "These rocks don't fit very well," observed Jessica, pencil poised above graph paper.

"Yeah, I agree," said Meg, kneeling beside her.

"Why is that?" Jessica asked.

"Looks like a poor man's shitter to me," Meg said. While Scott snickered, Jessica just stared at her, apparently surprised to hear a professor say such a thing. "What I mean is rich folk of the era usually had nice, brick-lined privies that might be several meters deep. What we have here is a pretty basic way to get the job done. Kinda makes sense for a poor farmstead, don't you think?"

Later that day Scott called her back over, amazement in his voice. "Hey Dr. H., you gotta come check this out—it's awesome."

Meg came over and knelt beside the unit. Scott and Jessica had excavated level 2 and had done an admirable job of removing the jet-black soil from a surprisingly dense layer of glass and ceramic sherds. They had exposed exactly the kind of debris Meg was hoping to find. Archaeologists excavate privies not to savor any possible remnant aromatic bouquet, but rather to recover a different kind of human waste: household garbage. In a privy, refuse from one year was heaped right on top of refuse from the last. It was stratigraphy: an organized, highly contained, nearly perfect sandwiching of time—even if sodden with evaporated human excrement.

Meg nodded as she observed their handiwork. "Good job, guys. Well done." She lifted up the labeled artifact bag to feel the weight of artifacts they had recovered from level 2. She peered inside at the contents, then smiled. "You guys feel like learning an important diagnostic technique?"

"Sure," Scott said.

Meg pulled several ceramic sherds out of the bag and held them out to him in her palm. They were all thin, undecorated, and off-white—virtually identical. "These look the same to you?"

"Yeah, pretty much."

"Well, there's only one way to tell them apart."

Scott looked at her, uncertain.

"The tongue test."

"No way!"

"Yes, way!"

"But there's you-know-what all over them!"

"Ah, that's all long gone."

"You're joking, right?"

Meg shook her head as again she offered Scott her ceramic-filled palm. "How else are you going to distinguish between ironstone and whiteware? They're identical except for firing temperature. High-fired clay doesn't stick to the tongue, but low-fired clays do. If it sticks to your tongue, it's a whiteware."

"Go ahead," Scott suggested.

Meg shrugged her shoulders and selected a sherd. She laid its broken edge against her tongue before drawing it slowly away. "Yeah, that one sticks," she said. She picked up another and brought it to her tongue. "This one also."

As she prepared to put another one to her tongue, Scott interrupted her, "Okay, I'll give it a try." Still looking at her warily, he touched the edge of the sherd to his tongue, held it there a moment, and drew it away. "It does kinda stick," he said in disbelief.

"Indeed. So, thus far at least, the evidence suggests we have a lot of what?"

"Whiteware. Can I try another one?"

"Be my guest," Meg chuckled, again offering her palm. "Of course, we could also perform this fun little analytical technique in the lab, once they're, you know, washed up and everything."

"Oh, yeah, right," Scott muttered.

"And especially since ironstone actually doesn't usually show up until the 1850s." Meg knitted her brow, suddenly feeling ashamed about luring her most willing student to taste the dirty sherds, when in this particular case there was really no reason whatsoever to do so.

Apparently, not quite grasping he'd been slightly duped, Scott's thinking had already veered off in a new direction. "Okay, I don't get it, why all the different ceramic styles and everything, anyway? A plate's just a plate, right?"

"A plate is just plate? Oh please, I can't believe you just said that. I suppose you think all pants are the same, too?"

Scott shrugged. "I don't know, I guess."

"I doubt that. How many times did you wear bell-bottoms last year? Plaid pants with cuffs, maybe? Those were cool in the '70s, so were hipsters. Do you like capris? But long, baggy shorts nearly falling off—you wear them all the time, right? Styles of everything come and go; it's no different with ceramics. Pants styles, tableware styles—it's all the same conceptually."

Scott nodded his head. "Yeah, okay, that makes sense."

Meg smiled at him as she dumped the ceramic sherds back in the bag, then looked once more at the dense layer of exposed sherds still *in situ* on the dark privy layer. The glass fragments were virtually all of the exact same type—a veritable sea of dark olive green. She could tell just by looking that such a large quantity of sherds represented way more than a handful of bottles. Meg stopped smiling. "That's interesting. Does that piece right there have something embossed on the side? I can't quite tell from this angle." She pointed to a small, raised section that protruded from the smooth surface of dark olive green.

Scott tilted his head to look at the sherd from the side. "Yeah, I think it does. Is that important?"

"I don't know—it could be," Meg evaded. She tried to think back to the photographs in her reference books on bottle glass, vaguely recalling a few examples of embossed whiskey bottles that dated mostly from the early to mid 1800s; but then a few other bottles of the era were embossed as well. Meg sighed as this new concern began creeping like a dark cloud across her mind, one that did not bode well for the fate of the people who had once called this place home.

Meg could hear her phone ringing as she fumbled with the grocery bags, hurrying to unlock her front door. She let the bags slide to the floor and then dashed to the wooden crate of a telephone table. The caller ID said Nicholas Harrington—her brother. She reached out her hand, hesitated. What if it was her sister-in-law, calling as she occasionally did? Meg drew her hand back, waited a moment as she listened to her own voice. "Hey, you lucky duck—you've reached my answering machine. I'm not here, so leave a message and I'll call you back. Have a great day! BEEP."

"Hi, it's Nick, gimme a call when—"

She snatched up the receiver. "Hey, Nicky!"

"Hey, Magpie! Screening your calls, huh?"

Meg plopped down on her futon couch, ready to chat awhile with her big brother. She loved it when he called her Magpie. "Oh, I just got in the door. Hey, what's goin' on? You guys done moving in?"

"No, not quite. We're still unpacking," Nick said with a tired sigh. "I'll be happy if I don't see another cardboard box the rest of my life. Too much damn stuff!"

Meg chuckled. She knew exactly where all the damn stuff was coming from. Nick's wife, Deborah, was the consummate shopaholic whose sole purpose in life seemed to be filling their home with elegant, high-priced bric-a-brac.

"How's the new house?" Meg asked. Nick's family had just moved to Chicago, to a gargantuan house in a new subdivision several notches more upscale even than Creekside. It must be costing them a bundle.

"It's wonderful," Nick replied. "I must admit I never thought I'd enjoy having a Jacuzzi in the master, but I really do. The kids haven't gotten out of the pool since we got here, and Deborah absolutely loves the built-in glass shelves for her knick-knacks."

"Sounds nice—I'm glad you like it," Meg said, glancing around her own sparse living room. Her eyes lingered on the sagging bookshelves made with lumber and decorative concrete blocks, one of many furniture remnants from her graduate school days. On the top plank was a baseball she caught at a Twins game . . . it was the top of the seventh, Phillies trailing . . . she'd stood up, raised her arm, and SMACK—it was in her mitt! Meg reached over and picked up the ball, tossed it lightly as she felt again the delightful tingle of that smack in her palm. She grinned at the prospect of Nick displaying a lowly baseball on Deborah's new glass shelves.

"How's the job going?" Meg asked.

Her brother's voice dropped a bit. "Oh fine, although I do tons more paperwork than before." Meg guessed he wasn't happy about his new job, despite the big raise.

"Yeah, paperwork's a drag. Maybe it'll just take some time getting used to," Meg suggested hopefully.

"Yeah, maybe. More responsibility, too. Can you believe I have two hundred people I'm supervising now, and regulations are tight."

"Wow—sounds like lots of changes."

Even though Nick had never said it, Meg suspected Deborah had forced her husband to take the new high-paid job in a high-powered Chicago stock brokerage firm. Her sister-in-law wanted all the trappings of affluence and her husband was the ticket to get them. Then she had the nerve to complain, call him unsophisticated because he didn't care about his appearance as much as she did. But then Deborah was the kind of woman who wouldn't emerge from her bedroom unless she was perfectly made up, hair washed, clothing and accessories flawlessly matched—even to go grocery shopping on the weekend.

"How's the dig going?" Nick asked.

"Good, actually. Although the peckers moved up the timetable on me. I have two fewer weeks than originally scheduled."

"They can do that?"

"Ah, hell, they can do any damn thing they want."

"Finding anything great out there?"

"Oh, you know, your typical early square nails and lots of blue, scalloped-edge pearlware. Looks like they date to the 1780s through the early to mid 1800s, but abandoned a decade or so before the Civil War." Meg paused a moment and considered her next question. She gazed out the window, watched as the neighbor pruned her rose bushes. She imagined their next lovely burst of blooms and then glanced at thin rows of the stunted marigolds in her own meager flowerbed. They needed water badly.

When she spoke again her voice had taken on an uncertain quality. "Nick, do you remember Mom ever wearing a locket?" Her brother was several years older and, as a consequence, had a much better memory of all things related to their mother. She frequently envied him for having those memories.

"A locket? Uh, no, I don't think so. Why?"

"Oh, I don't know, just wondering. We found one out at the site and I guess it made me think of her."

"Humm. No, I guess I can't say I ever recall her with a locket," he said. "Hey—change of subject. I gotta run, but I just wanted to make sure you know about the big shindig we're having, a Fourth of July cookout beside the pool. You know, invite the neighbors, some of the new folks at work and church. Should be a lot of fun, Magpie!" Nick was making an effort to sound upbeat.

"Yeah, sounds great," Meg lied. An awkward pause followed.

"Think you can make it? Come up and spend a few days with us at the new house? Deborah's fixing up a really gorgeous guest room. With a bit of luck you'll be able to find the bed underneath all the fluffy pillows!" He laughed hopefully.

Meg laughed with him, buying time. Although she loved seeing her brother, she dreaded being around his wife. Whenever she was, her sister-in-law more often than not took the opportunity to offer helpful advice. One time Deborah recommended a new hairstyle. Something a bit shorter would actually be more appropriate for a professor, she said with a knowing nod, indicating with her hand a mid-length cut about neck level. Another time she suggested that if Meg wanted to find a husband, she might think about a visit to the manicurist, and that claret might be a good color. On a different occasion, Deborah had even gone so far as to suggest Meg might consider a different career path—maybe opt for something a bit more *feminine?*

"Ah, July Fourth?" asked Meg, feigning uncertainty about the date.

"Maybe we can catch a baseball game. Wrigley Field. Still no lights! It'll be the Giants versus the Cubs that weekend. I can get tickets through the firm. I know you love those stadium bratwursts!" Nick was trying to tempt her now. He lowered his voice. "It'll just be the two of us," he promised.

Even though they had never actually discussed it, her brother certainly knew how Meg felt about his wife. It was the unspoken communication that passed between close siblings, even ones that had grown distant, particularly since his marriage.

But Meg knew Deborah would never allow her husband to get away with not making a baseball game on the Fourth of July weekend an event for the entire family. And in the end Nick would relent and they would all sit in Wrigley Field eating stadium bratwursts, Deborah complaining about their high fat and sodium content and nagging her husband about dripping mustard on his new Ralph Lauren shorts and chastising the kids for their overly eager participation in the wave as it swooped across the bleachers.

"You know Nick, let me have look at my calendar. It's, uh, it's up in my office. Can I get back to you?"

"Sure, that's fine. July's still a long time 'til Christmas—it'd be nice to get together before then. Chicago should be drivable in a day, not like Minneapolis."

"I'll try," Meg said, frowning into the receiver. Being around Deborah was always such a chore—she wasn't sure she had the strength to endure an additional visit that year.

Chapter Eight

They appeared suddenly, hundreds of them, that warm spring morning. Their long, shifting V emitted boisterous, intermittent honks as it glided low and un-hurried across the gray sky. Then the geese banked in the air and flew a slow, ample circle around the edges of the clearing, as if seeking a closer glimpse of the cluster of humans gathered below.

As one, the wedding couple lifted their faces, following the honking geese with bright smiling eyes. It was as if the birds had winged the long skies all the way from their southerly climes to join in the celebration of marriage between Lizzie Mullins and Isaac Tackett.

The young bride standing at the edge of the clearing wore her mother's plain muslin dress stitched by Ruth Tackett long ago for her wedding to the pastor. Estelle had re-sewn the neckline, adjusted the hem, and faced the entire bod-ice with the new cream-colored lace they bought the last time they drove the wagon up to Lexington. Estelle had even replaced the long line of simple bone buttons up the back with those cut from shiny white shells. But even more spe-cial was the silver locket that rested against the bodice's new lace. Estelle had presented her daughter with the cherished gift only moments before the cere-mony began.

The mother of the bride had just slipped the last button of shiny shell into its hole at the back of the collar, then slid her hand into the pocket of her own simple dress. She held the locket in front of her daughter, the silver oval freshly polished and gleaming, dangling from a new silver chain. "A family heirloom," Estelle said. "And now it's yours, honey."

Beaming, Lizzie reached out, held her hand behind the locket, and Estelle let the chain drop from her fingers. "But I want you to keep the hair in it, now," her mother continued. "It's from your own Aunt Elizabeth's head, you understand? You's named after her, you know that?"

Lizzie's lips lost some of their smile. She glanced at her mother, noted once again how fast the gray had overtaken the blond in the thinning coil of braid around her head, how the skin on her face had grown thin and crepe-like, blotched here and there with liver spots. She observed again the deepening of the creases at the corners of Estelle's eyes. Lizzie knew exactly what was coming next: Did her mother have any idea how often she told the story of the last-minute parting gift from her older sister and of the long and difficult crossing over the Gap?

"Don't you worry, Ma. I know how special it is." And how could Lizzie not know whose blond curl of hair rested inside the locket's silver shells? How many times had her mother clicked open the little, filigreed oval, the two of them sitting side by side on the bed, to reveal the treasure within? Those moments typically brought forth the same oft-repeated story told again with the identical words and identical gestures each and every time.

All her mother's stories were like that. Estelle always pursed her lips when she told how she and her sister caught frogs in the pond and raced them on boards laid out across the grass. She always closed her eyes real tight when she told how she and Elizabeth squirted milk at each other from the goat's teat, missing the other's mouth on purpose. Each time she waved her hands through the air as she spoke, her fingers now knotted and bending at the tips from arthritis. There was little doubt her mother still saw those same racing frogs, that same goat and worn wooden milk pail, and the white stream of milk across her beloved sister's face.

But occasionally she spoke of a man whose handsome face loomed up from the reflective surface of a pool of water, a face that hung beside the pale sickle of the moon. At those times her voice was low and filled with foreboding, her eyes glazed over with uncertainty and longing. Lizzie never understood what she meant when she told that particular story, and her mother never could explain.

"I sure do wish you coulda met your Aunt Elizabeth," continued Estelle. She leaned her head to the side and studied the locket now hanging around her daughter's neck. "She's who give me that locket—I tole you about how she had it all wrapped up in a kerchief when me and your pa headed over the mountains, didn't I? But now you cain't never meet her, not 'til we're all gone to heaven." Lizzie recalled full well how her mother had cried and cried the day she got word that Aunt Elizabeth had died the previous year during a typhoid outbreak that swept through Virginia.

"Don't you worry, Ma," Lizzie said, putting her arm around her mother's shoulder. "I'd never even think of takin Aunt Elizabeth's hair out of the locket—you know that. Even though I never did meet her, she means as much to me as she does to you, even passed away an all."

"Always guard it well," Estelle smiled. She patted Lizzie on the cheek, then reached up and planted a quick kiss on her daughter's forehead. Tears brimmed in her eyes as she plucked up some fresh sprigs of pussy willow and began tucking them into the coiling blond braid at the back of her daughter's young head.

Lizzie leaned against the porch rail, and called over to her husband, "Isaac, come an' get yourself some pie while it's warm!" She smiled as she watched her husband's curly dark head turn from stacking lumber at the edge of the clearing, nod in her direction. Still newlyweds of several months, they had settled with ease into married life at the cabin beside the creek.

That morning, Lizzie had baked a pie with the latest crop of fresh peaches from the orchard. Just as her mother had taught her, the woven latticework crust across the top was golden, flaky, and perfect. Estelle sat on the porch and rocked back and forth in her chair. She looked out over all that remained of the irises after their great crescendo of glorious bloom.

"Here's your'n Ma," Lizzie said, handing her mother a plate with a large juicy slice of warm pie. "Is that big enough for you?"

Estelle looked down at the slice of pie on the plate. "Oh, honey, you know I cain't eat all that!"

"You want a cup of sassafras tea to go along with it?" Lizzie asked.

"Why sure, honey, a cup of tea would be mighty nice." Estelle said, pleased with all the attention. She turned back to look over the rail, watched as Isaac strode across the clearing, headed for the porch.

Several months before the wedding, Isaac had built a small timber-frame addition at the back of the cabin. Since large trees were becoming scarce on their land, building the addition of whole logs would have required too much wood. Instead, Isaac had felled a few trees, then hired a man to help him saw the logs into planks. After they nailed the planks to the frame, the new addition enclosed the entire rear of the cabin and formed Lizzie and Isaac's sleeping room.

It was the next addition that was going to be the problem. The cabin's front porch had rotted in several places, mainly along the northern edge, where the wood always stayed damp. The base of the riser of the first step had deteriorated so badly that the soft, decaying wood gave a bit with each footfall.

Lizzie and Isaac had already discussed the possibilities. The simplest option would be for Isaac to replace the rotting riser and the planks along the northern edge, but several more planks would be in need of repair in another few years. Besides, the newlyweds had decided the porch was just too small for a young family likely to grow with a hoped-for batch of lively children.

Ever since the wedding, Isaac had been busy cutting and sawing more logs into planks to build a completely new and much larger front porch. A larger porch, however, would jut out further into the yard, and that meant the first section of the irises would need to go. They expected Estelle would raise a commotion about the larger porch, particularly since she now spent most of her time there, gazing out over her long curving pathway of irises.

Now that all the planks were ready, the squabble could not be put off any longer: Estelle had to be told. Shrewdly, the pastor had decided it best his next ministerial round correspond to the day Lizzie and Isaac broke the news. Now that day had arrived, and Lizzie had risen early that morning and baked a fresh peach pie—her mother's favorite—hoping it would get her in a good mood. So far, their strategy seemed to be working.

"Here's your tea, Ma," Lizzie said, handing her mother a cup. She watched as her mother took a sip. "Would you like another piece of pie?"

Estelle glanced at her daughter from the corner of her eye. "What you tryin to do, honey, fatten me up for the kill?" she chuckled and took a loud slurp of tea.

Isaac leapt up the steps and sat down in a chair beside his mother-in-law. "How're you feeling today, Ma?" he asked, as Lizzie handed him a plate of peach pie.

Estelle looked at him. "Oh, just fine. Why you askin?"

"Oh, no reason." He stuck his fork in the pie, took a bite. "Well, actually, Lizzie and me got somethin we need to have a talk with you about," he began. He glanced at his wife as she came to stand at his side.

"Ma, have you noticed how bad them steps is gettin?" he asked, pointing with his fork, his mouth full of pie.

Estelle took a quick look, followed by another sip of tea. "Yeah, not too bad."

"Ma, theys gettin dangerous." Isaac said.

"They look plenty fine to me."

"Ma, how can you say that?" Lizzie asked. She strode down the steps and kicked at the rotting riser. "Look at this! This here wood's so weak it's gonna fall to pieces right soon."

"Well, maybe they needs a little fixin," Estelle admitted. What was going on here? Why were they talking to her like this? Isaac didn't need her permission to fix a step!

Lizzie spoke next, her voice defensive as she strode back to stand at her husband's side. "Ma, it's time we built us a bigger porch. We's gonna tear this one down, startin today."

"Well, you go right ahead, honey. I hain't stoppin you!"

Lizzie and Isaac looked at one another, stunned. "You don't mind?" asked Lizzie.

"Well, of course not. What's all this fuss about anyway? What are you two up to?"

"Okay, well, good then," said Isaac. He leaned back in his chair and stuck his fork in his pie and took a big contented bite. But as he chewed, he realized his mother-in-law had simply not grasped the implications of building a bigger porch.

"Ma, why don't you stand up and I'll show you where the porch's gonna go— out front there," he said, standing up from his chair. "Are you done with your pie? I'll take the plate for you." He took her plate and handed it to Lizzie, along with his own, the pie only half eaten.

Estelle got up, walked to the porch rail, slurped again on her sassafras tea. Isaac jumped down the steps and stood in the middle of the pathway, sad rows of drooping yellowed iris stalks on either side. They had made sure to wait until the irises were at their ugliest so as to reduce the potential for bickering. Lizzie put down the plates and came to stand beside her mother at the rail.

"Ma, the edge of the new porch will come out to right about here," he said, indicating a distance of some ten feet into the line of irises. He waved his arm back and forth crosswise to the winding rows of fading stalks and then looked up at her as he continued to swing his arm.

Estelle peered over the edge of the porch and nodded her head, still not certain what all the fuss was about. Only when she noticed her son-in-law glance over at Lizzie did Estelle realize the terrible horror of what he was showing her. "Oh no, sir! Not there you don't! Ya'll have to cover up my irises an' I won't let you do that!"

"Ma . . . " Lizzie began.

"I'll be dead and buried before I let you cover 'em up. An' I won't let you tear 'em out neither, you hear me?" She marched down the steps, Lizzie close on her heels.

"Ma, it's alright; we'll only dig 'em up and move 'em over to the side of the clearing," Lizzie pleaded. "You'll still be able to see 'em from the porch."

Estelle turned, shook a crooked finger in her daughter's face. "Oh no you don't, missy!" Then she strode down the drooping iris pathway to confront Isaac. When she stopped before him she hoisted her fists on her hips and narrowed her eyes to glare face-to-face at her son-in-law.

"Ma, we promise, you'll still be able to see 'em from the porch. We'll make sure a that," Lizzie begged.

"I have an idea," Isaac said all of a sudden. He didn't address his mother-in-law but instead looked directly at Lizzie. He walked to her side, leaving Estelle standing in the middle of the wilting pathway. "We'll dig 'em up and plant 'em at the far ends of the rows—make 'em curve the same way an' everythin'. Then the rows won't look so short. She won't even realize nothin's happened, because it won't look no different. I think that's what she's objectin' to. I can't believe we never thought of that before."

Estelle turned her back on them and huffed loudly, her arms crossed over her chest. Lately, she had noticed that people had begun talking about her as if she wasn't even there, sitting right beside them in the room. They talked right past her, as if she was invisible. People nodded in silence when she spoke, then exchanged knowing glances with each other when they thought she wasn't looking. She had recently come to the conclusion that people were treating her as if she were losing her mind. They were wrong, of course, she just tended to get a little confused from time to time, that was all.

But her son-in-law was such a fine boy—so helpful, really, and so considerate. Isaac was so strong and even-tempered, and his brown curls looked so nice beside Lizzie's thick blond coil of braid. He tended the farm so well—always had. Ever since he was a little boy he had been such a hard worker, living with them in the cabin. Had there ever actually been a time when he hadn't lived there?

Whatever he just said about the irises sounded fine. It was a good idea. What had he just said about them? Besides, hadn't it been Isaac who had helped her plant the irises? She didn't quite remember—a little fog had just come and descended down around her, and she couldn't quite see through it at that particular point in time. At that exact moment she didn't honestly recall why it was she didn't want anyone messing around with her irises, she just knew she wanted them left alone. Oh yes, Isaac had helped her plant them; she remembered now. Of course he had—how could she have forgotten?

Long before Lizzie and Isaac married and took over running the farm, it had been clear that neither of Lizzie's two half brothers would be taking over the place.

Although the boys were both bright enough—adequately if not enthusiastically learning their letters and numbers—they were never able to stick to even their simplest chores around the farm. More often than not Lizzie continued to milk the cow and fill the thick red milk pans in the springhouse, even though milking had been reassigned to her younger brother since the previous summer. Why did Isaac still end up mucking out the smelly wet hay from the stalls, when that chore belonged to the older brother?

One warm spring day Isaac had optimistically called the boys out to the barn. He would make one final, determined effort to teach them how to plow, because plowing was a task every farmer needed to know.

"Now pay attention, boys. First you harness up the mules," Isaac explained, taking down the oiled leather tack from the wall. "But now you gotta remember old Queenie always goes on the right, else the team won't pull." The boys watched as Isaac slid an oval hame of rigid black leather over the neck of each mule and buckled the harness straps into place.

"I'll even show you a little trick I figured, but don't tell your ma," Isaac said, lowering his voice, smiling at the brothers conspiratorially. "Ya grab a handful of dry peach slices from a gunny in the springhouse and feed it to 'em as a treat." He pulled a handful of dried peaches from his pocket, held his palm flat for the mules. "It'll make 'em easier to work, but you gotta make sure to give the first handful to Queenie, else the ol' gal's liable to get jealous and not pull at all," Isaac warned, chuckling a little as Queenie nuzzled his palm.

He turned to the mule on the left, patted his neck affectionately. "Besides, this one here's just a young 'un; he's still gotta wait a good spell to be first with some peaches, don't you?" He tussled the young mule's long fuzzy ears, his rich brown fur not yet struck with gray. He turned his attention back to Queenie, rubbed his large, calloused hand gently against the long whiskers and soft velvet of her silvery muzzle. Pleased with Isaac's attention, Queenie snorted and shook her head, her long silvery ears flapping from side to side. Isaac clapped her affectionately on the neck. "Yep, old gal, pretty soon we'll be gettin another young 'un, then you'll be able to go rest awhile out in the pasture."

Isaac turned to the brothers perched on the barn rail. "Ya wait 'til theys done eatin and then bridle 'em, like this," he said, guiding a metal bit into the mouth of each mule and sliding the leather up over their ears. "Then you lead 'em over here."

The mules plodded obediently behind Isaac, swishing their long brown tails as they walked. "Then you hook up the plow to the harness, like this. Once they drag it out to the field, then you hook up the hitch to set straight the plow."

The boys followed along in silence as Isaac guided the double-harness team out to the burley patch. He hitched up the plow and flung the long heavy reins full around his right shoulder and back, to loop firmly around his left arm. "Now walk along beside me, boys, and keep close watch on my hands."

The brothers observed as Isaac's strong and capable left hand slid along the black leather reins and then pushed down hard on the plow's smooth and worn wooden handle. They listened as he hollered "Gee!" when it was time for the team to turn right and "Haw!" when he wanted them to turn left. They watched as he draped the heavy reins against their necks as the mules rounded each turn, hitch chains clinking with the steady motion of the plodding animals. With each slow pass the plowshare turned under the dry stubble of last year's crop and carved a fresh, clean furrow through the rich earth.

When the brothers tried their turn at the reins, they seemed to catch on fast. Isaac was so pleased with their progress he brought them out to the far cornfield, a somewhat trickier area to work not only because the land sloped toward the creek, but also because it didn't form a perfect square. But even there, the brothers did well.

"Okay, boys, I want you to keep plowin on your own. I'll be back after a bit," Isaac called to them from the side of the field, confident he had at last succeeded in teaching the boys something useful.

They worked steadily at first, but once the plow neared the middle of the cornfield, the brothers lost interest in turning the soil in neat rows. Instead, they became fascinated by the things the heavy plowshare kicked up from the field. After their discovery, the older brother drove the team while the younger walked behind, picked up arrowheads and other artifacts, and stuffed them into pockets that soon began to bulge.

By the time Isaac returned, both boys were down on their knees in the middle of the cornfield, their heads bent close together, grubbing deep with their hands and tossing dirt back up behind them.

Isaac could see from the pattern of furrows that instead of straight lines across the field, they had circled around and around at a broad dark stain where the plowshare had hit upon the greatest trove of Indian artifacts. To the far edge of the field, the mules were still in harness, grazing with their bits in their mouths, plow tipped and wedged tight in a thick grove of chinquapin and green briar. As the contented animals ate, Isaac saw great clumps of purple thistles and dry cockleburs tangled in their long manes and swishing tails. It would take hours to brush them out.

The brothers were so preoccupied with their digging that they hadn't even noticed Isaac standing at the edge of the cornfield. He put his hands on his hips and shook his head in frustration.

His first impulse was to march over, order the boys to dislodge the plow, and demand they groom down the animals. But as Isaac thought again about the disgraceful scene before him, he decided against it. No, it was best he himself unhitch and back the mules calmly out of the grove and brush them down, simply because he knew full well it would be the mules that suffered most under the brothers' careless handling.

After that disappointing day in the cornfield, Isaac had finally felt obliged to discuss the matter with their mother, and Estelle had dutifully thrashed her sons. But, of course, she had already thrashed them countless times before, all the while hollering and threatening until she was red in the face, but they still had not listened.

Finally, she had even felt it necessary to discuss the matter with her husband, who, of course, thrashed them once again, but this time hard and long and mercilessly with his thick leather strap. Their father's punishment motivated the brothers to do better, but only for a while, and soon they once again only managed to complete the most simplest of tasks, and even then in the most perfunctory of manners. As a result, the brothers were given fewer and fewer responsibilities, just because it took too much effort to force them to comply.

But it was the discovery of arrowheads in the dark soil of the far cornfield that day that changed everything. After that, relic collecting was the only thing the brothers could think about.

At first they were content to stay on the farm, walk their own newly plowed fields. They learned the pickings were best right after a heavy rain, even if they returned home with mud caked thick on their boots and clothes. They lugged heavy gunnies full of new-found relics to the barn, where they laid them out in the empty part of the loft. There, amidst rafters draped with drying burley and tall piles of cut hay, they sorted their spoils: stone axes with deep grooves; large pieces of broken pots with incisions along the rims; tiny triangular arrowheads no bigger than their dirty chipped thumbnails.

As they grew older, they expanded their range to include the fields of other farmers. Sometimes they asked permission to search their land, but if permission wasn't forthcoming, they'd sneak back in and hunt anyway, pack their gunnies full of loot, and sneak back out through the woods.

Once they heard a man tell a story about John Swift's lost silver mine, and the thousands of dollars in silver crowns the miners buried when they fled from Indians. After that, the brothers began searching the woods for the old mines as well as the treasure, running their hands across the trunks of every large beech tree near a south-flowing creek, hoping to hit upon the rough outlines of the miners' carved names, and thus the first clue in locating the hidden hoard.

It was in searching for Swift's lost treasure that they first came across the Indian burial mounds that dotted the landscape. There were large mounds with stone facings and small earthen mounds in the center of deep encircling ditches. They found mounds on riverbanks, mounds nestled at the graceful curve of a creek or at a small falls, and mounds that rested high on a ridge to peer down a long, steep valley. None was spared the sharp eager edge of the brothers' shovels.

They dug as well in the little caves and rock shelters that pocked the sides of the knobs. If the caves were too deep and dark, they'd bring bundles of cane torches, light one after another as they burned down to nubs. Sometimes they'd pack old Queenie with shovels, pickaxes, and food and head down the lane for a long day of mining, for that's really what it was. They were prospectors searching for the world's richest treasure trove, and they quickly learned it would likely be found in Indian graves. They became little more than ravenous dogs digging hysterically in the dirt, sniffing for bones, and then burrowing deeper when they caught the scent.

And bones they found. Long bones that once were arms and legs; shorter bones that once were fingers and toes; long flat curving bones that once were ribs. Skulls. Bone rendered light brown from centuries—or millennia—of quiet rest in the rich Kentucky earth.

Buried with the bones were artifacts of many shapes and sizes. They gathered them all, returned with them to their dusty lair in the loft of the barn. Even at night they continued sorting their plunder, even though their mother hollered at them from down below, afraid they would burn down the barn with their careless candles.

So good were they at their trade that they became known as the Relic Brothers. And the Relic Brothers always had plenty of relics to sell.

Once they sold a skull with two perfect round holes on either side of the head, at the thin delicate bone of the temples. The older brother pointed to each hole as he recounted his tale, encouraged the listener to raise the skull close to his eye, peer through one hole to sight the other.

"That's where a bullet gone plumb through he's head and out the other side," the older brother said, even though he had drilled the holes in the skull himself. "I even found the bullet that kilt him layin right beside he's head—this bullet right here, all the way in the back of the cave," he lied, holding up an old bullet, twisting it in his fingers. "It musta bounced off the rock before it dropped to the ground where I dug it from. I can only sell it to you as a set—the skull and the bullet together. Cain't part with 'em separate, now, since I found 'em like that, you know."

And people bought what the Relic Brothers had to sell. The brothers soon realized a tall tale brought a higher price, so their tales got taller all the time, and they did ever more inventive things to the artifacts and bones to make them match. Although once they went too far.

"That's the sign of the devil you's lookin at," said the younger brother in a hushed voice. He raised one pale, ragged, conspiratorial eyebrow for effect. As he spoke he looked earnestly into the face of the man holding the skull, considering its purchase. The older brother leaned over, tapped his thin grubby finger next to the burn mark in the skull's forehead, a long dark line smack in the middle between the gaping black eye sockets.

The prospective buyer's face grew ashen, and his eyes widened in sudden panic. He almost dropped the skull on the floor before he ran from the room, hollering something about the devil's servants in their midst. He hollered all the way down the street so loud that no one ever came to peruse any of the Relic Brothers' merchandise in that little community ever again. After that, the brothers worked to revise that particular tale so as not to scare folks too badly and lose out on a prospective sale.

In due course, they came to understand that if they hauled their loot to the city, they could get even higher prices. Many times they made their way to Lexington to sell their goods and returned home with new shovels and other tools with which to continue plying their trade. Once the brothers even made the long journey all the way to Cincinnati, where they had heard of an antiquities dealer who sold artifacts to collectors back in the eastern cities, and that sometimes the better pieces even traded as far away as Europe.

The dealer operated from a brick row-house storefront off Third Street in Cincinnati, in the city's commercial district. Hand lettering on the window proclaimed the proprietor's business: *"Curios and Rare Indian Relics."* Below that, *"Buy, Sell or Trade,"* in bold yellow script.

When the brothers opened the door, a long curving sleigh bell mounted high on the doorframe announced their arrival with a deep persistent ring. The dealer emerged moments later from the backroom.

He was a short, heavyset man with jowls that jiggled as he walked. He wore a white shirt that strained at the buttons from his girth, and damp circles of sweat radiated out from the pits of his arms that hot summer afternoon. A stiff brown mustache hid the man's thick upper lip.

As the dealer approached, the brothers jerked off their dusty felt hats, stood awkwardly inside the entrance. They clutched and curled their old hats in anxious hands, forced expressions on their faces—expressions they hoped conveyed a much greater worldliness than was, in fact, the case. This was their first trip to this sprawling river-port city, and they did not want to be mistaken for common country bumpkins.

"What can I do for you today, gentlemen?" said the dealer genially, jowls jiggling as he spoke. Behind his broad smile he eyed the brothers up and down, took stock in one quick glance.

"Well, we thought we'd just look around at what all you got for a bit, if that hain't no trouble," the older brother said.

"No trouble a'tall, fine sirs, be my guests." The dealer swept his meaty arm graciously toward the main part of the store.

Tall glass cases hugged the walls of the cavernous room, while shorter cases stood in rows in the center. Some held long strings of shiny shell pendants and beads, many with intricate designs carved deep in their brilliant surfaces. Other cases held row upon row of arrowheads made from different kinds of flint— glossy red flint, gray translucent flint, and flint that glinted like coal, except it wasn't. The case furthest from the door held several creative arrangements of carved stone pipes, smooth and shiny in a wide array of colors, some shaped into strange, unfamiliar beasts whose cavernous eyes glimpsed distant unimaginable worlds.

About twenty pairs of worn leather moccasins dangled from a pole suspended from the ceiling. Each moccasin was beaded with reds and blues and greens in intricate floral patterns. When the brothers stood directly below, a faint smoky scent drifted down toward their nostrils. Wooden and beaded cradleboards hung from the wall alongside bows and arrows and quivers made of thick brown animal pelt. A dank musty smell permeated the entire store.

High shelves held whole clay pots, some painted in fading whites and reds, others with broad, fanciful incisions, some of which may have depicted ducks—

or perhaps they were some kind of supernatural bird the brothers had never seen? The dealer even had a small case featuring shrunken heads from the Amazon, painted bullroarers from the Australian desert, and mummified cats from Egypt—all mere samplings of the rare global antiquities the dealer anticipated would fetch the very highest prices of all.

A strong beam of sunlight slanted in through the shop window. Its bright light illuminated tiny dust particles that drifted back and forth, suspended aloft in the warm, lazy air of summer.

The brothers looked toward a shelf on the far wall, where an assortment of old baskets was propped on their sides. A few of the baskets were frayed on the edges but were otherwise in good shape. Some had bold symmetrical designs in light browns and deep earthy reds. Other designs seemed to capture the essence of a leaping deer—or perhaps those were antelopes that ran across the neat rows of spiraling coils? Certainly, none of the baskets looked at all like those their mother and sister wove from split oak. No, the baskets propped on the shelf must have been made by Indians, but their years of digging had not yet produced anything even remotely like them.

"Where're those from?" asked the younger brother, pointing up at the baskets.

"Oh now, those are from a place called Spanish Arizona," said the dealer with just the barest hint of condescension. Something in his tone made the brothers turn back and gaze up at the baskets as if they were pieces of the holy cross itself. The brothers nodded their heads in unison, hoping to give the impression they knew all along that the baskets were from a place called Spanish Arizona.

The younger brother narrowed his eyes, peered intently at a basket whose tight coils bound the short red feathers of a songbird. "They dig 'em up like that?"

"Well, no, not exactly," said the dealer. "They were found just like that, in stone houses under dry cliffs. Quite valuable, they are. May I pull one down for you to take a closer look?"

"We got some things you might be interested in lookin at," blurted the older brother. "Things that'd go pretty good in these here cases."

"Oh, and where're they from, may I ask?" enquired the dealer, cocking his head with mock curiosity. He was glad to finally be cutting to the chase; he was a busy man.

"Ther from a ways outside a Lexington."

"The best things we got come outta mounds down ther," added the younger brother. "Although some good things come outta caves, too."

"Ah," said the dealer, his interest perking up. "And you have them with you?"

"We got 'em out in the wagon in some big ol' boxes. Too heavy to lug very far, theys so full. Would you care to come on out to the wagon and have a look?"

"Ah," said the dealer, feigning disinterest. He paused for effect, tugged a gleaming gold pocket watch from his vest, clicked open the gold face cover. He raised his eyebrows as he noted the time.

"Well, I guess I could close up a tad early for the day. Business is unusually slow—probably too hot," he said, fanning his face a moment. "Shall we then, gentlemen?" He flung his generous arm toward the door. He reached over to the hat rack at the entrance, plucked up a bowler and plopped it on his head, tapped it once, and locked the door behind them.

The brothers turned left outside the store and led the dealer across to the other side of the paved street.

When they first arrived that day in Cincinnati, the brothers were impressed by the quantity of planking and paving—both cobblestone and brick—on the streets of this noisy river-port city. In Cincinnati, even streets off Main were paved, whereas in Lexington it was only Main Street, and even then it was just one short stretch of cobblestone, and all the other streets were deeply rutted and still turned unbearably dusty or impenetrably muddy, depending on the whim of the weather. Many of Cincinnati's streets had new wood plank walkways, while only Lexington's Main Street had any, all of which were old and narrow and splintering badly. Of course, their tiny crossroads town had no cobblestone or brick paving or even any plank walkways. The brothers were also amazed with the vast throngs of people they saw in Cincinnati; the burgeoning popu-lace of that great city seemed to bustle along its busy walkways or glide across its smooth streets nonstop. Many rode in polished black buggies with enormous wheels or in fine carriages with plush velvet seats, their proper ladies adorned in showy white ostrich feather hats, driven to their important engagements by stiff-backed, uniformed coachmen.

Even the mighty Ohio River fascinated them, strong and determined in its inexorable westward flow.

So busy was the river traffic that when the brothers had arrived at the ferry crossing they had been forced to wait for well over an hour. Although the day was hot, they hadn't minded the delay because it allowed an opportunity to watch as keelboats and flatboats, pirogues, canoes, and barges plied back and forth along the busy riverfront, loading and unloading their endless cargo of goods and people from the wharves. When their turn finally came, the brothers had to prod the old farm mules—skittish in their unfamiliar surroundings—

onto the ferry's hollow wooden floor, the sound of their own nervous hooves frightening them anew as they boarded the strange listing vessel.

The dealer sniffed the air as he followed several paces behind the brothers. A disgusted expression crossed his face as the smell of rancid blood on a hot summer day hit his nostrils: The brothers had let the cheapest livery in town, the one just downwind from the slaughterhouse.

They entered the dark, shadowy stable, walked across the straw to the brothers' dusty old farm wagon. The youngest brother untied the rope from a heavy piece of hempen cloth and flung it back. Below were several wooden boxes topped by wooden lids with simple metal hinges. There were so many identical boxes they lined the entire wagon bed like a row of miniature coffins.

The younger brother lifted the lid of the box at the rear of the wagon. The dealer peered inside, gave his eyes a moment to adjust to the dim light of the dusty stable after the brightness of the summer outside. Slowly the dark contents took form.

Whole clay pots were stacked one against the other, with wadded linen wedged between them. The dealer reached his hand, grasped the rim of a pot, and pulled it from its cozy circle; a careful curving design adorned its sloping shoulder. The dealer grunted, returned the pot to its nest of wadded linen. He pulled out another; faint lines of red and white paint graced the cool surface of the fine, exquisitely burnished clay.

The next box held arrowheads. Although the brothers had wrapped their very best specimens in cloth, thousands lay loose at the bottom of the box, left to jostle and knock with the shifting of the wagon during their long journey. They had a box full of carved stone pipes and polished bannerstones and shell pendants and long strings of shell beads, all sorted into smaller boxes. Another box was filled with their entire collection of skulls. The brothers had coated each one with thick applications of wax and oil to make them sleek and shiny and more appealing to potential customers.

As they opened box after box of ancient Indian treasures, the dealer was careful to maintain his feigned indifference. From time to time he pointed out various flaws—a tiny chip, a faint line or crack—in whatever wondrous artifact he inspected, commented how such defects negatively affected the value of the object in question. Sometimes he shook his head, clicked his tongue at how nearly worthless some object had been rendered due to this or that regrettable blemish or some other deeply unfortunate deficiency.

At last, after he had examined all the boxes, the dealer stood up and slapped the dust from his hands. With a weary sigh, he leaned his hot fleshy arm against the wagon rail. He pulled a neatly folded handkerchief from his pocket and blotted large heavy beads of sweat from his forehead. "How much do you boys want for all this?" He swept his hand to indicate all the boxes on the bed of the old wagon.

The brothers were silent for a moment. They had only ever sold their pieces one at a time, and even then those sales were accompanied by their fanciful tales, none of which they had yet recounted to the dealer. They had not expected to sell their whole inventory in one fell swoop, nor had they calculated the value of every item in every box. They had not even counted all the individual objects. How could they have come so unprepared?

The younger brother turned to the box closest to him. "Well, let's count 'em real quick," he said, and began rifling through its contents.

"Oh boys, boys," said the dealer, exasperation in his voice as he shook a meaty finger in their direction. "I'm afraid I don't have time for all that." He tugged out his gold pocket watch, raised his eyebrow as he noted the time. He snapped shut the gold face-cover and slid the watch back in his vest pocket. "Now, what's your price? But remember boys, you've got a whole lot of defects in there, I hope you realize that."

"Ten dollars," blurted the younger brother.

The dealer began to cough and splutter, his jowls shaking violently. It was only with great effort that he finally regained his composure. "I'd say that's mighty high for what you've got to offer," said the dealer, a crease of incredulity across his brow. "I'll give you five. Cash."

"Eight," blurted the older brother.

The dealer shook his head, chuckled. "You drive a hard bargain, boys. You're pretty good at this, aren't you?"

"We've been working this trade for a while now," said the younger brother, as if to explain their superior bargaining skills.

"Alright then, let's make it seven," offered the dealer, reaching a hand into his pocket. "Including the boxes. But you've got to drive them over to my store and unload them. You're lucky, I just happen to have some space available in my backroom at the moment."

The brothers were mesmerized as they watched the dealer open his pocket purse and extract the silver coins. As he counted them, each gleaming coin chimed against the next: It was more money than the brothers had ever seen. Four sets of thin pale lusting fingers reached out to seize hold of the shiny round pieces of silver the dealer proffered in his palm before their greedy faces.

What the brothers didn't realize was that as soon as they drove the wagon from the alley behind the dealer's store, gloating as they patted their clinking pockets, the dealer left through the front door to visit to another man. That man was of the social class that wore a luminous black top hat when he walked the streets, tipping it in polite greeting to others of similar high breeding. The dealer clapped the collector on the back and suggested he stop by the store later to peruse a new shipment of some quite unique and exquisite pieces. By the end of the day, the dealer had sold many of those artifacts to the man with the luminous top hat for nearly five times what he had paid the brothers for the entire lot.

Estelle and the pastor were both fully aware of their sons' relic digging, and neither one of them approved.

"Just leave the bones in peace, that's all I ask," their father always shouted as they headed out the lane.

But the boys just waved and nodded their heads, bound for yet another grubbing operation, poor old Queenie in reluctant tow, the aged mule hauled out of retirement and pressed into unwilling service. More than once the pastor had stomped his feet, red-faced in anger at his sons as they hoisted skull after skull up the narrow wooden ladder propped against the barn loft.

The pastor laid most of the blame for his errant sons at his own feet. He should have set a better example for them, been a better farmer himself. But then in their youngest, most formative years he had been gone so often—too often, perhaps—that his sturdy hand of guidance was not present frequently enough to provide sufficient direction for their unripe and willful souls. Perhaps he should have applied his thick leather strap more consistently, and from a much younger age. As he reflected back, he should have been with his family more, instead of always tending the ceaseless spiritual needs of his wayward flock. Inwardly, he knew he had failed his sons, like a cobbler whose children ran barefoot—and then cut their feet.

Besides, a woman raising boys was unnatural, and the outcome bound to fall short. It had been a mistake to leave them in his wife's care. Boys needed a firmer hand; Estelle had evidently allowed them to have their way far too often. What's more, his wife had always favored her daughter from her first husband above her two sons from him. Perhaps that was where the true difficulty lay.

For her part, Estelle had tried to love her boys every bit as much as she loved her first two children—Lizzie and Thomas—but they had not made it easy.

Even as babies they were unaffectionate by nature. Colicky from birth, they fussed and cried for hours at a stretch and nothing she tried could soothe them. As children they had whined and complained, left a mess wherever they went.

As her sons grew, they favored their father in looks—tall and lanky and bald-ing, even in their teens. They were hushed and devious, always scheming to get out of chores and quick to place blame on others. Although she confessed it to no one, Estelle wasn't disappointed when they took their leave from the farm one day, the very same morning they announced they were headed to a place called Spanish Arizona.

Chapter Nine

Each slab of heavy limestone had fallen flush with the earth, embedded beneath a thick layer of sod. Trapped below, each slab was little more than a strange swelling scarcely discernible in the soft rolling green.

Her eyes glued on the slab in front of her, Meg set her paintbrush on the ground. She reached out her hand, made hopeful contact with the cool surface of the stone. Braille-like, Meg pressed her fingers across the undulations. She stroked each rise, examined each promising protrusion in the roughness. She studied each dip, inspected each tight swirl in the hard folds of ancient stone. She sought any hint of initials—maybe a name, perhaps a month or a year, however faint—chiseled into the hard rock with inexpert hand.

"Nothing," she murmured, kneeling on the gentle rise of land at the edge of the creek. Not one slab carried the least indication of its service as monument to the browning bones buried deep in the soil before it. "Nothing," she murmured again.

No, the initials EEOM were not carved across any broad face of cool stone; just silence blared back at her from the ancient gray rock. Cretaceous. Jurassic. Devonian. Meg's fingers continued their searching, but touched only the remnants of fossilized sea life, those tiny mute vestiges of a primordial era far beyond the scope of human life, a deep and misty epoch, vast and unfathomable to mere human comprehension.

"May as well make yourself comfortable," Meg said, glancing at Bob as he knelt in the dirt. "This'll be your home away from home for the next few days."

"Great," muttered Bob, not at all pleased with this new turn of events. He slid his glasses back up his sweaty nose, then scanned the immediate vicinity for spiders.

Meg took off her Dodgers cap and blotted up little beads of sweat on the sleeve of her T-shirt. She ignored his displeasure. "Just go slowly. Start at the feet and work up, removing about two centimeters each pass up the skeleton. Plan to take about six or so passes. Expose as much and as many of the bones as possible while still leaving them in place."

"Okay," he muttered. After Meg stood up she paused a moment to consider Bob's hunched back. She felt only a slight pang of sympathy for him, in part because he was so darn persnickety, but also because this was a task he simply needed to be able to accomplish.

"Don't worry—you'll get used to it," she said, hoping to provide some small measure of encouragement as she walked away. "Oh, and if you hit anything unusual, be sure to let me know right away."

Excavating a human burial wasn't particularly easy either physically or emotionally, but it was part of the requisite skill set in archaeology whether you liked it or not. It demanded concentration and attention to detail to meticulously expose an entire skeleton with just a dental pick and paintbrush, all the while confronting your own mortality . . . and then break for a ham and cheese sandwich. The good news was it got easier.

As a graduate student, Meg worked on a project that required each crew member to excavate, record, and remove one complete burial each day. The breakneck pace was ludicrous, but then no one had expected to encounter a cemetery with over eight hundred graves the morning construction began on a new bridge abutment. Poor early-stage planning was to blame, but as usual it was the archaeologists who ended up taking the rap. The delay was costing the Department of Transportation thousands of dollars a day as an entire fleet of yellow bulldozers sat idle in a gravel lot while engineers wearing white hardhats and worried expressions peered through the dusty chain link. It had been an exhausting project, but by the end of it, excavating human burials had become routine.

"Dr. Harrington, what's this?" Bob asked about an hour later. He had not yet completed one entire pass.

Meg walked over and knelt at the edge of the unit. Bob pointed his dental pick at a flat, metallic surface on the skull's forehead, where a plunging eye socket was scheduled to appear. "Humm, what *is* that?"

"I don't know; it's hard. Right at the eye," Bob said. He kept his eyes on the worrying skull as he spoke.

"Okay, let's see what we've got," Meg said, stepping down into the unit. She took the dental pick from Bob and crouched low over the skull.

Even from level 1, this particular burial had been different from all the others currently under excavation on the gentle rise of land near the creek. Even the limestone slab associated with this particular individual was taller and more massive. Once surface stripped, the rectangular soil stain of this grave shaft was noticeably longer than any of the rest. Excavations revealed the shaft was outlined with dark rotting wood. Apparently, this individual had received a coffin, while all the others had been laid to rest directly in the ground.

Meg plucked away some dirt, then shifted her hand to pick away some soil above the other eye socket, and then returned to dig a little more at the first. Then she tapped the hard surface with the pick and listened to the reverberation—something thin and metal above something almost hollow. "Wow, Bob! You know what we got here?"

He didn't respond. Even as she waited for his answer she recalled Bob didn't like to admit that he didn't know something. She hummed deliberately, then said, "We got coins over the eyes."

"Coins?"

"Yeah, an old Irish burial custom. This is excellent, you know why?"

He shifted his position a little beside her, but said nothing.

"Because there'll be dates on them, and we'll be able to know this person died around the dates people were using those coins. Isn't that fantastic?" Bob continued looking down at the coins, an uncertain sulk on his face.

"Go ahead and clean them off a little more—but not enough to dislodge them. Then we'll get photos." She handed the dental pick back. "A date. No, *two* dates. This is excellent!" Meg said walking away.

By early the next afternoon, Bob had made several complete passes over the entire skeleton and had succeeded in exposing most of it. After being buried for so long, the bone itself had taken on a light brown hue. "Dr. Harrington, what's *this?*" Bob asked. He pointed his pick at a short stretch of smooth gold wire at the skeleton's right side, close to the hip.

Again Meg took the pick and crouched low beside Bob. She began plucking the soil from around the gold wire, following its path as it plunged into the earth. "Well, isn't that interesting. I'd say it looks like this old guy wore glasses."

Earlier that day, they had identified the pelvis of this particular individual as male, and the length of the long bones suggested he had been a very tall one. Massive bone lipping at the knees and ankles revealed he had suffered from severe arthritis. His bones were light and porous, indicating he may have had osteoporosis as well. While the man certainly had lived to a ripe old age, he was probably in a lot of pain toward the end.

"Glasses. Okay. What do I do with them?" Bob looked up at her through his own thick lenses, then slid them up his sweaty nose.

"Expose them just a little more, then we'll get some photographs. Humm, I wonder if he had the glasses tucked in a pocket? Couldn't wear 'em because of the coins."

When she checked on Bob later, she was pleased to find he had the entire skeleton exposed. The old man's glasses—wedged tight between his hip and radius—had tiny oval lenses that had cracked by the weight of the soil over time. Bob had taken the initiative on his own and was sketching the burial on graph paper, assisted by two tape measures at perfect right angles. "Good job," Meg said looking over his shoulder.

"Thanks," he grunted, without looking up.

She stepped down into the grave and squatted closer to peer at the skull. The mandible and maxilla gaped apart as the jaw hinged wide, the cranium tilting back to balance at its heaviest spot. The cheekbones were long and thin and the coin-covered eye sockets stared blankly skyward. Meg examined the old man's teeth: long yellow teeth gaped back at her, except for the dark stretches where teeth were missing. "So, did you have a good look at his teeth?"

Bob didn't stop his sketching. "Yeah, I know, they're real worn—almost down to the pulp."

"That's right. But did you check out his upper and lower incisors, and the bicuspids on the left side?" Bob paused, his pencil in mid-draw, and then lowered his face until he was nearly eye to tooth with the old man. "What do you see?" she asked.

"Ugly teeth," he replied.

"Yeah, well, I bet your teeth'll look like that when you're his age, too," she said, as a fleeting image of Bob as a spider-phobic old curmudgeon crossed her mind. "What else?"

Bob leaned forward, studied the teeth. "They're real long, and it seems like the bone around here rotted away," he said, pointing his pencil at the dark gaping root sockets along the left side of the jaw. "And this side too," he said, moving to the right jaw.

"Now you know they don't call it 'long of tooth' for nothing. That's a bad case of gum disease you're looking at—massive bone loss. Not much dental care back then," Meg said. "But what else do you see? Look on the front left teeth."

Bob shifted his position a little and cocked his head to get a side view of the jaw. "Are the edges of those teeth more rounded than the others?"

"That's right. Notice anything else?" Meg took the pencil from Bob and pointed with its tip. "Look close—what's that?"

"Is that a chip out of the enamel?"

"Sure is," Meg said. "Any idea how someone might come to have chipped enamel and worn edges on only those particular teeth?"

Bob was visibly eager to provide the answer, but again would not admit he didn't know it. Instead, he just sat staring into the skeleton's gaping mouth. Meg handed him back his pencil as she rose from her crouch. "Well, I'd guess our old fella here smoked a pipe for a mighty long time."

Lunchtime at the creek became a great deal quieter once the burial excavations had begun. The crew just sat in the shade, watched as the water trickled past, and ate their lunches in silence. Even Scott, the class comedian, stopped telling jokes for a while.

"So, do we even know who these people were?" asked Jessica after several days of hushed lunches. The previous weeks of excavating stone and glass and ceramic—even the privy remains—had not yet elicited that question.

"You mean do we know their names?" Meg asked.

"Yeah."

"Nope. No names. No known descendants."

"Why not?" asked Jessica, a puzzled look on her face.

"Well, one reason is that during the Civil War the county courthouse burned to the ground. The whole thing up in smoke—nothing but ashes. But even so, it was unusual if early land ownership was legal, at least in the sense we understand it today, so it's hard to say whether these folks ever actually held an official title." She paused to take another sip of Gatorade. "The first *known* deed for this specific area was taken out by the Hennesseys following the Civil War, when it became part of Chestnut Grove. But all our artifacts pre-date that by far."

Meg paused to look down at the water. For the inhabitants who had once lived in the cabin beside the creek, the link with the present had been broken.

"So, archaeology's all there is for these people?" Jessica asked.

"That's right," Meg said. "But even then, archaeology's incomplete. We are only able to build a picture of the past based on the preserved remains, which we know represent a pretty small fraction of what life was really like."

"What about the bodies?"

"If you mean what'll happen to them, as per law, a notice ran in local newspapers identifying the location of these graves, but no descendants came forward."

"What if descendants *had* turned up?" Jessica wasn't letting up in her questioning. Meg was pleased her young, tongue-studded student was so interested in the human remains. The girl had spent the last two days excavating the skeleton of a small, young adult female—probably a woman about her own size and age. Jessica had also helped Emily with the infants, whose graves were particularly difficult to excavate since the delicate bones had scarcely even formed before they were buried. Jessica had not spoken much during that entire time.

Meg smiled at her. "The descendants would need to provide some kind of evidence they were who they said they were—you know, related to the folks in the graves. But if they could, after adequate study, they would receive the burials."

"What about the grave inclusions?"

"They would go to the descendants also."

"Then what?"

"Typically, they rebury the remains in a family plot somewhere," Meg said.

"But since there are no descendants what will happen to all, all this, uh, this stuff?" Jessica asked, waving her hand in the general direction of the cemetery on the rise.

"After analysis, the state will eventually rebury it. Most cemeteries have rear sections for unmarked graves. When KYDOT surveys for roads, they often try to avoid old farm cemeteries if they can, by routing roads around them; but more often than not, they just dig 'em up, like here."

Meg's eyes traveled along the curve of the creek and then followed the slope of the land as it rose from the banks and up toward the odd scene on the rise. A stack of limestone slabs, dark mounds of earth, a cluster of cardboard boxes with gaping flaps, and several long shadowy rectangles were what now made up the little family cemetery. A row of modern Creekside houses formed the backdrop for this strange sight. "Lots of small farms once existed around here—but they just couldn't make it."

"Dr. Harrington? I need to talk to you." It was Tonya, calling from the grave down slope and closest to the creek. Her voice had a troubled sound.

Meg walked over and squatted next to her. The girl's dragon tattoo extended from wrist to wrist over her back and shoulders, always displayed in full by her halter-top. The sun had turned the dragon's red scales several shades deeper and made its green talons more vivid against her tanned skin. Tonya offered her cupped hand to Meg, a crumble of dirt in its palm. "I'm sorry, Dr. Harrington."

Tonya had been excavating the rib cage of an older adult male with multiple and unmistakable fractures throughout his entire body. Both collarbones and one of his femurs were broken. Although it was difficult to tell, it looked as if his spine may not have been in proper alignment at the time of burial. Not one of the breaks had been set, and there was no re-growth of bone at any of the fractures: The man had died as a result of massive injuries.

Meg frowned as she peered into Tonya's hand, not pleased with the implications of an apology. She held out her hand, and Tonya transferred the contents with care. Within the crumble of dirt were several small pieces of corroded metal. At first, as she pushed the dirt around with her finger, Meg registered only the corrosion of the metal—the white bulbous growths on thin green fragments. But then she noticed the broken pieces were round in cross section, and straight, only a centimeter long at most. One broken section had a tiny round ball of corroded metal.

"I'm sorry, Dr. Harrington; it just broke into pieces."

Meg adjusted the bill of her cap and sighed. As if she had never broken an artifact before! However hard you try not to, it's inevitable it'll happen sooner or later, especially when dirt needs to be moved fast to meet a deadline. She understood how the girl felt. "I know you didn't mean to, metal this thin preserves so poorly," Meg said, still concentrating on the crumble in her palm. "Don't worry about it, but do try to be more careful."

"Okay."

"So, do you know what this is?" Meg peered into her face.

"No," Tonya admitted.

"It's a shroud pin. You know—the poor man's coffin," Meg said. She looked back at the dirt and fragments of corroded metal in her hand. "First one we have. Where'd it come from exactly?"

Tonya showed her an area midway deep along the right side of the ribcage. It was a ribcage in which several ribs were snapped completely in half, their sharp edges looking painful even now.

"Make sure you draw and label that location on your map, and write it in your unit notes also. Get a little box with cotton from the yellow trunk to protect it from more damage, and label the box separately. And keep a sharp eye out in case there's more."

Tonya nodded, but made no move for the yellow trunk. "So, what do you think killed him?" she asked.

Meg paused a moment to contemplate the fractured body in the ground. "Hard to say. Must have been a pretty bad accident though."

As soon as the fractures had become apparent, Meg had checked the sex of the skeleton. She was thankful the pelvis was narrow and tall, with a rounded iliac crest, and thus could not have been the remains of EEOM. She was glad her friend had not met her death in some terrible accident. Even though the crew had already exposed all eight of the adult burials present, thus far she had not been able to narrow down which one might have been EEOM. As Meg gazed at the shattered bones, she tried to imagine the face of the man whose broken remains lay in the ground before her. Had EEOM witnessed this tragedy? Surely she must have known this man. How did she take his death?

"Like what kind of accident?" asked Tonya.

"Well, I don't know really, maybe a horse fell on him—crushed him on the spot."

"How long do you think he lived afterwards?"

"I'd guess the break in the femur might have been a compound fracture— the broken end tearing right through the skin. That big of a wound, he could have bled to death pretty quick, I'd think. They didn't have ambulances to speed people to hospitals back then. A major accident on a farm this remote would have been a death sentence."

A plane in the air caught Meg's attention. She watched its sleek silver body as it sped through the sky, its wake a thin vein of white painted on the cloudless blue. Had such a terrible accident happened today, a helicopter would have air-lifted the victim to a well-stocked hospital and the specialized care of surgeons in sterile white coats.

Meg's eyes were still fixed on the sky when she felt a light tap on her shoulder. She turned to find Suzy looking at her. "Dr. Harrington, could you please help me with something a minute?"

"Sure," said Meg. "Is anything wrong?" Everyone else on the crew just yelled for her when they had a question. Only Suzy, the shy girl, was polite enough to get up, walk over, and kindly request her assistance.

"There's something I think you should see." As Suzy spoke, Meg was pleased to hear a growing confidence in the shy girl's voice; it was a quality that had not been there before field school began.

As they walked, Meg noticed again how careful Suzy was with the sun. She always dressed in long-sleeve shirts buttoned at the wrist and full-length pants tucked in white tube socks. She wore dainty garden gloves and the widest brimmed sunhat Meg had ever seen. During the past week the girl had proven herself a particularly capable excavator of burials. She had an endless supply of patience as she removed clumps of dirt from the tight spots at the joints of toe and finger bones or the dark spaces between ribs.

Without qualm or complaint, Suzy had excavated the burial of an older woman with clear evidence of rheumatoid arthritis in her hands: Her knuckles were round and bony, and severe bone lipping in her digits must have bent her fingertips at the ends. After completing the necessary sketches, photos, and documentation, Suzy had removed the bones, wrapping each one in paper and placing them in a brown cardboard box for transport to the lab. During that entire process, this was Suzy's first request for assistance.

When they reached their destination, the cardboard box sat on the sod beside the grave, flaps open, waiting for its final installment of wrapped bones. Suzy pointed downward. The very base of the old woman's grave was visible in the floor of the excavation unit, and it was there Suzy's eyes were fixed. As Meg squatted and peered into the shadows, she too saw the long, straight line of small, round, evenly spaced white marks on the blackness of the soil.

"Wow," said Meg, glancing quickly at Suzy. The girl had a keen sense of observation; a lesser excavator may not have noticed them at all. "Good work, Suzy."

Grabbing a dental pick, Meg stepped into the darkness of the empty grave. She tossed her Dodgers cap on the ground and squatted down above the long line of white marks. She extended her hand and drew the pick gently against the edge of a spot of white. As she did, abruptly and without explanation, her vision began to change and a chill prickled her skin.

At first it was only the very slightest of clouding, but then an opaque veil began to gather substance within odd blurs of shifting mist. It worked itself into a hazy curtain pulling open to reveal the edges of an ancient portal. Just beyond that portal Meg recognized those same white shapes. It was the distant, smoky image of a long line of tiny shell buttons gracing the length of a woman's curving back, sewn tight to the fabric of her long white dress. At the nape of her neck dangled loose ethereal strands and the sparkle of golden braided hair.

Her apparition, vague and indistinct, strode the olden ground in the clearing beside the creek. The shells twisted as the woman twisted, the shells bent as she bent. The quiet flash of iridescent nacre—the glisten of pale pink, a faint swirl of light emerald green. The shimmering buttons reflected the bright flicker of a cooking hearth and a pale sickle of moon in a still pool of water. As Meg beheld this vision, she understood that the frail, aged body in this grave was that of EEOM. It was this woman, the owner of the special silver locket, who had been laid to rest within the coolness of this rectangle of shadowy earth.

Amazed, Meg stood up, but continued to gaze downward. "What are they?" Suzy asked quietly. The shy girl had come to kneel at the edge of the unit and had waited as her professor studied the little round spots of white.

Meg whispered the words. "Shell buttons." Then they both were silent, gazing down into the shadowy grave before them. "They once ran along the back of her dress," Meg continued, still in a whisper. She lifted her arm, gestured in the vague direction of her own back. As she did, sudden tears welled up in her eyes.

She blinked hard and crouched back down: Meg was not ready to let go of that wondrous portal just yet. She hovered her fingers just above each tiny spot of white, pausing over each one, and again the coolness began to enter her hand. As her fingers moved they felt the smooth shell surface and the gentle slide of each thin button into its slit of ancient fabric. Meg sensed the bodice tighten around her own waist, firm along the length of her ribs. With deliberate breaths she took in the musty air of this woman's decayed dress, a smell that still lingered in the dark soil of her open grave.

Stunned, Meg stood up again. She turned, wondering for a moment whether Suzy might also have felt anything unusual. The girl smiled faintly. "What do we do with them?" she asked, and EEOM began her quiet retreat back across that portal, back into the silence of the cold grave.

Meg turned her eyes back to the grave with regret and sighed as she felt EEOM depart. She pursed her lips as the weight of responsibility returned to its customary place on her shoulders.

Meg turned her head away from Suzy for a moment as she collected herself. She fixed her gaze on the rough bark of a mighty oak whose branches must have shaded the little cemetery for many long years. Its trunk was so broad it had likely been witness as each and every grave was dug on this gentle rise of land. This tree had outlived them all. Meg forced her gaze away from the rough trunk and sighed as she grabbed her Dodgers cap and stuffed her hair back inside its confines. Without looking at Suzy, Meg crouched back in the unit and peered intently at the buttons.

There was barely anything left of them. The shell was soft and flaking from long years of contact with the moist soil. She tried to excavate a button, but its edge disintegrated to powder at even the first touch of the dental pick. She tried another, but the fragile shell again crumbled into many fine particles of white. They would not come out intact. It was as if the ancient shell buttons had chosen to stand their ground, remain steadfast in the dark earth, maintaining their vigil as the last vestige of EEOM's grave.

"They won't come out whole," Meg said. "Clean it up a little, then let's go ahead and photograph and map. That'll probably be it. You can try to excavate them, but it's likely they'll just stay right where they are."

Suzy nodded, but didn't move.

Meg looked around and assessed the needs of her crew. They were all occupied with their various tasks and didn't appear as if they would require her assistance anytime soon. She looked at Suzy. The girl was a truly excellent mapper. Meg had no doubt the girl would produce an accurate and beautiful map all on her own.

"Would you like me to help you?" Meg asked.

"Sure," Suzy said, and smiled.

Midway through the afternoon, the old woman came tottering down the slope, picking her way with care over a particularly uneven section of pasture. It was rough going for a woman her age and weight, even without the added burden of the balloon-decked baby carriage she pushed in front of her. As the carriage rolled down a hefty bulge of sod, the colorful balloons bobbed sharply in the air.

As soon as Meg saw that odd sight, she leapt up and sprinted toward her. Could this woman really be wheeling an infant over the pasture?

"Are you okay? Let me help you with that!" Meg offered, taking over the helm of the carriage.

"Why yes, thank you, honey," said the old woman. She spoke slowly, pronouncing her words with a Kentucky accent.

"You're coming to visit us, I guess?" Meg asked.

"I sure am, honey."

As she pushed the carriage, Meg glanced inside. Jammed in where babies normally rode were several large, round, flat Tupperware containers. At the sides of the carriage several tall Tupperware containers swished and gurgled with icy liquid. "What have you got in there?"

"Peach pie." The old woman said "peach pie" with a delightful singsong—a somewhat proud, somewhat jesting tone that sounded like music to Meg's ears.

As they reached the excavation area, she prepared to launch into her site tour. "I'm Meg Harrington. I guess you're probably wondering what we've been doing here all this time," she began.

"Oh no, honey," said the old woman, smiling and shaking her head. "I know exactly what you're doing here. You're taking care of our old things."

Meg smiled, unsure exactly what she meant. "Yeah, that's right."

"Good for you, honey," continued the woman, gently patting Meg's hand. "And I thank you for doing such a mighty fine job of it. We sure do appreciate it!" Her expression didn't waver as she spoke, but it did let Meg know she really wasn't interested in the details; apparently for her, "old things" was detail enough. "Now, I do believe you folks take your breaks down at the creek? I think this would taste right good in the shade."

"Ah, great idea. Break time everybody!" Meg called.

Immediately after arriving at their shady spot along the bank, the old woman began slicing and serving up the pies. "I'm sorry, Ma'am, I didn't quite catch your name," said Meg a little too politely as she helped hand the pie out to the crew. She felt strangely small and humble beside this woman.

"That's because I haven't thrown it your way yet," the old woman replied with a mischievous twinkle in her dark eyes. Meg blushed. "I'm Mrs. Elizabeth Kenton," she added with a more serious tone, although still with that singsong of mocked formality adorning her words.

"Are you from around here?" asked Meg. It was a typical Kentucky question. It generally inquired in which county someone was born. Despite over a decade of living in the Commonwealth, Meg's Midwestern accent still betrayed that she was "not from around here" and never would be.

"Oh yes, honey," was the woman's enigmatic reply. "I'm from right here." She smiled as she handed Meg a plate with a generous slice of pie. "This one here's for you."

The pie was mouth-watering. It had a perfect, flaky crust with a perfect, golden-brown, melt-in-the-mouth latticework crisscrossing the top. The perfect proportion of peaches to syrup in the filling. The perfect consistency—sweet but not sickeningly so. Mrs. Elizabeth Kenton had baked exactly enough pie for everyone.

The crew, always happy for a break, couldn't believe their luck. They devoured each slice until nary a crumb remained, gorging themselves as if they had been on the verge of starvation, gulping down the iced tea as if they had been on the brink of dehydration. After they finished, they lounged about on the shady grass, grinning with satisfaction.

Meg stuck her fork in her final bite. "This pie's delicious. Is it an old family recipe?" she asked.

"Sure is—my momma taught me how to bake pie. I can teach you, if you'd care to learn?" She made her offer to everyone, but looked right at Meg as she spoke, her dark eyes narrowing. "Come to my house Saturday afternoon." It was a proclamation rather than just a polite offer. "I live right there," she said, pointing her pudgy finger toward her house. "But you already know that, don't you, honey?" She winked.

Meg blushed; she had hoped the embarrassing binocular incident wouldn't be brought up. Then she turned silent, suddenly becoming very interested in a blade of grass.

"Oh, darlin', bakin' a pie really isn't as hard as you might think," chuckled Mrs. Kenton.

How did this woman know that baking had always struck Meg as vaguely mysterious? Although she was proud that she managed to bake muffins from time to time, a pie was entirely out of the question. So many fussy things to do with the ingredients and in such precise order. The strange enigma of finicky dough. Besides, why spend so much time on something you just turn around and eat? Where was the efficiency in the baking of a pie?

"Honey, if you can do what I've been watching you do out here, you sure got what it takes to bake pie."

There was that mildly mocking tone again, but infused with such kindness and sincerity it was impossible for Meg to take offense. Mrs. Elizabeth Kenton was not what she had expected. But then, what exactly had Meg expected from the old woman who watched from the rail of her back deck?

"Let's go, Dr. Harrington, it'd be fun," urged Emily.

"Oh, I'm really not that good in the kitchen, Mrs. Kenton," Meg confessed, hoping to shrug off the invitation.

"Nonsense! And call me Miss Eliza. I'll expect you both about one o'clock Saturday. Just bring yourselves."

"Oh fantastic!" Emily said, as Meg forced the corners of her mouth to turn up in an unconvincing smile.

Even after they had packed up the Tupperware and everyone had said their thanks and good-byes and Emily was pushing the baby carriage up the slope toward Miss Eliza's house, Meg's reeling mind was having difficulty with Saturday's unexpected pie-baking extravaganza.

What was making her so anxious? Was it really the simple act of baking that had her so concerned? Was it only just the bewildering complexity of dough? She was reasonably sure she could follow a recipe, even a rather difficult one, without too much trouble. Besides, it would be a good learning experience, not to mention a welcome change of pace.

No, it was something else, something she would rather have left buried, an inconvenient and deliberately ignored relic of her past. As she watched Miss Eliza's bright balloons bob and wend their way back across the bumpy pasture, Meg could not deny the source of her uneasiness regarding Saturday afternoon's get-together.

As the oddly disconcerting proposal of baking permeated her mind, so too did the image of the gaping hole in her heart where a warm oven should have been. There she stood peering through the oven's open door—a smiling, apron-clad mother with flour dust to her elbows. Standing on a chair at the kitchen counter, young Magpie dropped fresh dough from a big wooden spoon onto a greased baking sheet. The wistful, comforting scent of cinnamon and nutmeg hung in the air. A bowl of eggs on an old wooden table. A sunlit window with gingham curtains.

These were the mother-daughter baking sessions that had never been. Had her mother ever baked pies? Cookies, even? Meg just couldn't remember.

Chapter Ten

"Ma, I reckon Pa needs help settin out the 'bacca today," Caleb said hopefully. He kept his eyes on the floorboards and kicked at the edge of his boot, miserable at the prospect of another day in school.

Lizzie put her fist on her hip and shook her head as she opened the cabin door. "Son, you get yourself down to that schoolhouse right now, and I don't wanna hear another word about it."

"Yes, Ma'am," Caleb muttered, dejection in his voice.

She glared at him as he slouched past. How many times had she needed to put her foot down with her youngest? Her other two boys had gone willingly to school, but ever since she could remember, Caleb always preferred to stay on the farm and work alongside his father.

"And when you get home I want you to finish choppin the firewood for me," Lizzie added as he thudded down the porch steps. She knew her son loved to chop wood; she could at least give him a task he could look forward to.

A schoolhouse had been built on the edge of the growing crossroads town several years earlier, and the county authorities had hired a teacher—a proper, energetic, young Christian woman—to instruct all grades in the same small room. The community was so proud of their new school that a few of the surrounding families had taken up a collection to buy an iron bell for the yard. On a clear winter day Lizzie could even hear the bell's toll from all the way at their home near the creek.

Although Isaac often kept his boys out of school to help set the burley or break the hemp or stir the sorghum, Lizzie argued with him if it became too regular. She felt it important her children get at least a minimal level of schooling. The value of education was something her stepfather, the old pastor, had instilled in her as a child, even though she hadn't managed to get much of it before marrying Isaac and starting a family of her own.

Her aging stepfather was her staunchest ally when it came to his grandsons' schooling. After the old pastor finally retired from preaching, he walked the boys all the way to the end of the lane on school days and met them there in the afternoon. He backed her up without fail when it came to help with instruction, taking great pleasure in drilling them on spelling and the rules of grammar or quizzing them with questions of arithmetic, sometimes threatening to withhold some treat or other if they failed to answer correctly.

Even beyond schooling, the old pastor went to extraordinary lengths to teach his three grandsons the gospel—to know the word of the Lord and to fear His mighty wrath. For exactly thirty minutes before bed each evening, he pulled up a straight-backed wooden chair, arranged his three innocent lambs side-by-side in their narrow bed, and had them follow along as he read aloud from the Bible. "We shall commence at Luke, chapter 18," the old pastor would begin, nodding his head and glowering over the rim of his spectacles at his grandsons.

"Yes, sir," muttered Caleb, the youngest and most obedient of the little lambs. He flipped quickly through the thin pages to find Luke 18, lest his grandfather accuse him of not knowing by memory the order of Scriptures in the Good Book. He listened dutifully as his grandfather's booming voice droned the solemn words, his own small index finger tracking the strange words on the page.

"'Then he spoke a parable to them, that men always ought to pray and . . .'"

The old pastor was insistent his grandsons attend services at the meetinghouse with complete regularity—every Sunday morning and evening and every Wednesday evening—always and without fail. No exceptions were ever made, not even during the long, difficult days of the harvest when they worked endless stretches in the field, cutting and baling and heaving their produce onto the bed of the wagon, sweat spilling off the brow and stinging the eyes. It was not unusual for one or perhaps all three boys to sit dutifully in the pew, their heads jerking upright as their bodies fought against fatigue, seeking to claim even a fleeting instant of well-earned sleep.

"'. . . know the commandments: Do not commit adultery, Do not murder, Do not steal, Do not bear false witness, Honor your father and your mother,'" intoned the pastor. While he read, the boys were obliged to follow along in silence, struggling to comprehend the strange and empty words their grandfather uttered, lest he stop and interrogate them on the content.

"And he said, 'All these things I have kept . . .'"

For the boys' baptisms, the old pastor presented them each with their own black calfskin edition of the Bible. The first thick page listed every family member's full name, date of birth, marriage, and death as far back as the pastor could account, all recorded in his own tight flawless script. So that they would not lose their places, the pastor had been careful to provide a calfskin bookmark with each Bible, complete with a small brass cross stitched tightly onto the stiff leather by the pastor's own diligent hand.

"'. . . those enemies of mine, who did not want me to reign over them, and slay them before me.'"

When they finished the Bible's last verse, reverently closing the back cover, he instructed them to open the front cover in the same reverent manner, commence again from the beginning, even if they had nearly completed their allotted reading time that evening. The old pastor seemed most determined his grandsons never stray from the Lord's narrowest path; it was a most stubborn, most unyielding doggedness, almost as if he were attempting to redeem himself for some undisclosed failing of the past.

Lizzie and Isaac had been blessed with three sons, but a farm too small to divide. Lizzie knew two of her boys would need to leave the farm, perhaps go off to work at the crossroads town, or perhaps even all the way to Lexington. She hoped to give them at least the possibility of finding good employment; with an education they might even become clerks in one of the many new establishments popping up along Lexington's Main Street.

Lizzie was amazed at how the city had grown in recent years. Stone now paved not only the length of Main Street but many streets in both directions as well. Many tall brick buildings now stood where it seemed only last year log and wooden frame structures had been. Shops lined not only Main Street and Main Cross, but Water and First and Spring and Short.

Ever since the *New Orleans* had steamed down the Ohio from Pittsburgh way back in 1811, an overwhelming variety of fetched-in merchandise was now available for purchase. Millineries now carried silk gloves and stockings and thick bolts of shiny taffeta and chintz and plush French velvet brocade. Thread and buttons of many sizes and colors and all kinds of intricate bric-a-brac could now be had, although for a dear price. Many store windows displayed elaborate English Spode and shiny bone-white porcelain dishes with brilliant transfer prints—cups and saucers, bowls and plates and elegant serving dishes all in the same fancy patterns.

Although Lizzie and Isaac had expected their oldest son would take over the farm, he was turning out to be the boy least suited to the physical demands of farm life. Although strong enough, he was uninterested in the heavy monotonous work of farming and quickly grew impatient with the boredom of the place. He preferred instead to head his horse up to Higbee Tavern for a tankard or two of ale and to try his hand at poker at one of the back tables.

Lizzie and Isaac's second son was the one who took best to schooling. He and his grandfather derived great pleasure in long evenings passed beside the hearth, paging through the yellowed leaves of thick, leather-bound books or reciting Scripture and discussing the life of the apostles in the Holy Land. The boy had a remarkable memory and skill in ciphering with chalk and slate, even if a weak body. Although for completely different reasons, he, too, was ill-suited to the difficult life of a farmer.

But Caleb, Lizzie and Isaac's youngest, was unlike either of his brothers. Even as a small boy, it was Caleb who spent long days in the forest with his father, hunting deer and turkey and squirrel over toward the base of the knobs. Between them both, rarely did they return empty handed.

By the time he was ten, Caleb could drive the double-harness mule team as well as his father—Gee! and Haw! in tight perfect turns as the heavy plowshare carved furrows through the spring fields. Together with Isaac, he scrambled up to the highest rafters to hang the cut burley after harvest, and was quick to grasp when best to open the long windows for the breeze to come and cure the drying leaf. As long as he could work alongside his father, Caleb even enjoyed the bloody task of slaughtering the hogs for winter and packing the meat in rock salt in wide wooden barrels or hanging it from sturdy iron hooks in the smokehouse.

How many times had father and son worked side-by-side on some difficult farm task, their two heads of brown curls—Isaac's now streaked with gray— bent toward the other in happy concentration? And in a sure sign of friendship, Isaac even let Caleb wield his favorite hammer, its long wooden handle worn and stained dark from countless grips and countless swings onto the heads of countless nails.

Of the three brothers, only the eldest enjoyed the Saturday night barn dances. For him it was there, swept up in the excitement of the surging crowd, that he was able to taste freedom—and it tasted sweet.

Each Saturday afternoon in summer, he spent hours in the washhouse eliminating any trace of farm labor from his body. He stood in front of his mother's tiny wall mirror, combing pomade in his hair and directing it back against his head. Then he would saddle the horse and ride like the gentleman over to Mr. Anderson's barn. He was partial to the reels—the fast, frenetic dances that spun spiraling circles of people around the room. In the well-earned pauses between sets, he and his friends talked of the Arkansas Territory, spoke in hushed tones of adventures to be found there—a place where fast fortunes could still be made.

Since his grandfather did not approve of the dances, on Saturday evenings the middle brother accompanied the old pastor to his staid play parties; and, like his grandfather, he managed to finger out a few Irish tunes on the old man's tin whistle.

But Caleb had little interest in the Saturday night barn dances for other reasons. They were too much fuss, too many people crammed in too tight a space, too much noise and commotion. He was content to just relax on Saturday evenings, sit on the porch step and tinker with tools or whittle on wood, listen quietly as his father and the other men told tales of the old days, and nod with understanding as each shared their helpful advice on one subject or another.

As Caleb got older, Lizzie and Isaac did their best to encourage their youngest to go to the dances—to saddle up a horse and ride along with his brother over to Mr. Anderson's barn—but he had no interest. But once it became clear to all that it would be Caleb who stayed and worked the farm beside the creek, Isaac finally felt compelled to intrude in his son's private affairs.

Unlike the old pastor, who was not in the least reluctant, Isaac had always been disinclined to impose his will on any of his sons, most especially his youngest. He figured it was one of the reasons he and Caleb had forged such a strong bond. But apparently his youngest was now in need of a little guidance. They were walking in silence toward the burley patch, along the dirt trail that curved past the old chestnut tree near the creek, when Isaac broached the issue.

"Son, since it's you whose gonna be stayin on the farm, you know you'll need to be gettin yourself a wife?" Isaac asked, making sure not to look up.

"Sure, Pa."

"But she's gotta be one who really likes this life, which hain't too many these days," his father continued, genuine concern in his gravelly voice. "Theys all lookin for somethin better nowadays."

"I know, Pa. I will," Caleb said with little conviction. "I just hain't seen one I like." He reached up a strong hand and scratched the back of his curly brown head.

From the corner of his eye his father watched him do it and noticed the momentary look of bewilderment on his son's face. "Well, sure, son, I know it. But you hain't gonna find yourself a wife just settin around here with us old folks. You gonna need to go out and look some." Isaac said. After a moment he added, his voice lowered, "I'll talk to the new pastor for you, if you'd like."

"No, sir, I don't."

"Alright then." And that was the last Isaac spoke of the matter to his son.

But Caleb did find a wife. Or perhaps it was Rebecca who found him.

It wasn't just Lexington that had grown over the last decades. Even the crossroads town had burgeoned, spilling two blocks deep either side of Main Street. The town now boasted its own courthouse, a postmaster station, a bank, several solicitor's offices and blacksmith shops, a hardware store, and two dry goods stores. Tight rows of new houses lined each street, many occupied by the new immigrants that seemed to spring up from the dusty streets each day.

The newcomers had begun arriving in earnest after 1811, when Henry Harrison defeated the Indians at Tippecanoe, killing hundreds of warriors and putting an end to their hope of retaining the Ohio Country. Winning the War of 1812 spurred efforts to remove eastern Indians west of the Mississippi ... and new settlers came in veritable droves.

Young Rebecca Hennessey and her family were among those newest settlers who arrived soon after the war, making their way down the Ohio to Kentucky's rich Bluegrass on a steamer, and then by stagecoach on Maysville Road, rather than struggling overland by pack train or in rough wagons over rugged Cumberland Gap.

Like so many of the new arrivals, Rebecca's family was accompanied by a daunting mass of chairs and tables and bedsteads piled on top of heavy crates and trunks, a thick rope net thrown over top. Rebecca's mother had even insisted on shipping their upright piano and its matching red velvet stool, so her daughters could continue their lessons, and thus greatly improve their marriage prospects as respectable young ladies.

Although not exactly wealthy by East Coast standards, the Hennessey family was better off than most who had settled earlier in Kentucky. Like so many of the newcomers, the Hennesseys were prosperous enough to bring slaves, ten in total, among them two married couples. Most of the slaves labored on the land, while the two married women worked in the house, scrubbing the floors, washing the clothes, and pressing out the wrinkles with a heavy iron. Rebecca's mother supervised the cooking of each meal, glowered over them whenever they polished the silver; and, certainly, she was wise enough to keep the key to the sugar chest tied to her waist at all times.

Mrs. Hennessey prided herself as charitable because she allowed the married couples to remain together, even though whatever children were born went to the auction block. She even came to fancy herself a slave breeder, even if modest in scale, driving her own one-horse gig to Lexington to scrutinize each sale, making sure she got a decent price for her troubles. It was many a young Hennessey pickaninny was sold on that Cheapside auction block on Court Day, while the aging bucks and wenches were sold down the river to end their years on a cotton plantation in the hot South.

Rebecca's family purchased six hundred acres of land, including the original acreage surrounding the old Whitaker farm. Old man Whitaker had been the patriarch of one of the earliest settler families that had struggled into Kentucky over Cumberland Gap.

"Theys taken over the old Whitaker place," the neighbors muttered indignantly, shaking their heads. "That farm's been in the family near three generations."

But Mr. Hennessey owned the land now and made sure to hire a trained surveyor of superior reputation to document its boundaries with rod and chain. Then Mr. Hennessey himself accompanied a reputable solicitor, whom he paid well, to file all the proper deeds and papers at the courthouse and retain a copy himself in case the courthouse burned. He made known throughout the community that if the Whitakers had not been so foolish to rely on corn patch and cabin to claim the land, they would not have lost it.

Rebecca's family built their new mansion not far from the old Whitaker cabin, and again the neighbors muttered, "The old home place hain't even good enough for 'em. Can you imagine? Slaves is livin in the cabin now. What a disgrace! Why, old man Whitaker would just spin in his grave."

The Hennesseys constructed a tall two-story brick house facing the main wagon road down a long front lane. Rebecca's mother was adamant their home be fronted with a long row of tall, round, fluted columns, newly painted white each year. The columns could be seen all the way from the wagon road; when they loomed up through dense fog from the river, they resembled the bars on some ghostly, ethereal prison.

Many of the newcomers referred to their grand homes with lofty names like Fair Oaks and Meadowview and Pleasanton. The Hennesseys decided their home would be Chestnut Grove, named for a fine forest on the property. The naming of homes was a pretentious tradition that the early settlers—the first-comers over the Gap—had hoped to leave far behind, back east across the mountains. What they could not have known, given their short human life spans, was that their own forebears had once hoped for just that—to leave the same ostentatious custom back across the wide eastern ocean. But that pernicious symbol of social class had tracked them, hiding like a cunning thief biding his time. It bobbed stealthily across the salty water, lurked unseen in the thick forests, and made its quiet way even here, to the far side of the mountains.

And it was slavery that made possible the construction of the grand houses and the tilling of such vast parcels. Not that there hadn't been slaves in Kentucky before the new arrivals, for certainly there had been. Nor as a rule were Kentuckians necessarily opposed to slavery. Mostly, the small farmers were just too poor to be able to own slaves for themselves.

More quickly with each passing year, the original wave of determined settlers, whose courage and brawn had chopped and burned the thick Kentucky wilderness and transformed it into farmland, was being pushed aside by this new wave of wealthier settlers from the East. These new, landed gentry were equally ambitious, although in entirely different ways. Of course, the early-comers resented this intrusion. It annoyed them as they drove their wagons, looked out across the rolling land, and saw the fine, new pedigree livestock grazing in pastures where the previous owner's humble cattle and mules had grazed the year before.

"Those cattle were descendants of the original breeds who crossed over the Gap," they scoffed with pride, even though they were well aware that the newer, fancier breeds—shorthorn cattle, merino sheep, and Thoroughbred horses—fetched a much higher price at both auction and slaughterhouse.

Caleb swung his leg slow and wide as he dismounted. He tied the reins over the rail in front of the crossroads town hardware store, headed there to buy a sack of nails. He paused a moment to straighten the sorrel mare's forelock out of her bridle. When he turned and leapt up the step of the plank walkway, he smashed full tilt into the girl.

The suddenness of the impact knocked her down on her backside, and Caleb stood gaping as white stockings and tiny black boots began kicking from an amazing sea of frothing white ruffles. His face flushed as passers-by turned to gawk, but still he stood there, mesmerized by the oddly amusing scene before him. A few people paused to watch as the kicking black boots gained an accompaniment of angry, unintelligible utterances from beneath the vast layers of heaving crinoline.

Finally, Caleb gained his composure and bent down to help the struggling girl, a slight grin across his face. "Here, Ma'am, let me help you."

He grabbed hold of both arms and began drawing the girl to her feet, but then a thousand utterly alien sensations rushed over him all at once. The softness of the fabric, the way it rustled against his callused hands. The curve of her arm beneath the thin sleeve. The surprising hue of the dress matched the girl's eyes as they neared him—the way the color enveloped her in sky-blue brilliance. A sweet smell of roses wafted from her hair as it rushed over his face; a wisp of light chestnut brown tickled his bristly cheek. He had never been so close to anything so lovely.

Caleb pulled her to standing with one strong heave, but she was lighter than he expected, and the momentum of the pull propelled her into his chest. Again he smelled roses, heard the rustle of fabric, the flash of bright blue eyes as her head whipped back. He gazed down at her curving pink lips and creamy skin and knew them to be tender without a single touch. He stood at the edge of the walkway still clasping her arms, staring at the unexpected vision before him. It was all so staggeringly feminine.

"You idiot!" Rebecca hissed, wresting herself from his grasp with an angry jerk. She began straightening her bonnet, re-tying its wide ribbon under her chin.

"I'm sorry, Ma'am," Caleb muttered. "I wasn't looking where I was going." Still he stared at her.

"You clumsy *oaf*," Rebecca raged at him, and then began to slap the skirt of her dress with quick annoyed hands.

"Here, let me help you," Caleb offered, reaching his hands toward her. Never before had he seen anything so beautiful in his life. She was so small, but so feisty. Supple but strong.

"Get your hands off me," Rebecca roared at him, much to the amusement of the gathering crossroads town onlookers, who always welcomed the opportunity to witness something out of the ordinary. Caleb pulled back his hands, but still he stood there staring.

"What are you gawking at, you stupid *ape?*"

"Oh, nothin, Ma'am," he muttered. The crowd laughed.

Rebecca started straightening her lace gloves, repositioning the seam back to the underside of her wrists, then glared back up at the man still standing before her. "Well, aren't you going to apologize?" she demanded.

Although Caleb had already apologized, he began stumbling out another, since that was what she seemed to want.

"Ah, yes, Ma'am, I mean Miss," he stammered. "I's real, real sorry. I didn't see you there. I promise I'll be more careful in the future. Are you hurt?" Finally he had managed to pull his wits about himself. He yanked his old dusty hat from his head, stood there crushing it in his hands, unsure of what to do next. Suddenly he offered a stiff bow, and the crowd laughed again.

"Oh, get out of my way, you buffoon," she said dismissively. She drove him aside with a quick jab of her elbow, buffeted through the circle of onlookers in the same haughty manner, and marched down the walkway steps. As her departing profile passed, he was struck by the passion, by the determination in the soft but adamant curves of her nose and chin.

"Again, I'm sorry, Miss," he called after her, followed by another round of laughter from the crowd.

He stood transfixed as he watched this amazing creature storm and stomp her way across the dusty street. He followed every movement of her proud arching back as she lifted her skirt and strode up the walkway steps on the far side of the street. She marched past the bank and post office and finally disappeared around a corner.

Only when she was out of sight did his face begin its astonishing transformation. Caleb's eyebrows lifted and the skin of his forehead soared with the sudden recognition of a new delight. His eyes took on a fresh gleam, sparkling in places where they had never before even considered a shine. His mouth formed an enormous grin; even the corners of his lips jumped to life, dancing with the delicious taste of newfound purpose.

He turned to his sorrel mare and planted a mighty kiss on her startled neck before he leapt up into the saddle. Then he flapped the reins and galloped home with thundering hoofs, great clouds of dust billowing up in his long and merry wake.

It was two days later, seated on the bench at the supper table, that Caleb remembered his errand, but even then only following his father's perplexed inquiry: "Alright, son, go ahead an' tell me where you hid that sack a nails you rode to town for. I just cain't find it anywhere."

Over the next several months, Caleb sought Rebecca out at every opportunity. He invented the most ingenious of excuses to ride the sorrel mare to town, looking as dapper as was possible for a farm boy.

He asked his mother to cut his hair and then sat stock still on the porch as her sharp scissors snipped and shaped his brown curls. With the tip of his knife he cleaned the dirt from under his fingernails and then trimmed each one to the same length. Before he went to town he shaved in front of Lizzie's tiny wall mirror and asked if he could borrow one of his eldest brother's clean, white shirts.

"Well, I'll be," Lizzie declared one Saturday afternoon. She stood chuckling at her youngest son as he sat on the top porch step. He had borrowed his brother's brown shoe polish and was buffing down his old leather boots. Despite their age, he had actually managed to coax a shine from the worn leather.

"Son, what in the world has gotten into you?" his mother asked with amusement. But he just smiled up at her, lifted his eyebrows dramatically, and started whistling like a lark.

A few days later, Caleb made his mother laugh out loud. "Ma, can you teach me to dance?" he asked her.

"Why sure, son. But why you wanna learn all of a sudden?" Lizzie asked, winking at her husband and breaking into a fit of laughter.

"Oh, no reason. Maybe I'll go over to the dance this Saturday. I reckon I oughta get out a little more, don't you think?" Caleb said, also winking at his father.

"Well, that's a fine idea," Lizzie said, grinning. She stood up and raised her arms out to her son. "Alright, just move your feet the way I do—it hain't hard." And Caleb and his mother turned a fast waltz as Isaac leapt about clapping time, doing his best to sing the melodies to their favorite songs as they twirled and spun around the happy little cabin in the clearing.

Usually Rebecca rebuffed him as soon as she spotted him, but by midsummer his persistence began to pay off. At first, she merely nodded coolly at him. One day she actually smiled, flashing her big blue eyes at him as she passed. And finally, after he hung around behind the corner at the dry goods store, she at last accepted a wilting bouquet of field daisies from him.

Caleb became a faithful attendee at Mr. Anderson's barn dances, awaited each Saturday evening with newfound eagerness. Eventually, Rebecca consented to dance with him. At first she moved warily, but by the end of summer they were spinning smoothly together in as many polkas and waltzes and reels as they could, always taking care to dance with others in between to keep Rebecca's mother off guard as she glowered like a badger from the corner of Mr. Anderson's barn.

The last Saturday of August was a particularly hot evening. Sweat poured from the brow of every dancer, and all the windows and doors had been flung wide to let in as much cool night air as could be found. Saw-stroke fiddle ballads floated through the night, along with the quick twangs of a fretless banjo backing up the melody. The little string band had already played "Lord Thomas and Fair Ellender" but planned to save the sad tale "Pretty Polly," a sure crowd pleaser, for their final set.

Rebecca peered from the opposite side of Mr. Anderson's barn from where her mother sat, fanning herself and chatting with a small group of older ladies. When she was sure the moving bodies of the dancers obscured her mother's view, she grabbed Caleb by the arm, tugged him in the direction of the side door. "Come on," she whispered.

Caleb let himself be led without hesitation. He followed along as she looped her way around the little clumps of people who stood and talked, fanning their hot faces and surreptitiously staking out their next partners. Once out the door, Rebecca led him behind the barn, winding her way past a grove of trees. There was just enough moonlight that Caleb could make out the silhouettes of couples locked in passionate embraces—some standing, some sitting, some even sprawled on the ground beneath the trees. He thought he recognized his older brother's silhouette as it tipped its head back to take a long draw from a flask, its arm flung casually around a silhouette with long ringlets. No wonder his grandfather disapproved of the dances.

Rebecca laughed and flung her head, tugged at his arm to quicken his pace. She led him toward a shed at the far end of the trees; she seemed to know exactly where she was going. "My mother won't find us here," she whispered as they rounded the corner and disappeared into the shadows.

"Good," said Caleb, grabbing her around the waist and pulling her to him.

How many times had he envisioned this moment and now it had finally arrived? He kissed her hard and strong, but her mouth matched his own with equal and unashamed insistence. Immediately, her hands grabbed his head, then tugged at his brown damp curls. She dropped her hands to his back as she rubbed against his sweaty shirt, as if admiring the strength of a fine racehorse. He walked her backwards and leaned her against the side of the shed. She rested her head against the wall, lifted her chin in the air, revealing to him her long slender neck. His mouth lunged for it.

After several minutes he forced himself away. He raised his arm against the shed, perching himself above her. He looked in her eyes; even in the moonlight he could make out the soft contours of her proud cheeks and the fluffy tufts of chestnut hair fallen loose and damp around her face with the hot exertion of dancing. Her eyes glowed in the dimness.

"Marry me," he whispered.

She jutted her chin into the hot night. His tongue moved back across the soft and salty skin of her throat. Then he kissed her again, slid his mouth over her eyes, her cheeks, her chin, and back down to her throat. Her body moved and arched in response to his every caress. She was a graceful willow, folding and unfolding in the quiet of the night.

How many times had she envisioned this moment, and now it had finally arrived? She had come to love the feel of his rough calloused hands as they held her on the dance floor. They were big hands—strong and solid. She craved their strength even more now that they rushed with bold daring across her skin. Those were the hands that spun her with ease, guided her toward the next step, lifted her from her feet and up and around when the caller hollered, "Swing your partner!" at the long climax of a fast dance.

His rugged backwoods ways intrigued her. He cleaned up well. She nestled her face into the dark hair that spilled from his sweaty white shirt. He was confident and determined. His smile was deep and alluring, twinkling. He would be imaginative.

"Yes, I'll marry you," she whispered back. But her words were nearly unintelligible as they stumbled hard against glistening wet lip and swift-moving tongue.

Most present at the wedding that late October afternoon likely agreed the bride and groom made a most unsuitable pair. The ladies gossiped behind their church fans, clutched in their meaty, disapproving hands: Why would a girl like Rebecca Hennessey, one with such good prospects, ever marry such a simple farm boy like Caleb Tackett?

Rebecca's mother sulked through the entire service. She had been determined to wed her prettiest daughter to one of the prosperous young solicitors in Lexington, or perhaps one of the new instructors at Transylvania University. She fully intended her daughter to live in a proper city home, one with appropriate amenities and a suitable number of servants. Her daughter would hold afternoon teas in her front parlor, where respectable women from the community—herself included—would sit on red velvet settees and discuss art or the latest fashions of the day. They would attend concerts at newly built Morrison Hall, ride there in a fine black carriage. They might even take a steamship to England one day and ride across London Bridge.

In the months preceding the wedding, Rebecca's mother was relentless in trying to dissuade her daughter from making such a dreadful mistake.

"You will be revealing exceptionally poor judgment if you go through with this," she hissed, still pacing the room, her heels angry thuds against the floor. As she spoke again, she threw her hands derisively into the air. "Live on such a small farm! Preposterous! I should know; I was born on a dreadful place like that," she reminded her daughter, her voice struck with indignant pride.

Rebecca stared out the window, elbow propped on the sill, head drooped in her hand. "I love him, Momma," she said again, without emotion. They had already been through this discussion a hundred times.

Mrs. Hennessey stopped her pacing, spun to confront her daughter. "Oh, you love him, do you?" she exploded in sarcasm. "Well, I have news for you, little missy. Marriage is not about love; it's about bettering yourself. And it would be a step in exactly the wrong direction to marry a man like him!"

"I don't care, Momma."

"Oh, you'll care soon enough! Believe me, I know the hard work that life entails, and with no slaves to lighten the load. I know you better than you know yourself, young lady. You simply aren't up to it. Mark my words—you'll regret this sooner than you think! The isolation of a farm in *Kentucky*"—she nearly spat the word—"is no place for *you!* Just imagine, no more tight corsets and fancy hoop skirts for you, little missy."

Rebecca sat and looked blankly out the window. She had long since resigned herself to the barrages of her mother's harsh words. The thought of not being strapped into a corset anymore caused a smile to flicker across her lips. Besides, she already knew rather well that Caleb was a man who preferred a more natural woman.

But her mother was far from finished. "You won't inherit one cent if you go through with this, I tell you. Nor will you get one single solitary acre of Chestnut Grove!" her mother threatened, shaking her finger in her daughter's face. "That'll teach you to sully the Hennessey name!"

Rebecca continued to stare out the window. Chestnut Grove meant nothing to her, and the Hennessey name meant even less. Once more she counted off the days until the wedding, when she could at last escape this pretentious house and such a striving, mean-spirited woman. Regardless how many times her mother tried, once Rebecca—always the stubborn child—had made up her mind, there was no changing it.

Nor did all of Caleb's family in the meetinghouse that afternoon approve of the match. Caleb's middle brother and grandfather sat together in the front pew, disapproving scowls smeared across their uncompromising faces. In a month, the middle son was scheduled to leave the farm to attend a seminary in Cincinnati, to confront the double evils of Catholicism and the godlessness of city folk, particularly those who inhabited that wicked river port. Caleb's oldest brother was already gone, bound for high adventure in Arkansas Territory.

It was only Lizzie and Isaac who sat hand in hand in the front pew, beaming as they watched their youngest son marry his beautiful bride. They had both taken to Rebecca right away, and she to them.

Despite their misgivings, no one present in the meetinghouse that afternoon could deny that Rebecca glowed in her fine dress of white taffeta. As she walked up the aisle she held her head high and tossed her chestnut hair with youthful confidence. To her mother's great displeasure, Rebecca had insisted she wear the family heirloom silver locket that Lizzie—her soon-to-be mother-in-law—had given her as a wedding gift, although it hardly matched the elegance of her finely tailored dress.

Of course, in the end, the naysayers were proved wrong. Rebecca enjoyed the rigors of farm life and adapted to it quite well. Although she kept a few nice dresses and wore them to town or to the dances, around the farm she took to donning the simple, practical, homespun cotton smocks her mother-in-law also wore.

Soon after she moved to the cabin, Rebecca and Lizzie cleared out the wooden cupboard beside the cooking hearth to make space for their new dishes. Rebecca's father had demanded his daughter receive a full and fine set of dishes, even though Rebecca's mother had been opposed to such an expensive fetched-in gift for such an ingrate of a daughter. Lizzie and Rebecca beamed as they unwrapped each luminous plate and bowl from the shipping crate, traced their slow, admiring fingers across the bright clumps of lavender willows and lavender pagodas of some distant and unimaginable Chinese landscape.

That fall, the two women decided to finish old Mamaw Estelle's quilt. They dragged the quilt frame to the porch and, with thimbled thumbs, began the long task of piecing together the remaining colored squares. Side by side they drew their sharp needles, at last completing the intricate Kentucky Pinwheel top, even though it was many an evening the dim light of the setting sun caught them squinting to count their stitches—exactly twelve to the inch. That spring, Rebecca took up a hoe right alongside Lizzie and together they turned the warming soil in the kitchen garden. Later, yellow crookneck squash and bunch beans and thick, sliced tomatoes graced their table all summer, followed with latticework pies baked with peaches fresh from the orchard. That fall, the women worked as one to pick cabbage and grub potatoes for winter and put up many heavy crocks of greens in rows on the springhouse shelves, topping them tight with tied cloth and beeswax.

Contrary to everyone's expectations, even the ailing old pastor came to appreciate Rebecca's cheerfulness about the place.

Toward the end, when he became confined to bed, it was Rebecca who brought him tea in the extra-large English Spode mug she bought for him her first Christmas at the farm. The old man nearly shed a tear when he saw it, wrapped in bright calico and tied with a ribbon. How thoughtful of her to notice he always took a second serving, not because he enjoyed hobbling to the hearth on his cane, but because such a tiny cup of tea no longer seemed to satisfy; and how considerate that she should observe his arthritic old fingers had trouble grasping such dainty handles. The old pastor was at once fond of his extra-large mug with its English hunting scene, in the end refusing to drink his tea from any other. And Caleb, Lizzie, and Isaac all shook their heads in wonder each time they heard Rebecca clap out time as she sat beside the old pastor, gently encouraging the bedridden old man as he played a weak, off-key Irish melody on his old tin whistle.

But, of course, it was Caleb who made Rebecca's life at the cabin beside the creek so pleasant. At every chance they sought each other out and slipped away. Sometimes it was out to the woods near the creek, Rebecca's leg nudged up their favorite low-hanging chestnut branch. Other times they'd latch the smokehouse door, and Rebecca would giggle as she dropped to her knees before the pickling vat. Sometimes he would lure his wife to the dusty back corner of the barn with some imaginary ruse. And there, he'd bend her over the half-height stall dividers, wooden slats thumping hard and hasty, making sure they finished before Isaac returned from the pasture with the mules. They sought each other out most any place except in the bed at night . . . because it creaked too much.

Chapter Eleven

"Let's try the twenty-eight-inch," Meg told the salesgirl behind the jewelry counter.

The girl popped her gum, sighed under her breath, and reached below the glass countertop once again. She flicked through a few tags and pulled out a twenty-eight-inch silver chain. Meg held the ends behind her neck and turned back and forth in front of the countertop mirror, observing the length. It was a little too long.

Meg handed it back to her. "May I see the twenty-six-inch? Same style links, please." She was making the salesgirl work for this transaction.

First, she had requested the medium-grade twenty-four-inch chain, then the thicker twenty-four-inch chain, and then the medium-grade twenty-six-inch chain. She also liked the thicker-grade twenty-eight-inch chain, although the twenty-six-inch finer-grade was a possibility as well. Meg determined early on that she preferred chains with simple, even links, rather than the alternating large and small links with glittering surfaces. EEOM would never have owned a glittery chain. Whichever Meg chose, it would need to be just right, because not just any chain would suit this special piece of jewelry.

The salesgirl muttered beneath her breath, blew a big pink bubble as she reached back under the counter. Meg raised an eyebrow as she watched the girl's irritated fingers flick through the tags again.

EEOM would never have had such a problem deciding on a chain. There was likely only one silver chain option back then, perhaps increased to three or four in a large city. With so many options available today, the chances of choosing incorrectly were high. It was too easy to get confused and end up not choosing at all.

Ever since the locket had emerged from the soil and Meg cleaned and opened it in the lab, she often found herself comparing her daily existence to that of EEOM's. Even on the most basic aspects of life the disparities were enormous—even simple things like selecting a proper silver chain. When Meg cooked dinner on her electric stove, she envisioned EEOM cooking on a wood fire at the very fireplace pad she excavated. When she drove her car, she thought of EEOM riding in a wooden wagon. When Meg got Novocain at the dentist last week, she reflected on the wide variety of medicine bottles they were digging up and the pain EEOM may well have needed to endure. At any given moment, Meg paused to marvel at how different her life was from even the most mundane of daily experiences for EEOM.

Rather than allow the salesgirl to fluster her, Meg shifted her attention to the contents of her shopping cart: two fluffy white towels, some light green tapered candles, a fancy bottle of creamy honeysuckle-scented body lotion. She smiled at the appropriate extravagances befitting the wondrous occasion ahead.

In one way or another, Meg had been considering the upcoming evening ever since the locket first emerged, although she had only finalized the strategy several days after the discovery of EEOM's initials at the white enamel drain board. She took an unanticipated pleasure in contemplating the evening ahead, permitting herself to savor her new craving for nostalgia. Even if it went against all the rules.

What would her colleagues think? Certainly they would consider it a very unprofessional way to treat scientific evidence. Archaeologists were supposed to be coolly detached from artifacts they dug up, not drawn to them and compelled to engage in such inappropriate and amateurish behavior. Her field was rife with tales of anthropologists who had embarrassed their peers by "going native." They grew their hair, tattooed their skin, wore the clothing of "their tribe," and advocated for them at every turn, sometimes at the risk of professional censure. Such individuals had forsaken scientific objectivity and allowed bias to overpower all sense of reason and impartiality. It was the cardinal sin of the discipline.

Archaeological textbooks often illustrated the earliest days of the discipline, with its clear and undeniable origins in antiquarianism. Vast artifact collections decorated the walls and cases of private villas while private gardens featured a plethora of Greek and Roman sculptures looted and pilfered from sites at will during the Grand Tour. "Archaeologists" of the era were independently wealthy, high-class gentlemen who found and dug the grandest of ancient tombs in dogged pursuit of the remains of their aristocratic kinsmen of civilizations past.

Heinrich Schliemann was one such gentleman archaeologist. Schliemann studied Homer's *Iliad* to determine the precise location of Troy, near Turkey's western coast. His excavations unearthed the Treasure of Troy, a remarkable cache of gold jewelry that may once have adorned the ancient royal head of the beloved queen of King Priam. A famous 1873 photograph depicts Heinrich's wife, Sophia, wearing the newly excavated, glittering gold jewels of the Treasure of Troy. Exquisite gold earrings dangle from Sophia's ears, with long layered lengths of gold beads, while an elaborate gold headdress crowns her long dark hair. Meg smiled at the contents of her shopping cart as she thought of lovely Sophia. She suspected at least a handful of her female colleagues envied lovely Sophia wearing the golden Treasure of Troy, although they would never admit it.

Meg lingered over her dinner that evening. Candlelight shone across her table, and she toasted the pale green wax taper with her glass of wine. Soft old-timey fiddle music played the ballad "Old Joe Clark" in the background.

After dinner and the music were finished, the house descended into silence. Meg picked up the candlestick and walked through the dark hallway. She placed the candlestick on the broad rim of her bathtub. Before long, steam billowed from the rushing water, flickering the candle flame and sending long wisps of jittering black smoke into the dim corners of the room. As the tub filled, Meg undressed slowly, then brushed her hair before the mirror, twisting its long brown lengths into a loose roll at the top of her head.

First one foot, one leg and then the other, first sitting, then leaning, and then finally sliding her way down. The water rose to form a warm shallow bay as it circled her body and hugged the gentle slopes of her breasts. Meg lay motionless, gazing through heavy lids as the lapping water stilled to a tranquil pool and not a single ripple broke its quiet glassy surface. When she raised an abrupt knee, the candlelight sparkled off the tinkling cascades of dripping water. Again silence returned to her secret baptismal font, luring her thoughts to drift away with the wafting of the steam.

Did EEOM splash up water from an old bucket in a washhouse? Did she haul wooden pails from the creek, a heavy yoke across her shoulders? Did she heat the kettle in winter, tip its spout toward a rough round tub, sit with knees drawn tight against her chest? Meg caught the image of a woman at twilight splashing in a dimly lit creek, cool water drenching grateful skin—a welcome respite after the toil of another long summer day. She loosed a long blond braid, dipped back her head, shook it out in cool water of the creek. The smell of rough lye soap. A white nightdress luffing in the evening breeze, laid over a leafy green branch, a disembodied life form suspended in the gathering dusk.

When Meg stood, fast rivulets streamed down, and there she remained until only cool droplets lingered on her skin. She stepped from the tub and dried herself with her fluffy new towel. She squeezed out a generous handful of honeysuckle-scented lotion, and her skin glistened as slick hands glided back and forth in the dim light. All around her grew the warm sweet fragrance of summer.

She wrapped the towel around her, picked up the candle, and shielded the flame as one foot followed the other down the hall, a thin black ribbon of smoke dancing before her as she emerged into the stillness of the bedroom. Meg set the candle on her vanity, the taste of anticipation sweet in her mouth. The vanity was the single valuable piece of furniture she had ever bought, an antique of honey brown wood, backed by an enormous round beveled mirror. The flame of the candle flickered in the mirror.

With an air of reverence, Meg opened the lid of her jewelry box. From its upper shelf glinted the polished silver locket. Nowhere to be seen was its more official container—a precisely labeled plastic curation bag. She picked up the locket and placed it on the honey brown wood of the vanity. She opened a drawer and pulled out a new twenty-six-inch silver chain.

Meg paused to consider her reflection in the round beveled mirror. She loosed her hair and shook her head as wide brown curls cascaded down to drape her bare shoulders. She picked up the locket and chain and gazed for a pensive moment at the four flowing initials. The flowing script dashed and arched like living leaping shadows in the candlelight. They bid her carry on.

She threaded the end of the chain through the loop of the locket and drew the polished silver oval to center. The chain poured over her fingers to dangle in midair. Meg pondered the old and the new as they joined together, glinting before her on the skin of her palm. They were perfect. Despite disparate ages—or perhaps because of them—the old locket with its new chain seemed like an old friendship blossoming anew, reuniting in welcome after lifetimes apart. It was a restored, reinvigorated friendship forging not back, but forward, right there in the quiet embrace of her open palm.

As Meg raised her arms to clasp the chain, the towel loosened its grip. She let it fall, nestle down in soft folds at her hips—and her pale swells of breasts mirrored back in the candlelight. Each clasp rushed toward the other at the nape of her neck, drawn together like powerful magnets begging for reunion with a beloved partner. Meg smiled as she felt the sudden spot of coolness, the touch of olden silver against the warmth of her naked chest, the patch of skin at her heart.

Then she was there—a different glowing woman sitting before her in the mirror. She, too, was bare-breasted, wore against her skin the same silver locket glinting in the candlelight. Her hair was thick and blond, the color of fresh summer hay, long and draped over strong round shoulders. The wall behind her was the gray of rough-hewn aged wood, heavy with chinking. As Meg gazed at the reflection in the round beveled mirror, she understood she sat in the presence of a woman from a time very different than her own. Meg knew at once this friend from long ago.

The woman looked back at Meg from the glassy surface of the mirror, her pale blue eyes full of surprise and uncertainty. At first they simply gazed at the other—inquisitive—the woman in the mirror just awakening from slumber, stirring once more with hopefulness as smiles of recognition crept across the face of each dim reflection.

A sudden spark from the black curling wick captured Meg's attention. It drew her gaze to the very edge of the great moon-like mirror—to the slanted round border of glistening beveled glass. Displayed before her was a line of women reaching from deep within the bevel's multicolored prisms. They stepped back through time—an endless swag of paper dolls cut from coarse white paper in a long enduring chain. Strong links of tradition and resilience bound each hand to the other. Some of the dolls boldly grasped the sturdy hands of their cut-paper sisters. Others clasped only lightly; still other hands brushed just the fingertips of their neighbors. Even in the dimness, Meg understood that only the very thinnest of delicate threads was all that now held together that precious and brittle cut-paper chain.

When Meg and Emily first entered Miss Eliza Kenton's Creekside home that Saturday afternoon, it wasn't anything like they had expected. Without help from the other, each of their minds had conjured up boring white walls and plush beige carpets and tastefully dull paintings of landscapes with bucolic horses grazing in tree-studded pastures. Perhaps there would be a few shiny Lladro figurines adorning the mantel of a never-used fireplace, two straight-back needlepoint chairs next to a polite table with a single elegant orchid.

Instead, they entered a cathouse. Some might even have gone so far as to call it a gaudy cathouse. There was nothing beige or white or boring about the place. The walls were festooned with bright washes of purples and greens in every room. The paintings were stunningly original, with great vivid bursts of flowers exploding off the canvas. The mantel had an abstract metal sculpture that might depict a breaching whale. The fireplace was well used and surrounded by comfortable overstuffed armchairs and couches that offered the opportunity to lounge in leisure. A forest of African violets sprouted from the window sills like a private exotic orangery. Four cats—only later did they learn it was only three—roamed the place with impunity. It was the kind of home where laughter and informality reigned, in striking contrast to the dull exterior of the house and the blandness of its subdivision.

Miss Eliza directed Meg and Emily straight into the kitchen, a twinkle of delight in her warm dark eyes. "Let's get to work, girls. We'll chat afterwards, while we devour the pie."

Miss Eliza lifted her generous brown arms, tied the straps of a pinafore apron around Meg's neck. "Here, honey, this one's for you," she said. It had a bold cherry print with a bright red ruffle at the bottom. In other circumstances, Meg would have felt ridiculous wearing such a thing, but in such a fantastical kitchen it was perfect. Besides, there was no mistaking that Miss Eliza was in charge here, and Meg had enough sense to realize that any protestations regarding a gaudy apron would doubtless fall on deaf ears.

She put Meg and Emily—stunning in an apron with a daring daisy print with a yellow ruffle—to peeling and slicing fresh peaches. Their first few wedges dropped in the empty pan with tinny echoes, but soon landed with soft wet plops as their mound of peaches grew. While they sliced and peeled, Miss Eliza rattled around through cupboards and cabinets, noisily extracting the various implements required of their afternoon baking extravaganza. A wide smile covered her warm brown face as she rambled around the kitchen, sipping coffee from a lipstick-smeared mug. She directed the entire occasion like a maestro conducting an orchestra, never playing an instrument but producing breathtaking musical masterpieces through her sheer exuberance.

"All righty then, let's set these peaches to stewing," said Miss Eliza, placing the pot on the stove. "We'll just sprinkle a couple cups of sugar over the top," she said pushing a measuring cup in Meg's hand and pointing at the bag of sugar on the counter. "Along with a bit of butter and cinnamon," she said to Emily, pointing to the cinnamon jar on the spice rack. "And we'll just keep the heat real low, so the peaches don't get mushy," she said to no one in particular as she adjusted the stove's dancing blue flame.

"Now, the pastry. If we want three latticework pies and it takes one and a half cups of flour for each pie, how many cups of flour do we need?"

Meg and Emily looked at each other. "Four and a half," they answered in unison.

Miss Eliza beamed. "See, you're both naturals!" They measured the flour into a big ceramic bowl. As they dumped it in, little white puffs of flour billowed back up.

"All right, time for salt and Crisco." Miss Eliza said, and then laughed and turned to grin at her pupils. She cocked her finger at them. "Now ladies, when I was comin up we used *lard,* but I guess such modern women like yourselves might be *appalled* using that." Moments passed as she searched their faces for a reaction, then chuckled as she hauled out the Crisco tub. After that she got serious again. "Cut the Crisco into the flour like this, with two knives. We can't use our hot little hands or it'll melt into the dough and the crust won't be flakey." Miss Eliza demonstrated the technique, then observed as her young apprentices reproduced her every movement.

"Okay. Now sprinkle the flour with a little ice-cold water," she said, pulling a chilled bowl from the refrigerator. "Use only enough to just dampen the flour— too much makes the crust tough but too little makes it crumbly."

As Meg and Emily sprinkled and mixed the flour into dough, Miss Eliza scrutinized their every move. She was a careful, exacting teacher, and meticulous about her baking. As instructed, her novices pressed the dough into three big balls and three small ones.

"Next, I want you to flour the board and rolling pin, then start with the big balls. Roll from the middle and radiate out." Miss Eliza lined up three glass pie plates on the counter. "We'll bake three. One to eat now and one for each of you to take home," she said with a twinkle in her eye.

Only once, after Meg and Emily failed to adequately roll out the dough, did Miss Eliza get exasperated with her inexperienced cooks. She backed them away and demonstrated the proper application of the rolling pin, her generous underarms flapping until the dough was uniformly thin.

"Meg, honey, now it's time to pour the stewed peaches into the crust," Miss Eliza said.

As she lifted the pan from the stove, Meg felt a rush of excitement as she tipped its contents onto the waiting dough of the pie plate. She smiled up at Miss Eliza as she ran the spoon around the pot. Miss Eliza smiled right back, reached over and gave her shoulder a little squeeze, and in that very instant Meg grasped the greater purpose of baking. She swiped her finger through the syrup on the side of the pan and thrust her dripping finger in her mouth. The luscious taste of peach nectar slid across her tongue, and she experienced the delightful flavor concocted by her very own hand. She wondered why she had ever been so reluctant to bake.

The smaller dough balls were for the delicate latticework over the top. Miss Eliza insisted each thin strip be woven together rather than simply placed on top of the first layer of strips. "Such is the latticework technique of mere amateurs," she commented to a passing cat. She watched from the corner of her eye as Meg and Emily struggled with the fragile weaving.

Finally, they slid the pies into Miss Eliza's warm oven, and soon the sweet aroma of baking peaches filled this amazing woman's astonishing home. After the pies baked and cooled, and as purring cats rubbed against their legs, the three women sat at the kitchen table. They ate pie, sipped coffee, and chatted like old friends. The pie had a perfect, tender, flakey crust and the peach filling was sweet and juicy—even if the latticework was a little crooked and broken in a few places.

Being there in that warm fragrant kitchen brought a simple joy to their gently opening hearts. Already that first wonderful Saturday afternoon, each woman's mind began flirting with the same delicious thought: We could almost be three generations sitting at this table as if we had done so every Saturday afternoon for years. But they didn't share those thoughts with one another, no—not on that day. Rather, it was a day that held out only the promise of great friendship, not of its fruition—not yet. That first Saturday afternoon, only the mere specter of deep friendship swirled between them, rose up from the table in great wafts, mixing with the mouth-watering aroma of baking peaches.

In time, Miss Eliza told them her story. It came little by little and usually around her Creekside kitchen table as they ate generous slices of warm peach pie. She told them about growing up in segregated Kentucky, where many on both sides of town shunned a light-skinned black girl. About how Eliza had been among those who sat at the downtown Woolworth's lunch counter and demanded service—the same Woolworth's that fell not so long ago to the wrecking ball right on Main Street.

Eliza told them of her first date with the man she married—how he took her to the Lyric Theatre, where they heard Duke Ellington play his blessed heart out. Her future husband had walked her home that night, beamed with joy when she allowed him to kiss her cheek good-night. She told them of her struggle to gain an education at Kentucky State University, how she spent long nights hunched over a table in the college library studying her nursing books.

After graduation, she worked her way up to head ward nurse and then, finally, to director of the entire nursing staff at Fayette General Hospital.

She told them of her husband, who died years ago, and of her children, who had grown up, gotten good educations, and left for better opportunities and were long since sprawled into demanding lives of their own far away. She told them about the gospel choir she belonged to, the one that sang with such passion she was certain God himself heard their heavenly voices and surely tapped His foot to the beat whenever the saints weren't watching.

She told them how pleased she was to own her own home in Creekside, how she bought it after a lifetime of frugal living. While it was true she had used up most of her savings to buy it, she considered it a sensible move after living in small shotgun houses most of her life. For Miss Eliza, Creekside was a quiet and peaceful place surrounded by refreshing green, in contrast to the dense gray and concrete of Lexington's East End urban core, where she was born and raised.

"Besides," she once confessed, "from the very first time I ever came here, it just felt like home."

But as the shadows lengthened that first Saturday afternoon, neither Meg nor Emily, pies in hand as they stood at the door, were ready to leave Miss Eliza's surprising home. So much delight and disorder, so much of life's joy seemed bundled inside these amazing walls. How could such unanticipated wonders exist behind such a bland facade?

And as they walked down the sidewalk, away from Miss Eliza's remarkable home, the subdivision itself seemed changed. They noticed the trees, small, certainly, but also strong and growing—dogwoods and willow oaks and scarlet maples and even ginkgos, all the way from Asia. A few houses over, a cluster of little girls had set up a lemonade stand, and a collection of chatting parents had come to partake of the refreshing twenty-five-cent drinks.

As Meg and Emily opened their car doors, a streak of raucous young boys sped past them on bicycles. By the time they drove midway down the block, they passed a group of children engrossed in a game of hopscotch, their alternating feet teetering in and out of colorful wavy-line boxes chalked onto the crackless cement of Creekside's new sidewalk.

On the way home Meg stopped at the store, the second time in as many days. She walked directly to the housewares section and selected the gaudiest pie plate on the shelf. It was the glass pedestal variety, complete with multi-colored glass fruit around the edges and a bulbous glass dome with a bright yellow banana handle.

When she got home she set the pie pedestal in the center of her kitchen table, then placed her first-ever peach pie on top. The ringing of the glass dome echoed through the room as its edge nestled into the groove. Meg sat down, propped her elbows on the table, plunked her chin on her hands, and gazed at the magnificent sight before her. Not only was she proud of her first pie—even if the latticework wasn't exactly perfect—it was stunning in its magical new home.

Meg's heart pounded as the library's reserve reading room door clicked open. Someone just came in. She bent over the papers spread across the surface of her secluded corner carrel, listened as footfalls approached, then continued past. She glanced over her shoulder at the retreating back; she didn't recognize it. She returned to her furtive task, prepared to toss a purposely positioned book over her reading material in a second if necessary.

Not that she wasn't supposed to be reading Oliver Kearns's promotion and tenure portfolio. Indeed, it was her obligation to read it, and read it thoroughly.

But was she really just getting a jumpstart on the semester ahead? If so, why hadn't she begun her careful portfolio assessment at the top of the alphabetically arranged stack? Why had she gone straight for Kearns? Did she hope to find some dirt on him? Discover she was right all along and he really was too good to be true, that he was some kind of alien imposter posing grave danger to Emily?

She read fast but with peaked attention, searching . . . for what? She pored over his teaching evaluations—made a quick note on a course that seemed a little problematic during his third semester. She checked back on the author order of a recent publication, found them in non-committal, unenlightening, alphabetical order. She scanned for errors of any kind, for inconsistencies, for potential indications of unlikely hyperbole in his self-evaluation, troubled with the turn of each page about the honesty of her motivations.

But the more she read, the more she concluded the portfolio before her was not particularly illuminating one way or the other about the dashing young professor. There was no dirt, no worrying pattern of student evaluations to uncover, no malicious peer reviews of his scholarly work or his service contributions that would suggest problems with his colleagues. No rays of brilliant sunshine, either. No promise of pending genius. No indication of overly ambitious, workaholic, martyr-like tendencies that universities thrive on. Rather, the sum of the accumulated evidence in the papers spread across the secluded corner carrel suggested Oliver Kearns was an average teacher, an average scholar, and an average departmental citizen. Not great, not terrible—just average. And average would likely be good enough for tenure and promotion.

Strangely disappointed, Meg shuffled up the papers, collected her things, returned Oliver Kearns's portfolio to the reserve librarian, and walked over to the campus coffee shop.

"Medium cappuccino, please," she said absent-mindedly to the barista. Meg leaned against the counter as she waited for her order, then let her eyes wander in boredom around the little coffee shop.

It was painted in suitably benign colors, with non-descript posters of Parisian café scenes hanging at the obvious wall locations. A few potted ferns—thin and yellowing—dangled before tall narrow windows. Folding floor screens divided the unremarkable room into a few semi-private alcoves with uninspiring clusters of tables and chairs.

As she surveyed the room, the back third of a coffee shop patron appeared from behind a floor screen. The man leaned back on the rear legs of his chair, balanced there for a moment, and then righted his chair to disappear into the alcove again. Although it had only been a quick glimpse, she was certain the coffee-shop patron looked an awful lot like Oliver Kearns. She heard low mumbling voices coming from that same alcove, voices she had not noticed before.

Had that been Oliver, and if so, who was he talking to? Meg knew it couldn't be Emily because her young friend had driven to Louisville for the day.

Cappuccino now in hand, Meg glanced over her shoulder, then began wandering casually toward the partially hidden alcove. As she walked, she became acutely aware of the noise of her heels and forced her feet to fall without a sound against the hard linoleum tiles.

Why did she care who Oliver was talking to? It was really no concern of hers. As she snuck across the room she kept the folding screen strategically placed between herself and her target of interest. She willed herself to stop where she was, turn around and sit at the table in front of the window with the yellowing fern, drink her cappuccino and mind her own business. But her legs seemed to have a mind of their own—they felt strangely disembodied, unaccountably noncompliant with her brain. They carried her forward, one snooping foot after another, propelled on by impulsive curiosity. Curiously killed the cat, she told herself, as she took another step.

Soon she was able to achieve a more complete view of her target. Oh yes, it was Oliver, looking handsome and tan, his boyish charm emanating from halfway across the room. She noted he was quite striking in profile, with a full head of wavy brown hair that shook when he talked. Emily was a lucky woman.

Meg observed Oliver's left elbow minus his hand as it pumped the air for emphasis. He was talking in a familiar, animated fashion to someone out of view behind the floor screen.

Now that she knew it was, indeed, Oliver, she could just turn around and leave—but only a few steps more and she would be able to catch sight of whoever was sitting at the table with him in the rear of the alcove. Again her inquisitiveness propelled her snoopingly onward, just one more tiny step and—Meg's foot halted in midair as she recognized Oliver's partner in conversation. It was Ross Landers.

It hit her like a hard blow to the stomach. A disagreeable taste filled her mouth as a wave of nausea washed over her. All the emotion of that promotion and tenure meeting years ago rushed back. Her heart beat faster, creating an uncomfortable bursting sensation in her chest. As she stared in disbelief, her mind flashed to the favorite part of her strangling fantasy—the moment where Landers's eyes first bulge from his distorted face against the backdrop of the library's faux wood conference table.

It had only been a second, but even as Meg wheeled away from the alcove, a knot was already tightening in her stomach. Of all the hundreds of faculty at the university with whom Oliver Kearns might share a cup of coffee, why did it have to be Ross Landers? Meg's regard for Oliver sank another notch as she slammed out the coffee shop door. She strode from the building, shaking her head in disgust. She only slowed once she rounded the far corner of the Science Complex.

She walked until she found a quiet shaded bench. She sat down, took the plastic lid off her cappuccino, and brought the cup to her lips. She closed her eyes as she blew across the frothy top of steamed milk. She took a sip.

The warm sweet liquid tasted good as it filled her mouth. It was calming, reassuring. She took several more sips. She leaned back against the bench, willed herself to relax, urged the knot in her stomach to undo. A slight breeze blew against her face; she heard the quiet rustle of summer leaves high in the tree at her side. She was starting to feel better. She took another sip.

"Well, hello there!" a jovial voice called from behind. Startled, she opened her eyes to see Oliver Kearns striding toward her, a cup of coffee in his hand. "Hey, would you look at that—we were just at the same place. I didn't even see you," he said. Oliver raised his cup at her in a toast as he plopped himself down on the bench. He was acting like they were the best of friends. "Great minds think alike!" he said with a grin.

"Hello," Meg said, managing a faint smile. She rubbed her forehead, hoping he might get the message that she was deep in thought or else just had a headache and wanted to be left alone.

"Haven't seen you at the Rosebud lately," he said in a cheery tone. "We've missed you."

"Yeah, well, I guess I've just gotten kinda lazy, you know, with the heat and all," Meg lied. Oliver nodded, waited for her to say something else, but she didn't. She took another sip of cappuccino and stared straight ahead.

"So, how are things going out at the site?" he asked. "Emily tells me you're finding some interesting things."

"Like what?" she asked, looking at him out of the corner of her eye. All of a sudden she was curious to see if he had any clue what they were doing out there. She wondered how much he bothered to listen when his girlfriend spoke.

"Well, let me think," he paused, cocking his head. "She mentioned a little brass cross and a whole bunch of dull ax heads. Six, was it?"

"Five," corrected Meg in a low voice. For a split second the thought crossed her mind that perhaps she had been mistaken about Oliver—or at least he listened when Emily spoke and bothered to remember what she said.

"Oh, and a silver locket, she mentioned that, too."

Meg's stomach churned. She didn't want Oliver to talk about the locket. It was too personal, too cherished for the likes of him.

"Yeah, some pretty cool stuff, alright," she said quickly. "And what have you been up to?"

"Oh, you know, same ole, same ole," he said. Oliver put his cup down, clasped his hands behind his head, stuck out his legs, crossed them at the ankle as he relaxed back onto the bench. "I've been working on an article with a colleague at the University of Georgia, on animal sexual behavior. We're focusing mostly on captive chimpanzees."

Meg nodded, waited for him to continue, as she knew he would. Behavioral psychologists loved to compare humans and animals, locate their relative positions on a sliding scale of the evolutionary behavioral continuum. It was a subject she was rather interested in—particularly in regard to chimpanzees, our closest living primate relatives.

"Did you know captive chimpanzees masturbate several times a day?" Oliver continued. "Both males and females. Although rarely to ejaculation—apparently just enough to stay stimulated at a low but constant level. They also simulate intercourse with various troop members, chimps of either sex in fact, several times a day, briefly clinging to a passer-by now and then just long enough for a few quick thrusts." He spoke clinically and looked straight ahead, but then shifted his gaze to observe her reaction from the corner of his eye.

"Fascinating," Meg said with flat affect. She sipped her cappuccino and stared at the hedge in front of her. She wanted him to go away.

"So why do you think humans are so different, so prudish in their sexual behavior, in comparison to chimpanzees?" he asked, a faintly provocative tone in his voice. "Might it have offered some kind of adaptive advantage?"

As she turned to look at him in disbelief, he flashed a sunny, ever-so-slightly suggestive smile. His teeth were white and faultless, his lips deep red and full—she couldn't stop her eyes from dipping to look at his lips for just a split second. They were that kind of excessively soft lips, softer even than rose petals they would be, softer than goose down or fluffy white clouds floating like cotton candy in a perfect sky—oh, they would be so delightful to the touch of a lip or the pads of inquisitive fingers. The slight shadow of his beard would have the strangely exquisite quality of fine sandpaper against her skin. He continued smiling at her, held her gaze longer than was appropriate in the normal course of platonic human interaction, and particularly so given the nature of the subject at hand.

Meg's eyes darted to the safety of her cappuccino cup. She raised it to her lips, took the last too-sweet sip of its contents. "Ah, I don't know," she stammered. Her mind scrambled for something to say, anything so that Oliver wouldn't think he'd succeeded in embarrassing her. "Maybe because we eat fewer bananas?" she offered lamely, and then regretted the comment immediately as she contemplated the shape of a banana.

She could feel her face flushing even before she spoke. She was embarrassed not only by the evocative topic of conversation but also by the undeniable sensation that had crept its way into her imagination. Her senses quickened at the thought of Oliver lying on top of her—the feel of his weight as it bore down on the length of her body. She started fidgeting with her empty paper cup. She tore off a section of the soft curled lip and shredded it into tiny pieces.

Smiling, Oliver watched her do it. Then, leisurely and by design, he pulled his hands from behind his head and placed them on the bench near his knees. He hoisted himself up and shifted himself just a little in her direction. It wasn't a lot, but just enough that they both instantly understood the intention behind that subtle movement.

Meg froze. Was he really coming on to her?

Confusion gripped her. She could feel her face flush anew, turn an even darker shade of red with a profound and deepening embarrassment. Her long-standing, poorly understood distaste for Oliver Kearns was now front and center, intermingling with a previously unarticulated, harmless attraction to him. It was a temptation that roared into her conscious mind—but it was far from harmless. It was tight and immediate in its grip, and potent in its great promise of risk-filled passion.

Oliver dipped his head, looked up at her with mock boyish innocence. He smiled again. No, there was no mistaking it—he was coming on to her. Meg's face blazed with the vivid scenes that flickered across the fast-moving screen of her imagination. Her nostrils flared as she caught his scent in the summer heat. A primal rush of male pheromones slammed her senses, a flood of dopamine straight to the center of her lizard brain. Suddenly Oliver was little more that a fast silver flash of a shimmering lure before the blurry eyes of a hungry fish.

And at that moment she knew Oliver Kearns to be a compellingly dangerous man, both repulsive and alluring. She was drawn to him like the sad, mindless moth to the perilous pull of the flame. She knew him to be the kind of man who thrived on sudden infatuation and all-consuming obsession—reveled in the exquisite thrill of the chase. He was the envied boyfriend of her former student, current co-worker, and budding friend. As he sat beside her on the lusty bench, his body called out to hers, summoned it to drink with him of the great soaring drama that could be theirs to savor.

He smiled an even broader, even more pleasing beam upon her, forced her to look again into his eyes. They were a stunning russet brown, with dark yellow streaks that twinkled in the afternoon sun. They were delightful—all but irresistible. And mirrored there in the wet of his eyes, she could just make out her own guilty desire.

Chapter Twelve

"Got some more nails?" Isaac called over to Caleb, feet braced wide against the wooden beam to keep his balance on the rooftop.

Isaac, his hair shot full with gray, creases etching his face, stood nearly eye level with the canopy of dull, wilting foliage that encircled the parched clearing below. Heavy clouds hung low on the dark horizon, stuck in the breezeless air of the distant knobs. Ominous rumbles of thunder echoed against the hard gray rock, held out promise of much-needed rain. The men were working fast to finish the roofing before the storm set in.

"Yup," Caleb said, sinking a nail into a roof shake. He straightened his back and wiped a heavy trickle of sweat from his forehead with his arm. "Right here, Pa—come get 'em," he said, shoving his hand into his old leather tool belt and grasping around for a generous clutch of nails to give to his father.

For several days, Caleb, Isaac, and a couple of neighbor men had stood balanced high on the wooden beams, bent at the waist, hammering down row after row, layer upon layer, of split cedar shakes. That previous winter, many new leaks had sprung in the roof and the family had grown weary of shifting the wooden pails on the cabin floor to catch the drips as they fell from the ceiling. By the end of that wet winter, father and son had decided they could put off the task no longer. They needed to re-roof the entire cabin, including the enlarged porch and back addition as well as the original two log rooms.

As soon as spring had come, Caleb and Isaac spent long days as they always had, working in contented silence side by side. Together they cut and hauled the wood, their two sharp axes swinging in perfect rhythm, their swift chops and splits echoing again and again against the cabin walls. They stacked the shakes in tall towers, each crosswise with the other so air could dry the wood flat and even. By August, the time had finally come to replace the roof. For such an effort they enlisted the help of neighbors, and as a team they worked to pry up and toss the old rotting shakes and hoist up and hammer down the new. During those days the constant rhythmic sound of tap-tap, tap-tap-tap filled the clearing.

Lizzie, Rebecca, and the other wives kept their men well fed during their long days of toil. Eggs, fried potatoes, thick slices of ham, and fresh cornpone with blackberry jam for breakfast. Hearty fried chicken with biscuits and sorghum for dinner. Thick slabs of pork chops for supper. Peach pie and strong coffee any time they wanted. For three days straight, the cabin's broad wooden table and cooking hearth had become a hive of chopping and slicing and stirring and baking.

In a brief lull between cleaning up from dinner and beginning supper, the women rested in the shade of the porch. As they fanned their faces, they too kept a wary eye on the storm hovering near the knobs on the dark horizon.

Rebecca sat on the top porch step and leaned against the rail. A rambunctious gaggle of children dashed across the clearing in a rowdy game of tag, while the older boys played a bone-rattling contest of Crack the Whip near the lane. The young toddlers tried their best to somersault on the hard dry ground.

Rebecca stroked her round belly and smiled as she watched the frolicking children. She thought of her own children—her own child, she corrected herself. Rebecca had given birth three times in quick succession, but only one, a son, had lived; the others lay buried in the cemetery on the gentle rise of land. She chuckled as her son attempted a somersault and tumbled off to the side, still too young to keep his little body propelled forward in a straight line. Each day, Rebecca said a prayer that the child she carried might live—and would be a little daughter.

As he had done so many times in the last days, Isaac began a careful shuffle across the cabin beam to retrieve another handful of nails from Caleb, transfer them to his pocket, return to hammering down shakes. First it was only a tiny jerking movement of Isaac's arms, a slight unsteadiness, a quavering in the trunk of the body. Caleb looked up as his father's arms began to spin in wild circles, as the man on the roof just beside him struggled to regain his balance. As one boot and then the other flew in the air Isaac fell hard, face first onto his son's just-completed row of shakes. Caleb thrust out his hand moments after Isaac's foot slipped, but his closing fist clasped only air.

The sudden, heavy thud shook the entire cabin. Bent at the waist, the neighbor men turned their heads in unison, their widening eyes forced to seek the source of that sickening thud.

The instant Isaac's body hit, it began sliding down the rows of new shakes.

As he slid, his hands sought to catch hold of each shake as it sped past—but his floundering hands were unable to seize anything at all, powerless even to slow his fall. His head struck hard against each row of shakes, pounding again and again in his plunge. Isaac's hammer tracked his fast descent, it too tumbling over each neat row, tracing the long, downward path alongside its trusted friend who had wielded it over his entire lifetime.

It all happened so quickly; Caleb could only stare, helpless, from his wide perch on a high beam as his father fell, watching as his arms thrashed about in their desperate bid to prevent the pull of gravity, flailing in their frantic attempt to stop the unavoidable.

The momentum of the sliding body increased as it neared the edge of the roof. For a long moment it glided through the thick summer air, smooth and graceful—man on wing soaring against a backdrop of open sky. The flying man made no sound as he plummeted through the air, apparently content just to feel the rush of wind as it ruffled his hair, caressed his face in its swift descent. It was almost beautiful—until the ground caught him.

Isaac landed hard on his side, followed by a fast dusty bounce against the hard dry earth. Even from the roof, every man present heard the unmistakable horror of cracking bone—and Caleb still stood with outstretched arm, his fist clasping only air. The entire accident had taken only seconds, but he would re-live it in slow motion for the rest of his life.

As the men clambered down the ladder, the women sprang from the porch, alerted by the too-quick cessation of pounding hammers. Despite the cry and the scramble of bodies, their minds were gripped by that dreadful instant of in-credulity that precedes the acknowledgment of sudden tragedy. Within mo-ments, a shrieking circle formed around the twisted man splayed on the dry ground—a great circle of grief-stricken humanity powerless to alter the past or to change the future, regardless of how shrill and heartfelt their wails.

Isaac lay face down on the ground in the center of their shrieking circle, loyal hammer resting at his side. He didn't move. A puddle of blood swelled from beneath his body, first bulging and feigning a bubble of mercury, before finally soaking into the parched earth below where Isaac lay.

A neighbor rode for the doctor, but by the time he arrived he was only able to confirm what everyone present that day in the clearing already knew: Isaac was dead. Multiple fractures. A broken spine.

Like the other family cemeteries on the other farms in Kentucky, the one on the gentle rise of land beside the creek was a small but growing one. Like the others, it was marked only by a collection of rough limestone from the creek bed, each generation burdened with the task of hauling their requisite share of flat heavy slabs up the slope and placing them upright in the grieving ground.

A long fresh mound of tamped dirt still stretched before its most recent headstone. The frail old pastor had only just been laid to rest beside the grave of his wife, grass long since green where her own mound of dirt once stood. Death had finally come even for him, as at last the Lord's most faithful servant had been allowed to cease his earthly toil and enter the land of milk and honey, sit humbly at the foot of his Maker.

When Lizzie had announced to the congregation that the ailing old pastor's time was near, his grateful flock took up a special collection, gathered sufficient coin to purchase a fine coffin, and hauled it by wagon on the rough road from Lexington. Even while the old pastor lingered on longer than expected, the coffin sat in silence in the dim light of the dusty barn, waiting in patience for its certain, future occupant.

Now it was Isaac's turn.

The storm hovered near the knobs longer than anyone had anticipated, but it finally moved in as they placed Isaac's broken body in the dark ground.

The storm arrived without haste. The wind rose to turn and twist the leaves on their stems, revealing their delicate white undersides. Then powerful currents of air whipped the trees, tossing their branches high and heaving them to the ground in great commanding gusts. Next came the lightning, flashing in short sudden bursts of tense orange light, followed moments later by the low anxious crackle of thunder. The rain reached them last of all. First it cast down in great solitary drops from the fierce rumbling sky, and then as sheet after sheet of stinging cold rain that pounded the tangled circle of mourners. Tear and raindrop joined across their stunned faces, their stormy fonts indistinguishable in their grief.

From dark sky and soaked dripping leaf the rain poured. It surged from the gloomy heavens, drenching the long heap of waiting dirt at the edge of the dim open grave. Water welled up at the foot of the wet mounded earth, slowly trickling its way across the dirty matted grass. Trickles joined to form tiny rushing streams that merged on the muddy ground, gravity demanding they spill only downward toward the cloudy roiling waters of the newly gushing creek.

Although it had been several days since they buried his father, Caleb continued his vigil at the edge of the creek. He glared at its dirty brown water as it traveled past, still swollen and thick from its recent pounding. As he stared at its churning waters, Caleb deemed the creek forlorn, as if it suffered the loss of the limestone slab pried from its rightful bed, now perched grimly behind him, upright in the gentle rise of land. It was a hasty creek that sought to flee the gloom that hung within its muddy banks. In places the fleeing creek seemed to contemplate escape from its slick groove in the troubled earth—a desperate bid to seek a better place.

What Caleb failed to realize as he sat on the creek bank was how the world around him had changed.

He did not notice how the ground had softened and relaxed after the heavy wetting of the storm, or how the scorched brown grass had transformed into a thankful shade of pale green. Nor was Caleb aware of the new scent of freshness in the air or the lightness that had returned to the trees or how the birds had once again taken to wing, flitting and chirping across the grateful clearing. The oppressive heat was gone. Even the sky itself was changed, now a vast and open expanse of blue rather than the tense ugly gray of the previous weeks. Nearby, the stunted roots of the corn crop lapped with delight at the sodden ground, quenching their long and terrible thirst. The heavy drenching rain had been exactly what the little farm so desperately needed.

Lost in sorrow, for Caleb the gloom still hung heavy, smothering all else. Intermittent waves of misery overcame him—one full of sadness, the next full of guilt. When he rode a wave too painful to bear, he crushed his head in his hands and wept. As that wave threw him to his knees, the only image that came to him—other than his father sliding and flailing and falling through the air— was of a river of tears gathering at his feet. As the river grew it joined the roiling creek, and on its brown frothy crest he rode its roaring waves all the way to hell.

His father—his best friend—was gone. Why hadn't he carried the nails to him? Why had he been so lazy—so inconsiderate? How could he have allowed his father to work on the roof at all? Isaac was too old for that. He should have demanded his father not climb up the ladder and work on the roof with the other men. How had he failed to catch him as he fell? He was right there—he could have saved him. He only had to reach out his arm just a little faster, just a little sooner—and Isaac would still be alive.

"Caleb, you need to eat."

He heard Rebecca's words, but they came to him from a distance, from an unclear direction shrouded somewhere in deep, immeasurable fog. She was shaking him, looking up at his face as it drooped from his neck, her hands tight around his arms. She had again carried a basket of food to him as he sat at the edge of the creek. He sensed her words were angry—that the pleading words had left her some unknown count of days past. He looked at her blankly, showed little sign of having understood the language she spoke.

"The Lord giveth and the Lord taketh away," were the words he heard next. Although he knew they came from his mother, her speech, too, seemed vague and incoherent, reached him from far away. Even Lizzie, herself grief-stricken from the loss of her husband and lifelong friend, had again trod the winding trail to the creek in an effort to comfort her son.

But he would not talk, nor would he be comforted, not by his beloved wife, nor even by his kind gray-haired mother.

When later Rebecca forced him to eat some sweet buttered bread, opening his mouth with her hands and pushing it between his lips, he was barely able to chew, to swallow it down his dry throat. As the bread hit the hollow of his stomach, he doubled over as spasms of dry heaves wrenched his body.

Even his nights he spent at the creek, alone and desolate. Most nights he became but a wanderer, and one forbidden passage into the soothing realm of sleep. The hours of darkness wore long and blank, full of stillness except for within, where an incessant buzzing accompanied a kaleidoscope of shifting grays that cast strange, disconcerting patterns against the insides of his trembling eyelids.

When daybreak finally rose to pale the eastern horizon, Caleb turned and watched the blush of dawn as it sharpened the dim gray stone of the knobs. Still he did not stir from his place of vigil by the dark creek. It was only when he heard the early swell of birdsong—and the first crow of the rooster—that he rose and returned to the cabin, a sleepwalker who yet again had not trod upon that golden land of renewal.

Eventually, he did eat. In time, sleep also returned, even if only fitfully, for his had become a thin gray slumber fraught with vague nighttime images of a man plummeting through air. Although he was able to return to his work around the farm, Caleb's soul had become a fragile one, drifting without aim as the wind punched it at will, lurching back and forth through the air like a crisp autumn leaf.

Rebecca bent down, drew another wrung bed sheet from the basket at her feet. She shook out the wet homespun, pegged one corner to the line, another in the middle, and a third peg at the final corner. The cool October breeze billowed and snapped the cloth as she snugged the last peg on the line. She stood back to admire the long row of flapping linens, white and confident against the bright reds and dazzling yellows of the autumn trees.

She reached up and stretched from side to side, her back tight from the constant weight of the heavy child in her belly. She smiled as the breeze again caught the fresh washing. Life was finally returning to normal after the trauma of her father-in-law's sudden accident.

Just yesterday she had at last persuaded Caleb to join her at their favorite low-hanging chestnut branch near the curve in the creek. After their lovemaking there—when she had once again felt his strong callused hands caress her thighs and the great mound of her belly—she was certain her husband was coming back to her and would soon be whole again. With the birth of their new child, everything would be set right.

But as she reached down to pull the last wrung sheet from the basket, her body jerked to a halt. Her hands clutched at her belly as a swift hot gush poured down her legs as her water broke. She caught her breath and waited as the pain passed. She could still manage to finish the last sheet. She reached down and grasped the wad of wrung linen, but severe cramps doubled her over before she could peg even the first damp corner to the line.

"Lizzie!" She called toward the house. "Lizzie!" She yelled again, this time with more urgency as another quick spasm hit her.

There was no answer. Released again from her pain, Rebecca walked to the cabin, but found it empty. She walked to the barn, but no one was there. She found her mother-in-law down at the springhouse, arranging thick crockery jars on the shelves, figuring with her fingers how much they would need for the winter ahead.

"Lizzie, I think my time's come," she announced from the springhouse door.

Lizzie at once turned to Rebecca, grasped her by the arm, and started her gently toward the cabin. "Oh, child, you come with me. I'll take care of you. Don't worry none, honey; everythin's gonna be just fine."

She brushed the stray hairs from her daughter-in-law's flushed face as they walked arm-in-arm up the slope from the creek. Even though the words had never passed between them, both women felt the depth of their mutual affection—Rebecca was the daughter Lizzie always wished she'd been given, and the kind, now-aging woman was the mother Rebecca always wished she'd been born to.

Lizzie led Rebecca to the bed she and Caleb shared. A practiced midwife, Lizzie began preparations for the birthing. As she had with Rebecca's previous births, she boiled water, brought a pile of clean sheets, several soft blankets, and a thick braid of cloth for Rebecca to bite as she bore down. Lizzie was waiting as the next round of contractions hit.

Caleb appeared in the birthing room after the fifth round. "Son, you know you cain't stay here. Get on out to the barn and stay there 'til I call for you," Lizzie demanded. "The last thing I need is you gettin in my way!" It was Lizzie's philosophy that birthing was plain hard work that men weren't able to comprehend; she preferred they be all the way out of earshot.

Rebecca's labor continued as darkness descended. But after many long hours of Rebecca biting the thick cloth braid, Lizzie grew worried. She still couldn't see any of the baby's head. "It should be in clear view by now," she muttered to herself, shaking her head.

She lit several candles and began kneading the great mound of sweating belly that rose up from the bed. She tried pushing from the place just below Rebecca's ribs, but her belly felt hard and constricted, unwilling to move. Something was not right.

Worse, Rebecca was starting to tire. She was whimpering a little, although clearly making a valiant effort to be stoic as she bit down on the thick cloth braid again and again. She squeezed her eyes tight each time she pushed, her face hot and flushed, glistening from the exertion. Her hair was tangled and matted from thrashing her head against the pillow.

Between contractions, Lizzie ran to the barn. "Caleb!" she called into the darkness. "Caleb!" she yelled again, but the shifting and snorting of the livestock bedded down for the night was all that answered her. She hurried to the toolshed. Perhaps her son was sharpening an ax on the grindstone, a dim lantern on a stool beside him? But no light shone from the bottom of the toolshed door. Where was he? She ran to the smokehouse. Finally, she saw a thin line of faint yellow from under the door. She flung it back and there he was, shifting the hams on their sturdy iron hooks to let the air flow evenly around the curing meat.

"Caleb!"

"Ma, what is it?"

"Son, it hain't goin so well. Ride for the doctor—fast."

It was after midnight when the doctor's one-horse gig at last rolled up the dark rutted lane. Caleb clasped the man's arm, hauled him quickly up the porch steps, barely visible in the moonless night.

The doctor took one look between Rebecca's legs, felt along her stomach, and called for his bag. "Breech," he said, glancing at Lizzie before pulling objects from his bag.

The doctor opened several tiny glass medicine bottles, lifted Rebecca's head, and forced the liquid down her throat. She gurgled and coughed a bit, but before long she grew drowsy, and then eerily quiet. She flopped her head back and forth against the pillow, damp from hours of sweat and saliva.

The doctor drew a handful of thick cotton strips from his bag. "Here," he said, thrusting them at Lizzie and Caleb. "Tie her to the bedposts." Caleb stared at the man, incomprehension in his face. The doctor, rummaging through his bag, looked up when Caleb failed to carry out his instructions. "Son, I think you better wait in the other room," the doctor said, taking the strips of cotton from his hand.

"But doctor . . ." Caleb protested.

"Right now!" Lizzie screamed. She knew exactly what the doctor was about to do; she knew her son could not be there to witness it.

As soon as Lizzie closed the door behind him, they tied Rebecca by the hands and feet. The doctor drew a gleaming knife from his bag and turned toward the bed.

Lizzie stepped aside, nervously biting her finger as she watched the man lean over the body on the bed. Without hesitation, he drew a long, quick, perfect, curving slit along the full length of her rounded belly. The blade moved soundlessly as it sliced with ease through Rebecca's soft flesh.

The blood didn't flow immediately. Rather, it appeared in one long thin streak across the taut whiteness of her skin, lingered there for a short time as if uncertain of its next move. But then the streak grew thicker, wider, redder, until finally great crimson beads trickled down in steady streams from the entire length of the incision.

Rebecca had not flinched under the pull of the doctor's swift gleaming blade. Her head lolled from side to side, the whites of her eyes flashing as they rolled, lost and wandering deep in their sockets. A cold, clammy sweat covered her pale skin, the heavy dampness exuding a sour odor. She was breathing in short thin gasps, the thick cloth braid still clenched obediently between her teeth.

In one quick motion the doctor reached beneath the bleeding flap of skin, grasped the baby by the leg, and pulled it out.

He cut the dark purple tangle of umbilical cord and slapped the infant's behind. First a wheeze, then a little cough, and finally a loud wail, all in quick succession. The doctor handed the baby to Lizzie, then turned back to the bleeding woman on the bloody bed. She was barely moving.

Immediately he began sewing up the incision with quick tight stitches, hoping to halt the bleeding.

But the blood continued its steady flow. The basin that once held boiled water now contained a sodden pile of bloody linens. For every blood-soaked cloth Lizzie dropped in the basin, Rebecca grew paler, less alert. Her skin took on an ashen cast, and she no longer seemed aware of her surroundings. The doctor untied the restraints as soon as he completed the stitching, even though they had hardly been necessary at any point in his procedure.

Lizzie cleaned the baby, rinsing it with warm water. When she brought it over to the bed, Lizzie looked down, gently removed the wet cloth braid still clenched in Rebecca's mouth. The doctor had just finished bandaging the new mother as best he could.

"It's a girl," Lizzie said in Rebecca's ear as she laid the baby on her mother's chest. "You have a beautiful baby girl. And you did such a great job," Lizzie whispered as she dabbed sweat from her daughter-in-law's brow.

But tears were streaming down Lizzie's cheeks as she spoke. She was surprised at her ability to sound so calm when she knew Rebecca was dying and there was nothing either she or the doctor could do to alter that outcome.

As the doctor packed his bag, Lizzie began cleaning up Rebecca as much as possible without moving her. She swabbed her face with cool water, combed down the hair closest to her face, and sprinkled drops of rose water at her neck. Then she covered her daughter-in-law and the blood-soaked bed with a thin, clean quilt. Although only candlelight illuminated the room, she wanted Rebecca to look good.

The new mother struggled to focus her eyes on the infant in her arms. Lizzie bent low as she noticed Rebecca's lips move. Her words formed only the barest of murmurs: "I have a little girl!"

Lizzie kissed her daughter-in-law on the forehead and stroked her hair. "That's right, honey, you sure do!" she whispered.

Then she let Caleb back in the room. He raced to the bedside and dropped to his knees. He reached his arms around his wife and newborn daughter. He kissed Rebecca's face, sobbing into her ear. Fast tears streamed down his haggard face.

At the sound of her husband's voice, Rebecca's eyes fluttered open. Despite their beauty and blueness, they couldn't quite call into focus the face that hovered before her, although she knew it was him. She smiled weakly at the blurry image as she moved her hand from her tiny daughter and up to touch Caleb's cheek. Then her hand slid back down beside her, landing heavy and lifeless on the exhausted bed.

Again Caleb retreated to the edge of the creek as once more a torrent of despair rose up around him. But this time it was stronger, and this time it would hold him under.

It lashed out, smashed him hard against invisible rocks. It threw him down, shattered strength of mind and body. It tossed him high, gloated as he fell. Hopelessness came and crushed his spirit, and in due time it swallowed him completely. Where once he knew only happiness, all that remained was a misery that would not leave. At the edge of the creek sat a tender soul forced to dig too many graves in too short a time, a man who had hauled too many heavy slabs of rough gray stone up the short slope, obliged to place them upright in the grim and gaping earth.

It was as if the merciless hand of grief had reached out and grasped its next victim, instinctively seeking the most vulnerable of prey. Prey that would not struggle. Prey that could not struggle.

Rebecca's death, too, had been his fault. How could he have let her do the washing that day when her belly was so round? Why hadn't he been in the barn when his mother came looking for him? If only he had ridden for the doctor faster. And he never ever should have lain with her at their curving chestnut branch that day—not like that, not when she was so far along.

Left to wend its silent work, Caleb's remorse grew to anger, then to rage. It was a slow, grotesque transformation that turned a gentle man into a monstrous fiend. It was an unpredictable demon that seethed just below a deceptively placid surface but could rise without warning. Once when it rose, his wrath turned its accusing eye upon the Lord.

Caleb's grandfather, the old pastor, had always assured his family that the Lord would never burden His children with a heavier load than they could bear. But Caleb knew this time He had made a very great mistake. Why was the Lord punishing him? Hadn't he been a good Christian? What kind of a miserable God would weigh him down him with the deaths of his two most beloved in such quick succession?

Caleb leapt to his feet, countered his questions at the top of his lungs, "Only a *damned* God!" He shrieked his curse to the forest. He smiled as his accusation echoed against the hard bare trees of winter. Even after weeks of seething anger, his blaspheme surprised him, slipping out as it had from some dark murky place in his heart.

Once the echo faded, he screamed it out again, "Only a damned God!" He laid his head against the cold bleak air, reveled in the delicious sound of the forbidden words. Again he roared his magnificent blaspheme, huge white bursts billowing from his mouth, a great angry dragon standing on the bank of the creek. "Only a *damned* God!"

And at that moment Caleb became lost in his own deep labyrinth. It was a dim and shadowy maze of confusion and chaos where he would wander, shackled to its senseless walls and blind jumbled passages, for the rest of his life.

Later, when another fresh round of fury seized him, he yelled an endless string of curses into the cold empty forest, propelling them from his lungs with full force. Again and again he screamed at God, twisting his head in ugly obtuse angles with each horrible bellow.

His grandfather had always said that backsliders were the worst of all. Caleb knew the old pastor would have applied his thick leather strap for each and every utterance in his endless strings of oaths, but his grandson had traversed into a wilderness that lay far beyond perception of reason.

"What, old man? You gonna thrash me again?" he mocked. "Just try an' hit me, you old windbag!" He laughed, an almost maniacal ring in his voice. He turned and shouted toward the most massive of the stone slabs on the gentle rise of land. "May your damn bones rot in *hell!*"

Then he strode to the cabin, his boots pounding hard and heartless up the wooden steps and across the trembling porch boards. He flung open the door and rampaged through the bookshelf, tossing papers and leather tomes over his shoulder until he found what he sought: the Bible his grandfather had given him.

Caleb stomped back to the creek. He yelled and cursed again, held the Bible up to heaven, and shook it with all the rage that, despite weeks of fury, still surged through him. Then he hurled it far and deep into the utter bareness of the cold winter forest.

The good book turned and twisted in its soundless flight. Chapter and verse tumbled and spilled across the coldness, the distance, the vast gulf of space and time and emptiness that stretched out far ahead of its mere printed pages, until the black calfskin landed flat and stiff on the bitter frozen ground.

It was impossible for Lizzie not to hear her son as he began yet another round of bellowing, a new bout of frenzied hurling of objects into the forest.

But she remained in her chair on the wide wooden porch, rocked back and forth, wrapped warm in her woolen shawl against the deep chill of winter. After many terrible months, she had concluded that there was nothing she could do to comfort her son. There was nothing she had not tried—no amount of reason or pleading or threats or demands had reached him.

Her son was gone—a crisp autumn leaf lost and casting aimless on the breeze—a leaf that would never land back on the soil of the earth. By now Lizzie's own grieving heart was worn out, tattered and spent from the many hard blows of the last months. It called out to be granted its long and final rest.

But, He still needed her here on earth, the Lord told her. No—He would not bring her home now . . . not just yet.

As she rocked, she held Rebecca's precious baby girl, all swaddled and drooling, tight and safe in her arms. Rebecca's little toddler played marbles on the porch beside her, also now strangely accustomed to his father's endless ranting. Mamaw Lizzie leaned her head against the back of the rocker, closed her weary eyes. She hummed the tune, then whisper-sang the chorus to her favorite church hymn low and steady, just loud enough for their little cluster of three to hear.

"My fa-ith looks up to the-e, thou La-mb of Cal-vary, Sav-ior divine! Now he-ar me whi-le I pray, take al-l my guilt away, O let me from this day be who-lly thine!"

Little puffs of white escaped from her lips as she sang those familiar, comforting words. Her boot tapped slow against the worn foot of the old chair. She swayed as she rocked, the swaddled infant nestled in her arms. Deep, care-worn wrinkles pressed out from the corners of her sagging, lidded eyes. Only a single tear pressed across her cheek as the rocker moaned, slow and tired, against the aging wooden porch boards.

Chapter Thirteen

"This is such a fine opening, isn't it, Dr. Harrington?" the mayor asked, his eyes scanning the faces in the room. "And the Creekside exhibit is quite interesting." He waved and nodded to someone on the far side of the refreshment table. "But I dare say you'd have a hard time digging in that getup," he chuckled and gestured at her suit with his plastic cup before he again nodded and waved to someone across the room.

Meg sighed. She only wore her formal business suit once, maybe twice a year. Wearing it more often usually signified her lack of success in wiggling out of the myriad formal events that surrounded campus life. At the honors presentation that spring, Meg had sat on the dais and wondered whether the administrators of Bluegrass University ever noticed she always wore the same suit: a staid black-and-white hound's-tooth check.

Yet for the exhibit opening at the Bluegrass History Museum, Meg felt obliged to haul out her suit from the back of her closet. That made three times that year—not a good sign. She frowned at her reflection in the moon-like mirror when she snugged the fitted skirt over her hips, sucked in her breath, and wedged the button into its hole. She'd need to cut back a bit on the peach pie.

Meg laughed, smiled wanly at the mayor. "No, not hardly. I assure you I wear jeans when I dig." She glanced at the mayor's suit. Prominently displayed on his navy blue polyester jacket lapel was an "Unbridled Spirit" pin with the city of Lexington logo, a galloping horse and colt. She, too, scanned the room. Every city official was wearing the same lapel pin.

She looked back at the mayor. "So, you liked the Creekside exhibit? I'm curious to know what you found most interesting."

Meg knew the man had not even looked at the Creekside exhibit. She took a sip from her plastic cup, studied him over its rim. She detested formal events such as these, where small talk was expected, very little of substance was ever said, and people were wont to rubberneck, discreetly or not, in hopes of finding someone more important with whom to talk.

But the mayor had begun speaking again, apparently to some studio audience that only he could see. He ignored her question. "You know, the Creekside Subdivision is a vital addition to our growing community. It will bring a flurry of welcome economic development to a sadly neglected corner of our region. But, of course, it's also important we take every possible opportunity to preserve our past."

The mayor's words were smooth and flowing, deep and melodic, even if they lacked substance. Meg envied politicians their skill in oratory—how they managed to say so little yet say it so eloquently. She sighed. At least the mayor wasn't talking to her about dinosaurs. She gave him another wan smile. "Oh, yes, I agree; it certainly is important to preserve the past."

She felt the sudden urge to grab hold of the mayor's arm, ask him in great earnest if he had gotten word that KYDOT had unexpectedly reversed its plans and the Creekside Subdivision Expansion Site was now going to be preserved. The muscles of her face ached to leap into a feigned expression of incredulity, and then mocked astonishment, at the miraculous news.

Instead, she bit her lip, grimaced into her plastic cup. No, it was best she not use the present occasion to remind the mayor that their excavations in the pasture had nothing whatsoever to do with voluntary community largesse or some vague communal pride in the past. Rather, it was federal law—the National Historic Preservation Act of 1966—that required the work because the Kentucky Department of Transportation was a federal agency and because the Creekside developer was receiving federal housing loans. However tempted she was to edify the mayor on this critical matter, she decided instead that the moment held a perfect opportunity for her to practice discretion. No, she would wait for a better juncture than a formal museum opening to enlighten the city's elected officials concerning the laws that governed archaeology in the United States. She was working on holding her tongue.

Besides, she knew full well EEOM's early cabin home in the pasture would never be saved. It, too—along with thousands like it—was fated to disappear beneath the blade in one short day of bulldozing. Such was, after all, the fully anticipated outcome of the endeavor known to archaeologists as Cultural Resource Management. It was impossible to save everything, and CRM was the sieve that, ideally, captured data from the most significant sites before they were gone forever.

Meg took another sip of punch, and at the first opportunity she gave the mayor the slip—left him chatting with a lapel-pinned city council member, both of them holding polite portions of cheese and crackers on their plastic cocktail plates.

Safe for the moment, Meg wandered around through the exhibits, observing the people more than the displays. She was careful to keep her plastic cup strategically half empty in the event she needed an excuse to extricate herself from some conversation. She could take a quick swig, smile apologetically, hold up her empty cup, and make her escape in the direction of the punch bowl.

She glanced toward the refreshment table. Her crew was still making a valiant effort to nibble. For them, after weeks of Vienna sausages and Twinkies—and untold gallons of Gatorade—dainty cucumber sandwiches and broccoli with dip amounted to a veritable feast.

Most of the museum guests were paying little attention to the display cases. Meg noticed that fewer still were drawn by the Creekside exhibit, but that was fine; she was under no illusion. Meg understood this to be yet another official function from which the enamel lapel-pin officials would soon politely excuse themselves and rush off to their next cameo at some other semi-obligatory function. But at least funds had finally been secured—meager as they were—for the city's first and only history museum, even if it was housed in the musty converted basement of the old stone courthouse.

The basement's dank peeling walls now boasted a fresh coat of paint, cheap new aluminum window frames, and a new drop ceiling. Brightly painted pipes hung down through the ceiling tiles in an optimistic effort to add an air of edgy industrial contemporaneity to an unalterably backward-looking space. The warped and yellowing linoleum floor was the biggest giveaway that despite such hopeful window dressing, everyone nevertheless still stood in the musty basement of the old stone courthouse.

Meg and Emily had spent the last number of evenings pulling artifacts together to meet the formal opening deadline. They realized the Creekside display was only a filler exhibit invited primarily with the intention of rendering the echoing quality of the cavernous old basement less obvious. Their displays were tucked away in a dim corner of the main museum area.

The main exhibit was devoted to the history of the Kentucky Derby, arguably one of the most celebrated horse races in the world.

The walls in the main area were adorned with enormous black-and-white photographs of the famous twin spires of Churchill Downs, of great red rose blankets draped over gleaming horse withers, beaming jockeys resplendent in bright silks rendered gray and white in all but memory. Other photographs depicted the track's jauntily uniformed bugler blowing his long horn to announce the commencement of the next event. Behind, anxious excitement radiated from the gray faces of the racetrack crowd. One could almost hear "And they're off!" followed by the roar of thundering hoofs.

Case after case displayed polished silver trophies and colored ribbons, many awarded to Calumet Farm, one of the oldest, most renowned horse farms in the Bluegrass. Few visitors to Lexington could fail to notice the farm's white, green, and red horse barns spilling over thousands of acres, providing one of the largest remaining tracts of unspoiled green spaces in the county.

Yet as Meg strolled through the exhibit, she noticed the history of the Kentucky Derby as depicted on the basement walls of the old courthouse was not up-to-date. She could find no mention of the thousands of Mexicans who now walked and groomed and fed those fine Thoroughbreds and mucked out their roomy stalls several times a day. Low-paid migrant labor was only the most recent in a long string of major socioeconomic changes to hit the Bluegrass.

Scattered among the city officials was a healthy sprinkling of well-coiffed, blue-haired ladies. Thick coats of red lipstick lined their mouths, offering bright flashes of unexpected color amidst white powdered faces. Many wore their showy Derby hats in keeping with time-honored, blue-blooded Derby tradition. Some even wore buttons that read "Talk Derby to Me," although Meg wondered whether such respectable ladies grasped the true meaning of that catchy little phrase.

Most of the museum guests sipped virgin mint juleps: virgin because this was an official government function in a conservative blue-law region and mint julep because it was the *de rigueur* beverage at any Derby-related event.

That first Saturday in May, harried hostesses of Derby parties throughout the Bluegrass snipped bowlfuls of fresh garden mint in preparation for the elegant socializing of the Big Day. The well-heeled drank their juleps from polished silver julep cups, while the middle class sipped from special collectors' commemorative-edition julep glasses emblazoned with that year's official Derby logo. Compelled by tradition, everyone drank at least one mint julep that first Saturday in May, regardless of whether one liked mint juleps or not. Since this year's Derby had already come and gone, the required yearly julep intake for attendees at the museum opening had just risen to two.

The ladies in the Derby hats—and they truly were ladies—formed the city's stalwart historic preservation contingent. They had been the driving force behind the creation of the city's numerous historic districts, and through their vigorous efforts funds had been raised for the renovation of several important house museums in the city: the gracious homes of past luminaries such as Mary Todd, wife of Abraham Lincoln; Henry Clay, the great statesman and orator; and John Hunt Morgan, Thunderbolt of the Confederacy.

Although these ladies had certainly done much good work for the community, they seemed rather uninterested in the contents of the Creekside exhibit. But as Meg watched them stroll politely past, she was pleased they even bothered to look at all. Besides, why should they be interested in the humble artifacts from a small abandoned farmstead of some unknown, unnamed, underprivileged family eking out a living far removed from the center of civilized life?

Such ladies were unlikely to be impressed with a common assortment of broken medicine bottles and clay smoking-pipe fragments, a handful of children's glass marbles and a pair of broken rusting scissors, two crushed thimbles and miscellaneous scraps of cut tin. Or the partially complete, glued-together sherds of an unusually large English Spode mug with a hunting scene, despite the fact that it was one of the later and more expensive items of ceramic manufacture to come from the site. Or the partially complete, glued-together sherds of a redware pitcher recovered near the cemetery, even though it was actually one of the earliest artifacts recovered. Or the only slightly fancy brass coffin hardware from the grave of an exceptionally tall and exceptionally old man. A few people did glance at the coins recovered from the old man's eyes, although no one actually bothered to read the dates: 1834 and 1835. Certainly, the display of a worn hammer head and five dull ax heads was not likely to hold anyone's attention, particularly since their patterning in the pasture appeared to be random.

Meg noticed that even the case holding a meager assortment of Indian artifacts—found, oddly enough, inside the stone piers of the barn—did not warrant a second glance.

Over the years local collectors had amassed great quantities of fine projectile points, the best of which were usually glued and shellacked and hung in picture frames on basement walls. No one read the text explaining the very late dates for the Creekside arrowheads. Although many present-day Lexingtonians knew Indians were here at the founding of Fort Boonesborough in 1775, they usually preferred the myth that Kentucky was merely a hunting ground.

The only display that managed to hold any degree of interest—even if for only a few seconds—was the one with the little brass cross.

Meg and Emily's text told of the Second Great Awakening and the 1801 Cane Ridge Revival, an important local event that transformed the religious countenance of the Bluegrass and cast a fundamentalist, evangelical, and conservative pall to most of today's regional as well as southern religions. But, unfortunately, since the cross had not been recovered in direct association with more readily datable objects, their text had to admit that the date for the little brass cross remained uncertain, but likely fell within the timeframe of the other artifacts. Nor, sadly, could the little brass cross be connected with any of the early church founders with prestigious genealogies, many of which stretched all the way to the present.

But a few hardy souls—her crew among them—read the text of every display, Derby, Creekside, or otherwise. Some of the crew had invited their parents, who attended in an effort to support their children in their chosen careers, even if many had tried to dissuade their sons and daughters from going into archaeology, attempting instead to steer them toward more lucrative careers in business or accounting.

Meg smiled as she watched her crew wander the exhibits and stalk the refreshment table. She was thankful Tonya chose to conceal her tattooed dragon under a blouse, and she hardly recognized Scott without his red do-rag. And there was Bob, engaged in animated conversation with a councilman reputed to be one of the most boring individuals in the city, while shy Suzy stood and listened attentively. Miss Eliza was also in attendance, her bright red Derby hat festooned with long black ostrich feathers. Oliver Kearns was there as well, looking dapper as always, behaving uncharacteristically contrite as he stuck close to Emily's heels.

The low hum of polite conversation continued as Meg strolled to the case housing the silver locket.

Her text explained the probable date of the locket's manufacture—before 1805 but after 1770—and its place of manufacture: Boston, but not by Paul Revere. A book open to a photograph of a much better preserved example provided an opportunity to envision the Creekside locket in its heyday. Suspended above the locket was a mounted magnifying glass positioned to allow the initials to be examined by any would-be viewer.

Meg leaned her head against the glass. She gazed at the polished silver oval isolated so far away on the other side. It seemed strange that some transparent, arbitrary boundary now separated them from one another, their once intimate relationship now so unequivocally severed. Woman and locket stood on opposite sides of the glass, each now positioned on their appropriate legal sides of the vast gulf of time and ownership.

Meg sighed, her breath condensing for a moment on the glass. At least there was one good thing about it. The message of the glass was unambiguous. There was no way she could fail to grasp its implication: The locket was not hers, nor had it ever been. Meg had briefly toyed with the thought of keeping the locket, surprising even herself when that idea first rose in her mind. Keeping an artifact was something that had never occurred to her with any of the untold thousands of artifacts she had dug up over her career. But could she really emulate beautiful Sophia Schliemann, who, after having adorned herself with the Treasure of Troy, spirited the priceless gold relics out of Turkey—although even in the late 1800s it had been illegal to do so? The Turkish government still had not managed to retrieve its stolen treasure and repatriate its unique cultural patrimony to its rightful country of origin.

Meg figured the crew might easily have forgotten about the locket. She could have deleted the pictures and renumbered the photographs and drawings and changed the dataset. Although it would have taken time, it could have been done and she would have covered her tracks. But Emily would have remembered the locket. If she didn't see it discussed in the report or itemized on the artifact inventory or contained within a neatly labeled plastic curation bag, surely she would have inquired about it. Could Meg really have denied its existence?

As tempting as it had been to entertain the possibility of keeping the locket, she knew she'd never do it. The days of Sophia Schliemann were long gone in archaeology, even for a small, unassuming, broken-edged locket from some poor, nameless, soon-to-be-destroyed farm site. That little artifact, however humble, could never be private property again. It now belonged to everyone— a piece of our communal past. A cultural resource that was part of our collective heritage, shared by all citizens of the great Commonwealth of Kentucky. As a steward of the past, the locket was not hers. It never had been and never would be.

Even as Meg gazed at the locket on the far side of the thin glass, she had the vague sense that whoever EEOM was, she wouldn't have minded letting Meg wear her locket. Even from across the sterile boundary of glass, she still had the feeling that EEOM had been pleased to see her once-cherished locket around Meg's neck, to witness it worn again, polished and shining once more as it dangled from a new silver chain, revived after an eternity buried beneath the dark soil of the pasture.

But what would EEOM think of the display case with its bright impersonal light, or the blatant intrusiveness of the mounted magnifying glass? How would she feel about rank strangers filing past, gawking at it—or passing it blithely by? The dry, objective text that revealed nothing of the locket's true meaning? Of her prized jewelry rendered mere data, off-limits behind the glass, soon to be packed inside a carefully labeled, standard-sized cardboard curation box and buried again on a dusty shelf in the state repository? But then, what did it matter what EEOM might have thought? Finders keepers after all—although not quite in archaeology.

While Meg was lost in thought, a man walked up to stand quietly beside her. To her surprise, he didn't perform the customary glance and shuffle. Rather, he stood in front of the case, his face close to the glass, reading all the information about the locket. Then he peered through the thick lens of the mounted magnifying glass. He scanned the text again, returned to look at the locket under the lens. He took it all in with great curiosity, his breath condensing and evaporating on the glass.

As he did, Meg studied the man from the corner of her eye: medium height, medium build, maybe about forty, dark, thinning hair, a kind face.

"Do you know anything about this locket?" he asked, turning toward her.

Meg jumped a little at the abruptness of the man's question. He had been so absorbed by the contents of the case she didn't think he had even noticed her standing there.

"Ah, well, actually I do," she replied.

"This came from that new subdivision they're building, right?"

"That's right. It's called Creekside. Although, actually, it's an expansion project."

"What are those little broken ends coming off the edge?" He bent back over and looked through the magnifying lens, tapping the glass a little as he spoke. "Are those what's left of the filigree decorations?" He asked, answering his own question.

"That's right. They once went around the entire locket, attached to the back section." She too, leaned toward the locket as she spoke, glimpsed again the ragged edge of broken filigree. From her oblique angle of view, the flowing EEOM initials loomed up unevenly through the thick lens.

"How far out do you think the filigree extended?" he asked.

Meg moved thumb and index finger to indicate half an inch, even though neither could see the distance she measured. She glanced at him again. It was unusual for a layman to display such a keen interest in such details.

"About half an inch or so?" he asked, again answering his own question.

"That's right, at least according to the better preserved examples."

"How common are such lockets? I mean the ones with filigree?"

"Well, back East they're not too terribly unusual during this time, but in Kentucky they're a good deal rarer because there weren't as many wealthy people here at the time."

The man nodded as she snuck another peek: No navy blue jacket. No enamel lapel pin. This man was no city official.

"Was there anything inside?"

Meg was stunned by the man's question and paused for a moment before answering it. How did he know she'd opened it? "Ah, no, nothing inside. But then, anything organic would have deteriorated anyway." She hoped he didn't ask if she'd tried it on.

He nodded. "You know, this locket looks familiar to me. If I'm not mistaken, this is like the one my great-great-grandmother is wearing in a photograph."

Meg turned slowly to look at the man. As she did, he turned his head to meet her astonished gaze.

"I'm sorry, what did you say?" She couldn't have heard him correctly.

"Well, I have a very old photograph of my great-great-grandmother. I really don't know much about her, but if I'm not mistaken, she's wearing a locket like that," he said gesturing with his hand to the display case.

"Are you joking?" There was a sudden eagerness in Meg's voice, and her eyes grew wide. She was only vaguely aware of her jaw dropping open. She felt an odd urge to hug this stranger.

"No, I'm not joking. I think it's identical, but I might be wrong. I haven't looked at it in a while. I'll have to look again."

"When was the photograph taken? Was she from here? What was her name?" Meg was the one peppering the man with questions now. "Yeah, yeah, for sure, look at it again. Uhmm—do you think I could take a look? I'd love to see your great-great-grandmother's picture, even if it isn't the exact same locket, I mean, it'd be really great to see someone from the times actually wearing it, or even just one that only looked kinda like it." Meg had begun stammering. She very desperately wanted to see that photograph.

The man was smiling at her, amused.

"Are there any initials engraved on it?" She blurted, and then stood there blinking. She may as well have asked, *Does it have EEOM on it?*

"Well, now, I don't know about initials. I'm not sure it's that close up. I'm sure there's filigree around the edge, though, and I know we have kin that came across Cumberland Gap, which would place the locket very early—matching the dates for lots of these artifacts." As the man spoke his hand swept broadly to include the rest of the Creekside displays.

Meg was astounded. While she had been caught up in her reminiscences with the locket, this man had looked at and read the text of each Creekside exhibit. In that instant, the fact that even one person had willingly attended the museum opening and had taken the time to read and understand her display made the weeks of digging and the weekends and evenings of exhibit preparation seem worthwhile. Maybe her efforts made a difference after all.

She just stood there, speechless, staring at this very surprising man, an odd, puzzled expression on her face. This man's kin had crossed Cumberland Gap? His slight Kentucky accent became more apparent the longer they spoke.

"I'm sorry, please allow me to introduce myself," said the man, smiling. He pushed his right hand toward hers, started pumping it. "Tom Ballard."

"Meg Harrington," she smiled back, still staring.

She, too, pumped his hand, clasping it tightly. She held onto it just the slightest instant longer than one might normally for a regular handshake. But even after their hands parted, still she stared at him.

"So, you dug all this up?" Tom asked.

"Ah, yeah," she said. To keep herself from staring at him, she forced her eyes to the yellowed linoleum at her feet. "Well, I mean, my students and I did," she said, waving a hand in the general direction of the crew.

By now the crew was buzzing around the refreshment table, an excited swarm of bees busily demolishing the remaining food now that most of the officials had left. Scott's plate was stacked with a teetering pyramid of broccoli, while Tonya's held an enormous slice of Derby pie. Emily and Oliver were heading toward the exit, Oliver bounding up the basement steps, clearly in a hurry. Emily paused and waved at her with a big grin on her face. Meg lifted her hand, waved vaguely back.

"Well, how exciting. In a non–Indiana Jones kind of way, of course," Tom said.

"Well, yes, actually it is exciting, although absolutely in a non–Indiana Jones kind of way." They laughed, followed by an awkward pause.

"Well, here, let me give you my card," he said. Tom pulled out his wallet and poked through the slots. "Give me a call sometime and we'll investigate my great-great-grandmother's jewelry."

Meg smiled at his sense of humor. "Oh, that'd be great!"

"Here, I'll put my home number on it." He turned the card over to the blank side and began to write. She glanced at his left hand: Tom Ballard was not wearing a wedding band.

"Oh, I will. When are you free?" asked Meg as he handed her the card. "Maybe we can set a time now?" she asked, blushing. "I'm sorry, but I really do want to see the photograph. I'm still writing the report, and, uh, it'd be great to get a chance to see it before I'm done."

"No, that's fine. I understand," he said, chuckling a little.

"Anytime that's convenient for you—I wouldn't want to disturb your family or anything," she said.

"No family, so anytime's good. I'm free this Saturday afternoon. How about then?"

With a quick flicker of temptation, Meg almost agreed to abandon her Saturday afternoon peach-pie-baking extravaganza with Emily and Miss Eliza, but then realized she didn't want to miss out on all the fun.

"Well, actually, I can't make it then," she said with a little cringe of the shoulders. "I have a regular baking engagement with this great old lady. She just left, actually—did you see her, the one with the bright red hat and black ostrich feathers? Every Saturday afternoon. She's teaching me how to bake peach pie. I think I'm actually starting to get the hang of it. In case you can't tell." Meg said patting her belly.

Oh Jesus! She was nattering on like a fool, like she always did when she got nervous. No family—good. By now, Meg had decided that Tom Ballard was quite good-looking. Even more important, he had bothered to read her Creekside text. And he had a great-great-grandmother who had a locket like hers. Like EEOM's, she corrected herself.

"Sunday around noon, noon-thirty? I'll make lunch; you bring peach pie. You know, my mother always used to bake peach pie for Sunday dinner. They were delicious."

"Really?" said Meg, staring at the man again. All of a sudden she felt dubious of her newfound baking ability.

"Here, I'll draw you a map to my house." He retrieved the card from her hand and proceeded to sketch on the back of it. Meg watched as he drew a series of smooth, perfect lines and printed the street names in tiny perfect block letters. Not many people drew maps anymore—it was one of those rarely used traditional skills that was disappearing as fast as baking a pie.

"Okay, Sunday's great. I'll bring the pie. Hopefully, I'll get the crust right. That's where I've been having the most trouble." Meg made that little cringing movement with her shoulders again. "You can't knead the dough too long or else the crust gets tough."

He winked at her and smiled. "I'm sure it'll be wonderful. See you Sunday." Tom Ballard thrust his hand at her again, pumped it a few time before turning on his heel.

Meg followed him with her eyes as he walked toward the warped steps leading up from the basement of the old stone courthouse, his receding footsteps hollow against the yellowed linoleum tile. She watched him disappear up the steps with a strange mixture of disappointment and anticipation.

But then, out of the corner of her eye she saw someone approaching her. It was the councilman Bob had been talking to earlier. Up to that point she had successfully avoided him all evening, but now she was hopelessly caught with no plausible means of escape since the caterers had already removed the punch bowl. The most boring city councilman had just seen his next conversational victim and was striking.

"Say, have you heard about that new *T. Rex* fossil they found in Ethiopia?"

Chapter Fourteen

Lizzie bent her head, dabbed her eye with a handkerchief. "I's just gettin too old for all the work," she confided to the new pastor, her voice shot with emotion. "I just don't believe I'll live to see the day those young 'uns are all growed up."

The new pastor pursed his lips and nodded, running through the available possibilities. "I'll do some askin, see what I can find out," he said. "There's a recent widow that's close to your son's age I'll inquire about. But you know you've got to get Caleb back to church. The Lord can help, if only your boy will allow it."

They sat in the front pew of the cold, empty, crossroads town meetinghouse. Outside, the trees were bare once more, and sudden gusts of winter wind were starting to whip up a few flurries of fresh snow. Mamaw Lizzie had taken good care of her two grandchildren for several long years since Rebecca's death. She had raised them well, but the strain of caring for young children, in addition to all the exhausting work of running a home, had grown too strenuous for her aging body.

"Reverend, Caleb hain't set foot in no meetin'house ever since his wife died. Lord knows how I've tried, but he won't listen—he just won't listen to nobody no more." Lizzie shook her head, circled by thinning coils of long gray braid. The skin on her face had grown thin and crepe-like, and liver spots covered her sagging cheeks.

"I'll talk to him," the pastor promised. "I'm sure I can find a way to get to him."

The new pastor was a young and vigorous man, still optimistic and confident in his ability to save lost and wayward souls. He had listened with rapt attention to the old pastor's fiery sermons many times and had proven himself a quick study in the delicate, deliberate art of preaching.

"He knows I'm here talkin to you, Reverend. He don't like it none, but even he knows we cain't go on like this no more. That *I* cain't go on like this." Lizzie's voice trailed off as she looked up through tired eyes at the new pastor. The young man seemed so full of vim and vigor—maybe he *could* save her son, even though she knew it wasn't very likely.

The pastor reached out and clasped her arm. "I know, sister, I know."

Lizzie got teary with the pastor's touch. "I love those children so much. But I just hain't got the strength no more—it's not that I don't love 'em." She dabbed again at her eyes.

"I understand, sister," the pastor said. "You've done a fine job with them, and I know they love you right back."

Lizzie broke into sobs, something she had been hoping not to do. "I've tried so hard to give 'em all I got. It's just gettin too much. And now winter's here again." Lizzie glanced out the frosted window, bowed her head in defeat. "I just don't think I cain do it much longer."

When Caleb and his mother arrived in the old wagon, a long row of glistening icicles hung from the eaves of the meetinghouse like daggers waiting to break and impale the frozen earth below. Slick layers of ice coated the front steps, and hundreds of passing feet had trod new paths through the crusty snow, all merging dutifully back at the front door.

The new pastor creaked open the heavy wooden entrance door and peered out as mother and son traversed that slick path.

"Brother Caleb, I'm so happy to have you here," the pastor said as they crossed the icy threshold. "Please come in. This is God's house, but it's your house, too. You're always welcome." A broad smile of greeting shone from the young pastor's excited face, his arm eagerly outstretched.

Caleb reached his hand to the pastor's. "Reverend," he muttered. When he took off his hat he revealed a worn and haggard face with great dark circles below red watery eyes. He smelled of stale drink.

"We all remember your grandfather with great admiration," the pastor said. Caleb nodded his head, kept his eyes cast down at the wooden floorboards. "We pray for him every Sunday. We pray for you, too, son." The pastor's voice was low, imploring. "You know you need to come to church with your ma and your little ones. They sure are mighty fine children."

Caleb nodded, grunted, said nothing.

"Would you like some coffee, son? I brewed a fresh kettle for you."

Caleb shook his head.

"You sure? I'd be honored if you'd let me get you a cup? Well then, take a seat, please, right here." The new pastor opened a gracious hand toward the nearest pew.

Caleb stayed standing, remained silent.

The pastor waited a moment before he spoke again. "You know, your grandfather would be mighty disappointed in you, son," said the man half Caleb's age.

Caleb said nothing, kept his eyes fixed on the floorboards.

The pastor had requested the widow arrive only after he had ample opportunity in which to save Caleb's wayward soul. He took out his pocket watch and clicked it open. He had plenty of time, and apparently he would require each second of it.

Lizzie sighed as she eased herself down in a pew. She was certain her wait would be long.

"The Lord has no mercy for backsliders," the pastor began, his tone growing less genial, a little more menacing.

No sound came from the standing man.

Lizzie pulled her handkerchief from her coat sleeve. She looked toward the window and shook her head.

The young pastor's zeal grew as the mute standing man with downcast eyes resisted one after another of his foolproof, well-practiced entreaties. But although he continued to preach and scream into Caleb's expressionless face, after several hours even the new pastor began to grasp the futility of his wasted words: Before him stood a soul that could not be touched.

Admitting defeat, the pastor pulled a folded handkerchief from his pocket and mopped his brow. He looked at his pocket watch, frowned. Several hours of toil had failed to even begin to stir the emotions of the obstinate man who stood before him staring at the floor.

When Abigail arrived with her two small children, she and Caleb shook limp, indifferent hands. Neither looked at the other. The pastor married them that very day, at the altar of that cold, empty, echoing meetinghouse.

Abigail Crenshaw was born to a tenant family who turned over a portion of their crop to their landlord after each harvest. Not long after her marriage to another tenant farmer, a man who owned no plow and no mule, Abigail's parents left aboard one of the new iron-horse steam trains to try their luck further west. Her husband had been a hard-working man but, like so many that year, had died in an outbreak of scarlet fever, as had her youngest child. After her husband's death, she could no longer meet the landlord's demands. Abigail and her two sons had nowhere to live.

The newlyweds did not speak on the cold wagon ride back to the cabin. Instead, each sat huddled beneath their separate layers of heavy horse blankets as if cowering from whatever bitterness the future was certain to bring. That cold ride home marked the beginning of a joyless marriage in which husband and wife would exchange little except necessary information. It was a marriage in which neither Abigail nor Caleb was able to find any consolation in the losses of the other, nor did either seek the body of the other for whatever comfort might be found.

Once pretty enough, Abigail's perpetual drawn smile did little to belie her mirthless existence.

Throughout her years at the cabin, she took to sitting on the porch, looking out over the beauty of the irises, and breaking beans into a bowl with a ferocity that Lizzie had never before witnessed. She swept the house in a similar manner—harsh and angry—as if punishing the floorboards for some unforgivable transgression. She performed only the minimum tasks of cooking and cleaning, and the cabin soon took on a dank odor. Under Abigail's negligible care, the linens no longer received their proper boiling in lye soap and grew badly yellowed. Rips in britches or shirts or dresses were poorly mended, if at all. Lizzie did her best to make sure all four children were clean when they went to church or school, but their attendance dropped little by little, despite several visits from the pastor and the school's concerned teacher.

For Caleb, his only contentment was at the woodpile. It was as if the sway of the swinging ax, the brightness of the chop, and the rip of dry wood on dull stump might bring back his former joy. Hour after hour he chopped. Through his ceaseless efforts, high stacks of precisely arranged firewood rose under the eaves of each building at the farm. Every cool night he built a blazing fire in the cabin's cooking hearth and sat motionless beside it, dark circles beneath puffy eyes, staring into the dancing blue flames as he tipped his head to swig from his bottle.

From time to time, as if to defy sadness itself, the peal of children's laughter managed to pierce the despair that hung heavy over the clearing.

Despite her advancing age, Mamaw Lizzie was one of the few sources of happiness for the children that lived there. She took them to pick blackberries, small purple-stained baskets slung over their thin child arms. Other times she clapped her hands in encouragement as they swung from the long, knotted rope and dropped in the pool below when the creek ran high.

She instructed young Rebecca—named after her mother—how to stitch a sampler, her tight little Xs joining to form the familiar names of all her family.

Side-by-side, grandmother and granddaughter baked a peach pie for each Sunday dinner. Together they snipped the blooming irises, arranging the tall stalks in old redware pitchers and jugs and placing them on all the graves in the family cemetery on the gentle rise of land beside the creek.

But despite her valiant efforts, Lizzie knew that these children would be the last to grow up in the shadow of the cabin below the knobs—that they would all eventually take their leave of this sad place.

One late fall day, after years of unrelenting silence, Abigail finally lost the will to go on.

With chilling forethought, she sawed a narrow slot into a cabin floorboard and rammed Caleb's rifle down until it rested firm on the ground below. She perfected the rifle's angle, repositioning it until it was just right. She took a short length of twine, tied one end to the trigger and the other to the door latch. She sat in a chair before the rifle, nestled the muzzle high to her stomach, cocked the rifle, and kicked the door. The shot went straight through her body to lodge high in a rough-hewn log on the wall behind.

They buried Abigail near the low mound of dirt just beginning to harden overtop old Mamaw Lizzie, her grave joining that of the others who had lived and died in the shadow of the knobs. Even the least of each generation—the stillborn, the infants, the toddlers—had come to take their place within the dark soil of that gentle rise of land.

Although the process had begun years before, it took many more for life beside the creek to unravel completely. But piece by piece, strand by strand, that tattered fabric wore thin. Then it frayed on the edges, grew threadbare in the middle, shreds dangling from its open gaping wounds. Then it ripped apart entirely.

The children quit the place as soon as they could.

Abigail's sons left together for the Iowa Territory—two dirty ragamuffins earning their passage on a westbound paddle wheeler by hauling heavy cargo on their slight backs. Rebecca's son moved to Lexington, where he found work in a dusty ropewalk near Main Cross, tarring and twisting long strands of hemp into rope for use in the steamships that now plied the high seas in ever-wealthier merchant fleets.

Little Rebecca—the youngest of all the children at the cabin—also moved to Lexington. She was fortunate to find a live-in position in a big brick house on Mulberry Street, where she worked as a kitchen servant, scouring pots and peeling potatoes under the exacting eye of the cook. Her employers were a prominent abolitionist family who hired poor whites to work right alongside free Negroes. But regardless of their color, the household help were all required to use the small door that faced the back alley.

Alone at the farm, Caleb passed his days much as he had passed them before, sullen and silent. Despite several visits from the pastor, he refused to remarry, and by now only the most desperate of women would have agreed to such an arrangement.

Once a strong and vibrant man, Caleb had grown disheveled and erratic, despite his mother's efforts to keep him otherwise. Once she was gone, there had been no one to slow his slide. By his last years, he was capable of achieving only the minimum of basic human survival, and the little farm withered without his attention.

One by one he sold off or slaughtered the livestock. Because he had neglected to open the tall barn windows, great patches of mold grew on the curing burley leaves, rendering them of minimal value at auction. Where once he picked peaches and sold them by the bushel, now ripe fruit dropped from the trees and rotted on the ground. The gaunt, aging mules could no longer pull the heavy plow through the fields, and he had no money to purchase a new team. A sudden drought sorely diminished the hemp crop, so he ended the season with not even two complete bales. Caleb's debt at the crossroads store continued to mount, and the storekeeper had become more adamant in his requests for payment.

The shakes on the cabin roof had again rotted, and innocuous drips had become steady streams in heavy rain. The rear section of the springhouse washed away in a flood, and Caleb had lost an entire wall of the last remaining crocks of vegetables. Termites had taken up residence in the cabin timbers and a musty, sour odor permeated the dirty rooms. Weevils had invaded the sacks of flour stacked beside the cooking hearth, although he failed to notice their presence when he made his biscuits.

But what Caleb didn't realize was that many small farmers, even those who had not suffered his terrible personal losses, were all experiencing declines similar to his.

As the value of land had risen, so too had property taxes. At the same time, the price offered for grain and burley and hemp at auction had dropped. Many years before the Civil War broke wildly across the land, the long fingers of industrialization had already begun to extend far from the northern cities, insinuating their reach even to the little cabin near the creek. Railroads and steamships now transported great quantities of hemp and wheat and corn across immeasurable distances—from places they could be produced cheaply to places where they brought top dollar. Anyone not in that loop was left standing by the wayside.

Wealthier farmers with more and richer land and superior livestock were better positioned to withstand the periodic jolts of recession, and were better able to adapt to such changes than those whose lives had always been lived closer to the edge. These were universal processes under which the small farmer was always at a disadvantage, and Caleb was just one of many who lost. In the end, he was crushed beneath the weight of many different wheels, few of which he could fathom, and none of which he could fight.

In the end he did little more than sit on the creek bank and look toward the night sky. He watched as constellations turned and shifted upon some immense unseen axis. Through bleary eyes he observed the filling and the shaving of the moon and planets that blazed strong and bold and then, after a while, didn't. The greatest solace he found in the darkness above were the stars that fell, those chosen ones that grew exhausted from the pointless effort of remaining in the sky and hurled abruptly out of it—tiny streaks of white flashing across the dark dome of the night.

It was a new neighbor who found Caleb. The wide black circling of buzzards against the blueness overhead drew his attention. It was obvious the miserable, grizzly, old man must have finally fallen over and died right beside the creek. The stench, the stirring swarm of blackness, and buzzards on wing—all told him the body must have laid there for quite some time.

Season follows season, spiraling without haste. Greening leaves, falling leaves, rotting leaves. Falling snow, melting snow, rain. Rising heat, falling frost. Decay linked to rebirth, silent in its inexorable passage, now unobserved by inquisitive human eye. Only the creek continues to bear witness.

No longer any resistance—no grasping, no clinging, no pushing for movement in any unnatural direction. Not of human or of animal or of land, all now devoid of incessant struggle. Even the orchard reverts to wilderness as domestication departs, her footsteps fading as the great hush descends.

Time melts and melds the visions and dreams, the joys and sorrows that hover in this strange place. It leads them deep into darkness, to the damp of the quiet land, to old and ancient. Forsaken now, indistinguishable now from soil and rock, earth and stone. Elemental. The disparate whims of ephemeral human longing crack and crumble, embedding deep in the stillness of the dark ground.

Drops of individual identity seep out and drench dust and sand—identities now gone, inscrutable in their passing. It is a deliberate muting of the specific and the precise, now awash in generalization, distinctiveness collapsing and at last irretrievable. Uniqueness, once so prized, vanishes into the vast and impersonal. The facelessness of decay; decomposing flesh. Indeterminate sherd; nameless glass. Anonymous browning bone.

Time dulls the arcs of individual lives. Short arcs. Pious arcs. Even the shattered arcs merge with the soil beneath to rest in the darkness, the immensity, the silence, even the longest human arcs mere flickers beside the long arc of the land. That human presence persists only in sherd and metal, lingers on in brick and bone—ghostly remnants, strange voiceless memories of the past. Layer upon layer of human action and striving grow forgotten here. Deep and heavy they groan, weighing down and crushing all below with the immensity of their terrible burden.

And it is a welcomed relaxation into the ground of that incessant human will, the last repose of ceaseless human striving. The final retreat into the sweetness of mud and earth.

Only dormancy watches over the land, guarding it as it sleeps, a great she-bear curled in her warm winter cave, waiting in the dark. Only dormancy watches the invariable movement of the creek as it trickles, aloof and distant on its steady seaward path. The knobs, gray stone sentinels soaring skyward, sweep their piercing vision across the land. Majestic watchtowers. A constant surveillance of all that passes.

Season follows season, and no son or daughter returns to claim the land. Not indifference. They are the sons and daughters—still arcing and individual still—casting broad across the land. Neighbors come and cart off stones and logs. Not vultures with wagons, but the pragmatic hardscrabble descendants of pragmatic hardscrabble pioneers who punched through the Gap and carved farm from wilderness. They come and they take.

Season follows season and the scars of scavengers merge with scars of the inhabitants. Scars of nature visit as well. Sweep of flood. Scorch of lightning. Soot and char of burning forest. Heavy ice on fragile groaning limb. The unthwarted advance of Virginia creeper.

Chapter Fifteen

Meg held up the pinafore apron, turned to catch her reflection in the department store mirror. She liked the mixed fruit pattern with a bright blue ruffle. She set the pinafore apron down, held up the simple skirt apron with the yellow daisies and green ruffle. Her eye roamed the shelf: matching dishtowels, oven mitts, tablecloths, and toaster covers were available for both patterns. Meg was coming to love the gaudy look.

She finally settled on the pinafore apron with the mixed fruit and blue ruffle, along with the entire matching set. She decided to buy the skirt apron for Emily. She considered getting one for Miss Eliza, but then decided she probably didn't need another gaudy apron.

Meg pushed her shopping cart through the aisles. She selected a rolling pin and flour board, nesting Pyrex measuring cups, a sifter, several glass pie plates and a pie lifter, along with other assorted kitchen wares she'd neglected to even realize were missing from her gaping cupboards and empty drawers. A soft and fluffy light green bath mat caught her attention, reminded her of the color of fresh honeysuckle. She picked up a bright print tablecloth of purple and yellow.

As she aimed her cart toward the cashier that Friday evening, her eyes wandered over the pile of assorted household items, a smile on her lips. Perhaps she was finally sinking roots in this place, creating her own home here in Kentucky rather than remaining several moving boxes away from her next destination.

Meg threw back the covers and jumped out of bed that Saturday morning. As she sipped on a cup of coffee, she looped her new apron around her neck. She fully intended to bring her first solo peach pie to Tom's for Sunday lunch.

She took out the recipe she'd managed to piece together after several Saturday afternoons in Miss Eliza's marvelous kitchen. She lined up all the ingredients and utensils on her counter, arranging them in the precise order in which they would be used. Meg paused to study the recipe again.

Miss Eliza never used a recipe, apparently didn't have one. She never arranged her ingredients and utensils on the counter in a neat organized line. Instead, Miss Eliza preferred the more spontaneous method of banging around in her cupboards and finding what she needed at the exact moment she needed it. Meg looked doubtfully at her organized row of new utensils and ingredients, and all of a sudden she felt completely ridiculous in her gaudy new apron. An unexpected lack of self-confidence swept over her as she studied the neat row, feeling more and more uncertain about her first solo peach-pie-baking attempt.

Meg sighed as she picked up her new paring knife. She peeled and sliced and stewed the peaches with sugar. She measured flour, salt and Crisco, cut them with cold water. She rolled the dough, cut the round bottom and lattice strips. It all seemed simple enough in Miss Eliza's chaotic kitchen, but in her own she grew lost and indecisive, second guessing herself at each turn. The texture of the dough confused her; had she kneaded it long enough or too much? The consistency of the stewed peaches didn't seem quite right; had she added sufficient sugar? When she finally slid the glass baking pan in the oven, little optimism remained.

After the pie cooled, Meg cut a slice and took a bite. After chewing a few times, she put her fork on the counter. The peaches were overcooked—mushy rather than firm. She had selected poorly from the peaches in the produce section, since there was little natural sweetness to her pale runny syrup. The dough was tough and tasteless rather than flaky and light. Each latticework strip had broken at least once in her weaving, and thick wads of patched dough made even the pie's appearance unappetizing.

She frowned. She wouldn't be bringing this disaster to Tom's house.

She walked to the sink and stood before it in her ridiculous apron. What did she do wrong? Had she forgotten some crucial ingredient? She turned the disappointing pie upside down and scraped the baking dish with her fork. She turned on the water and watched as the undesirable crust and the flavorless peaches slowly ground their way through the indifferent gears of her garbage disposal.

From the moment she arrived at Miss Eliza's that Saturday afternoon, both women teased her mercilessly. Emily, it seemed, had been quick to spill the beans to Miss Eliza about the mystery man at the museum opening. Meg knitted her brow. Had her behavior been that transparent?

"Just remember the poster on the lab wall," Emily laughed.

"What poster?"

"My how quickly one forgets!" teased Emily. "Since you seem to have temporary amnesia, let me remind you. It says, 'Love Is Fleeting. Stone Tools Are Forever.'"

Miss Eliza loved the joke. She whooped with laughter, slapping her leg and rocking back and forth. As she repeated the phrase, tears of laughter squeezed through the thick creases of her eyes.

While Miss Eliza amused herself with this cynical snippet of archaeological humor, Meg was obliged to recall how fleeting love, indeed, could be.

Her last romance had certainly been brief. The first clue to its brevity might have been that her thirty-seven-year-old boyfriend lived in his mother's basement. At first, Meg was willing to overlook what she thought was minor—a small pink flag of mild concern. But, as weeks progressed to months and her beau was unwilling to invite her to his house or stay out past midnight, that once avoidable pink flag transformed into a wailing red siren. At least it had ended quickly.

Nor had Meg's early exposure to love been idyllic. Her father had spent many nights and weekends at the office, leaving his wife alone with kids and chores. At times, arguments erupted and bitter name-calling ensued. As a child Meg learned the art of retreat: quick flight to the relative safety of her bedroom, bury herself in a book, at least until a rising migraine transformed the page into painful starbursts.

However fleeting love may be, for Meg it also seemed persistent and recurring. How many times had she found herself certain that some new man was Mr. Right—only to be proven wrong? Against her better judgment, her faith in love surprised her anew as each time it rose to claim her, only to dissolve again like sugar in rain.

The only true constant had been her work. Over time, it had proven her most steady and reliable companion.

More than once, withdrawal into the safety of cerebral space had calmed the mounting emotional turmoil that followed disappointment. That cerebral world made so much sense. The rewards of inhabiting that predictable, rational space were so tangible: articles, a book, grant money, maybe a plaque to hang on the wall. Over time, Meg's pattern of cerebral retreat had become well established, much as it had with her father. It had become a time-honored Harrington family tradition.

The map on the back of Tom's business card brought her to one of the historic districts of Lexington. His was an inner-city neighborhood that had recently undergone a sorely needed spurt of gentrification. At least in that corner of the city, Lexington's downtown decay was in hard reverse as old Victorians were bought up and remodeled by urban pioneers in flight from the endless monotony of suburbia.

Tom lived on a cul-de-sac off Broadway. Hundreds of cars sped past the little side street every day, but few noticed the urban Shangri-la hidden there. Tom's street was wide and lined with gracious trees, old oaks and mature tulip poplars grown tall and broad, spreading their branches across sun-dappled sidewalks, beckoning neighbors to stroll and pause and chat. Even some of the original curbs remained—rows of limestone slabs worn smooth by years of footfalls in and out of horse-drawn carriages.

Meg parked her car, walked up the steps to Tom's front porch, a peach pie fashioned in Miss Eliza's chaotic kitchen in her humbled hand.

A gray and white cat sat perched between two white porch columns, gray tail curling daintily over perfect white front paws. As Meg climbed the steps, the cat blinked, and two huge yellow eyes disappeared and then reappeared and then turned to gaze at the new arrival. Meg walked over and stroked the cat behind the ear; instantly there was purring. "Oh, aren't you a sweetheart!" As she petted the cat's sleek fur, she read the tag on the collar: Cinderella.

"And such a little princess, aren't you, Cinderella?" The cat flopped over on her side, exposing her furry white belly in case her visitor chose to rub it a little.

As Meg tickled Cinderella's belly, she glanced around Tom's front porch. Tucked behind hanging begonias and wind chimes were two wicker porch swings that faced one another from an easy conversational distance. A wicker table and chairs completed the cozy ensemble. It was a perfect spot to pass a lazy summer afternoon reading a book or sipping iced tea, or both.

Meg gave one last rub to the purring cat before she walked over and rang the bell. Tom opened the door right away.

"Hi! Wow, you sure do have a great house!" Meg said. "I didn't even know this neighborhood existed."

"Yeah, kinda off the beaten track. I like it that way. Come on in." He held the door open as Meg walked past him into the foyer. Tom took the pie and placed it on the hallway table. "This looks yummy!"

"I hope you like it. Sounds like you know your peach pie. How old is this place?"

"This house was built in 1905, but it was actually one of the last on the block. The houses on the other side all went up in the early 1890s. If you go just a few blocks south of here, those houses even predate the Civil War."

Meg nodded, gazing around the old foyer. A respectable woman once descended the staircase on the side, lifting her long taffeta skirt with a little bustle at the back. A date of 1905 could have made her one of the first on the block to run an admiring finger along the gleaming black steel of her family's new Model T.

"It's in great shape," Meg said, still looking around.

"Completely remodeled in the late '80s—this was a dying neighborhood not long before that."

"Did you remodel it?"

"No, that was before my time. I've only had the place for five years. The biggest thing I did was hire some guys to replace the roof. There were four layers of roofing up there—including the original cedar shakes."

"Wow—the original roof."

"You want to see the rest of the place?"

"Sure! If that's alright—I don't want to disturb you." Meg was dying to see the place. She loved old houses, but on a professor's salary she could never afford one, unless she was willing to buy a fixer-upper, but then she didn't have the proper skills—other than plenty of elbow grease—to repair a fixer-upper.

"Not disturbing a thing. Want to start in the attic?"

They toured the entire house, from the slanting dormers of the attic to the rough-cut limestone foundation in the cellar. As they walked through the rooms, Tom pointed out his favorite antiques from time to time, including some from his own family. He rested a hand on the wooden sideboard in the dining room. "I bet at some point this old sideboard must have housed some family's prized silver," he mused.

"So this piece wasn't in your family?" Meg asked. She brushed her fingers across the brass handles, restrained herself from opening the drawer.

"No, my family wasn't of the silver-service class, if you know what I mean."

In his bedroom, he walked to the far wall, where a folded quilt hung over a tall wooden frame. "My mother made this quilt when she got married," he said. "All by hand."

"That's amazing," Meg said, leaning closer to look at the stitching. Each one was tight and even. "Can you imagine doing that? I mean, hand sewing a quilt?"

She peered at the little squares of fabric. The colors reminded her of the pasture, and the view to the knobs. The pattern was one she didn't recognize—elongated triangles radiating out from a central point like a series of spinning pinwheels.

"Hard to believe, isn't it? My mom told me my grandmother insisted it be twelve stitches to the inch."

As they passed through the house, Meg scanned the walls to find Tom's great-great-grandmother's photograph. She didn't see it anywhere, nor did he mention it. Clearly, Tom was a patient man. Many people assumed archaeologists had an abundance of patience, perhaps even an overabundance, but Meg thought those people probably watched too many reruns on the Discovery Channel. She willed herself not to mention the photograph first.

"Are you hungry?" Tom asked. "I hope you like gazpacho."

They were standing in the old pantry behind the cellar steps and had just finished inspecting the layers of crumbling plaster overtop of rough wainscoting. "Gazpacho? Love it!" she said, following him up to the kitchen.

Tom opened the refrigerator, pulled out a Tupperware tub of the chilled soup, and ladled it into bowls. He uncovered a cast-iron skillet and cut thick wedges of cornbread from it. He placed a crock of butter on the table as well as a plate with thick red slices of tomato.

"You're not a church-goer, then?" Meg asked, but as soon as the words left her mouth she felt awkward. "I mean, uh, you suggested lunch on a Sunday and all."

Her question was an important one in Kentucky. Many people, especially those in rural areas, attended church each week, and sometimes on Wednesday evenings, and often looked askance on those who didn't. Meg had learned that many of her students were quite religious. An image from her first year of teaching in Kentucky was of a girl eagerly completing a lab exercise comparing *Homo erectus* and *Homo sapiens* cranial capacity, with silver crosses dangling from her earlobes. Moments like those never ceased to amaze her—how human beings have the capacity to hold two contradictory beliefs at once.

"No, not really," said Tom. "Once in a while I go, more out of tradition than anything. My mother was a big church-goer though. You?" he inquired.

"Ah, not recently."

"Somehow I didn't think so," Tom said and winked.

It was only after they finished lunch and cleared the table that he walked down a hall, opened a closet, and slid out a trunk. As Meg sat at the table she listened as he rustled through various objects; some knocked, while others sounded softer, and she willed herself to stay exactly where she was and not go peer over his shoulder into the trunk. At last, he brought a framed photograph back to the table. "Here she is, my great-great-grandmother," he announced.

Meg took the frame in her hands and gazed at the photograph. "She's beautiful."

The frame housed a very old sepia daguerreotype of the bust portion of a handsome young woman. She wore a simple white blouse underneath a light jacket of darker, heavier material in some kind of floral-patterned brocade. The woman was stylish but not elegant. Her dark hair was pulled behind her head, although little dark wisps had managed to escape and fluff softly around the sides of her face.

The picture was somewhat blurry, but not bad for such an early era of photography. Despite the distancing of the medium, Meg was drawn to the woman's eyes—they were bright and brilliant even in the drab of the grainy old photograph. The woman wasn't smiling, but it looked like she had only recently been doing so and just the slightest trace of it remained. Picture-taking was serious business in those days, and not cheap. Meg imagined a grumpy photographer hunched beneath his dark cloth, cranking a huge metal knob to bring his subject into focus, aiming a colossal bulb that at any moment would roar into sudden, terrifying brightness.

And there was the locket, dangling on a simple twenty-six-inch chain. It was a perfect fit, locket to chain and to this beautiful woman. "What's her name?" Meg asked.

"Rebecca Tackett."

A sigh escaped Meg's lips and her shoulders slumped a little, disappointed that this woman was not EEOM. Without fully realizing it until just then, she wanted these two time periods—then and now, the past and present, the woman and the locket, the woman and herself—to connect. Meg wanted to discover that missing link with the past and put right that broken chain of cut-paper dolls. She wanted the nameless to become named, the rip in the fabric mended and made whole, and she had wanted to be the mender, that diligent seamstress who drew the needle through the ancient cloth and stitched it back together. Regret washed over her—a brass ring just out of reach.

Even in her disappointment, Meg considered the dates. She wasn't sure exactly, but daguerreotype photography would probably have come in sometime in the mid to late 1830s, which was quite a bit later than the manufacture dates for the locket. But Meg suspected such a valuable piece of jewelry would likely have been passed down through the generations, which could actually mean that someone by the name of Rebecca Tackett could have ended up wearing it in an early sepia image. The dates could still fit. But how had it gotten lost?

Meg was silent for a moment before she spoke again. "Do you know much about her?" she asked.

"Not much, unfortunately. She was my mother's great-grandmother, and my mother died when I was twenty-five—still too young to appreciate much about family stories."

His tone conveyed a sentiment Meg understood. It suggested that now that he *was* old enough to appreciate such things, they were no longer available. At this point they were the names and faces of people he had never known and never heard stories of, people to whom he should feel a familial connection, but somehow didn't quite. Photographs and antiques were precious, but they usually lacked stories to go along with them. For Tom, that was the missing element.

Meg reflected on an assignment she had developed for one of her classes, a kind of family tree and oral history rolled into one. The project asked students to draw a kinship chart and record at least one story for every individual over sixty. Some students used tape recorders to capture the frail voices of their elders as they told long tales for their descendents. Meg's lectures explained how various social and economic forces—nursing homes, couples marrying later, and the changing role of women—all meant that today's generations didn't mix as much as they used to. Birth control meant smaller families and higher education that raised expectations far beyond subsistence farming. Technology played a role as well, as television and the Internet replaced the storyteller. Greater affluence allowed single-family homes—like those at Creekside—rather than multiple generations living under one roof. Since big farm families had remained the norm in rural Kentucky until recently, some of her students produced kinship charts that were surprising in their depth and breadth.

"I only knew my maternal grandfather well," Meg said. "But I remember his favorite saying: 'Moderation in all things.'" Although Meg loved her grandfather's adage, she found she had to remind herself of it constantly. Even so, she considered it responsible for bringing at least some balance to her life, even if that balance was hard to maintain.

Tom nodded. "My grandfather always said, 'Youth is wasted on the young.'"

They both sat in silence for several moments, each contemplating the wisdom of their grandfathers, the importance of moderation, the indifference of youth, and the swiftness of its passing.

It was Meg who finally broke the silence. She did so by rummaging in her purse and pulling out her magnifying glass. She offered it for Tom to admire.

"Now isn't that a beauty," he said, chuckling. He twisted it in the sunlight, and they both watched as the green-and-gold-tinged ivy handle twinkled against a jet-black background. The handle was Spanish damascene, a Moorish metalworking technique that had survived since the Middle Ages. Meg's father had bought it for her on a trip to Spain, to replace the plastic magnifying glass she usually carried in her purse.

"Never leave home without one!" she said as he handed it back to her.

Meg studied the photograph, paying special attention to the locket underneath the thick lens. Unfortunately, the locket rested against Rebecca Tackett's white blouse, washing out much of its detail. Nevertheless, she could clearly see the filigree along the curving edges of the silver oval. Meg spoke without looking up. "Yep, that's filigree alright. Just like what we found at Creekside."

Then she turned her attention to the face of the locket, searched for any sign of initials beneath the lens. She scanned back and forth several times. The bright blaze of the photographer's flash reflected off a portion of the locket's face, rendering that section little more than a brilliant sunburst. Meg set down the magnifying glass, sat up straight, and looked at Tom.

"Well, I guess I can't honestly say I see any initials on it." This time disappointment clearly rung in her voice.

Tom said nothing but gave her a warm smile.

Meg made a sincere effort to smile back at him and envied the easy detachment he now demonstrated. But then she heard her own voice as it spoke. "Although who knows? I'm not convinced we'd be able to see any initials even if they were there—the image just isn't clear enough."

Yes, it was Meg's voice, and it was refusing to let the hope slide completely through her fingers that the woman in the photograph was connected to her locket—to her friend EEOM.

Without legible initials there would be no way of knowing whether or not Rebecca Tackett's locket was the one they'd found at Creekside. Meg could never be certain. Even though she hated to admit it, the logical side of her brain told her there could easily have been at least two filigree-edged silver oval lockets in the greater Lexington area during the time period in question. In fact, there could have been many more than two.

"Do you think we should look on the back?" Tom asked out of the blue. "I've never taken the picture out of the frame. Sometimes people write on the backs of photographs, so maybe there's more information . . . you never know?"

"You never know," Meg agreed.

Tom retrieved a pair of pliers and turned the frame upside down on the table.

He pulled the little nails that held the thin cardboard backing in place against the glass.

"That's a beautiful frame. Is it walnut?" she asked.

"Yes, it is. My grandfather made it. An old walnut tree on his property came down in an ice storm. He salvaged a lot of it and built all kinds of things with the wood. I have a little box he made, too." Tom chuckled and then, mostly to himself, said, "Well, I guess maybe there are some family stories there some-where."

After he drew the last nail, Tom removed the backing from the frame. As the thin piece of yellowed cardboard tipped open, a musty smell escaped from underneath. Her head poised above it, Meg breathed in the ancient fragrance trapped within. For a moment she thought she smelled the scent of old lace and rose water. Perhaps it was the light fragrance of sweet honeysuckle on a hot summer day?

"Okay, let's see," Tom said, turning the photograph upside down. "Hey, there *is* writing."

"Really?"

"It's pretty faded though. Let's see that magnifying glass." Meg waited as he deciphered the faded writing.

"Humm. Rebecca Tackett. June 28, 1835."

"Are you kidding? That's my birthday! Not 1835, of course."

"Of course," Tom chuckled, continuing to look at the date through the mag-nifying lens.

"Yeah, 1835. That sounds about right," Meg said, half to herself. "Based on the artifacts we have, that would be toward the later part of the occupation." She tilted her head back and forth in the air as she again considered the dates. "Yeah, that works."

"It also says 'Lexington.'"

"Well, Lexington in 1835 could have had some photographers," she guessed. Even though date and place fit, there would still be no way of knowing whether EEOM's locket had anything to do with beautiful Rebecca Tackett, the smil-ing woman in the sepia photograph.

"Yeah, I suppose so."

"Would you mind if I scanned this for the report?" Meg asked. "I would love to have a shot of a woman from Kentucky wearing a similar locket. Maybe I could put it on the cover, if you wouldn't mind?"

"Sure, no problem. I've got a scanner right here—I'll e-mail it to you." He turned the photograph right side up, gazed at the image of his great-great-grandmother. "I don't know why, exactly, but I think she'd be happy to be in your report, especially on the cover," he said, smiling at Rebecca Tackett, then up at Meg.

"Is it time for peach pie yet?" Tom asked. "It's a beautiful day; let's eat out on the porch. How'd the crust turn out, anyway? Not too tough, I hope?" He winked at her.

"Well, you'll have to tell me, since it seems like you're the true peach pie connoisseur around here!"

The crew stopped digging, watched as the man in the crisp white shirt got out of his car and headed their way. Once Emily recognized the man from the museum opening, she sauntered over to Meg, a mischievous look on her face. Emily motioned with her head at the man walking toward them across the pasture, pointed to a wide cone of fine brown dirt beneath a screen, and raised her eyebrow a few times. Meg looked at the dirt cone in confusion, looked back at Emily for explanation.

"'Archaeologists do it in the dirt,'" Emily whispered.

Meg blushed, suddenly regretting teaching her students all those silly archaeological phrases, and then snickered along with Emily. As she watched Tom approach, she was glad he was already taking her up on the offer to visit the site.

They greeted in the pasture with a friendly handshake. Meg introduced him to the crew, after which they all pretended not to pay attention to the odd couple: the visitor in crisp white shirt and shiny black shoes and the woman in dirty jeans, work boots, and an old Dodgers baseball cap. If Tom noticed her transformation from a business suit to a pure dirt grub, he didn't mention it.

"I'll show you what we've been doing out here." Meg said, launching into her layman's version of the Creekside Subdivision Expansion Site tour. But as she spoke, her narrative became increasingly more detailed as she noticed Tom's level of interest remained high, even to the point of asking relevant and intelligent questions.

She showed him the charred stone fireplace pad of the log cabin, the two original rooms and the rear addition that came sometime later. She pointed out the small, early porch and the later, bigger porch. She showed him the rough stone circle of the privy, the square foundation of the smokehouse, the rectangular piers of the barn, and the remains of the other outbuildings.

For their last stop Meg led him up the gentle rise of land to the location of the little family cemetery. By this time all the graves were excavated, and all the human remains removed from the ground to cardboard boxes in her lab. Eight large and six tiny shadowy rectangles gaped from the greenness of the sod. Long dark mounds of fresh dirt stood again in wait, participants in some peculiar, poorly understood, reverse funerary ritual. The limestone slabs that once served as grave markers were stacked off to the side.

"What'll happen to the gravestones?" asked Tom, squatting down and running his fingers across the cool gray rock.

"They'll go into the metal boxes the funeral home will use to rebury the bones. All of these will be marked as 'Unknown' and buried with the others in the less-than-affluent section of a cemetery."

"Any idea how any of them died?"

"No, not really," she said, walking over to gaze down at a dark, open rectangle at the edge of the cemetery. "Except in unusual circumstances—like the man from this grave with multiple, likely fatal fractures—we rarely get much evidence of death." Meg's eyes swept across the tight gathering of dark, open rectangles on the gentle rise of land and fell silent.

Tom came to stand beside her. "It's good you came now," Meg said softly.

As they stood on the gentle rise they observed the trees that hugged the creek and the long line of gray stone knobs that stretched deep into the horizon. As they watched, a faint breeze ruffled the grass, bending the long blades as it climbed the rise, spilled back down the other side. A bright red cardinal swooped past, low and close, and then landed on one of the stacked limestone slabs. The red hue of the bird was brilliant against the gray of the rock and the vast expanse of summer green behind it.

Meg spotted it instantly. "Hey, pretty bird. Birdy! Birdy! Birdy!" she tweeted.

The cardinal sat perched on the stone, cocked his bright head back and forth, chirped at her in return, then flitted to land on another slab of stone.

"Hey, pretty bird," she called again.

The cardinal sang back to her several moments more, then it took wing and vanished into the line of trees along the banks of the creek. Meg stood and watched until it disappeared.

"Well, I guess I'd better call lunch," she said finally. "You can stay, I hope? I took the liberty of packing a lunch for you, in case you came. Round two for peach pie?" Meg asked, leading him back to the main excavation area.

"Thanks, I'd love to stay."

As they had each day since the dig began, the crew trod the well-worn path to the cool shade of the creek. Creatures of habit, each day they sat in virtually identical places as the first, as if drawn by some powerful magnet deep within the earth. Only Bob and Suzy had shifted places since the start of the dig, sitting closer together, chatting to one another as they ate, as if an even stronger magnet drew them from their previously assigned places. It wouldn't be the first time romantic sparks had flown on a dig, nor the last. Even despite the sweaty, dirty, sunburned, and repellent-soaked skin, the appeal of working closely outside together, sharing in all daily experiences, forged a bond rare in today's world.

Meg, too, sat in a different place that day, drawn with Tom to the very edge of the creek bank, the strength of a new magnet shifting her from her usual spot near the trunk of a tree.

"Here you go—I hope you like stir-fried chicken with broccoli," Meg said, handing him his own Tupperware container.

"Sure do, thanks." Tom stuck a fork in a spear of broccoli, turned to look up the creek bank. "Did you notice that huge old stump? You can barely see it for all the honeysuckle vines."

"Yeah, I think that's what's left of an old chestnut tree struck by the blight. Must have been something when it was alive."

Tom nodded, and then they sat in silence, watched as the creek trickled past, listening to the water's quiet gurgle as it flowed around cobbles and jutting slabs of stone. After half an hour, Meg forced herself to check her watch. "Well, I better get the show back on the road," she said. She zipped open her pack and tossed in their empty Tupperware containers. "I'm really glad you came."

He smiled at her. "Thanks for inviting me—it was great to come out and to just sit beside a creek. How often does that happen anymore?"

"Yeah, I know. I'll walk you back to your car," Meg said, standing up and turning to the crew. "Alright everybody, back to the trenches!"

After Meg herded the crew up the creek trail and back into their units, she and Tom chatted as they crossed the pasture. They walked slowly, observing the placement of each footstep, drawing out their walk a little rather than pushing ahead to their goodbye. As they neared the car, both fell silent.

Ever since the evening of the museum opening their conversations had flowed effortlessly, but now a little tension hung in the thickness of the summer air. Their prior interactions had all been embedded in some safe, external context— a photograph and a locket, the renovations of an old house, peach pie, the stone foundations at a soon-to-be-destroyed pasture site. Any future interaction—if there were any—would be less safe and not at all external.

It was Tom who spoke. "I'm out of town this weekend at a conference, but would you like to go out for dinner when I get back? There's a French restaurant downtown I'd like to check out. Are you free the following Saturday?"

They had stopped at the edge of the pasture, standing at the place where the green sod met the glistening black tarmac of the new road. Meg raised her hand against the bill of her Dodgers cap, squinting up toward the bright glare of the sun. The mechanical pencil behind her ear cast a long, dark shadow across her cheek. She looked at him through narrowed eyes, hoped her gestures helped obscure her beaming smile.

"That'd be great," she said. "I'd like that."

Chapter Sixteen

"Dr. Harrington? Can I bother you with a problem?" Emily asked. Immediately, Meg stopped sorting through the plastic curation bags and looked at her. Emily's voice sounded timid and forced; and she didn't just swivel around on her stool in the archaeology lab and ask her question, the way she usually did.

"Sure, Emily, of course you can."

Emily, too, stopped sorting through her stack of curation bags. Heavy rain that day had kept the crew in the lab, cataloging—inking tiny codes on artifacts—and sorting them out into separate curation bags by artifact class. By late afternoon the crew had left, and quiet had again fallen over the lab.

Emily said nothing, just stared down at the curation bag in her hand.

"What's the problem?" Meg asked, hoping to ease her young friend into whatever it was she wanted to discuss. But even as she waited for Emily to speak, she already had an inkling of what the problem might be—was herself reluctant to engage in that particular conversation. Meg stared back at the curation bag in her hand.

By Emily's behavior over the last couple of weeks, Meg knew Oliver had not mentioned the incident on the bench to his girlfriend. But she needed to know. Meg had not broached that difficult subject and had used the preparations for the museum opening as an excuse to avoid discussing the matter. Meg knew she couldn't simply continue to pretend the bench incident hadn't happened . . . or maybe she could. Perhaps it was really none of her business and it would be best to just keep her mouth shut. She glanced over at Emily, whose hand still clutched a plastic curation bag. Then again, maybe her assistant had simply discovered an error with a provenience code.

Emily fidgeted on the stool. "Well, it's kind of personal, I guess, but I don't know who else to talk to about it." She paused and fidgeted some more, but then finally she came out with it: "What do you think about Oliver?"

Meg had turned to look again at Emily, but when the blurted question was out, her eyes darted back to the relative safety of the plastic curation bag. She really did want to talk to Emily about Oliver, but then she really didn't. Awkward silence descended as the buzzing of the wall clock grew louder. It echoed against the beige concrete block of the lab in an unmistakable sound of antiquated institutionalism.

What should she say? Should she tell Emily the painful truth about Oliver and the incident on the bench? Had Oliver already said something, painted her as predator and he as innocent prey? If he had, it would be his word against hers. Whom would Emily believe?

"Is there . . . something going on?" Meg asked, pretending to study the provenience codes on the bag.

"Yeah, I guess there kinda is. You remember a couple weeks ago, when Oliver and I were supposed to drive up to Cincy—you know, to meet my parents?" She paused, her voice beginning to tremble.

"Yeah, I remember."

Emily knitted her brow. "Well, at the last minute he called and said he couldn't make it. That he had just gotten some revisions back on some article and he really needed to get them made . . . you know . . . before tenure and everything."

Shoulders slumping, Emily stopped talking. She looked down at her hands, poked at some skin on the side of her fingernail. It was only then Meg noticed her young friend's eyelids—they seemed a little puffy. She looked closer: There was no doubt about it, they were puffy. Meg at once recognized that telltale sign. Emily had been crying the night before, and crying hard. Puffy eyelids only came from crying hard.

Meg looked back at the plastic curation bag in her hand, weighed for a moment the important demands of tenure. "Well, I guess that does make some sense. I mean that he would want to get the article accepted by fall."

Emily turned her head to stare out the window. "Yeah, I guess," she mumbled.

"But I'd think he could've spared a day to meet your folks," Meg continued. "One day out of the summer isn't going to make or break an article."

Emily threw her hands in the air. "Well, that's what *I* thought!" she said, exasperation clear in her voice. "And then I come back from Cincy a little early on Sunday—just before noon—and I stop by his office. I was going to surprise him with Subway sandwiches for lunch. Dr. Harrington, he *loves* Subway sandwiches, and he *never* eats lunch before one o'clock, but you know what?"

"What?" Meg cringed, fearful of the answer. She dreaded what was coming next as her mind flashed to the evening she surprised her boyfriend in graduate school with pizza when he was supposedly grading papers late in his office, only to find his naked butt going a mile a minute as he screwed his office mate on the floor.

"He wasn't there," Emily said, and Meg breathed a sigh of relief. "So, I go over to the coffee shop to see if he's there, and lo and behold, there's Oliver! He's just lounging around at a table, drinking coffee with some woman—this disgustingly skinny peroxide blond. I couldn't believe it. And this woman was awfully interested in him; I mean, jeez she was practically drooling all over him! I was embarrassed for her!"

"And Oliver?" Meg asked in a monotone.

"Oh, he was just loving it—eating up all that attention like a freaking puppy dog." Emily sighed, looked down at her hands. "I feel like such an idiot."

Meg nodded, reflected for a moment. Peroxide blond and disgustingly skinny? Oh Lord, Oliver was flirting with Stacy Clemment, the ditzy professor from the English Department!

Meg raised her eyebrows. "What did you do?"

"Nothing," Emily admitted, her voice full of remorse. "I did absolutely nothing. I just slunk out of the place."

Meg pursed her lips. She had thrown the box of pizza on the guy's naked butt and, after shouting a few choice epitaphs at the top of her lungs, stormed out of his office. But the rest of her time in graduate school she had to live with the notoriety of having been cheated on.

Then an appalling scenario flashed through her mind: Stacy Clemment . . . she's on the promotion and tenure committee this fall. Meg's stomach turned as she considered Oliver and contemplated a truly horrible prospect. Could his machinations possibly stoop so low? But then, Oliver probably knew Meg was serving on the committee as well, thanks to Ross Landers. Her head throbbed: Had the incident on the bench been about offering her some kind of sordid favor—a sleazy "I rub your back; you rub mine?" God, did he really think she was that desperate?

Meg frowned. Could she really tell her young friend she thought Oliver Kearns was a weasel?

"What the hell was I thinking?" Emily was saying, speaking quickly now.

"I should have walked right over and sat down—interrupted the happy couple, pretended like nothing was wrong," she said, her voice full of sarcasm. But then she sunk her chin in her hands. "And now I can't even bring it up . . . confront him with it. God, I feel like such a coward. And now I'm starting to wonder if I'm over-reacting. I mean, this could all just be an innocent misunderstanding, right?" Emily asked.

Silence returned as the two women, one older, one younger, sat on their stools in the archaeology lab, each contemplating the complexities of this convoluted situation. They weren't looking at one another; rather, their eyes had remained discreetly averted since Emily began revealing such unusual personal intimacies to her mentor. The current topic of discussion reached far beyond any realm they had shared as professor and student, as field director and field assistant, and even as newly forming friends.

The clock on the archaeology lab wall still buzzed, but its sound now held less tension, more compassion than it previously had.

As they sat in silence it occurred to Meg that Oliver Kearns might actually be Emily's first real love. Throughout her four years at college, Meg had seen Emily with several young men, but no one about whom she seemed serious. Certainly, she had never detected any puffy eyelids or slumped shoulders or witnessed her voice full of sarcasm and self-doubt.

But Emily was only beginning the lifelong journey of romance that, if Meg's experiences were any gauge, would lead to heartache and confusion as often as it led to joy. Meg's thoughts jumped to Tom, a man who—at least for the present—also seemed too good to be true. Which would Tom end up being, heartache and confusion or joy? And if the latter, how fleeting might it be this time around? Maybe in the end it would be better to not become involved at all—undoubtedly that would make life simpler, as the young woman perched on the stool in the archaeology lab was just now beginning to fathom.

Meg turned to look at Emily. "You asked me what I think of Oliver?"

"Yeah," she said, chin in hand, eyes cast down on the counter.

"I'll tell you under one condition."

"What?"

"You stop calling me Dr. Harrington. My name's Meg." She smiled a little, hoping to ease the pain of the immediate situation and buy a little time.

"Okay," Emily mumbled. She nodded her head, smiled faintly, waited.

Meg knew that whatever she said next would carry great weight with the bewildered young woman on the stool at her side. Even though she was still uncomfortable with the notion of being a role model to countless young people, particularly to young women—what exactly was she supposed to model?—she had gradually come to accept that reluctant duty. It was one she recognized as carrying enormous responsibility, and it had to be wielded with great care. Like it or not, she had come to understand that both her actions and her words spoke louder than she might ever have wished or imagined.

When Meg spoke, her voice was flat, emotionless. "I think you're too good for him."

Silence again prevailed as Emily took in the honesty of her mentor's words. Meg waited while her young friend pondered those words, viewed them through the painful lens of truth, turned them over in her mind, and considered their implications for her future.

"Emily, although it might not seem like it right this instant, you have your whole life ahead of you, and there are really fantastic things waiting for you. I just know there are," Meg said.

She started to reach out her hand, to rest it reassuringly on Emily's slumped shoulder, but then doubted whether she should. She hesitated, returned her hand to the edge of the archaeology lab counter. That kind of physical affection had not passed between them before—but then the situation had never called for it. As a rule, Meg was not wont to initiate such intimate demonstrations, particularly with students—she found them uncomfortable, their reception un-predictable, the danger of misinterpretation ever-present.

But then she just did it. She reached out her hand and placed it on Emily's shoulder. Instantly, she was glad she did. She could feel Emily's carriage shift a little under her hand, find some resolve, and gain a new source of courage—a glimmer of determination that moments earlier had not been present. Embold-ened by the change, Meg rubbed her hand on Emily's troubled shoulder in kind circles.

"And there'll be better guys out there too; I just know it."

There was a new protective quality, an unforeseen caring in Meg's voice as she spoke. Even though she wasn't entirely certain that such would be Emily's future, she truly wished it for her young friend; and at that moment, wishing it strongly enough—like a magic wand waved in the hand of a fairy godmother—made it the truth.

It was Saturday morning, and again Meg walked the long hall to the archae-ology lab. She opened the door, flipped on the light, and batted for the gnawed pencil stub hanging from the clipboard's dirty string. She cursed Ross Landers as she scrawled across the clipboard's smudged paper.

As she pulled a stool up to the lab's main analysis table, Meg's thoughts were on Emily; she would miss her company that morning. During yesterday's lunch at the creek, her friend told her she was driving to Cincinnati for the weekend, where she planned to roam around the University of Cincinnati campus—that maybe she would apply there for graduate school next year.

Meg sighed as she settled in, prepared herself for the morning's work. But then she grew nostalgic, reflecting back on her own days in graduate school and the many months of isolated fieldwork in the overgrown Maya ruins of the Guatemalan jungle. She smiled a little, shook her head wistfully, then looked back down to the task at hand.

On the table before her stretched row after row of Styrofoam meat trays, each brimming with artifacts. Each artifact had been washed and inked with tiny catalog codes. Each one awaited her analysis. Over coffee that morning, Meg decided to choose a task that would fill up the time until her dinner with Tom. She had already completed the nail analysis with the crew; Emily had nearly finished the metal artifacts. She still had the bulk of the ceramic analysis data entry to go, but that would take longer; that task could begin another day.

Bottle glass. Yes, she would go ahead and tackle the bottle glass. Like ceramic analysis, bottle glass analysis was an undertaking that required long stretches of solitary confinement; yet, if she worked hard, it was a task she could complete in a week of evenings, plus some time on the weekends. It would be good to get it out of the way; as well, it would thwart her mind from conjuring up ridiculously romantic, happy-ever-after scenarios that would never be.

Meg clicked on the table lamp, and her work area flooded with a warm circle of strong yellow light.

She pulled her old plastic magnifying glass from the drawer and, with a final sigh, picked up a sherd of bottle glass. She brought it under the brightness of the lamp and adjusted its distance relative to the magnifying lens until the dull mat of the patinated surface of the old glass jumped into clarity.

She turned the artifact over in her fingers a few times, looking at it from all angles. She gazed right through the film of patina to examine the diverse qualities of the glass itself. Although at first the many variables flooded toward her all at once, her methodical mind progressed to the next analytical stage. One by one she teased each variable apart from the others, urged each to find and enter its own separate category.

She assessed bubble size and bubble quantity. She noted glass color and overall body shape. She searched for the presence of a seam on the fragment in her hand. She pulled out her calipers, measured the overall thickness of the curving sherd. She scanned all outer surfaces for any evidence of a maker's mark. As she worked, she recorded the value of each variable on the inventory sheet on the table at her side. She put the piece of bottle glass down, picked up a second. She noted the same variables, recorded their values on the tidy lines of the inventory sheet. She clicked her favorite mechanical pencil, then on to the next sherd of broken bottle glass.

Even by mid-morning, an irrefutable pattern had begun to emerge from the numbers block printed in her own precise hand on the inventory sheet at her side. She frowned as her eye combed through the troubling quantities. She scowled for a moment at the many still-unanalyzed piles of glass sherds in the rows of Styrofoam meat trays on the analysis table. The inventory sheet had already begun to reveal a surprising overabundance of a particular—and a particularly disturbing—glass type, the cheerless implications of which she simply did not wish to acknowledge.

When Meg opened her front door Saturday evening, Tom stood holding a bouquet of flowers. "Happy early birthday," he grinned, thrusting them toward her.

"Oh! Thank you! But how did you know my birthday's coming?" Meg asked. She stuck her nose in a generous spray of bright pink carnations.

"How could I forget? After all, it's the same day my great-great-grandmother had her photograph taken. Although not the same year, of course," Tom said.

Meg smiled at him, pleased he had remembered. She was happy to see his kind face again and wondered if he had developed a new twinkle in his eye or whether it had been there all along.

"Oh, yeah. Wow—you have a good memory! Come on in. Let me put these in water—they're beautiful," she said, carrying the flowers to the kitchen. "How was your conference?"

Meg opened and shut a few cupboards, searching for the appropriate vase. She decided on a clear glass milk bottle, the kind that in bygone days was left on front doorsteps by neighborhood milkmen on their morning rounds. She filled the bottle with water, opened the bouquet and laid it out on the counter. She snipped off the bottom of each stem and placed it upright in the wide-mouth bottle. After half a dozen stems accumulated, she repositioned each one, added several more, then turned the arrangement to observe her handiwork. Meg surprised herself as she poked and prodded at the flowers longer than she might normally have, but she was enjoying the moment. She could tell that Tom was trying not to watch her too closely as he told her about the conference and an amusing incident from the plane flight back. But she felt the quick glide of his eye up her shoulder—now bronzed and strong in her sleeveless dress—felt it linger for a moment at the crook of her neck.

With daily attention to the task, Meg had succeeded in dissolving most of her farmer's tan—a common occupational hazard of archaeology. Just a half-hour before, sitting in front of her round beveled mirror, she had pinned her hair into a loose bun and tugged on a few brown strands so they would fall about her face. Earlier that day she had given herself a manicure. Although a far cry from the professional treatment her sister-in-law received on a regular basis, she had nevertheless managed to eliminate the worst evidence of four weeks of field-work. She smiled as she observed her own moving fingers as they fussed with the last few carnations. Deborah had been wrong: Clear nail polish was a better choice than claret.

"So, what have you been up to?" Tom asked after they settled in. They sat at a window table at the new French restaurant downtown. The windows were tall, with full-length folding shutters, and opened to the street this warm summer evening. They both sipped chilled white Chardonnay from tall-stemmed goblets; in the heat, tiny beads of condensation had risen up on the surface of the thin rounded glass.

Around them the place was bustling. The waiters wore all black with long white aprons tied at the waist. They scurried back and forth with trays raised a bit too high for Lexington, but the establishment's upscale clientele seemed appreciative of the highbrow affectation. The notes of a languid saxophone from the bar side of the premises drifted about the room. The music created an atmosphere that resembled a Depression-era speakeasy, although absent the thick air thanks to the city's recent smoking ban. It was the cozy, intimate kind of restaurant where the diners leaned inward, heads tilting toward one another as they conversed.

"Oh, gee, what have I been up to? Well, to tell you the truth, I've been analyzing Creekside bottle glass—but you don't want to hear about that," Meg waved her hand to dismiss the subject. "Tell me more about your conference—it sounds really interesting." She took a sip of wine, hoping Tom would change the subject.

"Oh, but I do want to hear about the bottle glass. It's not a topic they ever discuss much around my office."

"No, actually, you don't—it's . . . about as dry as it gets."

"Try me."

"Wouldn't you rather talk about dinosaurs?"

"Dinosaurs?" laughed Tom. "I hate to break it to you, Dr. Harrington, but archaeologists don't dig up dinosaurs; paleontologists do."

"Well, okay, maybe not dinosaurs, but how about the Red Sox? Do you think we're lining up for another pennant this year?"

"How about bottle glass?" he said smiling. "I'm curious to know how you spend your time," he added. He spoke with the perfect amount of sincerity, such that a little place in her heart softened.

"Okay, but remember, you asked for it!" As Meg cleared her throat she willed herself brevity.

"Well, glass analysis happens in two steps. First you date the glass with one set of variables, and then you type it with another set. Typing means what kind of a bottle it was—like what kind of liquid it held. Dating identifies the timeframe in which different glass-manufacturing techniques were invented and came into common usage. Bubbles in the glass—that's the easiest. Lots of bubbles mean hand-blown glass, which is always early. All our Creekside bottles have lots of bubbles, so we know we have an early historic site."

She took a sip of wine, glanced across the rim of her glass at Tom, gauging his level of interest. It hadn't waned. Meg set her glass down, pointed at the bottle of Chardonnay in the silver wine chiller beside their table.

"Another thing to look at is the base of a bottle, to see if it has a pontil mark—the place where the bottle attached to the blowpipe and then was snapped off when the vessel cooled. Bottles with pontil marks date prior to the Civil War—so before the early 1860s. Each and every one of our Creekside bottle base sherds has pontil marks, so, again, they're all pre–Civil War."

As she spoke the waiter came to the table to fill their water glasses. When he caught the gist of their conversation he shot her an inadvertent glance. Tom caught it too, and they both laughed when he left the table. "See, I told you; most people think this stuff is pretty dull," Meg chuckled. Then she paused, again allowing Tom the opportunity to change the subject.

"Please carry on," he said, smiling as he nodded in feigned solemnity.

"Well, okay. Another thing to check for is a seam. If there's a seam on the side of a sherd you know it was made in a mold. Like this," Meg said, plucking the Chardonnay bottle from the ice. She twisted it until she located the seam, showed it to Tom, who ran his finger across the long ridge that extended the length of the smoky light-green glass.

"This seam is faint because the technology is now perfected, but not so in the past. Blowing glass into one *single* mold only appeared after the Civil War, although a few *two-part* molds did exist earlier, but those early mold-made bottles still had blown-glass necks and lips." Meg paused a moment as she shoved the bottle back down in the ice bucket. When she spoke again, her hands dashed through the air with each word. "We don't have one single completely mold-made bottle sherd at Creekside; hence, again, we know nobody lived there after 1861. Probably nobody lived there during the decade prior, either, since not even one itsy-bitsy piece of ironstone showed up, and ironstone was just all over the place in the 1850s. And, of course, that general end date matches up with all the other artifacts that appeared—or didn't appear—at the site."

She glanced up. Tom was still listening attentively, nodding from time to time to indicate his continued comprehension. "Archaeologists like redundancy, in case you haven't noticed," she admitted with a wry smile. "We're a tad dense sometimes," she added, tapping her index finger against the side of her head.

Tom chuckled. "Redundancy can be a good thing."

Years ago, when Meg decided to enter graduate school and earn a PhD, Deborah—then her brother's girlfriend—had tried to dissuade her from continuing her education. With Nick out of earshot, she had cautioned that an advanced degree would intimidate men and thus cut down on her marriage prospects. Time had revealed that Deborah had been right; Meg had encountered more than a few men who were put off by her education, as odd as that seemed. But Tom didn't appear to be one of them.

She took another sip of wine, chuckled along with him, encouraged by his sense of humor as well as his genuine interest. "You want to hear more?" Meg asked, although this time not in an effort to evade the issue of glass analysis. Rather, this time it was just a simple question.

"I would."

"Alright. Then comes typing the bottle glass. Typing is about figuring out what the bottle contained. You know—snake oil or soda pop. Illustrated reference books do that trick. We've got the standard quantity of medicine bottles and other assorted jars at Creekside. But . . . " she paused, all of a sudden disconcerted to be talking about bottle typing, "we also have what I think is clearly going to be a statistical overabundance of cylinder whiskey bottles. I'm afraid they stick out like a sore thumb, as well as quantitatively speaking."

"How so?" he asked, noting the change in her voice.

"The color for one thing. Dark olive-green glass, hand-tooled mouth. Complete bottles stand about nine inches." She raised her finger to indicate the height above the top of the white tablecloth. "We even have one with XXX embossed on it—it's hard to suggest that anything other than whiskey was in that one." Meg said, a bit of cynicism creeping into her voice.

"So, what does that mean?" he asked, his tone suggesting he already suspected the answer.

"Well, I'd say it probably means someone was drinking a lot of whiskey at one rather specific, relatively narrow window of time quite late in the site's occupation."

Tom nodded his head, still listening.

"I'd say it wasn't inexpensive stuff either. Good ole homegrown corn squeezin's would've been a whole lot cheaper and a whole lot easier to come by. Looks like they eschewed the old copper kettle in favor of professional distillers— certainly, Lexington would have had several of those." She paused a moment, dabbed her mouth with her napkin, returned it to her lap. "I would guess the drinking took a serious bite out of the household budget, which was likely already pretty close to the bone."

"An alcoholic in the family?"

Meg shrugged. "Heavy drinker anyway." She had compared the date ranges for the locket and whiskey cylinder bottles the very day the disturbing glass patterning became evident. They didn't overlap. While that probably meant it hadn't been EEOM who took to the bottle, one of her descendants likely had.

Meg's mother had started drinking toward the end of her life, and it hadn't left pleasant memories for young Magpie. Those memories were the last she had of her mother before she just withered away in her bed. As Meg sat on the stool in her lab and recorded the presence of yet another dark olive-green whiskey cylinder fragment, she had marveled at how broken bottles from an old cabin site in Kentucky were able to stir up painful memories of a childhood in suburban Minnesota.

As Meg had continued her work, she decided to take some unusual creative license when she compiled her report for KYDOT. Although she would certainly include all the accurate quantities of the different bottle glass types in her data table, she would just fail to highlight the unusually high amount of dark olive-green whiskey cylinder fragments in the actual text.

There were plenty of other interesting data patterns her text would emphasize instead. First, there was the solid numeric presence of utilitarian redware vessels, like milk pans and pitchers, which indicated an initial founding date somewhere in the early 1780s, a date substantiated by the creamware sherds. Then there was the quantitatively irrefutable replacement of the common blue scalloped-edge pearlware with dishes of a lavender Chinese willowware transfer print sometime in the early 1830s. That unexpected ceramic transition apparently marked a sudden but brief rise in household wealth, a rise that was not, however, mirrored in other artifact categories, with the sole exception of the unusual occurrence of a large and valuable English Spode mug. It was a clear instance in which the lack of artifact redundancy indicated some kind of behavioral incongruity, but one that could not be readily explained by the fragmentary nature of the evidence at hand.

Her decision concerning the report had been a protective urge that arose bit by bit, keeping pace with the mounting tally of dark olive-green glass on the unequivocal lines of her inventory sheet. By the time Meg had analyzed her last sherd of dark olive-green bottle glass, she had come to the conclusion that there was just nothing to be gained from airing other people's dirty laundry in her report. Surely, she could do this small bit to safeguard this poor farming family from the resounding community disapproval that would fall on them even to this day, once their shameful secret became public knowledge.

Besides, the drinking was just one of many apparent causes for site abandonment. Overall, the Creekside Subdivision Expansion Site fit a broader pattern in which the early effects of the Industrial Revolution caused the decline of countless small family farms even decades before the Civil War. It was a decline that continued in rural areas of the Commonwealth to this very day.

She also reasoned that if anyone wanted to inquire further about the relative quantities of differing bottle glass types at the site, the raw data were available in her report, contained in the clearly captioned Creekside Historic Bottle Glass table, printed plain as day in black and white for any KYDOT bureaucrat to consult should the fancy ever strike.

"My father was an alcoholic," Tom said suddenly.

And Meg breathed a small sigh of relief, but not because of the opportunity to change the subject—she no longer felt the need to change the subject, and she was glad he had pushed her on the bottle glass. He had listened, he had understood, and he had appreciated. Rather, she breathed a sigh of relief because Tom didn't seem reluctant to bring up his painful past. If he didn't need to be reluctant, neither did she.

Tom turned his car key in the passenger door lock. "I have an idea. Let's go out to the site," he suggested.

Meg turned to him. "The site? Why?"

"Why not?"

"Well, there's nothing left to see out there. We backfilled a little already. Besides, it's dark," she said, gesturing at the night.

"There's some moonlight," he said glancing up at the sky. "And it's a nice night for a drive. You said Monday the bulldozers come, didn't you?"

"That's right. First thing Monday."

"Let's go see it one last time. Besides, the night is still young."

They turned left past Triangle Park, where an entire city block of commercial old Lexington was razed to build a fountain, and travelled along the Woolworth block, recently demolished to make way for a modern glass monstrosity that was "Coming Soon." They drove in view of the long corner park where the grand Phoenix Hotel was torn down in 1987 and, before that, where old Postlethwaite's Tavern burned in 1819. They bounced across potholed blacktop and railroad tracks before leaving the city, then sped past wide empty pastures where hours earlier multimillion-dollar Thoroughbreds grazed on rich bluegrass and crossed the concrete highway bridge spanning the dark Kentucky River far below. Then the hum of rubber on tarmac changed as their wheels rolled across flat new road. As Tom parked the car, his headlights shone on the new swirling brass sign, CREEKSIDE. The bold script stood in sharp contrast to the rough limestone of the grand entryway bridge that now arched across the dark creek.

The coming and going of booted feet over the weeks had worn a trail winding from road to creek across the soft swells of the pasture. Even blindfolded Meg could have walked that trail; Tom followed as they made their way along the shadowy dips and rises. She turned her head, gazed into blackness as they passed their dark perfect squares, now empty and eerily silent.

It was the sweet smell of honeysuckle that hit her first. Warmed from the day, the fragrance hovered along the banks of the creek, bathed her in an unexpected bouquet. Standing wordless beside the creek, they watched as the moonlight glinted off the gurgling splashes, content to be still as the dark flashing water journeyed past in its unhurried tumble to the sea. From time to time, wisps of cloud crossed the bright face of the moon, offered up an endless changing kaleidoscope of dappled splendor.

Meg had never been to the site at night, and now she wondered why she hadn't. She gazed about in awe, marveling at all she had been missing, taking in the new and wondrous world all around her. She was surprised to discover how different the place looked at night: softer, velvety, and infinitely fragile. Each shadowy tree, each swale of silvery moonlight held a kind of innocence she had not noticed during the brightness of day.

Even the creek itself seemed transformed—a dark glossy ribbon laid across the land, draped perfectly in its tender cradling banks. It was a long narrow window peering deep into the heart of the earth, honored witness to her most intimate of secrets.

It was a quiet paradise lit only by moon and stars. The knobs in the distance jutted up, their stone of ancient gray now rendered black, their jagged edges sketched in charcoal against the surprising brilliance of the glittering sky. The place reminded Meg of a painting by an old Dutch master hanging in a giant gilt frame. A mythic portrait of some vast lavish landscape—rich enticing textures, deep alluring colors fashioned by brushstrokes both generous and extraordinary. It was the kind of magical illuminated canvas you stand in front of, are drawn into, and never want to step back out of.

The longer they stood, the greater rose the din of night. Bullfrogs belched their lazy croaked calls from a distant pond. From somewhere along the shadowy creek an owl began its low guttural hoots, built up to a mighty crescendo of ancient primal sound, and descended back into stillness. Nesting doves cooed to one another, their calm low murmurs of contentment drifting out over the dark glistening ribbon of creek.

Meg's head spun with wonder. It was as if she had sipped the nectar of some mysterious elixir and the world around her had changed. How had she failed to imagine such finery? How had she not even dreamed of such splendor and delight? And now, as this darkened magical landscape reached out to greet her, she loved it even more.

It was at that moment the cottonwood trees along the creek chose to open their woody pods and release their seed into the black velvet of night. Thousands of white fuzzy seed-bursts appeared all around them—tiny intricate spirits hovering in grace on the warm night air. Without haste they drifted, gliding with ease across the broad starry darkness. It was as if a colossal hand had reached out from the heavens and tipped a warm summer snow-globe just to admire the magnificence of that slow-motion miracle.

Standing on the creek bank, Meg and Tom drank in the swirling marvel all about them. They turned to gaze at one another in shared awe. In silence they acknowledged the sheer wonder of this place, and of each other's wordless presence in it. Tom stepped behind her and encircled her shoulders with his arms.

She reached up, cupped her hands at his wrists, leaned her head back to rest at his shoulder.

He smelled good. He smelled warm and sweet and salty like the taste of the earth. Again she breathed, and his scent mingled with the delicious perfume of honeysuckle, whose dense, generous vines adorned the trunks of trees gracing the banks of the trickling creek. As they stood, both sighed in pleasure and release. It was in that moment that any lingering doubt was gone, drifting away like a cottonwood seed vanished into the darkness of night.

"Happy birthday again," he whispered into her ear.

"Thank you," she whispered into the air.

"I have something else for you," he said. He slid his arm from her grasp, slipped his hand in his pocket, pulled out a small white box. It was the kind of small white box that jewelry comes in, pillowed within a piece of soft cotton.

Meg lifted her head from his shoulder, accepted the box from his hands. "My, aren't you full of surprises tonight," she said, shaking her head in amazement.

His arms encircling her again, she opened the box a crack. She peeked beneath the lid as if she wanted to make sure that whatever promise rested within didn't escape before she could claim it. Nestled in the soft cotton was a plain silver oval locket with a plain twenty-six-inch silver chain running through the loop. She reached inside, clasped the chain, and drew it from the box. The moonlight glinted off the shiny oval surface—a hypnotist's magic ball dangling before her eyes.

"A locket. You got me a locket," Meg mumbled in disbelief. She felt an unexpected tightness in her throat, a sudden watery sensation in her mouth. Tears began stinging her eyes, blurring the shiny magic dangling ball before her, fracturing it into hundreds of shimmering silvery prisms. She blinked to keep her tears from falling.

"I could be wrong, but I had this sneaky suspicion you really liked the one you dug up, so I thought maybe you needed one of your own. Do you like it?"

"A locket," she repeated, still hypnotized by the shining oval, by the unbelievable thoughtfulness of the surprising man who stood just behind her. "Of course I like it. It's beautiful."

"No filigree to be found, though," he continued, his quiet words warm and jovial beside her ear. "Shall I help you put it on?"

Meg nodded, her vision still blurred by fractured silvery prisms.

As he took the dangling locket from her hand, she bowed her head, baring the soft nape of her neck. And there she stood, offering up that bare open

neck—exposed and vulnerable—the trusting assent of a wild animal present-
ing a most tender stretch of vital flesh. She felt the cool caress on her skin as
he blew away the stray brown strands of her mane. Despite the warmth of the
evening, she shivered in delight, closed her eyes, and beamed into the darkness. When he finished clasping the chain, his hands slid to her shoulders. He
brought his head beside hers, nudged it like a playful lion.

And she was turning to him, moving effortless within the loose circle of his
hold. She drew up her arms, embraced the back of his neck with calm hands.
She reached up and kissed him—neither soft nor hard, neither timid nor demanding. It was a confident kiss, unafraid in the midst of this magical luminous
place. And he kissed her back—there, standing beside the long curving creek
drenched by the warm scent of honeysuckle, its quietly trickling water dappled
by the splendor of moonlight.

Chapter Seventeen

Early that Monday morning, Meg and Emily stood at the edge of their old excavation units. They stared down at the perfect dark squares, spread with a few pointless shovelfuls of backfill dirt flung toward their centers. They awaited the fullness of that graying dawn in silence.

It was often a melancholy moment when the time came to end a project and backfill units—or else leave them open and gaping for the inevitable. On Friday afternoon, Meg had instructed the crew to toss a few ceremonial shovelfuls of dirt back into their units—a temporary, symbolic reburial prior to the destruction of Monday morning.

The moment the bulldozers arrived was the hardest of all.

When the women saw the machines rounding the curve in the road, they walked to meet them. Waiting at the road, hard hat under her arm, Meg kicked the dirt at the edge of the pasture, contemplating the inevitable events that lay just ahead.

Of course, she had always known this day would arrive, the day she would watch that sharp blade tear across the land. But it was not quite that simple. She would not just watch from some remote distance; no, hers was a burden that required pacing right alongside that tearing blade for each and every moment of destruction.

As the heavy machinery operators parked their enormous trucks at the side of the road, she knew herself as someone who had lost the benefit of objectivity. She could no longer be considered some detached figure, aloof and reliable. She had allowed herself to become too close, been rendered ineffective, unable to reason, her logic invaded by sentiment. She was no longer certain she could carry out the task that lay just ahead.

As Meg waited for the men to descend from the cab of the truck, she understood why doctors never perform surgery on their loved ones. How could they wield that sharp scalpel in a hand rendered shaky by emotion? And why a death-row prison guard has only minimal contact with the condemned as they await the sweeping hand of the clock. But then, sometimes, against their better judgment, guards end up caring for their prisoners after all, and weep inwardly in silence as they walk the doomed man down the long bleak hall.

As they stood at the edge of the pasture, Meg did her best to explain to the two inexperienced bulldozer operators how they would proceed. Operators who worked with archaeologists knew the drill and were masters at their craft. They were able to peel off shallow, consistent layers of earth with their powerful blades. Even though their task was one of demolition, operators who had worked with archaeologists understood well the significance of their callused hand as it rested on the trembling gearshift; and they were able to carry out their destruction with care, always alert and ready to throw the machine out of gear if any final evidence came to light—even in the eleventh hour.

But the two men standing at the edge of the road that morning were new and would have to be broken in at Creekside. Both stood with hands thrust deep in their pockets, caps with trucking company logos drawn low on their foreheads. Wads of chew bulged their cheeks; from time to time they turned their heads to squirt thin streams of tobacco spittle against the ground in fast brown splats.

The older man was wide and round across the belly, short, with a heavy shadow of gray whiskers, and played with a tinkling handful of coins in his front pocket. The younger man was tall and long limbed, fair haired, with a scraggly goatee. He fiddled with the Skoal container that had worn a round white mark in his front left jeans pocket. Both studied their dusty work boots as they listened to their instructions.

With the bulldozers idling beside them, Meg had to raise her voice to be heard above the roar. "I'll work with you and we'll start at the far end of the pasture and head north," Meg gestured to the younger man.

"Yes Ma'am," he replied, not taking his eyes off his boots.

"The two of you work together," she continued, gesturing to Emily and the older man. "Start in the middle of the pasture and work north. That way we won't get squeezed up against each other in the middle." Emily and the older man nodded.

As they spoke, a sense of finality hung heavy in the early morning air. It permeated even the very last drops of dew on the pasture sod, glistening like crystal beads in the sharp slant of new sun.

When they had arrived at the site just past daybreak, Meg and Emily had both remarked on the dew. It was heavier than any other morning they had ever witnessed there. It was as if the very earth itself was weeping, shedding infinite tears in silent lamentation of its own imminent destruction. A thick fog had blanketed the pasture as well. When they first arrived it was still billowing up from the creek as if making a final desperate attempt to conceal the land and keep it safe from harm.

But it was a futile effort: The land would not be saved that morning. When the destruction commenced, that lingering mantle of fog transformed itself into a shroud.

Even though they had spent four weeks excavating the Creekside Subdivision Expansion Site, it was still completely possible more cultural material remained hidden beneath the pasture sod. But as time had pulled its burden forward, anything exposed by the bulldozers now would have to be excavated in a matter of minutes, as the massive idling machines belched their great impatient plumes of black diesel, their heavy buckets of steel hovering in wait of the archaeologist on bent knee before its path. At that extremely late date, much depended on the dexterity—and the goodwill—of the man whose callused hand rested upon the trembling gearshift.

"We'll walk to your right and about six feet in front," Meg shouted above the roar. "But don't worry about us getting in the way. We'll be close, but not too close."

She wished she didn't have to talk, to speak out loud their impending course of action, to reveal to the pasture and the earth below how systematic the demolition ahead would be. It was as if uttering the words made the act itself seem even more premeditated, even more diabolical.

"We'll match your pace, but stay in first gear. Obviously, you need to watch where you're going, but also keep an eye on us. If we throw up a hand, stop as fast as you can. But don't worry—if it comes to that, we'll be quick about it."

Her instructions were finished. The men had understood. They had nodded their comprehension, climbed up to their cabs, placed their callused hands on their trembling gear shifts. As Meg lifted her hand to signal commencement, she couldn't look at any of them. She pulled the bill of her Dodgers cap low over her face, then firmed her hard hat overtop and into place. She walked along the green edge of the pasture as the bulldozer rumbled along behind her—an innocent puppy lacking awareness of its own immense strength, its own ability to cause profound and irreversible harm.

As she walked, Meg braved one last look across the soft swells of green, blurring quickly as tears brimmed in her eyes. She looked back down at the dusty shoulder of the road and put one foot before the other. She stopped at the far fence, again raised her arm. Without looking up, she nodded her head, and the bulldozer lowered its broad sharp blade.

A rev of the engine, a great plume of black diesel belch, a thundering grind of gears—the merest touch of the blade, and the first stretch of sod folded. Then it rippled and cracked, tore apart as the great yellow lurching hulk moved forward.

At no time during the day did the incessant biting blades show mercy. They offered up neither leniency nor sympathy, neither regret nor compassion. Beneath the power of the relentless machine, the soil severed with ease from the earth, shorn away from its time-honored repose—a faithful mantle of constancy sheltering over the ancient land.

With each cut the green disappeared, replaced by thick clods of brown. With each slice the swells of rolling pasture vanished, replaced by endless flatness. Even the gentle rise of land where the denizens of the little farm had rested was no more. In its wake the bulldozer left only uninterrupted rows of unremitting treads—tank-like impressions crushed deep into the tender brown of the earth.

The ceaseless reverberation of straining engines crashed hard against the distant line of knobs—those mute and astonished sentinels of ancient jagged stone that touched the horizon, whose long rock roots stretched to the very core of the earth. Forced to witness such a vast scene of destruction, even the knobs wept that day, long wet streaks seeping down their broad gray faces.

One final time, Meg and Emily sat beside the creek to eat their lunch. At the edge of the road, the operators ate theirs, while the machines idled nearby, their task nearly finished.

The women sat in silence, for there was little to say. They ate slowly, chewed slowly, their food tasteless in their mouths. In front of them, the creek trickled on—peaceful, cool, shaded, oblivious to the annihilation of the quiet blanket of land beside it that morning.

As they ate, two young boys emerged from a Creekside home on the opposite bank and ran the gentle slope to the creek. Meg and Emily watched them enter the ribbon of trees downstream, their voices faint in the distance. They wove their way through the thick tangles of honeysuckle and past the dark, rounded form of the crumbling chestnut stump. The boys wandered down the creek, moving little by little away from the women. They picked up stones and tossed them in the trickling creek. The older boy skimmed a rock across a stretch of flat water, then the younger one, unable to duplicate his older brother, reverted back to tossing his stones and waiting for the splash.

The older boy knelt and turned over a rock, called to the younger. Together they studied whatever it was they found beneath the rock. The older boy pulled a slingshot from his back pocket, fit a stone in the rubber, and thumped it against the crumbling old stump. They sat on the bank, took off their shoes and socks, and waded into the cool water. Faint sounds of distant laughter floated above the banks as the cool mud oozed between their toes. They walked a way down the creek until the older boy remembered his slingshot on the bank, dashed back to retrieve it. Then they splashed and laughed, meandered their way along the creek, until they disappeared around the bend.

"Oh, no!" cried Meg.

Emily jumped. "What?"

"The irises! What about the irises?"

The women stared at each other for a moment, their mouths hanging open, eyes wide. They had forgotten all about the irises. Unmistakable in bloom, the yellow and purple flowers had again shriveled and wilted, their once-tall stems now yellowing and withering toward the pasture sod. How could they have forgotten those two beautiful rows of thick, brilliant color?

"Oh God—we've got to dig them up!" Meg said, throwing her half-finished Tupperware container in her pack. "Now, before the operators finish their lunch."

They jumped to their feet and dashed back along the last section of remaining trail to the truck. They pulled out shovels and plastic garbage bags and returned to the last broad swath of remaining pasture. Even withering, it was easy to spot the lines of irises—the women were pulled there by the strength of tradition, the pressing call to rescue these final living vestiges of the past before their destruction.

Emily sunk her shovel alongside a clump of thick bulbous roots and, with care, loosened the soil around their yellowing shoots. Meg dropped to her knees, her fingers working fast to coax soil from gnarled root, to encourage the irises' gentle departure from their old home in the disappearing land. They worked in silence, diligent liberators salvaging priceless gems.

"You know, I bet Miss Eliza would love to have some of these," Emily said after a while, her voice deep in thought.

"Yeah, she would," agreed Meg, her voice resolute but quiet. "We can plant them for her next Saturday. I bet she'd love the idea of having them grow just a stone's throw from their original home. You know, come to think of it, she must have been able to see them from her back deck all along."

"You're right," Emily said. "Humm, I never thought of that before." They stopped talking, once more directed their full attention to their urgent mission of recovery.

After several minutes, Emily spoke again. "I bet my mom would like some, maybe my aunt, too." Meg could tell her friend was making a mental list of people who would appreciate a gift of irises, especially these heirloom bulbs. She noticed Emily didn't mention Oliver.

Meg again plunged her hands into the earth, gathered up another handful of dirt and bulb. She watched her moving fingers, following the path of the dark soil as it dropped to the ground. She began making her own mental list. Tom would love to have some of these bulbs; he would appreciate their story, whatever it was.

Meg laid another brown gnarled root in the bag at her side and thought of her own sparse flowerbed. Surely she could manage to grow irises, particularly since they had succeeded in growing themselves for some two hundred years. Maybe these old beauties would inspire her to become a better gardener. Deborah and her brother might like to have some bulbs, too. She could offer to plant them anywhere her sister-in-law wanted in their new Chicago yard . . . drive up for their Fourth of July cookout . . . make an effort to reconnect with family and take a break that summer, prepare for the onslaught of another academic year.

As they dug down through the last strip of remaining pasture, it never occurred to either woman to pack up the irises and turn them over to the Commonwealth of Kentucky.

They had dutifully mapped and photographed the two thick rows in their precise spatial relationship to the cabin's stone foundation, recorded the exact grid location for each row. What more was there to do? Should they really stuff the irises in carefully labeled plastic curation bags, pack them in carefully labeled, standard-sized cardboard curation boxes, and store them on a shelf in the state repository to let them rot? It would be better to let the bulldozers rip them from the ground, leave them to shrivel and die in the searing sun.

Besides, the irises weren't artifacts in the standard sense. They were living things—breathing tethers to the lives of earlier times. Human hands hadn't made these—no, these irises were part of nature—human hands merely placed them in the ground in that stretch of land beside the creek, in two long rows up to a front porch step.

Sure, the locket had to go. But, no, these bulbs belonged to Meg and Emily. They would not be relinquished to the state.

As Meg's fingers worked the soil, a quiet coolness rose up from the earth. It evoked for her a subtle portal of opening that felt familiar. It invited her to enter and share, to partake of that immense beauty of nature, and to drink of its great antiquity. And there, kneeling on the final sod of the pasture, digging with her hands in the cool rich soil, holding the thick, fleshy bulbs of brown gnarled root, Meg knew she held the promise of continuity, season following season of persistent splendor, in the very palm of her hand.

It was then she smelled the wood smoke. It was there from one instant to the next, strong and close and immediate. She looked up to see where it came from, here, now, in the middle of the suburban summer. But there was no thin pale thread of blue twisting up to the sky—she could only make out an imprecise haze where it once rose long ago, under the slanting shadow of the towering gray knobs.

She heard the crash and split of dry wood chopped on a stump, but when she turned to see who wielded the ax, the form remained vague and indistinct against the green backdrop of trees.

A barn door squeaked on a slow rusty hinge. Chickens clucked nearby. She heard the quick snap of ripe summer beans and the muffled pop of a sharp needle drawn through taut fabric, the quiet rhythmic creaking of a chair as it rocked back and forth across worn wooden porch boards. And just there, riding on the little breeze that licked up the rise, was the very faintest of melodies played on an old tin whistle.

Meg gazed down at her open hands, saw the rich soil spilling about her bended knees. And as she plunged her hands back into the earth, a cool ripple began its slow passage through her fingers—and coursed up her arms. She listened as a voice rose on the air, pleading to be heard. It called her, invited her to join hands in an ancient chain that was now linking forward.

She watched in wonder as her hands began a quiet transformation. They became stronger, but smaller, their nails dirty and short and chipped, their knuckles red and rough. They were sturdy, capable hands, skilled and resilient. They were hands from another time. Hands not her own and yet strangely familiar.

Meg recognized these hands. They belonged to the woman from long ago who had also worked this land—the very soil that now fell through her fingers and gathered at the crook of her knee. It had been she who once cradled these very bulbs in her hands, nestled them into the fertile ground. It had been she who doted over them, guarding them fiercely. And it had been she who rejoiced each year as their color burst forth from dormancy once more, signaling the renewal of the land, the promised cycle of rebirth.

Another set of hands appeared against the dark grains of earth—similar hands, but less ancient than the first shadowy set. These hands, too, had worked the rich soil, held the gnarled bulbs, cut their radiant stalks, delighted also in the certain return of summer.

An ageless love of the land and tradition emanated from these most enduring of bulbs. That cool quiet love drenched the woman that knelt there on the last remaining swath of green near the edge of the creek, under the long shadow of the tall, gray knobs. And they were ancient tears of devotion, of humility, of lasting remembrance that budded and fell, splashed down upon that long chain of clasping hands, washed over those resilient gnarled bulbs, and soaked deep into the timeless earth.

The End